Counterparts

To my friend Ed —

You and I share a proud heritage that I enjoy remembering as we talk about our experiences.

I am proud to call you my friend.

Jim McDaniel

Counterparts

Jim McDaniel

Writers Club Press
New York Lincoln Shanghai

Counterparts

Writers Club Press
an imprint of iUniverse, Inc.

For information address:
iUniverse, Inc.
2021 Pine Lake Road, Suite 100
Lincoln, NE 68512
www.iuniverse.com

ISBN: 0-595-25405-5 (pbk)
ISBN: 0-595-65152-6 (cloth)

Printed in the United States of America

Contents

Act 5

FOREWORD

ABOUT THE LANGUAGE IN THIS BOOK

Anyone remotely familiar with the language of the Vietnamese people will recognize immediately that it is not being presented properly within the pages of this book. I have deliberately changed the written appearance of the language for two reasons: First of all, one needs a Vietnamese keyboard in order to produce the proper letters and punctuation; and secondly, I did it in order to give the reader a better "feel" and "sound" of the language. For example, the word for "man," or "sir" when addressing a man directly is "ong" (with a small triangle above the 'o'). However, the spoken word sounds as if (in English) it would be spelled "*um*." Throughout my book, I have used "*um*" in order to give a realistic *sound* of Vietnam at the same time I present as realistic a picture of Vietnam as possible. This same drive for realism also explains the excessive use of profanity throughout the book. To eliminate profanity, or even to minimize it in a novel about that time and place would have been quixotic.

TERMS

Anh: "Big brother" in Vietnamese

Arc Light: Code word for a B-52 heavy bombardment.
                            Also used to describe the target area of a B-52
                            strike.

Armed
Propaganda Team: A small commando sized unit of former VC
                            and NVA turn-coats. The Republic of Viet-
                            nam government habitually sent these teams
                            on very risky or even suicide missions.

ARVN: Army of the Republic of Vietnam. The South
                            Vietnamese Army.

Au yi: Phonetic spelling of the traditional garment
                            of the Vietnamese woman. It is a long, ankle
                            length, high necked bodice that is split along
                            both sides of the legs to the waist. Made to
                            wear over feminine trousers, the garment is
                            colorful and often brocaded or embroidered
                            with flowers or other designs. Women wear
                            this outfit for everyday wear as well as dress-
                            up occasions.

Ba: "Mrs." in Vietnamese; used in almost every
                            discussion with or about the lady in ques-
                            tion.

Cam On:	Phonetic spelling of the Vietnamese phrase for "Thank you."
C & GS School:	Advanced professional military course of approximately 9 months for career Army field grade officers (Major and Lt. Colonel).
Charlie:	Slang (from military phonetic alphabet), short for Victor Charlie, the Viet Cong.
China Beach:	Military hospital area near the City of Da Nang.
Chu Lai:	Large US military base near City of Ly Tin in Quang Tin Province.
Co:	"Miss," in Vietnamese; used in almost every discussion with or about the lady in question.
Cobra:	An armed helicopter designed to provide air support for ground troops.
CP:	Command Post.
Cai luong:	Modern Vietnamese theater, similar to western stage plays.
Chu Hoi	South Vietnamese government program to encourage enemy soldiers to defect and switch sides.
CIA:	Civilian Intelligence Agency.
CONUS:	Continental area of the Unites States.
COORDS:	Civil Operations and Revolutionary Development Support: A US State Department program during the Vietnam conflict which functioned in coordination with military operations. All province, and district advisors as well as other advisors to civilian organizations functioned under this program.

Dai Ta:	Phonetic spelling of the Vietnamese word for "Colonel."
Dai Wi:	Phonetic spelling of the Vietnamese word for "Captain."
DEROS:	Date of expected return from overseas.
District:	The equivalent to a US "County." Cities, villages (hamlets) and townships were given specific territories within the districts to farm and to defend.
DMG:	Distinguished Military Graduate. The top honors at a military school or course.
DMZ:	The "Demilitarized Zone." A space cleared of vegitation on the border between North and South Vietnam.
Dong:	Monetary base of South Vietnam. In 1968, one US dollar = about 110 Dong.
DPSA:	Deputy Province Senior Advisor.
DSA:	District Senior Advisor: Advisor to the District Chief.
FNG:	"Fucking New Guy." A sardonic title applied to any new arrival.
FAST:	Foreign Area Specialist Training: A military education program designed to train specialists for certain areas/countries of interest to the US government.
G1:	The personnel office of a general's staff.
G2:	The military intelligence office of a general's staff.
G3:	The operations office of a general's staff.
G4:	The logistics office of a general's staff.

G5:	The civic action office of a general's staff. This office performs liaison between the military and civilian communities.
Hat boi:	The traditional or "classical" style of Vietnamese dance theater, similar to opera.
Helipad:	Prepared landing pad for a helicopter.
Hoi Chanh:	An enemy turncoat. One who has switched sides under the terms of the "Chu Hoi" Program.
Hom qua:	Phonetic spelling of the Vietnamese word for "yesterday."
Home Guard:	A village or hamlet self defense unit.
Hooch:	Military slang for house (the temporary place the soldier currently dwells).
Huey:	The Iroquois HV-5 ( ) helicopter. The primary personnel carrying helicopter during Vietnam (and today).
IR:	Infra-Red: Heat sensing sensors usually mounted in special helicopters.
K-Bar knife	A commando knife, standard issue to the US Marine Corps.
KIA:	"Killed in Action."
Loach:	Slang term referring to a light observation helicopter with no troop carrying capacity.
Long noses:	A defamatory title used by some Vietnamese to mean westerners, especially, Americans.
LZ:	Landing Zone. The area designated for landing of helicopters, often during an airborne assault.

MACV:	Military Advisory Command, Vietnam. The headquarters for all advisor units.
Militia:	A reference to all territorial forces.
MOS:	Military Occupational Speciality: The career speciality of each soldier, i.e. "Infantry."
MP:	Military Police.
MPC	"Military Pay Script." Specially printed paper money issued to US military in Vietnam to preclude actual US dollars from being used in the black market.
MR1:	Main Route One: The chief highway running north and south throughout South Vietnam. This "highway" was often a two lane dirt road.
MSR:	Main Supply Route.
NCO:	Non Commissioned Officer:
Nouc Mam:	A processed fish oil, often mispronounced "nuke bomb." Used in Vietnam in the way soy sauce is used in other parts of the Orient.
NPFF:	National Police Field Forces; white shirted policemen belonging to a national police organization, but armed for combat against insurgent guerillas.
NVA:	North Vietnamese Army: regular army units from the north; quite separate from the VC.
OER:	Officer's Efficiency Report: A twice yearly report on each officer by his/her superior. Officers receive promotion or are cashiered from the service based upon these reports.
Pink Team:	A slang term for helicopter "Hunter—Killer" teams. One observation helicopter flying low

to draw fire and mark targets, and one or more armed helicopters (usually cobras) to respond to any hostile fire.

PNLF: Province National Liberation Forces. Province level VC headquarters.

POW: Prisoner of war.

Province: The South Vietnamese equivalent to a US "State." The Province Chief was roughly the same as the governor of a US state.

PSA: Province Senior Advisor: Advisor to the Province Chief.

PSDF: Province Self Defense Forces: Another level of militia, less "official" and less well armed than the RF/PF.

Purple Heart: Military award (medal) gained by being wounded as result of enemy action.

PX: Post Exchange. The military canteen/department store.

R&R: Rest and Rehabilitation: Military leave over and above the usual 30 days per year. In Vietnam, every soldier received at least one week of R&R, but some special programs (i.e. the FAST Program) allowed more.

RTO: Radio Telephone Operator.

Ruff-Puff—RF/PF: Regional, Provincial and District militia. Official National Guard units, highly militarized and composed of civilians on call to carry out military defense missions. Most of these units conducted constant routine daily and nightly missions. (These were different from the PSDF units).

RVN:	Republic of Vietnam. The official government of South Vietnam.
S1:	The personnel office of a military staff commanded by an officer below the rank of general.
S2:	The military intelligence office of a military staff commanded by an officer below the rank of general.
S3:	The operations office of a military staff commanded by an officer below the rank of general.
S4:	The logistics office of a military staff commanded by an officer below the rank of general.
S5:	The civic action office of a military staff commanded by an officer below the rank of general. This office performs liaison between the military and civilian communities.
Scrambler:	Military slang for secure radio frequency. The radio(s) in the TOC which were equipped with signal scramblers for military security.
Sin loi:	Phonetic spelling of the Vietnamese word for "I'm sorry."
Snifter:	A helicopter equipped with infra-red sensors to "sniff-out" enemy ground targets in heavy jungle areas.
Territorial Forces:	All militia units (Ruff-Puffs).
Thi:	"Little sister" in Vietnamese.
Tiu Ta:	Phonetic spelling of the Vietnamese word for "Major."

Tiu Wi:	Phonetic spelling of the Vietnamese word for "Lieutenant."
TOC:	Tactical Operations Center: The operations and communications hub of any level of organization; another equal term is "War Room."
Troom Ta:	Phonetic spelling of the Vietnamese word for "Lieutenant Colonel."
Um:	Phonetic spelling of Vietnamese title "Mr." Used in almost every discussion with or about the man in question.
VC:	Viet Cong. South Vietnamese guerrillas fighting against the South Vietnamese government.
VC legal cadre:	VC who carry legal South Vietnamese credentials. The covert forces of the VC.
VC Main Line Unit:	South Vietnamese regular units. Always armed, formed and ready (As opposed to legal cadre VC).
Victor Charlie	Viet Cong. This term was the (then) phonetic alphabet for "VC."
War College:	Advanced professional military course of approximately 9 months for Senior career Army officers (Colonel). (Some foreign officers of a more junior grade are admitted).

Act 1

SCENE 1

THE CASTLE

0600 HOURS
MONDAY, 1 JANUARY, 1968

"But Colonel, you didn't say deuces were wild!" Major Bill Clayborne's wide eyes showed both frustration and astonishment. His exposed hand revealed two jacks and two threes.

"Yes I did, Goddammit! I said it when I first got the deck. I can't help it if you-all got shit in your ears." The Texas drawl was pronounced.

"Sir, nobody heard you. One of the cards I threw away was a deuce. I ended up with three fives," Captain Hastings mumbled uncertainly.

"Well I said it Goddammit! And I've got two kings and two deuces, which makes four big mother humpers! Sure as hell beats your two pair, and would've beaten your four silly assed fives even if you had listened." he glared at the four men sitting around him at the table. All wore faded, olive drab tee shirts. None had shaved since the day before.

Major Buckingham, who had dropped out of the hand early, spoke calmly, soothingly. "Sir, you might have meant to say it, but nobody heard you."

"What about you Clarence? You heard me didn'tcha?"

First Lieutenant George paled. His single pair of aces stared weakly up at him from the green felt of the table. Everyone knew he didn't want to answer. The players glowered in silence. Finally, reluctantly, his voice softly whined, "Sir, I'm sorry, but I didn't hear you either."

"Oh, for Christ's sake! OK! We'll play the hand over. We'll leave this whole pot in for the ante, but it's still my fuckin deal!"

They all agreed with cowed and sullen faces.

Lieutenant Colonel Richard C. King pulled the cards on the table toward him and began cramming them together into a stack. "Clarence, pour us all some more coffee. It's too close to workin hours for a beer. Hastings, go out to the kitchen yonder'n tell Ba Mai to get her ass in here and clean out these fuckin breakfast dishes. This better be the last hand. Today may be a holiday back in round-eye land, but it's a work day in this shitty country."

The two junior officers pushed away from the poker table to do as they were told. King began to shuffle the cards, being careful, however, to covertly conceal his recent, almost winning hand on the bottom of the deck. Lucky for me, he thought, that I was last. I probably woulda called my hand just two pair if I'd laid down first. But I bluffed um! Bluffed um all. Haven't lost this fuckin hand yet. Shit, that's the name of the game in poker. Bluff um if you can, and by Christ I can!

Lieutenant George was still making his way around the table pouring from the huge brown porcelain coffee pot. Hastings hadn't yet returned.

"That's an unusual ring, Colonel," said Buckingham, evidently trying to ease the tension. "I've never seen a college ring that didn't have a stone in it."

"Texas A&M," King drawled. He placed his hand flat on the table for them to admire. He remembered that he had shown the ring to Buckingham less than a week before. Buck's tryin to be a diplomat, he thought. West Point social trainin comin through. Oh well, the others haven't heard about it.

"Every Texas A&M ring's the same." King's voice expressed pride. "All Aggies have um." The engraved eagle and shield on the flat gold face caught the light. "I earned this fuckin ring the hard way. Be'in an Aggie from Texas is tough enough, but, in my case it was harder. Even my classmates were against me. They tried to get me thrown outta school, but I showed um, by God! I stayed in and made DMG. In fact, I was the top Distinguished Military Graduate of my class. Been ahead of um ever since, the sons a bitches!"

"What do you mean being an Aggie from Texas is tough enough, Sir? Couldn't be harder to get through than West Point could it? Clayborne smiled. "Least that's what Buck always says." He grinned at Major Buckingham's squirming discomfort.

"Shit! West Point's a fuckin breeze compared to Texas A&M," King sputtered. He watched Buckingham's jaw twitch. "But that iddn't what I meant. Everbody in Texas hates us Aggies. They twist ever fuckin Polock joke into an Aggie joke, like how many Aggies does it take ta change a light bulb? Fuck um all! Fuck everbody from Texas!"

Ba Mai, the Vietnamese cook for the Americans in the castle, limped into the living room with an empty tray. She unhurriedly began gathering the multitude of used plates and cutlery scattered around the room. Hastings followed her in.

King stood up, holding the card deck in his hand. "Watch this guys." He bowed to her. "Chow Ba Mai."

The frail, elderly woman looked up from her task, obviously surprised by the greeting. Returning the bow, but with noticeable apprehension, she replied, "Chow, Troom Ta." She used the Vietnamese term for his rank title.

King bowed again and in a pleasant, deceptively charming tone asked, "Is it true Ba Mai, that maggots have eaten away all your pubic hair?"

Ba Mai stared at him uncomprehendingly. "Sin Loy Troom Ta, kum bic; kum bic." She shook her head from side to side.

"It's OK Ba; never mind; all OK; go ahead on." He waved his hand at the remaining dishes and sat down smirking.

Clayborne and George smothered sniggers of appreciation at the joke. The others smiled politely, suppressing their chagrin.

Ba Mai shrugged and resumed collecting the plates, but she had not missed the facial expressions. It was not the first time something like this had occurred since the American Troom Ta had become the Province Senior Advisor and moved into the house reserved for that office.

King readied himself to deal. "OK guys, for the last game, let's make the blood run red. All face cards and deuces are wild. I'll deal seven cards, but it's draw poker. Throw away two cards plus however many ya wanna draw. Aces are low. This is my special game. I call it the Imperial Orgy. Three of a kind never wins this fuckin game! Now, did everbody hear me this time, or should I repeat myself?"

All agreed that they had understood him. He began to deal. "Still rainin outside iddn't it?"

The others all paused, listening to the heavy patter on the roof. "Been raining like this all night." Hastings mused.

"Shit! It's always rainin; and hotter 'n holy Hell besides. I thought the winter monsoon season was supposed to be mild."

"Well Sir," Clayborne said, picking up his cards, "it's always milder than the summer monsoons. These rains now are coming from the west. In the summer wet season, the weather comes from the sea. Three months in each monsoon, but a lot more rain in the summer."

"Fuck! How can it rain any more'n it does now? Like we say in Texas, it's like a cow pissin on a flat rock!"

"Just wait and see, Sir. In the summer, we stand under elephants!"

King smiled to himself. The weather conversation had caused them all to concentrate on the intense sound of the storm. They hadn't noticed him dealing from the bottom.

"Want ya-all ta remember that today's special in more ways 'n one. It's my anniversary. I took over as PSA one month ago today. Kicked those fuckin civilians out and moved us over here that same day. Hand picked you guys ta live with me, so it's our anniversary a be'in together as a team within a team. Hope ya-all 'preciate it."

"Hell, who wouldn't Sir? Better bennies, and this villa sure beats the quonset huts of Camp Kronberg," Major Clayborne crooned.

"Good," King snorted. "Your bet Clarence."

"Yes Sir," Lieutenant George said. He had winced again at the sound of his first name.

"Oh, I forgot. You don't like me ta call ya Clarence do ya?"

"No Sir, I'd rather you didn't."

"Why not? It's your name iddn't it?"

"It's my name Sir, but I hate it. I've always been called Duke. My dad wanted me to be like John Wayne. He started it, and I still like Duke better than…."

"Well, OK Duke, quit whinin, 'n bet. Yore holdin up the game." King grinned at the others.

"I'll check," blurted George.

"You'd better not be checkin an raisin, you little fart. Yore bet Buck."

"A dollar."

"Big Buck bets a buck," chortled Clayborne for the tenth time that night. "OK, it's up to me huh?"

He called, and tossed a blue MPC dollar bill into the pot.

"OK, yore bet Earl."

Captain Hastings paused. His face twitched. "I'll raise a dollar," he said as if making an impulsive decision.

"And I'll bump it another buck," said King, as he tossed three crumpled script notes into the pile. "Three to you Duke."

George called, as did all the others.

King glanced at his cards again. The two kings and two deuces as before; a three from the previous hand, and two fours. He chuckled under his breath, six fuckin fours, but that's no good. I'll sure get somethin better'n a four. Only five ov'um'll count. He tossed all but his four wild cards into the discard pile. "Cards," he announced.

Lieutenant George flipped five cards into the pile. "Three, Sir," he said.

King dealt the cards. Clarence should be no sweat, he thought. I wonder if I could manage a quick peek to see what the bottom card is?

"No peeky, Sir," bawled Clayborne jovially. The others laughed. "I'll take two."

"I wasn't peekin," blustered King, glaring at Clayborne. "How many you want Buck?"

"I'll stand pat," Major Buckingham replied dryly.

"Oh shitttt!" King blurted. The cigarette haze in the room seemed suddenly thicker.

"I'll take three," Captain Hastings muttered.

"And dealer takes one," King ejaculated. He looked at his card. It was the ace of spades. Motherfucker! he fumed. I shoulda kept a four!

"Lets start this round with three dollars," Buckingham said calmly.

"Raise a buck," said Clayborne carelessly.

"I'm out," said Hastings.

"Call," King snarled.

"I'll call too," said George.

Buckingham also called.

Clayborne laid down the five, seven and eight of clubs, a queen and a jack. "Straight flush, nine high," he beamed.

George tossed his cards in face down. "Beats my full house," he said lamely. He had been the heavy looser for the night, as always.

"I've got five nines," said Buckingham.

"Not good enough; I've got five aces!" shouted King.

The smoke in the room hung in heavy, silent layers.

"You said aces were low, Sir," Buckingham reminded him.

"The Hell I did!"

"Yes Sir; I'm afraid you did. Your tongue must have slipped or something, but you sure as Hell said it," Clayborne chimed in, his wide smile transparently tenuous.

"I heard you too, Sir," whispered George, wide eyed.

Should I bluff it through again? King wondered. He knew he could, though even the coward Hastings was nodding in agreement with the others. At worst they would play another hand. He felt the tension in the room. Tight, restrictive. No; better not. They're all together. They'd go along eventually, but they'd be pissed. Fuck um. I'll give in this time and next game I'll raise the stakes. "Well," he said, as if the words hurt him physically, "I didn't mean ta say it. Shit! Aces are only low in Low Ball. Never played Imperial Orgy with aces low before, but if I said it, then that's the way it is. I'm a man of honor, and true to my word. Nobody can ever say that I go back on my word. It's yore pot Buck."

Air expelled from four pairs of relieved lungs. Everyone relaxed and smiled. Buckingham raked in his winnings. "Come to Papa," he crowed; "biggest pot of the night."

"Well, I still came out ahead," King groused. But only about ten bucks ahead, he thought. Fuckin lucky bastard. That last pot shoulda been mine. "OK, time ta go ta work guys," he said.

The others stood, stretched and wearily climbed into their fatigue jackets. Two of them slipped into ponchos; the others prepared to brave the storm with no rain gear.

"You-all go ahead," King called out as he headed for the bathroom, "cept you Bill, you stay awhile. I need to talk to ya."

In the bright yellow and white tiled bathroom, King stripped off his tee shirt, washed, and lathered his face for a shave. Major Clayborne appeared in the doorway, lounging against the door frame.

"We can talk here if you want Sir, if all you're going to do is shave; but if you're going to do anything else, I'd kinda prefer to wait in the living room."

"Just shavin," drawled King; his smirk acknowledged Clayborne's attempt at humor. "Wha'dja think a the party?"

"Well Sir, it was a great party. Could'n'a been better; 'cept maybe if we'd'a had some broads in."

"Fuck! The only broads we could'a gotten would'a been slant eyes. Whores at that! Buckingham would'n'a liked it, 'n George's probably a virgin. Would'n'a known what to do. Would've ruined our poker night."

"Maybe poker's OK for you, Sir; you're married and your wife's in the Philippines. That special PSA program you're in will let you get to see her every cuppla months or so. You've only been here about six months and you've already had at least three conjugal R & R's. Me? I miss women. I'm always horny. Hell, I've jacked off in the shower so often since I've been here, I get a hard on every time it rains!"

King grinned as he down stroked his razor. "I've only been back twice you Ass Hole. My third's comin up as soon as I get someone in who's competent to watch over this fuckin team while I'm gone." His eyes met those of his Senior Operations Advisor in the mirror. Clayborne hadn't taken the mild insult personally, as he could have. As he should have, King thought.

"Well," he said, "the party's over now, so my rule is off. We can talk shop now. Bring me up to date with what's goin on."

"OK Sir. First of all, your new Deputy PSA's in country."

"Hey, that's good news. Looks like I'll get ta go ta Australia for R & R this week. Who the fuck is he?"

"I don't know Sir. No one else seems to either. I checked with all the civilian sources I know of, and no one knows anything. CORDS Saigon says no new State Department civilian has come in country in the last two weeks. Best I can figure is that we're not getting an FNG, you know, a Fuckin New Guy; he's probably an in-country transfer."

"Good again. Maybe I won't have ta break him in 'n teach him how to work with these fuckin Dink nut scratchers over here. What else?"

"Well Sir, Da Nang G2 says their info still shows a North Vietnamese Army regiment about ten clicks west of Hau Duc, and they're burning our butts for not getting a Ruff-Puff patrol out there to check it out. They kept asking for you personally on the horn."

"You didn't tell um didja?"

"No Sir. I wouldn't do that. They'd shit if they knew you were out sunning yourself on the Ly Tin patrol boat. I told them you were with the Province Chief trying to talk him into it."

King again caught Clayborne's eyes in the mirror. What's Bill staring at? he thought; hasn't he ever seen a man shaving before? "What're the Vietnamese doin about it? Anything?"

"Nothing Sir. My counterpart, Major Hai, he's willing. Seems to think a patrol's the right thing to do, but he's just staff; the S3, like me. He's out of the chain of command; can't order a unit commander to send out a patrol. All he can do is make a recommendation. Colonel Tu, the Deputy Province Chief's been outta town, on leave or something. I think he's getting back today. Hai went over to the PC's office again last evening to try to get the Chief to reconsider, but he wouldn't. That fat fucker's dead set against it."

"Did he give the same reason as before, or did he come up with a new excuse this time?"

"Same ole shit Sir. The Dai Ta says that his stars say it's still a bad time to send a patrol outta Hau Duc."

"Motherfucker! That fuckin slope head won't take a piss unless his Goddamn stars say it's OK!"

"A lot of um are that way, Sir. Major Hai, my counterpart, he's a real chatterbox. He's been telling me about it. Even he believes in it a little bit."

"I'll go over'n see Colonel Biet this mornin. If his fuckin stars let him get outta bed today, I'll get him to send out a patrol one way or another." Finishing his left cheek, King reached across to downstroke the lather on the right side of his face. "Anything else?"

"Well Sir, you're looking a little ragged this morning. maybe you should take a nap after visiting with the Dai Ta. You know you older officers can't take staying up all night like us younger studs."

King smiled again, his mouth still slightly framed by shaving cream. He bluffed as if to flick the foam laden razor at his smirking subordinate, but Clayborne recognized the ruse and only pretended to duck.

He's a real smart ass, thought King. More of a clown than a soldier. Likes to fuck around; thinks he's a Goddamn comedian, but he does make me laugh. He's the only one with balls enough to even try to rag me a little; and he always keeps it humorous. Way down deep though, he's even more scared of me than the others. Maybe that's why I let him get away with it.

"You Sonuvabitch," he drawled, as he turned back to the mirror. I'm only a year older'n you, but I've been a lieutenant colonel for three years already. You, Pecker head, won't even be eligible for the list till next year. I'm as wide awake as you are, and if you wanna see how fit I am, I'll lay my rank down 'n take yore ass anytime you want. Now ya got any more news for me?"

"Only one thing Sir. I lined up an Air America flight from Saigon to Tam Ky to bring in the new Deputy, assuming he's not a ghost. So whoever he is, we oughtta see him sometime this afternoon. We also got a message that a replacement TOC Shift Sergeant has been assigned from Camp Alpha. I sent word that he should catch the same flight."

"Well I'll be damn! Sometimes you do get something right."

"That's it Sir. Anything you want done?"

"Yeah. Let's see how many real men we have around here after New Year's Eve. Call everbody out at noon, just before chow. Give um a half hour of PT. Make um all run at least a mile in addition to the exercises. I want you to lead it personally over here at the TOC, and pick someone else ta lead it at Camp Kronberg. Call the districts 'n get the DSA's ta lead their troops in the same drill. Then tell the club we'll have another party tonight. We'll call it a welcome party for the new Deputy Province Senior Advisor. We'll just see who feels younger tonight you shit for brains. And, by the way, be sure they have a billet for this new ass hole at Camp Kronberg. I sure don't want any candy-assed civilian livin over here in the castle with us; but don't give him the trailer either. That's for the senior military guy at Kronberg, the camp commander. This new civilian may officially be the number two man on this advisory team, but I'm never gonna let him be any kind of commander over my troopers!"

"Yes Sir. Willco Sir." Clayborne wheeled to his right in an exaggerated military about face. "As the abacus said to the Chinaman Sir, you can count on me! I'll carry you home and put you to bed nice and cozy after the party tonight. After that, some of us younger tigers, well, we'll really start partying then."

"Fuck off!" King shouted as he watched Clayborne's mirror image salute with the wrong hand and spin to the left, which made the joking move even funnier than intended. King's eyes returned to his own double.

The sound of boot heels clicking discordantly down the polished tile hallway of the old, majestic French villa stopped, followed by the rising squeal of the screen door opening. "OK Colonel, I'll find you if I get any hot poop you should hear." The screen door screeched again and banged shut.

King continued shaving. I wonder if the stars are the real reason that fuckin province chief won't send out a patrol, he thought. He might be tryin a power play to show me who's really the boss of this Goddamn province. I wish I hadn't told Lamar that I'd check out that G2 report. Of course, G2 is probably wrong. There couldn't be an NVA regiment that close to Hau Duc! What would they be after? Hou Duc is such a small district. Just one village. Just two or three hamlets. It's not worth nuthin. No skin off my balls if it does fall. Who the fuck would give a shit anyway? But by God, I told Lamar I'd get a patrol out there ta check it out, and I will! I'm too new at this job ta have anyone in Da Nang thinkin any negative thoughts about me. I'm the only light colonel in a full colonel's slot in the entire country, and I aim ta keep it! I'll show that fuckin Dink who's really in charge of this province, no matter why he's playin chickenshit!

His doppleganger in the mirror smiled in agreement.

King wiped his face clean and stepped back to study his image. From his trouser pocket, he pulled a lipstick-like tube of theatrical make up. Carefully, as with much practice, he dabbed at the red, mushroom shaped birthmark around and his left eye. Wish I could blot it out completely, he thought, but I can't. It always shows through, no matter how much I put on. Even worse here in the tropics; sweat really fucks it up. I've got to find some darker stuff when I'm in Sydney later this week; the rest of my face's gettin too much sun.

A separate thought struck him. Ahh, that's why Bill looked at me so perplexed just now. It's the first time he's ever seen my mark without make up coverin it. The silly ass hole's probably jokin about it right now at the TOC with the rest of the advisory team. Even the fuckin dinks are probably laughin their heads off. Clayborne'll do anything for a laugh, the stupid clown; I can just see him wearin a red ribbon or a fuckin orchid over his eye 'n drawlin like he's from Texas. Fuck it! I'll get the last laugh on him at OER time; 'n the rest of the bastards as well!

He stepped back again to evaluate his art work. There, that's better. I'd actually be handsome if Nature hadn't fucked with me, but this Goddamn blotch hasn't stopped me yet. I've been laughed at before, lots of times, but I always get even.

"You are the fuckin PSA of Quang Tin Province trooper." He said this aloud as he pointed at himself in the mirror. His jaw became rigid, and the red mushroom mark tightened around his eye as he squinted. "And no one can stop ya now!"

He and his reflection relaxed and winked at each other with their unmarked eyes. "Damn fuckin right!" they both said with one voice.

King donned a freshly starched fatigue jacket with black oak leaves embroidered on the collar; "King" over the right breast pocket, and "US ARMY" over the left. He pinned the Vietnamese rank equivalent badge, a gold bar with two silver pips over it, onto his jacket front, and meandered down the hallway to the living room. He was mildly surprised at the neatness. White stucco walls, several brightly colored easy chairs and two brown leather sofas dominated the high ceilinged room. A large green and yellow oriental rug sparkled on the white floor tiles. A tinsel "Happy New Year" sign still hung from strips of scotch tape on one wall, but the Vietnamese servants had already brought order to the chaos of the night before. Even the card table had been put away.

He pulled his web belt from the row of pegs on the wall and snapped it around him. The weight of the pistol felt solid and comfortable against his hip. Gotta find a reason ta use it soon, he thought. Hell, I've gotta win me some more medals if I'm gonna make general.

He strolled to the boxy wardrobe in the foyer. Opening the wooden doors, he grabbed his poncho from a hook and slipped it over his jacket. He started to reach for his ball cap, but hesitated. The hairs on the back of his neck prickled his skin. The tips of his fingers tingled. Something. What is it? He shuddered involuntarily. Something was wrong.

He glanced at the top shelf where his helmet, soft cover and two fatigue ball caps rested. Nothing out of place. Nothing moved. His field jacket hung on a hanger in the main section. Everything appeared to be in order. But? Something! He studied the bottom shoe dowel where a pair of extra boots and his old slippers sat suspended above the floor. The electric light bulb under the boots glowed eerily, protecting the leather from mildew. The trapped heat poured from the open door as it always did. Nothing seemed out of place.

But something was different. He felt it. He smelled it. He knew it. A booby trap? Could the VC have entered the Castle? Was Ba Mai VC? Or the hooch maid? Was it someone else? Could one of his men be planning to frag him?

He scanned for wires. No wires. Maybe it was just imagination. The jungle jitters. Maybe I'm a little hung over from last night. No, the feeling was real. He trusted the feeling, it had saved him before.

Carefully, gingerly, he clasped the bill of a ball cap and jerked it to the floor. Nothing! He grabbed the bill of the other and jerked. It plunked heavily onto a circular throw rug and tumbled. A brightly banded snake recovered quickly and squirmed frantically across the tiles toward the living room.

A krait! Motherfucker, someone put a fuckin krait in my cap! "Ba Mai!" he shouted.

The limping woman appeared immediately, drying her hands with a towel. He pointed at the red and black snake, which was just disappearing into the hangar-like gap under one of the easy chairs.

Ba Mai blinked with surprise and disappeared. The towel glided gently to the floor where she had been standing.

Shit! King thought. Damn Gooks can't do nothin. Afraid of their own shadow. He pulled the .45 caliber pistol from his holster. Hafta do it myself, like I hafta do everthing round here. He walked carefully to the chair, which now completely concealed the deadly viper.

He put his hand on the chair to push it, but suddenly realized that his canvas topped jungle boots were well within the krait's striking distance. Shuddering, he awkwardly hopped and danced backward watching his feet intently. Jesus! Standing as far away as he could, gripping the automatic firmly with one hand, he leaned and shoved at the chair with the other. The chair didn't budge. The damn thing weighs a ton, he thought. How in Hell am I gonna do this?

Ba Mai reappeared, limping resolutely toward him. Her thin rounded shoulders were set with determination. In one hand she carried a metal bowl, in the other, a machete. She stopped before him, bowed courteously, and, ignoring his drawn pistol, pushed him gently to one side with the bowl.

Facing the chair, she tossed the bowl over it so that it clattered resoundingly on the tiles. While the metallic clamor still resonated through the room, she padded softly to the chair, shoved it effortlessly to one side, and whacked off the snake's head in one flowing motion.

She turned, bowed again to King, and hobbled to retrieve the bowl and the towel. King stood dumbstruck with his mouth agape, his pistol still in hand, as she used the machete to scoop both parts of the dead reptile into the bowl. With the towel, she diligently wiped the tiles clean, and then, with no apparent exertion, pulled the large bulky chair back into its original position.

Bowing yet once more to the still open mouthed American, she limped with the machete, bowl and gory towel back to her kitchen.

King released a slow whistle. Racing thoughts flooded his mind. The krait's a nerve viper. You'd die within ten minutes without the antidote. Ba Mai's leg had been broken by the VC when her husband wouldn't join them. The VC had killed him. She sure as shit can use a machete! Kraits can climb. Found um on top of metal wall lockers before, and it's not unusual to find um in a heated wardrobe. She bowed to me like she always does, but her eyes are never respectful like they should be. She looked almost hostile. Fuckin Gooks are always hostile. Sure waddn't scared though! Fuckin Gooks. Can't trust any of um. Wait a minute! Who'd be the one who'd most likely put that thing in there? That Goddamn fat Biet! My fuckin counterpart! It would be just like that slope sonuvabitch. Rumor says he murdered his predecessor. Maybe so and maybe not. But I know he got ridda Gonzaga, my predecessor. Of course, I kinda helped with that. Why not? I'm a lot better PSA 'n he ever was. But whatever, Biet's a slimy fat turd who'll do anything to anyone who might stand in his way. He's obviously after me now, the gook motherfucker! I was gonna be nice 'n try ta get him to send a patrol on his own. Not now! I'll show him by God! There'll be a patrol tonight, 'n no more fuckin snakes or I'll stick a cobra up his ass. It's high time he learns who really runs this Hell hole of a province!

SCENE 2

SAIGON

0600 Hours
Monday, 1 January 1968

Hell! This sure is a weird way to start off the new year, Jake thought. I don't even know what I'm going to be doing this afternoon, much less beyond that. Here I am standing on a street corner in a war zone, waiting for a damn taxi because the general himself wants to give me my orders. I wonder why he needs this personal, one on one touch? It must be something he considers difficult or dangerous, or maybe secret. Hell! I hope he doesn't expect me to volunteer for some kind of suicide mission!

A baby screamed. The frightened, terrified wail pierced through the early Saigon traffic. Jake turned to glance behind him at the shabby shop which seemed to be the source of the sound. No one else paid any attention to the noise. The sky had brightened, but the infant's cry cut through the air like a night siren. Jake couldn't ignore it. He squared his shoulders and marched toward the closed bamboo door.

Sunlight streamed past and ahead of him as he pushed into the room, illuminating the tableau of tension, hatred and fear inside. The scene reminded Jake of a stage setting, with the actors as grotesque statues of frozen action. An old woman stood in a corner clutching the shrieking child to her frail body. The shopkeeper groveled on his knees, his bloody face jerked toward the door, torn between hope for rescue and fear of more violence. An American sailor stood over him with a fist poised to strike again. Another Sailor half leaned, half sprawled against a rickety homemade bar.

"What's going on here?" Jake asked, holding the glazed stare of the attacker's with his own steady eyes.

The sailor dropped his fist. He turned in confusion to the relaxed one. The old woman began to nervously bounce the baby in her arms, apparently making the first effort to calm the child.

"Shit, Sir, waddn't our fault. It's fuckin New Years, an these stupid slopes wouldn't give us no American booze. Can't celebrate New Years on Tiger Beer can ya?"

Jake took a deep breath. They were drunk, mean drunk. A waste of time to talk. Something else might set them off any minute. Glad there's enough light in here for them to recognize my rank.

"Outside," he ordered. "Now!"

He held the door as they stumbled into the sunlight. Following them, he saw an MP jeep approaching in the swarm of bicycles and old automobiles. He beckoned and the jeep immediately wheeled to the curb.

"These two clowns are plastered," he said, amazed at his luck that the police had been so handy. "They just beat up the proprietor of that little bar over there. You can handle this from here on can't you Sergeant?"

The Army MP sergeant saluted as he reached for the handcuffs with his other hand. His glance reading the name patch on Jake's fatigue shirt. "Yes Sir. We'll take um into the brig right now. I'll be back later to get the statement from the victim. Can we give you a lift somewhere Major Thorpe?"

Jake looked at his watch and then back at the shop. The baby still bawled. "No thanks. I need to do something before I leave here."

"OK, Sir. Happy New Year by the way."

The jeep pulled away with the two sullen sailors trundled into the back seat. Jake headed back for the tiny bar.

As he opened the door again, he noticed the silence. The infant had stopped crying. The two Vietnamese adults both came forward smiling and bowing. Their gratitude exploded from their eyes. The man clutched Jake's hand and pumped it vigorously. "Number one, GI, number one," he bubbled. The old woman held back, wiping a tear from her eyes.

Jake had come in to check on the extent of the man's injuries, and to tell them that the military police would soon return to square things away. Their unexpected display embarrassed him. "Thanks," he stammered, it's OK, OK."

He noticed the baby now propped into a sofa corner with a bottle. The sofa had a tear in one cushion, and at least one wooden chair had been smashed. Broken glass lay scattered across the floor. The sailors had vandalized the shop, they must have been in here longer than I thought. These people have suffered even more than I thought.

Jake tried to remember the few Vietnamese words he had learned during his first tour, two years ago, but his mind wouldn't cooperate. He did suddenly remember, however, that he had just exchanged his stateside dollars for MPC.

He reached into his pocket and drew out several crisp new notes. The Vietnamese saw his intentions and threw up their hands in determined refusal. "No pay, GI, no pay. You number one. You no pay!"

Smiling himself now, Jake strode across the room to the baby. He looked down at the face of hungry innocence. Calmly and carefully, for he really wasn't confident around children, he tucked several brightly colored MPC notes under the child's chubby arm, bowed his head to the thankful couple, and returned to the Saigon sunlight to catch his cab.

He waived one down, leaned back into the torn upholstery of the rear seat, and tried to relax. He knew he was already late for his appointment. His eyes caught the bustling groups of pedestrians crowding the sidewalks even at this time of day. Saigon hasn't changed at all, he thought. The Oriental men, who dressed blandly in either white shirts and black trousers or black two piece suits that everyone called black pajamas, hustled and pushed their way through. Color seemed to be reserved for the females, and it served them well. A few young girls paraded in multihued mini skirts or bright pants suits, but most women wore au yis.

Yes, the au yi; Jake grinned as he remembered. There is nothing like an au yi. The tight, long sleeved blouse with flowing ankle length panels hanging front and back over black or white silk trousers. The garment, unique to Vietnam, gave the effect of a long dress, enticingly slit to the waist on both sides.

This morning, au yis of every color sprinkled the streets: solids and polka dots; flowered prints and sequined flashes; cotton, silk and muslin; all blinking and swirling from the crowded sidewalks like neon lights on the dusty grey face of the city. Jake nodded to himself in the reaffirmation of his first tour feeling that, for women, the au yi was the most attractive and seductive national costume ever.

The women, however, whether in Western or Asian dress, almost all wore the conical straw hat of the Orient, and, in contrast to the scurrying males, walked unhurriedly with easy grace and unworried strides. He marveled at the differences he saw in the two sexes.

Yin and Yang, Jake thought. The Oriental theory of opposites. For male there is female; for fire there is water; and for good there is evil. Everything in this crazy world over here has a natural antagonist. All of the elements of nature are in a constant state of war. He remembered studying the concept back when he had been a university student. He had gained an A in the course, but it didn't really make sense back then. It had taken that first tour of duty, one full year in Asia, to make it at least somewhat understandable.

"No sweat GI," the driver shouted over the din. "We do easy. Number one; number one." He pumped the throttle with the clutch partially engaged, and the old engine roared with the high pitched scream of speed as the taxi continued to crawl through the clogged streets. He smiled to himself at the driver's broken English. Every Vietnamese he'd ever met knew how to say "no sweat", "number one" and "OK".

Jake's back felt wet. He smiled as he realized he was sweating despite the driver's assurance to the contrary. Son of a bitch, this tropical heat sure brings back memories. It's always so damned hot here in Vietnam, even this early in the morning.

He looked at his watch. Fifteen after six. I've only been in country for four hours! The spec-five who had been in charge of processing last night had expressed surprise to find no orders for him. Instead, there had been a note in his arrival packet.

"Sir, this says you are to report to General Elsin at oh six hundred hours this morning for your assignment. Must be something special. Do you know General Elsin Sir?"

Jake nodded that he did.

"That's great Sir. Maybe he'll give you a cushy job here in Saigon. Maybe he needs an aide or a gopher."

Jake smiled at that. Not bloody likely, he thought. I've served under Elsin twice before. The first time as one of his staff officers in the 82nd Airborne Division when Elsin had been a battle group deputy commander, and the second time here in Vietnam two years ago. We got along well, both times. He's a hard ass who expects results, and so far, I've been able to give them. But Elsin's not the type to cut corners just to do a favor for one of his old subordinates. He's got a job for me all right, but he's picking me because he needs someone he can trust. He thinks maybe I might be able to come through again.

He looked again at the scene outside. Bicycles swarmed like hungry insects. Motorbikes and motorcycles putt-putted before billowing plumes of exhaust smoke. In the midst of the demure pedal powered vehicles and the robust, flatulent two wheelers, ancient hump backed automobiles and Army trucks inched along in jerky motions like confused, clumsy beetles which have accidentally blundered into a stream of worker ants.

Jake glanced down at his stateside starched fatigue uniform. It's wrinkled from being packed in my garment bag, and this sweating I'm doing sure isn't helping. I'll look like a landed fish in front of the general.

He chuckled silently. What the Hell am I doing worrying about my appearance in Vietnam? Appearance standards are relaxed over here. It's a war zone for God's sake!

He slid closer to the open rear window behind the driver so as to catch as much of the breeze as possible. He rested his arm in the opening and gazed out at the teeming confusion which was Saigon. Yes, it's just as I remember.

He inhaled the aroma. Spices and fish, fresh flowers and perfume. Charcoal smoke, exhaust fumes, hot asphalt, and the smell of open sewers. The perfume of the Orient; the scent of excitement! He smiled with pleasure at the broad tree lined boulevards and statue dominated street intersections. Saigon! Such a magnificent, thriving, unique city!

The buildings, as in any metropolis, uniformed themselves in solid grey masonry. Here in the capital of South Vietnam though, temporary vendor stalls of every description squatted among them like ugly weeds in an untended lawn. Unsightly shacks of old wood, tin and pierced steel planking formed the best of these, but most were nothing but flimsy cloth awnings or faded burlap, draped over taut wire.

Hawkers stood in and around the stalls shouting and chanting their wares in melodic Vietnamese. They peddled pocket knives, pots, pans, fresh flowers, and garish paintings on felt or velvet. They sold tools and trinkets; sunglasses and souvenirs; cigarettes and sandals; jewelry and underwear.

Jake saw a jacket for sale, made from a US Army poncho liner, with the words: "VIETNAM—When I die, I know I'm going to Heaven, because I've spent my time in Hell," embroidered into the back.

Business begins early in Saigon, Jake thought, even on New Year's day. And war, he realized, makes good business in Vietnam, just as it does back home.

The driver raced his engine again. He raised his fist out the window and shouted what Jake took to be an insult at a young bicyclist who had daringly knifed between the taxi and the car ahead. Jake smiled. It's like San Francisco or New York, he thought. Taxi drivers the world over seem to be cut from the same mold.

Jake pushed his elbow further into the morning breeze so that his left shoulder protruded from the taxi. The books all say it takes two weeks to get acclimated, he remembered, but right now it seemed that he would never get used to the sweltering heat. He noticed the several billboards along the boulevard. Most of them painted red and yellow, the South Vietnamese national colors. Propaganda signs, he thought, "educating" or "motivating" the people. Damned right. The government should make these attempts to win over the people. They weren't doing anything like that last time I was here, but the Viet Cong did all kinds of "educating."

The taxi pulled into the left lane of the one way street so that Jake felt even closer to the people on the sidewalks. He searched their faces for expressions of fear, or oppression, or hostility, or desperation. There were none. The people looked busy and content. They laughed and smiled as people do everywhere. Jake stroked a bead of sweat from his chin. They're still taking it in stride, he thought. The war is just a hump in the road. Life goes on.

The driver pointed his left arm straight out in a turn signal, almost blocking the slight street draft. The taxi slowed almost to a stop and crawled hesitantly around the corner into another one way street.

Then the vehicle breeze did die, and Jake felt the stagnating heaviness of the tropics settle over him like a mantle. The people now stood scant inches away from his elbow as they waited for the taxi to pass. Faces blurred, but voices were clear. "Hey GI; you want girl?" "Hey GI; change money?" "How about doll for babysan GI?"

Suddenly, Jake felt a sharp tug at his arm. His Spidell wristband bit into his flesh. A violent jerk outward. The sharp snap of metal popping. His hand whipped involuntarily into the crowd, and his wristwatch was gone!

"Hey! Wait! Stop! Stop the car! Someone stole my watch!" he shouted. He grabbed for the driver's shoulder while trying to look backward to identify the thief. But the driver didn't understand.

"No sweat GI. We do easy. Number one; number one."

The cab eased into the heavy traffic in the new direction. It wouldn't do any good anyway, Jake thought. The quick fingered robber had already blended into the crowd. I wouldn't know who to chase even if the taxi did stop. He rubbed his sore wrist, noticing the ghostly outline of the missing timepiece on his tanned arm. "Welcome back to Vietnam," he mumbled ruefully. "That's a new trick since last time."

Sighing, Jake gazed again at the thronging street scenes. Uniforms appeared everywhere. A few tiger striped Vietnamese marines, and a few Americans in office-work khaki, but mostly, the combat fatigues of the ARVN or local militia dominated. Several were on duty with rifles slung over their shoulders.

This is the only sign of the actual war, Jake thought. No bullet holes, no starvation, no shell craters, no ruins. Only lightly armed, lethargic soldiers casually parceled out among the pedestrians; and none of them saw the son of a bitch who stole my watch!

They rolled past the My Cong floating restaurant. It had already been bombed five times. No one knew why. The Viet My restaurant next door had better American food and was less expensive, yet it had never been bombed. Jake smiled grimly. He'd heard a sergeant talking about restaurants last night. He'd said it was almost impossible to find a good Vietnamese restaurant in Saigon. French, Japanese, Italian, Indian, Chinese, American and Mexican restaurants could be found. All of high quality. But no popular restaurants which served Vietnamese food. He glanced at the sign of the restaurant they were now passing. "Greek Food and Turkish Cuisine" the marque advertised. Jake shook his head in wonder.

Three blocks later, they arrived at CORDS Headquarters; a new command, not in existence on his previous tour. "Civil Operations and Revolutionary Development Support," the gate sign explained. Jake puzzled at what the words really meant. Revolutionary Development? Hell, it sounds like we're the guerrillas.

He left his bags with the central receptionist and walked, as directed, down the long, polished wood paneled corridor to the far corner office. Ceiling fans hummed overhead.

Brigadier General Eugene P. Elsin greeted him at the door of his office. "Hello Jake. Happy New Year. I'm sure you're not surprised that we still work on weekends and holidays over here?"

Jake smiled. "No Sir, I remember."

Elsin placed his hand paternally on Jake's shoulder. "Looks like our paths are destined to keep on crossing."

"Yes Sir, General. Especially if you keep sending for me whenever I arrive at a new theater. Sorry I'm late by the way." Elsin shrugged, "Heard about your run in with the Navy. When you weren't here on time, I figured something must have happened, so I had my aide check with the MPs. They said you handled it well. How was your trip?"

"The flight was fine Sir. Had a little problem on the way here this morning though. Someone snatched my watch as we made a left turn."

Elsin grinned, "You sure aren't the first one to fall for that trick. You might set the record for being the one with the shortest time in country though. Had your arm out the window didn't you?"

"I sure did Sir. Won't do that again."

Elsin led Jake back into the interior of the spacious office with its massive mahogany desk, thick oriental carpet and dazzling European chandelier.

"You know why expensive wrist watches are the most stolen items in Vietnam don't you?"

Jake didn't.

"Well, these Vietnamese bandits are pretty smart. What they do is, they steal a good watch, say an Omega or a Seiko, any kind of good watch. Then they go out and buy a local cheap one for say a hundred piasters, about eighty cents. Then they swap the guts. Put the cheap works in the good watch and the expensive works behind the cheap face. You get it yet?"

"No Sir," Jake confessed. He waited for the explanation, remembering as he did so that Elsin had a penchant for details; that's how he had earned the nickname: "The Don't be General General."

"Well, they go out to some crony who's got a little savvy and they sell him the cheap face with the good insides. He'll pay through the nose for it because it'll be reliable and even more so. You see, since it looks cheap, nobody'll steal it from him. He's willing to pay a little more for peace of mind.

So now they've got the expensive watch with the low quality works inside to sell to some dumb schmuck, who'll pay double the PX price for a fancy hunk of junk he thinks is black market, but it won't keep time for shit. When the damned thing stops, he can't complain, cause the black market's illegal. Those guys who ripped off your watch'll make up to four or five times its PX value, and if they didn't get caught in the act of actually stealing it, they'll never get reported."

"I'll be damned," said Jake, a bit dazed at the ingenuity involved. "By stealing watches so often, they've created their own market for items that aren't appealing to thieves."

Elsin sat on the corner of his highly polished desk. His short jet black hair had begun to show a few grey strands, Jake noticed. He looks a lot older than I remember.

The general continued to talk in a rambling manner about how some thieves kept an expensive watch just for show while selling cheap watches with their original insides for fifty to one hundred times their value by just claiming the insides had been switched.

He has no tan at all, and he's lost weight too, Jake realized. Elsin had never been heavy, but now he looked as thin as a rifle barrell. Must be the Vietnamese food; or the strain of the job, he amended.

The general stood again and walked slowly to the center of the room. Jake knew the small talk had ended. Elsin's head bowed in concentration. Here it comes.

With his head still facing the carpet, Elsin began almost hesitantly. "I'm going to send you to Quang Tin Province Jake. You're going to be the Deputy Province Senior Advisor there. The number two man. It's supposed to be a civilian State Department slot. But I'm going to send you. You with me so far?"

"Yes Sir." Jake knew the curtain hadn't risen yet. This had been just the prelude.

"You've been on the promotion list for how long now Jake?"

"It's been slow, Sir; The list came out the first of August, I've been a major bow legs P for five months so far."

"That's what I thought, that means that at the present speed of the list, you'll probably make lieutenant colonel about April. The thing is though, I don't want you going up there as a major. I know these people by now; this is my second tour also."

The two men looked at each other, both remembering. The last time had been such a short two years ago, in the delta, when Elsin had been a full colonel and brigade commander. Jake Thorpe had been a captain and company commander in the same brigade.

"You were a bow legs P then too weren't you?" Elsin asked.

"Yes sir, I made major right after I hit stateside."

"Well, as I say, I know the Vietnamese. They are much more rank conscious than we are. If you arrive up there as a major, you'll be a major in their eyes your entire tour, no matter when you put on your silver leaves. That's why I want you to arrive as a lieutenant colonel. Co Bai...," he called. "Come on in here, and bring Lieutenant Bernardo."

His Vietnamese secretary and a tall general's aide entered the room.

"Co Bai and Lieutenant Bernardo will be our witnesses," he proclaimed.

He pinned a metal silver oak leaf over the gold embroidered major's insignia on Jake's collar and handed him a small parcel of emblems. A handful of the glittering metal badges and several new cloth rank patches lay in Thorpe's dumbfounded hands.

"That's one of my old leaves on your collar. I took the liberty of gathering all the others for you because I knew you wouldn't have time."

Jake felt a lump begin to form in his throat. With all the bluster, there was a warmth in this man that was unmistakable. Jake tried to say something appropriate but nothing would come out.

Elsin continued as if there had been no emotion whatever. "Your airplane leaves for Tam Ky City at oh nine thirty this morning. Make sure all your uniforms are changed over to the higher rank by the time it takes off." He paused, jerked up his head as if remembering something, and continued speaking in a low cautious voice. "Now you understand this is just a temporary promotion don't you Jake? It's officially called a brevet promotion. Doesn't change your official rank nor pay grade, but otherwise, as far as anyone knows or cares, you're an oh five all the way."

"Yes Sir, I know, and thank you Sir," Jake stammered.

"Hell, I'm not doing it for you. Well, yeah, I guess I am in a way. You're a damn good officer and I think this'll help you do even a better job than without it. And it's important. Even more important than you suspect." He turned to the two witnesses in the room, who by their expressions, weren't sure whether to offer congratulations to the new colonel or not.

"Thanks guys, leave us for a minute will ya?"

They both smiled awkwardly, and hurriedly left the room.

"I've got some more news for you Jake. It's the other reason I'm pinning you, and I'm afraid it's bad news."

Thorpe sat across from the general's desk. Now comes the real reason he's sending me there, Jake thought.

Both men lit cigarettes. Elsin leaned back in his high backed leather chair. "You're a friend of a guy named Doctor Raymond Gonzaga aren't you?" he asked.

"More than a friend General, he taught on the staff at Rutgers University when I went there as a student. He became my advisor as well as one of my professors. He helped me get my Fullbright Scholarship to Germany. He's like a father to me. We've kept in close touch ever since my school days. I saw him in Washington D.C. last year, after he started working for the government."

"Did you know he's in Vietnam?"

"Yes Sir. When I wrote him that I got orders for my second tour, he wrote back. Got it about six weeks or so ago. He said he'd make sure we got together a couple of times while we're both here. He's a

Province Senior Advisor somewhere, all I have is the APO number."

"Well not anymore," Elsin cut in. "He's in Da Nang now with a small desk job, restricted to his quarters when he's not working. Up until a month ago, he was the PSA of Quang Tin, where you're going. He's been relieved for cause!"

Thorpe felt stunned for the second time within ten minutes. "What happened Sir?"

"Several things. He's charged with stabbing and killing a national police officer for one. They say he stole an Army truck from the camp at Chu Lai and sold it somewhere, either on the black market, or to the enemy. And they even claim that he sold or gave one of our code books to Victor Charlie, you know, the VC."

Jake leaned forward to grip the front edge of the general's mahogany desk. A long ash from the cigarette in his fingers fell unnoticed onto the plush carpet. "Sir, I don't know who "they" are, but whoever they are, they're liars! I know Ray Gonzaga as well, Hell, even better than I know you. He's as honest as the day is long—more honest! He took this job because he believes in this country. He's an idealist. He'd never do a traitorous act. Never!"

General Elsin calmly flicked his ash into a polished 105 MM howitzer shell cut down to make a heavy military ashtray. "Hold your voice down Jake, I think you're right. I think someone has deliberately poisoned our ears regarding Ray, but they've done a good job of it. Right now there's not much I can do. The evidence seems to be very incriminating, and the Province Chief up there, Colonel Biet, is really pissed. He insisted that we move him out. At first I wasn't going to, but the State Department finally ordered it. There's a lot of confusion whether to send him home for a civil trial, arrange a civilian trial over here, or try him by military courts martial. I'm insisting on a courts martial because I know the State Department will never accept it, so it's helping to drag this thing on. That's all I can do. The thing is, my time is almost out. I can't keep on stalling. If no contrary information comes along soon, I'll have to fade out of the picture and allow charges to be filed."

Jake sat back in his chair and took a long drag, exhaling slowly. "Why me Sir? I'm not CID."

"No, but you're smart. Better yet, you've got common sense. You've got the personal motivation I need, and you're not one of those by the book types who are afraid to use their own judgement," the general said softly. "The former DPSA, a Lieutenant Colonel King, took over as the PSA which is what the Province Chief wanted, so we have reestablished good relations. King has a good record and seems to be getting along so far with his advisory job, but I don't know anything more about him. The open slot, in accordance with CORD's policy, is supposed to be filled by a State Department civilian, as I mentioned before, but knowing you were on the way, I pulled some strings. Our official line will be that no civilian is available. I sent a "For Official Use Only" letter to General Westmoreland to cover my ass on this thing and his reply gave me the green light to do what I can. But time is against us. The I Corps JAG officer is having kittens up there trying to find out what's holding up the whirling wheels of justice, and there's a lot of pressure from the RVN side of the house to get a trial going and settle this mess. That murdered policeman has their ulcers in an uproar."

"Tell me what to do and I'll do it Sir."

"OK, three things: First, here's a file copy of all the evidence against Gonzaga. Read it; memorize it; and then burn it before you get on that airplane."

Jake looked at the official folder in his hands. "Right Sir, but won't somebody miss this? This is an official file folder."

"No sweat. We're a headquarters down here in Saigon and we're expected to be inefficient. I've lost two of those already as part of my foot dragging program." He paused to make sure Jake had caught the humor. Satisfied, he continued. "Just be sure and burn that baby thoroughly. I don't want an investigation started around me because somebody finds fragments."

"I will Sir."

"Secondly, when you arrive, I don't want you to know Ray or know anything about his trouble. OK?"

"I'll try Sir".

"I changed your records this morning as far as rank is concerned. They show you to be an oh five for ten days already. I don't think anyone will question that. They'd catch it in the states because everyone watches the Army Times lists. But they're all too busy over here." He scratched his head thoughtfully.

"Now it comes down to this: I want you to poke around Quang Tin to see what you can find. There's something rotten up there, and you're the only one I can really depend on. We're fighting a God Damned war here, and this type of crap doesn't help at all."

"With your permission Sir, I'd like to ask you why you got so involved. Do you know Ray personally also?"

"I sure do. His office sat right next to mine in the Pentagon when he first came over as a Foreign Area Specialist on loan from the State Department. He, ahh..., he helped me out when I had a personal problem. Ahh..., Hell, no reason to hide it now. My wife was running around on me. I got pretty broken up about it at first; didn't know what to do. Ray stepped right in like my own brother or something. We got to be closer than kin. Hell, we got to be even closer yet after my wife finally left me. I posted him to Quang Tin when he first got here. Other than official reports, we haven't been in touch since, because neither of us wanted to shake up protocol; but I'm with you. I know Ray couldn't have done it. And I owe him a lot," he added pensively.

Jake nodded understandingly. "What do I do if I find something?"

"I don't know. If Ray is innocent, as both of us think he is, someone whose supposed to be on our side has gone to a lot of trouble to stick it to him. The ass hole may be Vietnamese, or he might be an American. So don't give your hand away by sending any message to me in the clear. And don't use the military code either. Every command level uses the same code book. We'll have to have our own private code. Let's see, I'm sending you up there to dig up the facts, let's see, treasure? No, that would get too many greedy people curious. How about coffin? No, I've got it. This is going to be a bare bones type of investigation. Use bones, or skeleton, or skull. Send me a message from Tam Ky about anything, and if any of those words, bones, skeleton, or skull, is in the body of the message, I'll know you've found something and need me to come up there and meet with you."

"Right Sir." The meeting had obviously ended. Jake rose, snuffing his cigarette in the artillery shell ashtray.

"How's your wife, Jake?" The general walked him to the office door. "Are you still separated?"

"Yes Sir; it's been quite a while now."

"Well, that's your business and not mine; but it's better for a promising young career officer to be married, you know. Gives the image of stability and all that. I got married again. Of course you have lots of time, but you ought to think about it before you come up for oh-six."

"Yes Sir," Jake nodded without enthusiasm. Everyone he knew was full of marital advice. He wondered if the general had married again just for the sake of his career.

The general opened the door and Jake saluted. Elsin returned the salute casually. "Good luck, Jake, and watch your own ass out there. Word has it that the VC are about to flex a few muscles all over the country, and Quang Tin has always been a political hotbed. Besides that, if you're not careful as you do your other thing...," he paused, glancing at his Vietnamese secretary; at her desk a few yards away.

Co Bai looked up, saw the general looking at her, and quietly got up from her desk. "I go for tea General Sir," she said.

Elsin smiled and continued with a voice just above a whisper, "As I said, if you're not careful, you're liable to piss off someone else just as dangerous as the VC." His voice then resumed its normal tone, "I've always thought highly of you Jake. You're one of my boys, and I wouldn't want to lose you."

"Thanks General, I'll do my best."

The general's voice dropped again, this time to an actual whisper, and he leaned into Jake's ear. "And don't you dare stop by Da Nang or go up there later to see Ray. I know you'd like to, and you're just rebel enough to try, but someone would surely find out. If you're going to help him, you can't jeopardize the whole thing for a few hugs and tears. I'm not going to let Ray know you're already in country either, because he'd try to get hold of you too, and spoil the whole God Damned thing. If you're successful, I'll put the two of you together somewhere on the same team and you can talk each other's ears off, but absolutely no contact now! That's an order Jake, you got me?"

"Yes Sir, I understand."

"And don't forget to get those rank changes sewn on before you catch that flight."

The door closed, and Major (P), Acting Lieutenant Colonel, Jacob James Thorpe, Infantry Branch, Regular Army, walked out into the heat of the South East Asian morning, in search of a tailor, an airplane, the honor of a friend, and an uncertain future in a foreign land.

SCENE 3

CAMP ALPHA

0600 Hours
Monday, 1 January 1968

Sergeant (E5) Mark Amory Fellogese settled into the comfortable theater chair. He sat next to the center aisle of the large lecture hall and looked around. The building had obviously been a former airplane hanger which had been remodeled and partitioned into offices, classrooms and this magnificent, modern, central auditorium.

Another briefing, he thought. They sure throw the information at you in a hurry over here. In his three days in country, he had already attended briefings entitled: "Know Your Enemy," "The Proper handling of POW's," "The Code of Conduct for the American Fighting Man," "Organization/Command Relationships of MACV," "Venereal Diseases of Southeast Asia," "Military/Indigenous Personnel Relationships," "Booby Traps of the Viet Cong," "Field Sanitation in Tropical Areas," and "The History of the Vietnam Conflict."

Yesterday evening at 2100, three hours before the beginning of the new year, he had been summoned to this same auditorium to be given his tour assignment: Operations Shift Sergeant, S3 Technical

Advisor, Team Two, Tam Ky City, Quang Tin Province, I Corps, CORDS, MACV. He knew the words by heart, but he still didn't really know what he was going to do; and had even less of an idea as to where he was going to be doing it. Someone told him it was just north of central South Vietnam, about five hundred miles from Saigon, but that sounded too confusing. He'd have to look at a map to find out.

He glanced at his brand new Seiko with the black face and bright luminescent indicators. The thick hands strained away from each other as if in a vertical tractor pull; yellow green arrows in a chronological tug of war. "Oh six oh one," he murmured, almost out loud, "they really start you out at Oh Dark Thirty around here." He smiled at his little joke, knowing full well it was broad daylight outside.

He reached into his oversized fatigue jacket pocket, pulled out his journal and a black "U.S. Government" ball point pen and began to write:

"Camp Alpha, appropriate name for the beginning of a journey, the birth of an experience; the raising of the curtain, and perhaps the introduction of man to his own mortality. I hope this isn't the start of my final scene."

Mark did not consider himself to be a real writer and had no future dreams of being one. He knew, however, that he could express himself, and that he was not destined to be a career soldier. This would probably be his only war. "I want to remember it." he wrote. "Or, if I don't live through it, I want the folks—and Rosaline, especially Rosaline, to read it and know that I had often thought of her before I...," his thoughts took a more dramatic turn: "before the poisoned VC punji stake ripped into my heart."

He shook his head. That was a silly thing to write. It's supposed to be a journal not an outlet for gloomy day dreams. He bent his head to write again:

"Despite the newness and excitement of being in a war zone, Camp Alpha is under a cloud of boredom. Everyone here has to fight being bored. Even the briefings which are supposedly designed to save your life usually can't even keep you awake. In addition to being the in-processing center and out-processing center for all replacements, it's also a rest and recuperation center for soldiers who can't afford to go to other places out of the country. I've only been here three days, and I know I'll never come back here for R & R!

No combat action around here for miles, and there hasn't been for years. Yet guards are everywhere; bored guards who know their jobs are unnecessary.

I learned a new word yesterday: "Remf", pronounced with much emphasis on the final f, it stands for "Rear Echelon Mother Fucker". (Wow! The language over here!) It's what all these guys who work in the Saigon area are called by the field troops. The Remfs even call themselves this.

The gloom and boredom here isn't on purpose. The movie theaters show three fairly current movies each day; one in the morning, then the afternoon, and the evening. I've missed several good ones because of my schedule: These damned briefings!

In Vietnam, they call home two things: "CONUS" and "The Real World." Some guys also call it the land of the round eyes, but I won't. It sounds too much like a backhanded ethnic slur against the Vietnamese.

I do think of Rosaline's round eyes though, as well as her hair, her face, her arms and legs,..."

He paused in his writing to make sure no one was looking over his shoulder, "as well as her other charms," he wrote.

I'd better watch what I say, he thought, my folks might have to read this some day. He continued in his journal:

"All kinds of soldiers are here: field, fat, frenzied, fuzzy and for-saken. New arrivals are mostly fearful, and the outbound veterans do everything they can to encourage and exaggerate this fear. The perpetual greeting among the transients is: "Are you goin' or comin'?" Whenever the two have opposite answers to this question, one gets congratulations, awe and envy. The other draws derisive laughter and graveyard ridicule. A nod of the head means that both questioner and respondent have the same answer.

Everyone uses the term, "No sweat" a lot, but they all sweat. A lot! It is so damn hot. Almost everyone you see is hauling heavy duffel bags from one place to another, or resting in the oven-dark shade before they pick up their bags again to continue their quest for quonsets.

There are two basketball courts, a tennis court, a swimming pool (this very new and very crowded), a parachute covered snack bar, a PX, mess hall, and an all ranks club. There's a tailor shop, gift shop, barber shop, shoe shine shop, luggage storage area, and most unbe-lievable of all, a steam bath concession. How could anyone choose to pay a dime to go inside to take a steam bath and then come back outside where it's just as hot, but free?

They say you can't pass through Camp Alpha without meeting someone you've met before. This was true for me at least. I ran into Joe Abraham and Benjamin Vohlio, former college chums. Neither of them knew that I had joined the Army after dropping out of the University. They have graduated and been commissioned as second lieutenants. I had to salute them and call them both Sir! Felt funny. All of us were in the school Thespian Club together and all three of us agreed that meeting like this, over here, in uniform, was kind of like we were just acting out different roles in a new play, but it also feels very different, very real. They're both already gone to the field with different units. I sure wish them good luck.

Somehow, in all this madness and chaos, I've kind of lost who I really am. This disoriented sweating shell is not Mark Fellogese. I don't know if I've grown up all of a sudden, caught a bad case of schizophrenia, or am just in the middle of someone's anxious dream. I think it's probably the latter, except the dream is mine, and it's just the beginning, but I seem to be awake.

The loudspeaker is incessant as it screams for urinalysis testing, movie calls, plague shots, money exchanges, and people who have missed formation. The raspy, amplified voice never changes its tone whether it's announcing chow call, a lost weapon, a sale at the PX or an intel report of possible enemy activity. It says to Follow the broken blue line, or the solid white line, or the double red line." I wonder if it will ever tell us to follow the yellow brick road."

Pleased with this last bit of literary allusion, Mark closed his journal just as a very petite WAC, wearing the rank of Specialist 4, walked past him down the aisle heading for the stage. She was a red-head; less than five feet tall with a curly Orphan Annie type haircut. She wore highly starched and neatly pressed fatigues; not jungle fatigues, but stateside fatigues, with the shirt tucked in and her belt tight around her tiny waist. Her shirt insignia patches were not subdued but in blazing technicolor. "US Army" was stitched in gold on a black background over one pocket, "Sabbat" in black on a white patch over the other. A colorful patch on her left shoulder sleeve, and the polished golden amazon heads of the Women's Army Corps on her lapels. She faced the audience of only ten or twelve men and assumed a rigid position of parade rest.

Mark saw that her freckled face was impishly waif-like. A child's face; a mischievous infantile face on a Barbie Doll body. She wore no make up that he could see, but her sea green eyes, flashed tidal waves of hyperactivity and devilment.

"Atten—Hut", she commanded with a small child's cry for attention.

Mark and the others sprang to their feet. He flicked his eyes to one side to glimpse the briefing officer as he walked past.

He didn't. She did! A towering black female Army officer strode by with a purposeful, intense aura that gripped the room. She assumed a commanding pose behind a lectern, which had magically raised from the stage floor. The puppet-like enlisted woman, a squire at her side.

"At ease men, take your seats please. I am First Lieutenant Warner, Chief of Briefing Team Echo, MACV Headquarters. All of you men in this room have been assigned to CORDS, that means you will be working in district or provincial advisory teams under MACV command. It is my role in this briefing, to tell you what to expect during your tour as a CORDS advisor, and to tell you what we expect of you."

Mark was transfixed. He had rarely seen such an imposing authority figure, and never such a spectacular woman, anywhere. Her ebony face was remarkably beautiful. The jet black hair had been straightened and was worn chin length with just a slight inward curl. He was close enough to see that she wore soft purple eye shadow and glossy crimson lipstick which made her full lips almost seem to be bleeding. Her eyes had no iris that he could see, only large, very black pupils; the whites of her eyes and her white even teeth accentuated the blackness of her skin. The stateside fatigues which clung to her form appeared to be new, and she stood in patent leather jump boots. Her figure would have done justice to Athena.

"To begin with, I will answer the questions all of you men have on your very easy to read minds. I am six feet, three inches tall and did indeed play basketball in college. I went to the University of Highland Hills in Indiana. I was an All American in my senior year, and I definitely do wish that we had a women's professional basketball league. I am dispensing this information first so that you can all relax now and concentrate on what I'm here to tell you."

Mark was too astonished to laugh as expected, for he had been thinking precisely along those lines. Evidently he was not alone. Only two men laughed out loud.

Undaunted, Lieutenant Warner went on: "Let me now introduce the other members of Briefing Team Echo: Specialist Sabbat will be assisting me on the stage with the lighted pointer." The red-headed doll, now looking even smaller beside her giant superior, clicked her heels to attention and whipped a previously hidden flashlight into a right shoulder arms position.

"And Corporal Messenger will be at the controls of the slide projectors."

A movement to his right caused Mark to turn to see that a metal table with three pre-connected slide projectors had materialized in the center of the aisle right beside him. Behind it, another WAC stood in an awkward stance which more or less passed for the position of attention. The woman, older than either on the stage, limply raised her right arm in acceptance of the recognition. Her dishwater blond hair hung limp, and a bit too long for Army regulations. She wore heavy make up, but Mark could tell that her face had been severely ravished by acne in her long dead past. Her badly faded and rumpled uniform clashed with the immaculate attire of the other two.

Mark's eyes caught sight of her sleeve where an unfaded patch of seaweed green was clearly visible. She had made corporal the wrong way. From the size and shape of the darker area, she had been at least an E6 or maybe even a Master Sergeant at some former time.

Lieutenant Warner snapped her fingers and the lights dimmed immediately. Behind her, three gigantic screens lowered silently to replace the entire backdrop.

"First of all men, I have a message for all of you from General Westmoreland himself." She paused dramatically and the center screen flashed on:

"Happy New Year—1968," blazed in bright red letters on a white background above the blue signature of General William C. Westmoreland.

The projector clicked and the center screen now illuminated the red and yellow MACV crest.

Lieutenant Warner's amplified voice purred out of the darkness. "You all should understand the symbolism of the patch you now wear on your left sleeve. The colors are those of the Republic of Vietnam which is the official name of this country. The yellow wall stands for the borders of South Vietnam. Note that the wall has an opening which allows the red background to flow from one side to the other. This indicates infiltration and danger from both without and within. The red flow is blocked by the upright sword, representing United States military aid and support. Note also, however, that the wall is arched upward indicating that the South Vietnamese are also taking offensive action to push the aggressor back.

This symbolism is accurate. Some opponents of this war, back in CONUS, shout that we Americans are over here fighting this war alone. They go so far as to use the term genocide, and imply that we are fighting all of the Vietnamese people. Nothing could be further from the truth."

The left screen illuminated a picture of South Vietnamese soldiers, armed and alert, patrolling along a bright green rice paddy. The right screen clicked on to show two helicopters with Vietnamese markings in a pale blue sky. In quick succession, all three screens flashed several slides of South Vietnamese soldiers, sailors, airmen and marines as they trained, advanced, guarded, fought and died in battle.

Lieutenant Warner's clear voice accented the images: "The Vietnamese people resisted the Japanese invasion of their homeland during World War II, and, after the war, united to fight the French. Now they are fighting each other in a war of ideology rather than patriotism. You have already been briefed on the history of this conflict, but you must remember that Vietnam has been constantly at war for over 20 years. You will all learn, first-hand, that war is not pleasant. The thing I want you to understand is that the South Vietnamese people would not continue nor support this war against their own people if they did not believe that their cause is right.

Remember this. Three months ago, in September 1967, South Vietnam held a nation-wide election. At that time, over 80% of the six million registered voters of the country actually voted, even though the VC threatened and carried through on its threats, to cause violence to the voters.

People don't vote if they don't believe in what they are voting for. Yet the Vietnamese faced or ignored the danger, and voted in larger relative numbers than Americans have ever done."

The right and left screens rapidly blinked scenes of government employees at work; farmers tending fields and walking behind water buffalo; people voting in cities, villages and hamlets; soldiers guarding poll booths; soldiers voting; and aftermaths of election day terrorism. The center screen held steady on the yellow and red flag of the Republic of Vietnam.

"And voting isn't the only indication of this nation's commitment to freedom. Because of this national emergency, conscription in South Vietnam is one hundred percent. Only a mental or physical disability prevents conscription of all males when they reach the age of sixteen.

Obviously, with the omnipresence of the Viet Cong, even though he cannot choose to refrain from fighting, each sixteen year old male has his choice as to which side he fights for. Yet our statistics show that over eighty five percent of these young men choose the South Vietnamese Armed Forces. This is especially remarkable when you consider that the VC are also actively recruiting, often at gun point, and are known to carry out violent reprisals against the families of RVN military personnel."

The center screen darkened. The left screen flashed the words "Regional Forces—RF" in red on a black background. The right screen blazed a similarly colored "Popular Forces—PF."

Mark stole a quick glance to his right. In the almost total darkness, Corporal Messenger hunched over the table adjusting slides and control buttons. The projector lamps' glow from beneath her chin

gave her tired face an even more haggard and loathsome appearance. Wow! I'd sure hate to wake up in the morning and find that
beside me, he thought, before turning his attention back to the
blood and black screens.

"Listen hard men, because this is where you enter the picture,"
Lieutenant Warner hissed seductively.

The center screen portrayed Uncle Sam fiercely pointing at the
audience, still flanked by the sanguine letters "RF" and "PF".

"Regular Army units of the RVN spend seventeen out of every
eighteen months in the field, carrying out mobile combat missions.
While they are away, Regional Forces..." (Specialist Sabbat's
lighted arrow flickered onto the left screen pointing at these words)
"operate within each of the forty three provinces, which are the
equivalent of American states; while Popular Forces..." (the lighted
arrow danced to the other screen) "provide security to each district,
which is roughly the same as an American county. Together, these
forces are called by several names: the Territorial Forces, the Militia,
the home guard and the "Ruff Puffs."

All of you men in this room will be working directly with the militia; training them, teaching them, going on patrols with them, and
totally depending upon them! Some of you have probably heard
that you cannot trust the Vietnamese people. But all of you must
trust them! You won't be protected by American units! These territorial forces will be literally the only thing standing between you
and Charlie. Look closely and recognize your protectors."

Black pajama clad men glowered from the screens armed with old
American M-1 rifles, 60mm mortars and Browning Automatic
Rifles. Other slides pictured rag tag units in mixed uniforms. A few
web belts with one or more canteens. A sprinkle of men with jungle
boots, but many wearing sandals. Most were barefoot. Some were
bare headed. A few wore helmets, but most wore the conical straw
hat of the farmer.

The thing that Mark noticed which was common to all of them was the intense expressions. Not a smile nor a relaxed jaw on any face.

The show continued. Occasionally, only one screen flashed; often, two blazed at once; but mostly, all three flared their brilliance at the same time, turning the darkness into rainbow colored light. Mark struggled to keep up and actually see each slide; a busy, dizzy, head jerking effort which caused his eyes to burn and blur.

Lieutenant Warner's now monotone voice marched on: "The vast majority of militia members have already served their full five years of mandatory time in the military; some have been wounded and even disabled, thus earning an early discharge from the national service, some are yet too young to be drafted; but nevertheless they volunteer for Ruff-Puff duty because of their love of freedom, their hate for the enemy, or their fear of Communism. They are farmers by day and soldiers by night."

Both side screens went black. The center screen displayed a sandbag bunker along a trail, the thatched roofs of a small hamlet in the background. Two small boys, appearing to be about twelve or thirteen years old, peeped over the dusty lip of the bunker, both sighting along ancient carbine rifles, which looked like huge cannons in their juvenile fingers.

"In some villages and hamlets, you may also find women warriors." She said this with ringing pride. Several quick slides of armed, black clad, women and girls on patrols with men, guarding a village gate, and lined up in ranks with similarly garbed males, snapped on and off.

"Some of you may know that the Vietnamese, as a people, tend to be more chauvinistic in regard to women's roles than even the Americans!" Here, Lieutenant Warner paused again, evidently expecting laughter or some other audience reaction. The room remained silent.

She continued: "The war is changing this viewpoint, as both sides have women who fight and kill."

Mark suddenly realized that there was no light at the lectern. Lieutenant Warner was in total darkness. She had memorized her lines for this entire presentation. What a performance, he marveled.

"You men should also know that there are still others in South Vietnam who are fighting Communism and protecting you in their own way. The National Police have an important security mission in cities, villages and hamlets, as well as the usual police functions of traffic control and preventing and investigating crime. Also, in many isolated areas, armed Revolutionary Development Teams, called RDTs, carry out civic action, protect medical teams, and conduct building programs. In other areas where the threat is especially high, villages have formed extra guard units called People's Self Defense Forces".

The slides showed units scruffier still, with weapons of even more vintage, including machetes and spears. The three flashing screens forcing eye balls to snap back and forth.

"Gentlemen," Lieutenant Warner's voice grew sharp and fierce in the now total darkness with all screens black. "The purpose of this briefing is to allay your fears about working with the Vietnamese. You are all going to small advisory units which will be engulfed by the Vietnamese language and the Vietnamese culture. You will have many strange and exotic experiences, but you must trust those whom you are called upon to help. By doing so, the life you save may be your own."

The center screen portrayed a wounded American soldier with his arms around the shoulders of two diminutive Vietnamese, both clad in black pajamas. The militiamen were carrying him out of the jungle directly toward the camera; their faces contorted with strain, the face of the American distorted with pain. The projector clicked and the scene was replaced by a large scale map of South Vietnam.

"Before you depart, you should all know that the lunar new year falls on the thirtieth of this month. This is the Vietnamese New Year, which they call Tet. In the past, both sides have ceased fire during this holiday because of its importance in the Vietnamese culture. A cease fire is planned for this year's Tet holiday also. However, G2 reports indicate that the NVA is massing for several large scale attacks either just before, during, or immediately after this year's Tet holidays."

A pause. Silence. Mark and the audience sat without sight or sound, staring at the giant, illuminated map.

Lieutenant Warner's voice ripped the silence with fury and venom. "The arrow, Sabbat, if you please!"

Specialist Sabbat's glowing arrow flitted on, danced like a trapped housefly over the entire central portion of the country, and came to rest on the Vietnam-Laos border directly west of a large blue dot named "Hue".

"Here is one of the three major concentrations"; Lieutenant Warner's voice was icy calm again. "And here is the second"; the luminescent arrow dropped immediately to the Cambodia-Vietnam border just west of another blue dot named "Pleiku". "And here is the third". The arrow moved to the concave border directly west of Saigon. "If these intelligence reports are accurate, and we think they are, it is the largest massing of regular NVA forces in the history of this conflict. We also have some evidence of increased VC activity near almost every major population center of the country. We think something big is up and it's going to happen soon. You, gentlemen, our newest CORDS advisors, have arrived just in time. Are there any questions?"

The houselights blazed forth, exactly on cue. The map of South Vietnam remained on but faded in the brighter than day brilliance of the ceiling lights.

Lieutenant Warner looked even taller and even more dominating in the renewed brightness. The pause for questions lasted exactly two seconds.

"No? Very well gentlemen. Keep your powder dry, your eyes sharp, and your libidos under control. Good luck to you all and I hope you find your tours here rewarding. Just do your jobs and don't try to be heros. Remember, Vietnam is a land of contradictions. Things are never the way they seem to be at first."

"Atten—Hut!" Specialist Sabbat's child-like cry shrilled through the auditorium and the audience shot to its collective feet.

Lieutenant Warner serenely and majestically glided out of the theater, while every man in the room violated his position of attention by openly turning his head to watch her until she disappeared at the rear door. Her two minions followed, one skipping almost playfully rather than walking; the other stalking out with hands thrust sullenly in trouser pockets.

Sergeant Mark Fellogese sat down in his seat like a fat man with weak knees and immediately opened his diary.

"I'm in a different world," he began, "and the future has been foretold."

SCENE 4

CA DOR

0730 HOURS
MONDAY, 1 JANUARY, 1968

Someone who didn't know him might have mistaken Lieutenant Colonel King's bent posture, as he barged up the grey stone steps of Ca Dor, Quang Tin's provincial capital building, as that of a person suffering from an arthritic spine. But it was fury! Raging, white hot, twisted fury.

His thoughts boiled with hatred. How dare that God Damned Dink, he fumed. Puttin a fuckin snake in my locker. Didn't do it himself though. Had a fuckin slope snuffy do it for him. I'll make him eat shit!

He charged past the saluting guard at the entrance to the gothic structure, and burst into the marble clad foyer. Wheeling to his left, he pounded through the double doorway of the Province Chief's outer office. The attractive secretary, Co Li, looked up with a start and stood immediately when she recognized him.

"Good morning Troom Ta King. The Dai Ta, him wait for you. Him say you go in. No wait; go in now." She bowed politely and extended her arm toward the inner door.

King nodded fiercely. "He's expectin me is he? I jist bet he is!" He stormed past her to the Province Chief's private office.

Colonel Than Mak Biet put his pen down and stood up from his high backed wooden chair as King walked in. "Good morning Lieutenant Colonel King. Allow me to wish you happiness on this first day of the western new year." As usual, Biet's fatigue uniform had been freshly pressed. The huge Vietnamese full colonel's rank symbol on his collar seemed to dominate the room.

Reaching into a silver cigarette case on his boxy, French style desk, Biet withdrew an American cigarette and lit it. He inhaled deeply, with the open mouth gasp which was one of his often mimicked personality traits, and smiled as he exhaled smoke through his nose. His tobacco stained teeth appeared to be almost the same color as his face. "Would you care for a cigarette? he asked.

The casual, yet overt friendliness caught King off guard. He had expected defensiveness. He stopped in the center of the large room. "I understand you were expectin me," he blurted with uncertainty, ignoring the offer.

Biet paused, his erect and powerful torso tensed. That he had been athletic in his younger years was evident. Too bad he's let himself go ta seed, King thought.

Biet was evidently waiting for the military salute due from the lower ranking officer. Perceiving that it was not forth-coming, the smile waned and the eyes hardened. His voice, however, was still cheerful. "Yes, I have been expecting you since approximately six o'clock this morning. I was informed that your headquarters in Da Nang is rather urgently requesting you to persuade me to send a patrol into the jungle west of Hau Duc."

King's jaw jutted forward. "That's not why you were expectin me you fat...." He cut his sentence short. Biet's entire body had straightened. The heavy hooded eyes had become slits of heated steel. Yet there was a hint of a smile; a faint trace of triumph. Whoa! Be careful Richard my boy, King thought. There's something wrong here. Biet out ranks me, even though he's only in the fuckin Dink Army. He looks like he wants me to jump his ass. Don't know who might be listenin. It might be a trap ta git ridda me.

With a deep breath, King mastered his temper and forced himself to smile. "Sorry about that Dai Ta. Don't take it personal. Been up all night playin poker. Guess I'm a bit tukered." He plopped himself on the cane seat of the chair reserved for Biet's visitors.

The Province Chief relaxed slightly and rested his rounded rump on one corner of his highly polished desk. "I had expected you to be aggressive, Lieutenant Colonel King, as your superiors in Da Nang expect you to be. But your absence of military courtesy was not expected, and I certainly did not foresee an actual insult to my face." There was an air of disappointment in his tone.

"Someone just put a fuckin snake under my hat in my hallway wardrobe Dai Ta." King reached into a side pocket of his fatigue jacket and pulled a cigarette from the package inside. He lit it with his black alligator skin Zippo. "Somethun like that tends ta gitcha a bit jumpy. You wouldn't know anything about that snake wouldja Dai Ta?"

"What kind of snake was it?" Biet seemed surprised. There was no sign of guilt, but he still appeared somewhat upset. Was it the insult? Or was it that the trap hadn't worked?

"It was a krait."

"Kraits are skillful climbers. To find one on a wardrobe is not unusual."

"This fuckin snake wasn't on my wardrobe. It was in my wardrobe, and it was under my fuckin cap."

"You are lucky you were not bitten; but why do you suspect me? You must confess that, to a certain extent, I am indebted to you. You have done me a favor. A good turn. Why should I wish to harm you now?"

King glanced around the room. The colonial French furnishings always reminded him of a stage setting for "Arsenic and Old Lace." He noted the closed door at the other end of the room. "Who's behind that door Dai Ta?"

King watched the Province Chief's eyebrows spring up and then back down to normal as the Vietnamese colonel belatedly masked his surprise. "What makes you think someone is behind the door?"

"There is somebody there, iddn't there?"

Biet swallowed nervously. "It is a closed door. I cannot see through it. I do not know if someone is there or not."

"Git ridda him Dai Ta."

"Well, there is the possibility that Major Hai might be there. I have an appointment with him after you and I complete our business."

"Tell him to go away Dai Ta. I'm not gonna say nothun that might git me inta hot water, knowin he's standin there listenin. He don't need ta hear what we might have ta say ta one another."

Biet sighed and struggled off the corner of his desk to a standing position. He gave a quick barking command in Vietnamese and turned back to King. "He's gone now. Would you like to open the door and check for yourself?"

King took a long slow pull at his cigarette. "Nah, Dai Ta, I believe ya, but...," he paused for another thoughtful drag from his cigarette, "but now we both know where we stand don't we?"

The Province Chief seated himself at his desk, making the ornate piece of furniture a barrier between them. His chair made him much taller than King as they faced each other. King wondered if Biet's feet were touching the floor.

"I did not have anything to do with placing a snake in your wardrobe, Lieutenant Colonel King. The thought never crossed my mind, and wouldn't have. If I had truly wanted to rid myself of you, there are far more effective ways. I don't know who might have done it; perhaps even one of your own countrymen. I have been told that several of them have ample motivation for such an act."

King opened his mouth to protest, but Biet raised his hand. "Hear me out please, Lieutenant Colonel King. I confess that I did ask Major Hai to be a witness to our discussion today, for you are here to persuade me to send a patrol to the jungle, and I am determined not to send one. I expected you to lose your temper, and was prepared to use that fact against you if you tried to make future trouble with me. But those who claim that you were born under a lucky star are correct. You sensed the danger and avoided it. So we are again on level ground. For what it might be worth, I apologize for attempting this type of…, how do you call it? One upmanship?" He gazed directly into King's eyes in the western way, to show his openness, to assert his innocence.

King relaxed. "OK, we'll forget about it for now anyways. Let's change the subject. Let's talk about the patrol."

Biet smiled and poured himself a cup of green tea from a glazed ceramic pot. "Yes, to be sure. We must indeed discuss patrols. It is an interesting subject. Would you like a cup of tea? Or do you fear that I might try to poison you?"

King grimaced. Jesus H. Fuckin Christ, he thought. They always do it this way. It takes forever to get to the point because they always talk in circles first. "No, I never drink that shit Dai Ta, and you fuckin well know it. I don't wanna talk about patrols, an I don't wanna talk about a patrol. I wanna talk about the patrol! The same fuckin patrol we been talkin bout for three days! The same God Damned patrol you expected me ta talk about! Don't fuck with me Dai Ta. What about it?"

Biet shrugged. "Hau Duc is a small district; our newest district. There is only one real village, consisting of only seven small hamlets. I have only thirty men, one platoon, of my regional forces there. A captain commands; he is the District Chief. He also has five undermanned platoons of district militia or popular forces there, about seventy five total personnel scattered throughout the seven hamlets; over the fifty square miles of the district. They have one old French howitzer and one 81mm mortar. If I should ask them for a patrol of even twenty men, the defense of Hau Duc will be severely reduced."

King listened intently as Biet took a long gulping drag from his cigarette and lifted his face to exhale forcefully straight up towards the ceiling.

"I could, of course," Biet continued, "send a provisional unit from one of the other districts, but they don't know the Hau Duc area and it would weaken the defensive capabilities of whatever district they came from." He paused again and glanced at King.

"Or I could send a unit from my forces here at Tam Ky, but as you well know, these are the reserves for the entire province, and I do not feel we should weaken our reserve element when we do not know when or where we might need them against an attack. It is therefore my opinion that, if the Americans think a patrol is needed, it should come from the U.S. units now stationed at Chu Lai."

King shook his head. The fat pig has a point, he thought, but I gotta show him that when I want somethun, I git it! "Sorry Dai Ta, the Americans are after bigger game down in Quang Ngai province. I Corps feels this is a job for the Ruff Puffs."

"I do not know what you mean by bigger game, Lieutenant Colonel King; as I understand the intelligence reports, the patrol is needed to confirm of refute the suspicion of an NVA regiment in the area. That is big enough game for anyone. Would you not say so?"

King bowed while sitting, mocking the Vietnamese custom. "You got me there Dai Ta," he smiled. For a Slope, he thought, this sloppy tubba lard is clever. I probably shoulda talked ta him first before I committed myself ta Da Nang bout this fuckin patrol.

"My last point, Lieutenant Colonel King, is that the militia have been organized to fight the Viet Cong guerrillas. They are neither trained nor equipped to fight a regular unit of the North Vietnamese Army. Quite obviously, this danger is a matter for the Americans or the Army of the Republic of South Vietnam, certainly not the concern of our territorial forces."

"If there's an NVA regiment out there, it's a damned big concern for everbody," King snorted. "Look, Dai Ta, you've made yer point, 'n I'm even inclined ta agree with most'a it. If I really believed that there was an NVA regiment out there, I'd throw a fuckin temper fit in Da Nang ta git an American unit or at least the ARVN; but you 'n I both know that whatever's out there ain't no NVA regiment. There's probably nothun out there atall."

"There is something there," Biet stated flatly.

"How d'ya know that? As if I didn't know."

"The stars are never wrong," Biet's monotone was barely audible.

"Well we've danced round long enough Dai Ta. I honestly don't give a shit what the stars say. MACV says we gotta send a patrol out there, and by God we will! I couldn't give a rat's fart less whether the patrol comes from Hau Duc, Tam Ky or Tim-buckfuck-intoo, as long as some kinda patrol gits out there soon."

Biet's mouth twitched ever so slightly. "And if I refuse?" he asked.

"You won't refuse Dai Ta, Sir." King's sarcasm dripped with venomous meaning. "And I might as well tell ya why. If there's no patrol out there tonight, I'll have yer ass outta that kiddie high chair by tomorra mornin; and I'll see to it that you're behind bars by tomorra afternoon!" King's eyes narrowed; his voice hissed.

Biet's eyes were wide. He was not accustomed to being confronted, much less threatened. King watched the Province Chief's face as it contorted with the effort to keep rage under control. It was only a short struggle. Biet sighed; his smile was cold and his eyes colder. "And what have I done that will cause me to be arrested at your request? he asked. His voice raspy with heated emotion.

The blubber butt still hasn't caught on, King thought, smiling to himself. No use draggin this out. I might as well shove it up his ass now 'n git it over with, it's sure as Hell the only way I'm ever gonna git a patrol out there tonight. He opened the flap of his slanted breast pocket, extracted a photograph, and tossed it onto the polished desk surface. "Try this on fer size Dai Ta."

Biet looked at the picture. A Vietnamese soldier was obviously studying a code book, while Biet sat beside him writing what appeared to be a letter. The two were the only people in the image. King knew that Biet could easily read the three words on the code book's cover: "November," "Secret," and "Gonzaga." King could imagine the thoughts in Biet's mind: recall of the scene, fear, confusion, curiosity as to who might have taken the picture. Biet's face, however, remained expressionless.

"You might notice there Dai Ta," King's drawl was confident, "the photograph itself is dated on the edge. Stateside film developers are doin that now as a new service. That pitcher proves you had Gonzaga's code book at some time in November, the month it came up missin. By the way, you can keep that one if you wanna. I made several copies."

"You cannot use this without to implicate yourself," Biet stated. His voice was calm, but his halting English grammar betrayed his inner turmoil. "It was you who steal code book and give it to me. This letter I write here is the one to your superiors, recommending that you be new senior advisor. You were in same room at time this picture taken."

King chuckled. "Look again Dai Ta. I'm not in that pitcher. It's your word against mine, an if this snapshot ever becomes public, everone would expectcha ta try ta shift blame onta someone else."

"Yes, but you have photograph all along, if you not reveal you have before now, you bring suspicion to your door."

"I'm still ahead a ya Dai Ta. My story'll be that somebody else took the pitcher, as he obviously did. You have already remembered that

I was in the room. Could'n'a takin it myself. But I'll jist say that this friend a mine, who happens ta be a snuffy I can trust, had this pitcher all the time without knowin it. Or rather without knowin what he had. Can I help it that he didn't give it to me till the day before I turn it inta the authorities? You can see that I obviously have such a man, who'll do what I ask. As far as he's concerned, I wadn't there atall."

After a long pause, Biet spoke, once again with his UCLA diction intact: "So you have what is called a trump card in the game of bridge, and you choose to play it now. For what? A patrol? Does this patrol mean that much?"

King remained silent, smiling, totally self assured. His hands lay folded in his lap. With his right hand, he began to slowly twirl the ring on his finger.

After a long heavy pause, Biet spoke in a somber half whisper. "Or is this just the time you have chosen to elevate yourself not merely to the status of equality, but as my superior; where you, in effect, will command all forces in Quang Tin? If so, I think you overstep yourself Lieutenant Colonel King."

King jumped to his feet. "You stupid Dink pig! You always make such a point ta use my full title!" His raised voice sounded too loud in the quiet tension of the room. He checked himself and glanced around. His next words were spoken in a low hiss. "I took over this fuckin province a month ago when we got ridda Gonzaga. I've been in control ever since. It's jist that yer so God Damned dumb and incompetent ya wouldn't know unless someone toldja. Well I'm tellin ya, Shit For Brains. You bet yer sweet ass I'm in charge."

Both men glared at each other. The electric overhead fan droned, aiming its ineffective airstream at neither. King noticed that Biet's forehead was beaded with perspiration. He felt a drop of his own sweat creeping down his jaw.

"Yes, I do always use your full title, Lieutenant Colonel King. And it has indeed been a small effort on my part to cause you to remember your place. I am your superior officer, but that has always been very difficult for you to recognize and understand. However, I speak English even better than you do, yet you always call me Dai Ta, which is my rank title in Vietnamese. Surely you know that I recognize this petty ploy; so clearly based upon racial prejudice, that you say Dai Ta rather than the English word Colonel because to you it sounds lower?"

"It don't matter what we call each other Dai Ta, what matters is who pulls the strings. That pitcher there says I do." Their eyes remained locked in ocular combat. Neither man blinked.

Biet broke away first. "I see that I made a grave error in enlisting your assistance in the Gonzaga matter. At the time, I thought it was for our mutual benefit," he muttered through stiffly moving lips.

King fell back into his subservient, advisor personality. "You didn't make no mistake Dai Ta Sir; you did the right thing. I donno why ya wanted ta git ridda Gonzaga, but let's face it, he was too soft fer this job. We're in a war here. You an me, we're soldiers. You needed me ta help move him out. I thought it was the right thing ta do, so I helptcha. You could'n'a done it without me."

"I must have misread the stars. I can see now that I may have more to fear from you than from the civilian. Destiny now casts me into the role of a puppet."

"Don't take it so hard Dai Ta. Your part hadn't changed. You'll still be the PC; I'll jist continue ta play my role as yer loyal counterpart 'n call ya 'Sir' 'n everthing. The only ones who'll know the real story are you 'n me." King's voice now lowered into a steely growl. "And that pitcher there says that neither one 'a us will forget the real story don't it?"

Biet dropped his head as if he were praying. His eyes closed. He held this position for some time before he spoke again. "Very well," he said calmly. "We will send a patrol to the area. I will send a unit from the province reserve here in Tam Ky. Will you please arrange for American helicopters to lift them to a landing zone west of Hau

Duc at dusk this evening and pick them up at another LZ tomorrow at dawn? Our operational planners can work out the details."

"Now yer talkin Dai Ta. Sure I think I can do that fer us. I'll lay on the choppers 'n tell my S3 guys ta git with yours ta plan the patrol route." King was all smiles now. He strolled to the door.

"Don't be so glum, Chum. Cheer up Dai Ta. We'll make a great team. Yer my counterpart ya know. I'll take care a you, 'n you take care a me. That's what counterparts do."

Biet had risen and was now staring out the high arched windows. It had begun to rain. He did not reply.

By the way Dai Ta," King's tone was even more cheerful. "My new DPSA's arrivin today. We're havin a little welcome party over at Camp Kronberg this evenin at the club. You 'n yer wife are invited ta join us. It would be a nice gesture if you could come 'n make the new guy feel ta home 'n all."

Biet turned to face him. "Am I to consider this a command appearance, or do I have a choice in this matter?"

King continued to smile, deciding to meet sarcasm with sarcasm. "Don't be so touchy Dai Ta, I'm jist bein neighborly. A party'd be good fer ya. It would be a break from the stress a yer position a leadership." He knew Biet would understand the dig. He opened the door without waiting for a reply and closed it softly behind him.

I shoulda slammed the fuckin door, he thought. The yellow butterball still don't know what's goin on. He thinks we're jist playin a game of one-upmanship. Hell, this is a game of pure power, 'n I've already won.

Co Li was just entering her office from the other side of the room carrying a tea tray. Her pink au yai flowed gracefully as she walked. King had a sudden inspiration. This'll really git to him, he thought.

Bearing the tray and freshly brewed tea, Co Li quietly entered the Province Chief's office. Placing them carefully on Colonel Biet's desk, she stepped back respectfully.

"Dai Ta," she said in demure Vietnamese, "the American Troom Ta has just invited me to a party this evening. He said that you were going, and that I should come also. Is it your wish that I go, um Dai Ta Biet?" She smiled with practiced shyness.

Biet was still seething with anger by the window, but the question knifed through. He realized immediately why Co Li had been invited. The mismarked pig wishes to embarrass me, he thought. By inviting a lowly secretary, he deliberately demeans my invitation and expects me to refuse it. Hmm, I had already decided to not go. My wife will certainly choose to stay home. She hates the vulgar Americans, and I did not relish being in an environment which King could control rather than I; but now? A new challenge! My mismarked advisor, or counterpart, as he likes to say, still plays games. Now if I do not attend, he will think he has won.

I will go! I will teach him that he has underestimated Colonel Than Mak Biet. But Co Li must also be there. If I should deny her permission, I again allow him to think like a winner.

He turned to Co Li. "I must go my child. A matter of protocol; but for you it is a matter of choice. It would please me to see you there, but it is not mandatory."

"I will act as it pleases you um Dai Ta. I will go." She bowed and gracefully withdrew.

Biet walked to stand under the airstream of the electric fan, his plan for tonight already formed. His mind now raced with other jumbled thoughts. Co Li is very beautiful. Too beautiful! It is true what we Vietnamese say, that if one is too attractive, he or she will attract evil spirits. The uncouth American pig is almost certainly an evil spirit, with the mark of Satan on his face, and that is why she attracted him today. The stars warned me of his evil, but I underestimated it. I thought that being military, he would naturally submit to my superior rank. The astrologers told me this would be the case, or at least they implied it.

He turned and walked to the office door and proceeded down the hallway to the stairs. I wonder if someone did deliberately place a snake in his wardrobe. If so, he thought, I hope they try again.

He slowly climbed the stairs to his living quarters. Ca Dor, he mused. The Americans think it means something in Vietnamese. The Vietnamese think it means something in French. But I have talked to the French. They say the building existed with its current name before they arrived. Its meaning is just one of the many mysteries of Quang Tin.

His wife was in the music room. He parted the beaded curtain which sufficed for a door and entered the room.

Madame Than Le Di glanced up from her fingernails, as one of the house maids kneeled before her, renewing the royal red gloss with methodical care. The elegantly clad woman waited for her husband to speak.

Instead, Biet marched across the room and sent the house maid sprawling by shoving her savagely with his boot. "Out! Now!" he shouted.

Scrambling to her feet, and desperately protecting the open bottle from spilling, the young girl sprang through the beaded curtain and down the hallway.

"Something has upset you My Husband," Madame Di remarked calmly.

"I have come to tell you that your fear of the mismarked American demon has been justified," Biet began.

She sat majestically silent as her husband recounted the conversation between himself and King. When he finished, she blew on her fingertips without emotion. "I still do not understand why you involved this blemished man with our family's destiny. I know you feared the civilian, Gonzaga, but he did not bear a mark of evil. He was a good man."

"Yes, but I was following the advice of the stars. The bearded civilian knew too much about the financial matters of our province. He knew of many places where I make profits. I worried about what he might be saying to the powers in Da Nang and Saigon."

Madame Di nodded her head. "Yes, but you had already acted against him. By your shrewdness, he was already under suspicion of theft and murder. I thought we were in accord as to what we should do, but without consulting me, you went further than we had planned, and you asked the blotched demon for assistance. Surely Gonzaga would have been taken away to stand trial for those other charges if you could have but waited. Why didn't you?"

Biet leaned his back against the wall, resigned that he must explain. "I am familiar with American justice. It does not act with the speed of Vietnamese law in these days. Suspicion is not enough. Their laws state that evidence must convince beyond a shadow of a doubt. The evidence we have contrived against Doctor Gonzaga is strong, but there are many shadows. At the time, I felt that the killing of a Vietnamese citizen during this time of war would not be considered a serious crime if committed by a high ranking American. I thought it would be just a small mark against him. I knew how zealously they guard their code books, and I felt that this was the way to remove him quickly. I therefore approached the spotted one. It worked quite well, for as soon as the loss was discovered, Gonzaga was relieved. I have since learned, however, that Americans think murder is a most grievous crime, regardless of who commits it, even in a foreign country at war."

"So I am right," she snapped. "He would have been sent away without the assistance of the blemished one. You should have consulted me before acting in haste. You know I would have advised you to refrain."

"Yes," he sighed. "I also ignored the old sayings of our people which warn us that anyone who bears a prominent birthmark which is not on the exact centerline of his body is either evil or a conveyer of ill fortune. Even the stars foretold of malevolence from a soldier marked by a demon, but my astrologers convinced me that I would never and could never be harmed by an American."

"Perhaps, My Husband, we should still have this American killed. It would be the safest way, and we would be ridding the world of an evil spirit. Doing so might bring blessings to our family."

"No Madame, I have already considered that, and I will not do it. The house of Than has seen too much blood. There was a time when the advancement of my career was more important than the lives of others, more important than my soul's survival. I see this same trait now in the American whose face is marked with doom. It causes the shadows of my past to haunt me with guilt.

My office requires me to kill the enemies of our young country. These enemies are all Vietnamese. I kill my brothers and former comrades daily. During my confession yesterday, the Catholic Priest of Tam Ky said there is a difference between killing in war, and murder. I believe what the father says. I am weary of killing but I must continue. My hands will never be clean of my brother's blood, but I shall not commit murder ever again."

"I have less fear for my soul than you, My Husband. I shall do this small deed for your sake and your hands shall remain clean."

"No, Wife; I know that you have done this before, but this time I forbid it! The mismarked American has duplicate pictures! Besides, he will not harm me. The stars have promised. Despite his uncivilized behavior, he is a good soldier and a clever tactician. He wishes to defeat the enemy as much as I do, and he has a unique ability to foresee problems. The stars have warned that there is a time of great danger approaching. This danger will be from war, not from greed nor power lust. Lieutenant Colonel King will be needed in the days ahead."

"You are weak My Husband. If I had not been at your side to aid you, you would not now be the Province Chief. You should not allow this foreigner to shame you before my eyes nor before your own."

"It is for a short time only, Madame. Time, as ever, will pass. The American will leave at the end of his tour, and we will stay. All will then be as before. Time heals all wounds, solves all riddles and relieves all sadness. We shall win by waiting."

Madame Di nodded, but her lips tightened with reproach. "Indeed, that is the saying of our people, but a demon marked by the Devil cannot be trusted. He may accuse you as he departs, or after."

"Yes, it is possible, even though the stars have indicated otherwise. But what can I do? If I do not do as he wishes, he will allow the photograph to become public. He has no scruples."

She did not answer. A helicopter droned somewhere overhead. A wasp hung for a few seconds in the open window, harmonizing with the louder, mechanized hum from above and then darted away. The gaunt but graceful woman continued to blow gently on her fingernails with an air of indifference.

Finally she spoke. "Do not be alarmed by the barking of a caged dog My Husband. There will be no real change of status. You must not only retain your office for him to have the feeling of power, but you must also continue to bear all trappings of power as well. He is as locked to you in your present position as you are to him in his. If you fall in rank or in death, he will lose his grip on the scepter as well. He may think he controls, but the tethered tiger cannot be managed. You will not lose face with our people." She paused and then added, "our people may never know; but I do, and so do you. You have lost face with me and with your mirror."

Biet ignored the last remark; he was accustomed to his wife's acid tongue in times of domestic tempest. "But how shall we deal with this peacock's thirst for domination? I cannot defy him openly without risking my own exposure."

"We will plan. I will obey your request, and refrain from killing the blemished pig for the present, but we will both seek knowledge of something he wishes to be kept secret. A man of his nature always has something to hide. When we find it, it will not only ensure his perpetual silence, but should also re-elevate you into a position of at least dual control. It will then become a different game we play. But in this new game, you shall own the board My Husband."

"As always Madame, your advice is excellent. The stars were most favorable when you became my wife."

"As always, My Husband, my only wish is for your greatness to increase."

"Thank you Madame. I will now return to my bloody task. I must send some of our brave provincial warriors to their deaths near Hau Duc." He turned from his wife, parted the beaded curtain, and clumped downstairs, dreading the orders he must give. He had not mentioned the party to his wife. He knew she would never agree to go. King, however, would still be in for a surprise tonight, after the patrol departs. He sighed. No matter how fast a man runs, he thought, he cannot break free from his shadow.

After returning from Colonel Biet's office, Co Li busied herself at her desk until she heard the Province Chief climb the stairs. As soon as she was sure he was safely at the summit, she walked to the arched windows of her office and opened the two outward swinging halves. The one on her right, she opened full, flat against the outer wall. The one on her left, she opened only half way, leaving it perpendicular to the building.

The light rain falling upon her arms felt soothing and cool. The smell of the wet sand was refreshing. She returned to her desk and waited.

Within minutes, her brother's head appeared over the window sill.

"Anh Ty," she whispered, quickly returning to the window. "I have news. Dai Ta Biet will send a patrol west of Hau Duc this day at dusk. They will be transported by American helicopters and are scheduled to return at dawn tomorrow."

"You have done well, as usual, Em, my little sister. Is there more?"

"There is much anger between the Dai Ta and the hateful American Troom Ta. I could not discern all the words, for they spoke English in low tones, but the one with the sinister mark was very disrespectful and insulting, yet the Dai Ta acquiesced to his wish for a patrol."

The boy's face grew thoughtful. "We must ponder the meaning of this together at a later time. You have done your duty; now I must do mine. The People's National Liberation Front will be proud of us both. Until later my Em, my little sister."

"Luck and good spirits go with you Ty, my anh, my elder brother."

He turned. His stride was purposeful but nonchalant through the drizzle, towards the city center of Tam Ky.

Co Li smiled pensively, and closed the windows.

SCENE 5

AIR AMERICA

0930 Hours
Monday, 1 January 1968

The sleek, white Porter Pilatus airplane climbed sharply into the hot clear Mekong Delta sky. The engine whined loudly and the screaming propeller blades bit into the air, as the dart-like craft fought its own private war against the eternal foe, gravity.

Jake felt himself pressed heavily into his seat back with the steepness of the ascent. The noise and the pressure forced him into the isolation of his own thoughts.

The heat of sea level Saigon dropped away, replaced by the refreshing coolness of higher altitude, yet the blazing sun played peek-a-boo, first blinding him from one forward window, then playfully stabbing into his eyes from the next window back.

Jake watched Ton Son Nhut Airfield dropping away. The panorama of greater Saigon seemed to expand in all directions as the airplane gained height. He continued to stare out the window, but even though his eyes focused on the crowded traffic of every twisting street, the slashes of green in park areas, and the jumble of a million irregular shaped rooftops, he saw nothing.

He was conscious only of the contents of the document file he had recently read and burned. His mood was sour. Being given a brevet promotion and told to pass for a rank he shouldn't be quite yet, should have been cause for pleasure, but this was a triviality in his recollections. The droning throb of the aircraft engine vibrated in harmony with the one syllable in Jake's mind: "Ray, Ray, Ray, Ray."

General Elsin had been right. The evidence was staggering. Several witnesses to an argument between Ray and the murdered man just two hours before the body was found; a truck serial number traced back to Ray's signature; Ray's code book missing and two POWs' testimony that a US code book had been obtained from "a very important American civilian in Tam Ky."

Ray has to be in agony over this, he thought. It's so damned wrong! It has to be a mistake, or a frame, but how the Hell am I going to find out? I'll try, Ray, but I've got to hold my tongue to do you any good. Hell, I'm supposed to investigate. But I'm an infantry officer, not a damned detective. How the heck am I supposed to find out anything? I don't know what to do. I don't even know where to begin!

Unconsciously, Jake glanced around. The young buck sergeant in the row behind sat rigid, gripping the seat ahead. His blanched and frozen features clearly indicated a very frightened man.

"You OK, Son? You see something I didn't?"

"Gawd Almighty, Sir," the man exploded, "we went straight up!"

Jake covered his mouth to hide his grin. He remembered his first take off from Ton Son Nhut, and the stomach churning surprise at the steepness of the ascent. That had been on a C-130. This zippy little power plant had indeed zoomed almost straight up, but because of the preoccupation with his task, and perhaps because he'd expected it, he hadn't even felt the climb.

"They always do that," he said reassuringly. "The Rice Paddy Daddies sometimes sneak in close to the air strip and try to shoot at planes when they're just taking off. They're more of a nuisance than a danger, but pilots don't like to take any chances."

"Jeez, I don't either Sir; next time I think I'll walk."

Jake relaxed. This young NCO's going to be OK, he thought. He really was scared, but he's already recovered his sense of humor.

"Going to Tam Ky, Sergeant?"

Mark cleared his throat, "Ahh, yes Sir," he stammered, obviously now ashamed of showing his fear.

Jake smiled again. "I'm Colonel Thorpe. Going up there too. Just getting back from R & R?"

"Oh, no Sir. Just got in country; like you. I got assigned up there too. They told me that we'd be on the same plane."

"Glad to meet you Sergeant...?" Jake twisted in his seat, trying to read the name on the man's fatigue jacket.

"Fellogese Sir. One fellow constantly followed by more than one goose."

Thorpe grinned broadly, "I won't forget it now Sergeant Fellogese, but your info sources are better'n mine. I thought I was going up alone."

"The EM pipeline Sir. Never fails. Your first tour Sir?"

"No it isn't." Thorpe glanced out the window at the turquoise sky. "I was here two years ago, but a lot's changed. Where you from in the states, Sergeant Fellogese?"

"New York City Sir, Little Italy. I'm a big city boy through and through. What about you Sir, where are you from?"

"I'm from a place you've never heard of, and after you hear it, you won't be able to pronounce it."

"Try me Sir."

"I'm from a little place in Washington State named Puyallup." Jake watched for the reaction.

"Well Sir, I haven't heard of it before and I'm still not really sure I have now. It sounded to me like you swallowed your tongue rather than naming your hometown." The sergeant's eyes twinkled merrily. "Where is this Pew—whatever it is?"

Jake grinned, this was one of his favorite games. He had been playing it ever since he left home to go the University back east. "Puyallup is close to Seattle. Whenever I don't want to raise eyebrows, I usually just say I'm from Seattle since most people have heard of that."

"Yes Sir. I've heard of Seattle. Of course, we New Yorker's still hold to the belief that civilization ends at the Hudson River, and the edge of the earth is just past Chicago. Smoke Sir?" He held a stateside hard box of Winston cigarettes toward the officer.

"Thanks Sergeant, I have my own. Jake pulled a package of Camels from his fatigue jacket and both men lit up.

"You've probably heard this question a million times before Sir, but I have to ask you anyway. Are you related to Jim Thorpe the athlete?"

Jake shook his head with amusement. "No. No relation at all. Jim Thorpe was an Indian. I think I'm mostly Scandinavian with a little English thrown in. My middle name is James though, but nobody ever calls me Jim."

Jake noticed that Sergeant Fellogese appeared to be slightly disappointed at not meeting the kinsman of a historic personality. His face sure shows everything he's feeling, Jake realized. The sign of a good man with nothing to hide.

"What's your MOS Sergeant?" Jake asked.

"Well Sir, I'm supposed to be infantry, but I've been an RTO ever since I've been in. My orders read that I'm to be an Operations Shift

Sergeant and Technical Advisor in Quang Tin. I'm guessing I'll be honchoing a radio set up there as usual."

"That's probably more than just a Radio Telephone Operator," Jake responded. "Sounds like you'll be in charge of a shift in the Tactical Operations Center."

"Yes Sir. I know what it sounds like, but I've been a shift sergeant before at Fort Carson. There, it just meant an RTO with stripes. The shift officer had all the say."

"Could be, but when I was here before, we didn't have shift officers in the field. Only at major headquarters, brigade and higher. In the field, the NCO's ran the shifts unless something hot was going on."

"I'd like that Sir. When were you here before?"

"I came over in early 65 as an advisor. Advised a South Vietnamese Army battalion operating around Pleiku in the highlands. Then, when the First Cav came over in mid year, I asked a friend who was with them to get me a transfer, and I got it. Spent the last six months of my tour with an American unit as a company commander, mostly in the jungle. I sure didn't see much of the country."

Sergeant Fellogese looked at his companion with new respect. "Kind of a bummer isn't it Sir, to be sent back over here so soon?"

"Believe it or not Sergeant, I volunteered for early rotation."

Mark's face registered his shock. "Gawd Sir, how could you do that? Do officers have to do things like that to get promoted, or do you really believe in this war?"

It was Jake who now blinked in surprise. He had heard anti-war sentiments expressed several times in the states, but to hear it here, from a soldier, seemed wrong, almost unpatriotic.

Mark leaned forward apologetically. "Sorry Sir, I shouldn't have said that. It's none of my business."

"The partial answer to your question, Sergeant, is that yes, I do believe we're right in fighting this war. And now I'll ask you a question: If you don't think we're doing the right thing, what the Hell are you doing here?" Even Jake could hear the acid in his words.

Mark moistened his lips and lowered his eyes. "Sir, I wish I could answer that. I just don't know. I don't even know if I'm really against the damn war. Sometimes I think I am, or at least I should be. But I'm not the type to run away to Canada, and I didn't want to go to jail. Everything is so mixed up."

"What happened, did you get drafted? asked Jake, a bit softer this time.

"Nothing as simple as that Sir, I joined of my own free will. Don't ask me why, I still don't know. Must've been out of my mind."

Jake raised an eyebrow. "What about basic training? That's tough. How'd you make it through feeling like you do?"

"Ahh Hell, Sir, almost everyone there felt the same way! I wasn't the only one. We all just gutted it through. Same at Fort Carson. The officers and senior NCOs all seem to be for the war, but you'd be surprised at how many of the snuffys don't. And the thing is, they all seem to think we believe in it too, just like they do, so nobody talks about it. I expected a lot of brain washing and crap like that, but it's just the opposite. Nobody says nothin!"

"You mean you've never heard anyone talk about why we're here; why we're doing what we're doing?"

"Well Sir, not until I got here. I'd heard what the anti-war people say are the real reasons we're in Vietnam. The Domino Theory and all that, but I'd never heard anyone who really believed in the war talk about it. I did at Camp Alpha though, three days worth. Hell, before that I thought I knew how I felt. But those briefings are convincing; they're pretty practiced; it makes you think. The one I had this morning was especially powerful. That's probably why I feel so confused right now."

Jake scratched his chin thoughtfully, his anger gone. "I'll tell you what Sergeant, if you were going to a US unit, where you wouldn't have much contact with the Vietnamese people, I'd probably try to persuade you to my point of view right now. But you're not. You're going to be in a job where you can see for yourself what this war is all about. Let's just forget about it for now. We'll be here a year together. We'll talk in about three or four months. See how you feel then. OK?"

Mark met Jake's gaze intently. "I'm sure sorry this came up Sir. I'm a good soldier. You probably can't believe that now, but I'll do my job."

Jake smiled. "No one makes three stripes in the short time you've been in without being a good soldier Son. You don't have to worry. I won't hold anything against you. I guess I'm just surprised the Army's doing such a lousy job at informing the troops of what's going on."

A massive, hairy civilian, dressed in sky blue trousers and a crisp, white, short sleeved shirt with epaulets, abruptly loomed over them, halting conversation. His blond, handlebar moustache and shaggy beard hid his lips, but Jake could tell the man was grinning, for his teeth peered through like fresh chicken eggs half hidden by nesting straw. "Coffee in the back. If you guys want it, help yourselves, but don't make a mess!" He proceeded forward into the cockpit area and handed the two steaming mugs he carried to the pilot and copilot.

"Gawd Sir, what airline is this anyway? I thought it was a general's airplane when I first got on, but then I saw Gargantua there, and no general would ever have him around."

"This is Air America Sergeant Fellogese. Believe it or not, we're flying to Tam Ky courtesy of the CIA."

Mark arched an eyebrow suspiciously.

"I don't know why either," Jake raised a hand and cut in quickly, "but we'll still have that talk in a couple of months or so, so don't jump to any conclusions just yet."

Both passengers groped their way down the narrow aisle, stooping to avoid the low aircraft ceiling, until they arrived at a small metal coffee pot on a hot plate next to the tiny, boxlike latrine. Jake poured for both of them into waxed paper cups with sharp fold out handles. He sighed as he watched a rainbow colored celluloid film spread across the surface of his coffee.

"I don't know Sir," said Mark soberly, staring down into his paper cup, "I doubt if I will change my mind about the war. If the CIA makes everybody drink wax in their coffee over here, maybe all those other horror stories are true too."

They both were still chuckling when they returned to their seats.

Jake looked at his brand new watch which he had hurriedly purchased before the flight at the airport PX. It had stopped. He now remembered that the same thing kept happening during his first tour. Something about electricity in some people's bodies which somehow was stronger over here and often caused wristwatches to stop.

"What time do you have Sergeant?"

"Eleven hundred on the nose Sir. Back home I'd just now be getting up on New Year's Day, probably with a big headache."

"No you wouldn't," Jake shook his head thoughtfully. "Eleven O'clock in the morning on the first of January here is, what…? Seven o'clock in the evening on December 31st back in New York. The party you'd have been to last night is probably just now getting started. It's not even 1968 back there yet."

"Hey, that's right Sir! I forgot about that." He grinned mischievously. "When you think about it, we're kinda time travelers aren't we? Kinda like flew into the future when we came over here."

Jake smiled sardonically, "We're certainly not in the future here. It's more like the past. No television, no modern conveniences, not very many places outside of cities which have running water or electricity. Everyone carries weapons like old time cowboys. It gives you a funny feeling like time has somehow passed this place by. People don't measure time by hours over here, the whole nature of time is different.

"I don't get your drift there Sir."

"Time doesn't mean much at all to the Vietnamese. They come late to appointments or don't show up at all, and you can't take offense by this because they don't mean any offense. They'll show up at some time or other because they are people of honor, and their word is good."

"Oh, yes Sir. I remember something about that from one of my briefings at Camp Alpha. But you said people Sir. You said people don't measure time by the hour over here. You mean Americans too?"

"Yeah I do. You'll find that all the Americans, especially the military, measure time according to their DEROS. I just got in country yesterday, so I have three hundred sixty three and a half days before my Date of Estimated Return from Over Seas. That makes me a long timer, and you too, you're a long timer also."

"I've got two days on you Sir. This is my fourth day. Let's see. That means I've got only, lets see, three hundred and sixty two, no, sixty one and a half days. God that makes a year sound long."

"It'll seem long till hump day, then it gets even longer."

"Jeez, you're full of good news. What's hump day Sir?"

"That's your half way point. You keep on counting backwards until you only have one hundred eighty three days left. Your one hundred and eighty third day is hump day."

"It sounds like forever."

"It'll feel like it too. You're going on shift work. That means either midnight to noon or noon to midnight. Seven days a week. No holidays. No breaks. Time gets so blurred and out of joint you won't know whether you're coming or going."

"I feel that way already just listening Sir. Now that you told me what time it is back in the real world, I think I'll wait a couple of hours before I wish you a Happy New Year. You know, just to be safe."

Jake laughed. "Sorry Sergeant. I didn't mean to boggle your mind. I was a teacher in one of the military schools between my Vietnam tours. I guess it's still in my blood. I sometimes think I'm still on the stage and can't help reeling off a lecture."

"No sweat Sir," Mark grinned. His long dimples creasing his cheeks. "This is good stuff for my journal"

Suddenly, the airplane lurched into a steep bank, straightened and screamed into a shallow power dive. The pilot and copilot stared intently out the left window. The copilot pointed. The two soldiers looked left just in time to see an evil stream of blood colored anti-aircraft tracers slicing upward about thirty yards away from the tip of the left wing. The pilot steepened the dive and whipped sharply into a left turn, directly at the deadly red torrent.

Mark gripped the arms of his seat with terror, "Gawd almighty. He's headed right for it. We're gonna die!" he shouted.

Jake reached out and touched Mark's arm with a calming pat. The menacing river of staccato scarlet swayed to the right, passed close behind the airplane and began to whiplash back to the left. Jake felt his buttocks tighten. He knew the tracers could tear through the air-craft floor like a paper target. All eyes pivoted watching the string of ruby death. The plane now banked sharply right, standing on its wing to pass behind the tracers. These pilots know their business, Jake thought. Ducking back and forth makes us hard to hit. If we did the obvious, turning away from the tracers, we'd be easy to bring down. A few more steep turns. A few more quick intakes of breath from the sergeant beside him, and the cascade of crimson ceased.

Mark exhaled slowly. Jake lit a cigarette and offered the pack to Mark who took one automatically. Jake lit Mark's cigarette with his flip top Zippo. My hands are a little shaky, he thought. I guess you never get used to somebody shooting at you.

The pilot and copilot were smiling and congratulating each other with pats on the back.

Mark took a deep drag of the strong unfiltered smoke of the Camel cigarette and coughed forcefully for several seconds. He snuffed the cigarette out in the ashtray.

Jake smiled at him, "Welcome to Vietnam Sergeant Fellogese."

Mark recovered and smiled back. "Hell Sir. I knew you'd try to get back at me because I told you how I feel about this Damned war. Now I know why you volunteered to come over here early for the second time. Those damned weeds aren't killing you fast enough so you decided to speed up the process."

Both men laughed and chatted for a while longer then lapsed into silence. Jake absently looked out the window, not seeing the passing geography beneath. The noise of the single engine aircraft droned on. The simian crewman walked to and fro past them without speaking. The pilot and copilot chatted to each other using microphones and headsets even though they were only an arm's length apart. Monotony and boredom again ruled the sky.

Mark reached into the side flap pocket of his fatigue jacket and withdrew his journal. Absently, he turned to the first page, written only a few days ago, as his airplane had taken off for Vietnam. He read the poem to himself:

> "SAN FRANCISCO—1967
> How often at night,
> as I rounded a bend,
> or peeped o'er the crest of a hill,
> Was I blessed with the sight
> of the breathtaking blend
> of the lights of a city so still.

> But the most beautiful sight
> of this type I have seen
> was different from all before.
> It was on last Thursday's flight
> over the city serene,
> as I was flying off to war."

It's incomplete, he thought, but I don't know how to finish it yet. Ah well, it'll come to me some day.

He flipped through the several completed pages. At the first blank sheet, he quickly jotted down his memories of the tracer fire and his favorable first impressions about his new boss.

Finishing these reflections, he paused and glanced out the window at the tropical scenery below. The VC are down there, he thought. He shuddered, and then, inspired, bent to the journal again:

"Below us, the Republic of Vietnam is a kaleidoscope of shapes and colors. Squares, trapezoids and triangles of green, blue and muddy brown mingle with splotches of amber. The dark blue ocean welcomes the soft tan and white beaches with white ribbons of wave action. A mountain range starts off to the left front and then slowly curls eastward to invade the sea. Beyond it, the coastal plain with its rice paddy patchwork begins again. The agricultural scene looks pleasant, peaceful and inviting up here. Yet I know now that the image is false. The inviting geography below is deceitful, filled with danger and death. Even the elements of nature are at war.

Rice paddies are in constant conflict with the encroaching jungle. Each tree of the rain forest fights against its neighbors for root space and sunshine, and the fight is always to the death. Tigers and other carnivores prowl to pounce and kill. Deadly serpents lay in ambush. The rain seeks to drown; and the savage heat knows no mercy. Poisonous spiders and centipedes lurk in every recess, while legions of other insects charge in random but vicious waves. Disease, like nerve gas, attacks silently, invisibly.

The petty war between humans, in this violent land, is insignificant and paltry in the universal fight for survival, in the overall struggle for life; while I continue my own inner battle, trying to determine right from wrong."

Satisfied with his prose, Mark put down his pen and lit another cigarette. If those classes at Camp Alpha didn't do anything else, they gave me enough information to make my journal more literary, he thought.

The clouds were even darker now. Lightning flashed off to the east, where the Gulf of Tonkin and the South China Sea blended their waters into an indistinguishable oneness.

The copilot turned in his seat, pulled his headphones off so that he could hear what he was going to say and pointed downward with his thumb. "Tam Ky City," he said.

Mark hoped fervently that the gesture only implied direction.

SCENE 6

CAMP KRONBERG

1600 Hours
Monday, 1 January 1968

The warm monsoon rain pelted furiously. It wasn't a steady downpour for there was a rhythm which pounded their senses: An extended rush of almost solid water was followed by an abrupt pause. Another long wave of wind driven, wetness preceded another lull. Again the slashing needles, and again the hesitation. It was as if they were driving along the edge of an ocean being lashed by sea waves. But the beach was a mile to the east and these rain cycles came faster and seemed to carry more water.

The jeep's ineffectual wipers clicked to a slower, futile cadence, while the Vietnamese driver raced the engine and accented the tempo of the storm with staccato horn blasts, as if he thought he needed a foghorn. The topless vehicle plunged south through the crescendo of the storm song toward Tam Ky City.

Lieutenant Colonel King, Jake's new boss, sat huddled in the passenger seat encased in a formless Army poncho. The shape didn't look like man, more like a wrinkled plastic mound of…, of what? Jake drew a mental blank in trying to think of what the hump in the front seat reminded him of. It was something familiar though. He and Sergeant Fellogese, without ponchos, sat in the back, their bags and gear uncomfortably piled on their laps. Their backsides, still aching from the six hour plane ride, now crushed into the sodden canvas seats.

A cart pulled by two water buffalo eased onto the main road from the right, directly into their path. The driver whipped to the left, straight into the path of an onrushing U.S. Army ten ton truck! With split second timing, he lurched the jeep back to the right through the swiftly closing gap with only inches to spare on either side. "Aiii Ha!," the chauffeur shouted, reminding Jake of a Disneyland roller coaster, or maybe a Kamikaze ride, he amended.

King did not turn around, but his bellowing voice carried back to the two passengers who already felt like survivors. "Get any buffalo snot on ya?" His voice revealed that he was enjoying the drenched, heart wrenching dash as much as his driver.

Jake didn't answer. He used his hand to partially shield his eyes from the stinging darts of attacking raindrops.

From beside him, he heard Sergeant Fellogese shouting through the downpour. "I always heard of soldiers getting their baptism of war Sir, but I never took it so literally before."

The monsoon drowned the sound of their laughter.

Farmers were still working in the rice paddies they passed. Men, women, children, and water buffalo peacefully harvesting the second crop of the year, apparently indifferent to the speeding jeep on the raised road beside them, oblivious to the army truck convoy heading in the opposite direction, and heedless of the slashing rainfall.

To the right, they passed along a vast barren field. Beyond this sandy desolation stood a gigantic gothic structure just visible through the downpour. "Ca Dor, the Province Headquarters," shouted King from beneath his plastic shelter. "We're just northa the city. Our TOC and offices are right behind it. That's where botha you'll be workin."

Sergeant Fellogese's voice was just audible through the storm and road noise, "Looks spooky Sir. It'd make a good movie set for Wuthering Heights."

Jake turned to squint at the big building as it slid to the rear. It was veiled by the tempest and indeed looked spooky, although, to him, it looked more like a monastery or an old Scottish fortress.

They entered the outskirts of Tam Ky. But it wasn't a real city, not even a small town. It's like an old wild west town, or a little mining town, he thought. I had forgotten how small the cities and towns are over here.

He saw wooden hovels patched with cardboard. Shacks constructed entirely from straw mats, or the short boards of ammunition boxes. Many corrugated tin roofs, and several brick dwellings with tin sheets used for one or more walls. He saw only ten or so substantial buildings of stucco or masonry, and two old Army trucks hollowed out for human habitation.

Bicycles with riders of all ages swarmed past. A woman in black pajamas and conical straw hat jogged barefooted along the street balancing a long pole on her shoulder. Hung from one end of the pole was a wire basket full of multicolored bags. From the other end hung another basket with two naked babies huddled inside. The pole bowed and straightened in time with her jogging pace, lulling both children to sleep despite the torrent of rain.

Just beyond the city, the jeep slowed and turned west along a mud river which evidently had been a dirt road before the day's downpour. The ragged and tattered south edge of Tam Ky was still visible on the right as the jeep bounced along for about a quarter of a mile.

To the southwest of the city, about 700 yards from the nearest civilian habitation, Jake glimpsed a large wire enclosure: Camp Kronberg, the defensive compound for the US advisors of Quang Tin Province. In the gloom and rain, Jake was reminded of the popular TV series back home, "Stalag 17." It looked just like the movie set.

Camp Kronberg was enclosed by a fifteen foot high chain link fence with a double roll of concertina barbed wire stretched along the top. At the four corners stood guard towers on stilts, each with a thatched roof. Sandbagged foxholes dotted the interior.

Two MPs in rain slick ponchos stood at the gate, each surrounded by a waist high sandbag barrier. The gate remained closed as the jeep pulled up. Jake noticed that both MPs were alert, brand new M-14 rifles held at the ready. King stepped out of the Jeep, "It's me guys, I'm bringin in some fresh meat."

Both MPs saluted with their right hands rather than giving the ceremonial rifle salute. They both grinned knowingly as if they knew something the newcomers did not. One raised his arm and the large gate swung inward, electronically controlled.

They proceeded into the center of the compound and parked with several other jeeps in front of a two storied white stucco structure with a red tile roof. Several metal quonset huts were arranged in rows on either side of the main building.

A large, corpulent soldier stepped from the porch of the box-like building out into the rain wearing a poncho with the hood down so that his soggy ball cap was visible. Three up, three down with a diamond in the middle; the First Sergeant! He flipped a cigarette in a glowing arc to the mud and snapped a parade correct military salute, his face split with a congenial grin.

King climbed out again, returning the salute. "Howdy Top", he drawled, "got some fresh meat for us."

"Yes Sir," the First Sergeant boomed with a basso profundo that reverberated around the compound. Jake was, by now, thoroughly accustomed to the thin butcher's reference that always introduced new arrivals to Vietnam. He absently promised himself that he would never use the trite joke no matter how long he remained in country.

Jake and Mark clumsily crawled out of the jeep to stand in the well trodden muck of the compound. As if on cue, they both stretched and rubbed their buttocks.

"Top, this is our new DPSA, Lieutenant Colonel Thorpe, and our new TOC man, Sergeant—, ahh, how do you say it again Sergeant?"

"Fellogese Sir, just one fellow followed by more than one goose."

"Oh, yeah, Fellogese. Well guys, this is the team topkick, First Sergeant Prescott."

Prescott saluted Jake, and then stuck out his enormous hand in a warm greeting. "Glad to meetchu Sir, I thought we were supposed to get a civilian for the number two job."

The two shook hands, but it was King who answered the implied question. "So did I Top, I guess they've run outta civilians who're willin ta leave Saigon. Personally, I'm tickled shitless. Hell, this is war. In a war, we need soljers. Da Nang told me jist this afternoon, an I been thinkin bout it since. The more I thought, the better I liked it. His counterpart's a Lieutenant Colonel. The God Damned Vietnamese don't put civilians in charge of provincial governments. Why should we? And, Hell, I get along better with soljers than civilians. I always have, ever since college."

While King prattled on about the relative merits of a military deputy rather than a civilian, First Sergeant Prescott shook hands with Mark, and then helped the new arrivals unload their gear onto the porch which was dry only in comparison to the rest of the world around them.

"This is Camp Kronberg," King was now saying. "It used ta be Camp Zulu, probably cause it's about as far away and different from Camp Alpha as it could get. We renamed it a couple or three months ago, after a Captain who was stationed here got himself zapped at Hau Duc." He glanced at the dripping newcomers. "Top, you take Fellogese there over ta his hooch and git him settled in. I'll take Colonel Thorpe round ta his quarters. Be sure ta tell him about the party at nineteen hundred tonight, and make sure he knows what ta do in case a emergencies. We don't wanna lose a fish on his first day just cause he don't know where ta go when the balloon goes up."

"Right Sir", Prescott saluted smartly and the two NCOs trudged off into the mud and rain.

King turned, smiled, and put his hand on Thorpe's shoulder. "Well, I feel like I jist popped my cherry. I've never had a lieutenant colonel working fer me before. What's your first name Thorpe?"

"Jake Sir."

King burst into a guffaw of derisive laughter. "Shit! Ya gave yourself away that time Jake! No lieutenant colonel calls another lieutenant colonel Sir!" He was grinning with glee.

Jake felt a lurch in his stomach, as if he were about to be violently sick. His mouth became instantly dry. Jesus, he thought. I did give it away. He knows! Damn it! All that work by General Elsin down the drain.

"Yup," King chortled. "Ya let the God Damned cat outta the sack that time. Anybody'd know ya jist got promoted. How long ya been wearin silver? A cuppla weeks? Maybe even lessen that?"

Jake blinked his surprise. He didn't know after all! "Yeah, less than that." he croaked. His voice sounded to him as if he were being strangled. He hoped King didn't press for details.

"I knew it!" King chortled. "Took me quite a bit too before I could stop sayin Sir ta all the other oh fives."

Jake smiled guiltily.

"Well, from now on, don't call me Sir. You call me Dick. That's my first name."

"OK, thank you Sir," Jake said automatically. Both men immediately laughed. Jake thought to himself that this indeed would be the first time he'd ever called an oh five by his first name. It would be difficult to do.

"To orient ya," King picked up Jake's soggy garment bag and stepped off the porch in the opposite direction to that formerly taken by the two enlisted men. Jake shouldered his duffel bag, scooped up his athletic bag, and followed. "This buildin here's the club. It's an all ranks club fer the whole team; it's where the party's gonna be tonight. Also houses the two dining rooms, one fer officers and one fer snuffies. The upstairs is the first sergeant's office. It's gotta small readin room too, if ya go in fer that sorta thing."

Jake smiled inwardly as the two trudged around the clubhouse toward the rear of the building. King obviously isn't the intellectual type, he thought.

"This camp and everthin in it is your baby," King continued, "Team Two here in Tam Ky has a strength a fifty eight men: thirteen officers now with you, twenty three NCOs, eighteen snuffies and four civilians. A course there's more out 'n the districts, but you'll be briefed on all that later. Me an three a the officers live in a fancy French villa over near the province headquarters. It's reserved fer the PSA. You'll shit yerself when ya see it. It's number fuckin one. I've only been 'ere a month. I useta have yer job, DPSA. The PSA was a civilian. He'n the other four civilians useta live in the villa. That's what they called it back then. The Villa. I kicked the fuckin civilians out when I took over; they live here in Kronberg now. Brought somma my guys over to the Castle ta live with me. Everone thought the Castle was a better name cause my name's King. Get it? The King in his castle? Kinda neat huh?"

He turned to assure himself that Jake had indeed caught the meaning.

"Anyway, since I'm over there, you're the senior officer here, so you're the Camp Commander. But I'm still in charge, so check with me before ya change anythin. That bunker over there's the commo bunker. Don't look very big, but it'll surprise ya. Mostly underground. Big enough for everone in camp to get in. You know, in case'a a mortar or rocket attack. There's other bunkers round too though. Here's your hooch."

Jake's head had been on a constant swivel during the short sodden journey. He had tried to see everything that King pointed out. The task had not been an easy one, as the bulky duffel bag on his shoulder blocked half his view. He was forced to twist his entire body to see anything on that side, while stepping lively to keep up with his commander's quick pace, and struggling to stay upright in the slippery mud at the same time. His vision was also impaired by the oceans of water which continued to cascade from above. He looked up at King's last sentence and was surprised to see that they were heading for an American made house trailer. It was surrounded up to window level with soggy sandbags, making it appear half submerged, as if in a bog. Two more layers of muddy sandbags adorned the roof for mortar protection, and these decorated the aluminum sides with irregular muddy streaks, reminding Jake of a filthy sandwich made with moldy bread.

King opened the door and stomped in ahead of Jake, who bumped and squirmed his way through, forcing rivulets of water to be squeegeed out of the duffel bag down the doorjamb onto the floor, and down his neck inside his collar. He dropped his sodden load on the small kitchen floor and looked around, relieved to be out of the rain at last.

Without asking permission, King opened Jake's garment bag and pulled out the single class B khaki uniform Jake had brought and the two pair of starched fatigues. The left shoulders, sleeves and sides of all three uniforms showed large damp spots where the bag had failed to live up to its watertight specs.

"Not too bad," King commented, "Why don'cha take a shower and clean up. We got runnin water here in the trailer. I saw ta that when I was here. It's real special, none a the snuffies have runnin water yet. Shit! You look like ya already took one with all yer clothes on."

Jake shivered and suddenly realized the window air conditioner was on and blowing cold air directly at him.

"Good idea Sir," he said.

"Dick!", responded King, smiling.

"Oh, right Dick, I'll get used to it."

"While yer in the shower, I'll go out'n getcha a hooch maid. Everone gets one ya know, it's a regulation. Helps their economy or somethin. I'll send her over here ta get on your gear ta get it dry 'n cleaned up. Are ya hungry? Chow call's not till eighteen hundred."

"To be honest Sir, er, Dick, I'm starved. I missed both breakfast and lunch. I think Sergeant Fellogese did too."

"OK, I'll get the kitchen ta rustle up a cuppla sandwiches for botha ya. Be back in a minute trooper."

King sailed out the door as if he were making an exit stage left, with the spotlight still on him.

Well, he seems like he might be an all right guy, Jake thought, I think I'm going to like working for him. He hurriedly stripped off his sopping uniform.

After the shower, he walked back into the central living space of the mobile home and noted that the air conditioner now felt quite soothing in the climate's muggy heat. First time since I've been here that I haven't been either too hot or too cold, he thought.

He laid out one of the fatigue uniforms and noticed that the wet spot had almost dried. I won't put on my skivvies, he thought. They're probably all wet somewhere in that duffel bag. He remembered that he never wore them during his first tour because they caused crotch rot unless one was able to bathe regularly.

He paused in memory. This tour will really be different. Looks like I'm going to be able to bathe every day here.

He had pulled his soaked jungle boots onto his feet, without socks, and was adjusting to the squishy sensations of his wiggling toes, when the poncho draped form of Colonel King walked in without knocking. It was still pouring outside.

"Ya look a little better", King said. He wiped his boots on Jake's cast off uniform and stepped over the duffel bag on the kitchen floor. Stopping at the counter, he carefully raised the dripping front of his plastic gown with one hand and revealed a plate of sandwiches in the other.

"Here ya go," he drawled. "I think I left some coffee over here somewheres." He rummaged among the shelves and found a tin can with several individual packets of C-ration coffee.

"How do ya drink it?", Dick asked.

"Black please," Jake responded.

"Good. We got plenty a C Ration sugar if ya want, but the reconstituted milk tastes like shit. If ya didn't drink it black already, ya would before ya DEROS'd."

King soon placed two steaming stainless steel cups with rolled edges on the kitchen table and Jake stepped over the soggy hurdles to join him. King stripped off his poncho and draped it over the counter before sitting down. Jake noticed the holstered 45 on King's left hip.

"Well Jake, ya probably want ta know about me, so I'll start off." He offered a cigarette, a Salem. Jake winced but accepted. His cigarettes were a mushy blob somewhere on the floor.

"This's my second tour," King began, "been an advisor both times. Went through the State Department's special trainin for this type a thing. First time, I was a district advisor down in the delta. Saw quite a bit a shit. Won my share a atta boys." As he said this last, his hand brushed back and forth over the top of his left breast pocket.

King related what he had been doing between tours, but Jake, for the first time, realized the presence of the birth mark around King's left eye. Somehow, with all the wind and rain, and perhaps because King's face had been obscured by the poncho, he hadn't noticed it before. He recalled how the Vietnamese had reacted to the small brown mole in the center of his own back. A permanent body mark in the center of one's body meant good luck. The larger it was, the more it brought.

Anywhere else was bad luck, and the larger the spot, the more horrible the curse. And, as every Vietnamese knows, the luck of the bearer always tends to rub off on those about him. Wow, I wonder how he's been able to do his job over here with the Vietnamese recoiling from him every time he looks at them?

"Came up here six months ago in your job", King continued. A civilian named Gonzaga was the PSA. He stepped in some shit and Da Nang thought he smelled bad. So they jerked him outta here a month ago today. Even the Province Chief recommended me. I mean, even while Gonzaga was here I was doin mosta the work. So when he left, the whole fuckin load fell on my shoulders."

"What did this guy Gonzaga do?," Jake asked carefully, gritting his teeth about the implied slander to Ray's abilities.

King snorted. "Fuck, what didn't he do? That's a better question. Looks like they got him for black marketeerin, stealin a truck, sellin a code book ta the VC, and even murder for Christ's sake."

"Did he really do all those things?" Jake asked, wishing that he were a better actor.

"Well, I only know bout two things for sure. It looks like he sure as hell sold a truck and that fuckin code book ta the dinks. As far as I'm concerned, that's enough for me. He's a fuckin traitor and I hope they tear his balls off and stuff um in his fuckin mouth for that alone."

Jake nodded, fuming inside.

"As for the murder though, I don't think he did that. I think somebody's framin him."

Jake snuffed his cigarette and waited.

King leaned forward. "I saw the body a' the gook that was killed. The knife was still stickin outta his fuckin back. Dead center, only a little off ta the left, and the handle was aimed down, towards the dead gook's feet. I got ta thinkin bout that after I saw the body. Ta me, it don't jibe that Gonzaga coulda done it."

"I don't understand," Jake confessed.

"Well look." King went into elaborate gestures with his hands. "If the slope was standin up when he got it, the guy who did it was behind him, and he stuck it inta him like this see?" King was using a vicious left handed uppercut motion into an invisible victim's back. "Now if the killer was right up behind him, he had ta be left handed cause the knife was ta the left side a the backbone. Of course that's no real evidence, cause the guy coulda been anywhere behind him, not just directly ta his rear. Hell, he coulda been huggin him from the front for all we know."

"I see," Jake muttered, trying to appear interested but not overly interested. "But how does that make—ah, this guy, your former boss, innocent?" That was a nice touch, Jake thought, pretending to forget Ray's name.

"Don't ya see? Gonzaga's right handed first a all. And he's about the same size as the gook that got stabbed. I think if a typical guy is gonna stab someone in the back, he's probably gonna use an over-hand thrust, like this." He demonstrated a downward lethal blow in absurdly slow motion. "Now a real pro or someone with military trainin would use a knife underhand, and Gonzaga didn't have no trainin. He wouldn't even wear a pistol over here. Said he'd never fired one. He had a K-bar, but it was so fuckin dull, it couldn't cut shit. If he was a pro, his knife woulda been sharp."

"I see what you're driving at, but it's pretty thin Dick, probably not enough to clear him." Jake mentally congratulated himself for remembering to say "Dick."

"Well, that plus his alibi probably would. See, I happened ta check the radio log fer the time a the killin, an accordin to the log, Gonzaga was talkin ta the Ly Tin District Advisor on the TOC radio! Nobody's asked me about it yet, and it's not really an official document so it won't stand up by itself; but I figure there's no way Gonzaga killed that Gook clear across town at that time anyways."

Jake started in surprise. He quickly smothered the joy which leaped in his soul. "And you haven't reported that yet?" he said, the words choking in his throat.

King didn't seem to notice Jake's emotion. "The thing is," he said, "Gonzaga's a God Damned traitor. I'd like ta see him hanged for that alone. We're sure better off here without him, so I'm not about ta speak up for him at this fuckin point. Let him stew a while first."

But I can and will, Jake thought. How about that? This might be easier than I thought.

King got up and prepared to leave, again draping himself in the formless poncho. "We got a ping pong table over at the Castle. Are ya an athlete Jake? What sports didja do in school?"

"My main sport was wrestling. I wrestled in both high school and college. Played football and ran some track in high school, but wasn't good enough for college."

"Where ya from in the states?"

Jake decided not to play his game. "Puyallup, Washington. It's a little place…"

King cut him off. "Hell, I know where Puyallup is. I used ta be stationed at Fort Lewis. So you were a Viking huh?"

"I sure was," Jake laughed.

"What were ya in college, a Black Knight of the Hudson?"

Damn! Here it comes, Jake thought. No way out of this, it's on the first page of my records. I've got to play it straight and hope I can carry it off. He attempted a small chuckle which, to his ears at least, sounded shallow and insincere. "Almost, I was a Scarlet Knight from Rutgers."

"Rutgers!" exploded King, "Gonzaga was at Rutgers! He was a professor there. Didja know him?"

Jake tried to look as surprised and puzzled as he could. "Gonzaga? Gonzaga? I think I might remember a professor by that name. What's his first name?"

"Ray. Raymond. Dr. Raymond Gonzaga."

"The name sounds kind of familiar." Jake felt his eyes shifting subconsciously to the floor. He looked up again, forcing himself to meet King's steady gaze. "No, I don't remember him by name. I might recognize him if I ever run into him though."

King's eyes were slits. "You ever serve any cross branch duty with the military police by chance?" he asked.

"No, I haven't Dick," Jake responded. "Why?" He knew the answer, but the question seemed the natural thing to ask.

"Just wonderin. Where ya been stationed before this?"

Jake told him, leaving nothing out. He even included the scholarship trip to Germany before he entered the Army. He knew he had nothing to hide with these facts, and he knew King would check.

King seemed to relax. Even with the poncho on, he found another cigarette, lit it, and began to talk about his own background and history. He told of his tough childhood in Texas, his high school athletic prowess, his academic achievements at Texas A & M, the national championship in fencing which he won as a senior, his graduation with honors, and his lustrous military career to date which included two promotions below the zone. Every story in the sequence was heroic, and Richard King was the hero. "I'm on my way up Trooper," he boasted. "Stick with me and I'll carry ya along on my coattails."

"Sounds great Dick, I'll do my best." Jake remembered the sandwiches still sitting on the counter and walked over to claim them.

"By the way," King put in, almost as an afterthought, two days from now, I'm goin on R and R fer a week. I'm gonna go ta Australia—Sydney. Never been there before. Really lookin forward to it."

"Sounds good." Jake took a bite of sandwich and nodded.

"It'll be a good chance for ya ta really getcher feet wet. Shouldn't be any problem. I doubt if anythin big'll come up. You'll be in charge."

If this is a test, Jake thought, I'm going to pass it. He wiped his lips with his hand. "No sweat Dick," he said. "We still have tomorrow for me to get snapped in. If there's anything special I should know, I'll be sure to learn it by then."

"Good man," Dick said, "I know that Saigon and Da Nang are wavin all kindsa warnin flags about Tet. They think there's gonna be a major offensive between now and then. It's not gonna happen. Just a buncha REMF's tryin to act like they know somethin. I don't wantcha ta be ancy about me takin off now."

"I'll handle it," Jake responded. But, he thought, those G2 types in Saigon know what they're doing. I, for one, will take their warnings seriously.

"OK trooper, you go ahead 'n eat now. I got a few things ta do first 'n then I'll see ya at the party tonight. I've already given your personnel file to First Sergeant Prescott. He'll square ya away with all the check in procedure tomorra."

"Thanks Dick, I'll be there tonight," Jake said with his mouth full of spam and cheese.

King departed into the still raging storm. Jake sat down and munched his breakfast. So what did I learn? he thought. King will lie to make himself look good and will talk about himself forever, but other than that, he's a nice enough guy; didn't like Ray, but he probably wouldn't have liked any civilian boss. He thinks Ray sold the code book that's for sure, but at least he gave me what I need to clear Ray of the murder charge. I wonder, who did kill that policeman? Dick King was a left handed fencing champion. No wonder he recognized an upward knife thrust. He doesn't seem like the type to stab someone in the back though. But if he were to stab someone, he'd do it with an upward swing. He's so prejudiced, he might not hold a Vietnamese life very highly, and the victim was

Vietnamese. And Jesus! Did he react to the Rutgers info. Suspicious as hell. Too suspicious, even if he feels guilty about not clearing Ray. He's either paranoid or he's got something else to hide. I guess I'll just have to try to find out which.

SCENE 7

THE CLUB

1900 HOURS
MONDAY, 1 JANUARY, 1968

The storm had softened to a dark steady drizzle when Mark Fellogese stepped from his quonset hut on his way to the party. The perimeter lights barely illuminated the damp polka dot pattern on his uniform, as he inhaled the fragrant tropical air hanging heavy over the compound.

He had been busy since his arrival at Kronberg. After dropping his gear in his newly assigned hooch, First Sergeant Prescott had issued him a rifle and taken him on a tour of the camp.

He was led through the slashing rain to his fighting position, a perimeter fox hole near the front gate. Prescott made him get down into the muddy crater and sight along his rifle so that he could see how all the defensive firepower could be directed under the raised chain link fence, where only the poles and a few strands of straight barbed wire protected the foot high space. He located the ammo bunker, the shower stalls and the centralized latrine. At the aid station, he drew one month's ration of malaria pills.

Back in Mark's new quarters, a bare room with only a cot and foot locker, the big, balding senior NCO had sat down with him and talked for an hour just getting to know him. Mark was captivated by the fatherly concern, the sincerity and the warmth of the man. First Sergeant Prescott was going to be a friend as well as a good boss.

After a bath in the communal shower stalls, Mark found the dining room at chow call hoping to meet others and make new friends. But each group had seemed closed. No one seemed to notice the hungry stranger with the alert eyes and lonely expression.

Later, he had written in his journal and even dashed off a long letter to Rosaline. Writing to her made him even more melancholy and forlorn. He was ready for this party. He needed it.

He climbed the porch and entered the club, surprised to find that the festivities were well under way even though he was precisely on time. In fact, judging from the riotous noise, the celebration had been going on for hours.

He looked around. It was just a bar, almost like a stateside bar. There were several cocktail tables, two poker tables at the rear, a tiny, deserted dance floor, a stage area on one side and the long polished wood bar along the other. Three Vietnamese men busily mixed and dispensed drinks to the shouting celebrants.

Mark recognized the typical macho drinking contest. The followers of Bacchus all seemed determined to out-drink, out-shout, or out-muscle one another, sometimes from across the room. One table erupted in guffawing laughter, then another three tables over. A reel to reel recorder behind the bar was bleating music into the din of revelry. Mark recognized the barely distinguishable tune. It was a current hit in the states. The record was by a group called Country Joe and the Fish. The chorus asked the question:

"One, two, three, four, what are we fighting for?"

He grinned at the irony of hearing the song here of all places. Someone's idea of a joke, he thought, or maybe not. Could it be a sly, impish way of rebelling in a place where rebellion is forbidden? Or does anyone even think about what the words mean?

All the stools at the long bar were taken and several standing men squeezed between the stools. It seemed that none of these were engaged in conversation. They were here to drink, and they took their task seriously.

A door length mirror sitting sidewise along the back of the bar made the room appear larger. Yet it also seemed to make it more crowded, as every man had a double.

Two men in a corner near Mark were arguing.

"Jesus H. Christ, Jack. You're already drunk."

"Am not," slurred the other, "You're drunker'n I am. You can't even stand up straight. You're wobblin all over the fuckin place."

"I'm not wobblin you asshole," shouted the taller one. "It's you. You're even spillin your fuckin beer."

The one called Jack steadied himself against the wall. He took a deep breath and almost slipped to the floor. "Listen, Weaver. I'm not drunk. Ever once in a while, I get a recurrin disease. It's heredi-hereditary. They call it the multiplyin eye. I usually only get it at taverns or places like that. Maybe I'm allergic to pretzels or the smell of olives or somethin. Anyway, I got it now." He ended this speech with a belch which would have made a bullfrog proud.

"What the fuck is a multiplyin eye? Are you tryin to bull-shit me?" Weaver asked. His own eyes blinking stupidly.

"No. No Weaver, no. Listen to me now. I got this multiplyin eye and that's what it is. I look double to you. I mean you look double to me. There's two of everbody when I get it, and I got it again tonight."

"A multiplyin eye sounds purdy fuckin serious," Weaver slobbered. "Have you been over to see the medic?"

"I'll go see him tomorrow. Hell, tonight, I wouldn't know which one of um to talk to."

They both guffawed, slung their arms around each other, and staggered to the bar for another.

Mark smiled, wondering whether the semi-staged comic act had been done for his benefit or not, and went to the bar himself. He self-consciously bought himself a beer for twenty cents. He had learned at Camp Alpha that throughout Vietnam, he could purchase beer, even though he was not yet anywhere near twenty one years old.

He found an empty table and sat down. He noticed that Lieutenant Colonel Thorpe and Lieutenant Colonel King were sitting together at a nearby table. Three other officers, a major, a captain and a lieutenant were sitting on the edge of their seats at a nearby table. Their attention was glued to the two senior officers, seemingly waiting for an opportunity to join the conversation, go on an errand for Colonel King, or be of some other service. Boy, Mark thought. If that's what you have to do to make it in the Army, even as an officer, I want no part of it. What a bunch of brown noses.

At that moment, a tall Vietnamese officer walked in. Mark heard King shout to Thorpe, "Big night Trooper. That's Lieutenant Colonel Tu, your counterpart. He's been outta town, busy somewheres. I didn't expect ta see 'm. Come on, I'll introduce ya."

Colonel Tu walked a few steps into the room, stopping just a few feet from Mark's table. The two American colonels stood and joined him there. Mark watched the Vietnamese officer's intense eyes bore into Thorpe, questioning, searching, measuring.

"Welcome Troom Ta," King said. "This is a big night. This here's yer new counterpart, and he's a solger, a lieutenant colonel jist like you. This is Colonel Thorpe. Jake, this is Troom Ta Tu, the number two man in Quang Tin. He's the Deputy Province Chief. He was my counterpart for five months before I moved up."

Colonel Tu smiled, rather guardedly Mark thought, and bowed from the waist. Colonel Thorpe followed his example and bowed in response. The two of them shook hands, and Mark thought that Colonel Tu's smile had become a shade warmer.

"I was told that a civilian would be my new counterpart," Tu said.

"That's what we-all thought too, Tu", King chuckled and glanced around for appreciation of the homonym. "Right up till Jake here got off the plane today. I guess we musta run plumb outta civilians in Saigon."

Tu was still studying Thorpe's face. "I cannot stay. I have learned that we have a long range patrol tonight, and several ambush sites near villages. Sentries from many areas report movement. I must return. But when one's counterpart arrives," he smiled again at Thorpe, very warmly this time, "one must make him welcome."

Thorpe and Tu shook hands again. "As I am your counterpart, shouldn't I be with you when you're on duty? Shouldn't I come with you now?" Thorpe asked.

"There is time for that. You no doubt still suffer from, what do you call it? Time lag?"

"Jet lag," King corrected him bluntly.

"Yes", Tu glanced briefly at King. "I also understand that the Province Chief might also visit you here tonight to present his welcome. You must be present when he comes. I will sleep at the radio center tonight. Our TOC as you call it. I will see you tomorrow during the day. We will speak then. Again, welcome to the Republic of Vietnam. I will be pleased to work with you and learn from you."

Thorpe bowed first this time. "It is my honor Troom Ta, I'm sure it is I who will learn most from you."

Tu smiled again, returned the bow and departed.

"Hey that's all right," King blurted, oblivious to others in earshot. "You really wowed him. Ya got him eatin outta your fuckin hand already. That's sure better'n I could ever do with 'im. That's the nuts. We'll make a great team, you n' me. The old 'tough guy, nice guy' routine. You grease those monkey fuckers up one day and I'll kick um in the balls the next. We can't miss. Whadda ya drinkin? I'll buy. Hey!" he yelled to the nearest bartender. "Bring us a cuppla drinks over here."

One of the three men Mark had identified as a brown noser appeared seconds later carrying a martini for King and a shot of something on the rocks for Thorpe. King scowled and reached reluctantly into his pocket. "It's OK Sir," the lieutenant said, "I've already paid. These are on me."

"Thank's Clarence, King drawled. "You're all right, No matter what everone else says."

At that moment, before the lieutenant had returned to his seat, the hubbub of the club quieted. Almost all talk stopped. The amplified speakers were now clearly audible as a group named Ten Years After crooned:

> "Generals gathered in their masses,
> Like witches at black masses;
> Evil minds that plot destruction
> Sorcerers of death's construction.
> In the fields, the bodies burning,
> As the war machine keeps turning
> Death and hatred to mankind,
> Poisoning their brain-washed mind!"

No one seemed to pay the slightest attention to the song.

All heads were turned towards the doorway. The Province Chief, Colonel Than Mak Biet, had made his entrance. He wore a snow white dress uniform, complete with gold braid, many heavy medals, and a slim bladed ornamental military sword at his hip. Co Li was at his side, radiant in white silk trousers and a white embroidered silk au yai.

The pair moved directly to King and Thorpe like two graceful swans swimming through the green clad crowd as if through lily pads. Biet spoke first, clearly audible from where Mark was sitting.

"Good evening Lieutenant Colonel King, I trust I am on time?" He turned to Jake, "I met Colonel Tu outside as he was leaving. He told me that his new counterpart is a military man, the same rank as you Lieutenant Colonel King." He stiffly bowed in Thorpe's direction. "I am Colonel Than Mak Biet, the Province Chief of Quang Tin. Welcome to my province. Welcome to my country."

Mark could tell that Thorpe was taken slightly aback by the impact of the colonel's magnificent appearance, but he recovered and bowed in return. "Thank you Sir, I am Lieutenant Colonel Jacob Thorpe at your service."

"At my service you say? Well Colonel Thorpe, we will see what we will see." He turned then to King. "Tell me Lieutenant Colonel King, do you serve alcoholic beverages at this club of yours?"

It was King's turn to be confused. "Oh, sure. I'll getcha one Dai Ta." He turned, and caught Lieutenant George's eye. "Clarence, git one fer the Dai Ta will ya?" George struck off through the morass of masculinity and intemperance with the air of reborn purpose.

Biet turned again to Thorpe. "My wife sends her apologies and regrets for not being able to welcome you personally. She is ill this night. However, may I present my secretary? Co Let Chu Li. Her father is a prominent businessman in Quang Tin. He owns a fish oil production plant in this city, and also a fish cannery in Ly Tin."

Co Li and Colonel Thorpe bowed to each other. Mark chuckled to himself as he watched Co Li duck and hide behind the Province Chief's bulk before Thorpe could speak to her. Thorpe looked at Biet with a smile and a raised eyebrow.

"It is wise and prudent for all Vietnamese women to be bashful," Biet explained. "However, Co Li is perhaps more shy than protocol demands. She is young yet, and her English is halting. Let us sit down and converse Colonel Thorpe. I wish to know your history. You may join us if you wish, Lieutenant Colonel King."

King flushed but said nothing. Mark's eyes were on Co Li, as the four sat down at their table. Its wet surface had three or four used glasses as well as two full ashtrays. She's like a princess, Mark thought. I've never seen such a stunner. I wonder if it's that dress, the whiteness of it. Wow, is she an eyeful!

Thorpe started to clear the table but Biet stopped him firmly. "No, Colonel Thorpe. You are not to do this. It lowers you in the eyes of others. Unless I am mistaken, you are the third ranking officer in this room. It will not do. Co Li, you will clean the table please."

Thorpe, embarrassed, relinquished the task to Co Li, who went about the job with efficiency. After clearing the ashtrays, she scooped up the glasses with the proficiency of an accomplished waitress and marched with them to the bar.

Lieutenant George arrived with drinks for all, just as she departed. The men began to talk. The party noise had returned to roaring cacophony. Almost drowned amid the shouts, laughter and cheerful blasphemy, the amplified speakers blared out the ending of another current song, this one by Peter, Paul and Mary:

> "How many times must the cannon balls fly,
> Before they're forever banned?
> The answer my friends is blowing in the wind;
> The answer is blowing in the wind."

Mark watched Co Li weave her way through the uniformed throng. A pearl drifting through sea grass, he thought. She deposited the glasses on the bar and turned to retrace her steps.

Two men blocked her path. Mark recognized them as Jack and Weaver, the two he had seen having the comic argument earlier. They were now well beyond simple intoxication, but still capable of juvenile male bravado. They pressed against her, jostling her. Mark couldn't hear their voices, but he knew it was trouble from the body languages and because of Co Li's fearful reaction.

He glanced back at the officers. They were engrossed in their conversation. He quickly scanned the club. No one else seemed to notice the plight of the girl. He stood and hesitantly started toward them trying to decide on a course of action. He arrived before one came to him.

"Hey guys," he said, tapping both soldiers on the arm. "Let me through please."

They automatically parted for him, but were careful to keep their feminine prey still trapped against the bar. Mark stepped through beside her and then turned to the two men. He then recognized one of them, the guy called Jack, as an MP who had been on guard duty at the gate that afternoon.

"Hey guys, let her go now. You're plastered and don't know what you're doing. You're going to get in trouble. She's the Province Chief's secretary. Why don't you just let her go?"

"What the fuck do you know Mother Fucker, you just got here." snarled Jack.

"Piss off Shithead. Who the fuck are you anyway?" asked Weaver, the tall one. "I've never seen your fuckin face around here before."

"I'm Sergeant Fellogese," Mark said, swallowing nervously. He realized it was too late for persuasion, so he lowered his voice in earnest sincerity. "I out-rank both of you, so I'm telling you now, go back to your table, or back to your hooch and sleep it off. Stop bothering this girl."

"Listen Fuckface. We saw her first. All we're doin is havin a little fun, so piss off!" This was said by Weaver, who pushed his nose within inches of Mark's.

Inhaling the alcoholic reek of Weaver's breath, Mark prepared to bring up his fists. They're so drunk, I should be able to take both of them without too much problem, he thought. "OK," he warned, "this is the last time I'm telling you. Back off now or I'll make you back off!"

The lights went out. At least they did for Mark. He had not seen Jack, on the left, pick up the brandy bottle. He hadn't even seen him raise it.

Mark was sitting on the barroom floor when he came to. The team medic, Sergeant Usher, who had given him the malaria pills earlier, was bandaging Mark's head. The tape recorder had been turned off. Co Li was gone. All the officers had departed, and almost everyone else had long since stumbled to their hooches and to bed.

A small group of men were gathered in one corner around one soldier who was strumming chords on a guitar. They were singing; or rather, they were absorbed in a beer bred obsession to croon, to serenade, to lilt, to harmonize like angels. Their glassy eyes stared vacantly into space. Swaying together to the rhythm of the tune, they entertained no one but themselves, and the lyrics were lost in the empty room:

>"Where have all the graveyards gone?
>Long time standing.
>Where have all the graveyards gone?
>Long time ago.
>Where have all the graveyards gone?
>Gone to flowers every one;
>When will they ever learn?
>When will they ever learn?"

Doc Usher taped the final gauze-end into place and inspected his handiwork with satisfaction. "Come on John Wayne," he said to Mark. "If you can stand up now, We'll walk you to your hooch."

First Sergeant Prescott helped the medic hoist Marc to his feet. "Do you believe in omens?" he asked Mark.

Act 2

Scene 1

THE TOC

0530 Hours
Tuesday, 2 January 1968

The helicopter pilot's voice, as usual, was garbled and broken. It barely penetrated the "whoomp, whoomp" of beating blades and the amplified background of turbine engine whine. The scratchy static of the speaker added its din, and everyone strained for comprehension. "Ec-ho Three-ee this is Pee-per One, I'm on sta-a-ation; a-bou...to star...search pat-ter-n now. O-ver."

Major Clayborne grabbed the mike with eagerness, "Roger, roger Peeper One. This is Echo Three. What do you see? Do you see anything? Over."

Jake held his breath and leaned toward the radio. The TOC was hot; oppressively hot. It's the humidity, he thought, and too many people in this damned bunker. He noticed the sandbagged walls dripping with moisture. The sour odor of human sweat hung heavily in the air.

Silence.

Jake looked around. Colonel Biet, the province chief, sat in the back; his face full of gloom; his arms folded in resignation.

Facing him, Colonel Tu squatted oriental style, feet flat on the floor. It was clear that Tu was trying to encourage, for he nodded his head affirmatively as he spoke. His smile was the comforting, placating type.

King was beside Clayborne at the radio, intently listening for the pilot's response.

Other officers, both Vietnamese and American, plus their enlisted TOC crews expectantly waited. Nervous hands scratched, twitched, fiddled aimlessly with paperwork and lit cigarette after cigarette, forgetting those which burned untouched in nearby ashtrays.

Clayborne tried again. "Peeper One, this is Echo Three. Do you see anything yet? Over."

The radio finally crackled, clearer this time, "Neg-ative Ec-ho Three. I'll do my job Grunt, you do your's. Out."

King exploded, "Who is that cocky sonabitch anyway? Anybody know who the fuck he is?"

The artillery advisor, Captain Marcellus hesitantly spoke up, "I'm not sure Sir, but it sounds like Major Forrest, this is his third tour over here, maybe his fourth."

King snorted, "Still no reason for cuttin us off like that. You'd think we-all were workin for him rather 'n the other way round." He paused, looking at Marcellus "We got the map coordinates a where they got hit?"

"No Sir," the young captain responded. "They were on radio silence. The choppers who took um in told us it was a cold LZ; no problems at all at the landing zone. Nothing til about 0400 this morning, when all hell broke loose on the Viet side." He pointed to the opposite wall, where most of the Vietnamese stood next to another bank of radios. "It took a while," he continued, "to get um to tell me what was happening. I figured the patrol was being hit of course cause I could hear the fire fight when our guy depressed his handset. It happened real fast. It was all over in about five minutes.

The Viets kept trying to raise um for a while. I kept asking Where? Where? So I could get some Artillery support for um, but no one knew. Colonel Tu was here for the whole thing. He told me later that the patrol was unsure of its position cause it was so dark out there, and that's why they didn't give a position report."

King walked over to where Biet and Tu were still in quiet conversation. "Leme ask ya Dai Ta, do your people know anythin about where the patrol got hit? Anythin a tall?"

Colonel Tu answered. "I called to the Hau Duc command post. They could hear the gunfire. They informed me that the action was taking place on an azimuth of Two-seven-zero from their village. They estimated the distance to be at least two thousand meters although it was sound only. They could not see gunfire flashes. The area is heavily forested, thus they could not use the flash to sound distance estimating method."

King recoiled back to the radio and jerked the microphone from Clayborne's hand. "Ah, Peeper One this is Echo Six Actual, Over."

The gargling voice responded immediately. "Ro-ger Six Ac-tual, this is Pee-per One, over."

"Ah, Peeper One this is Echo Six Actual. Take a hard look about two clicks due west a Hau Duc's main village. New report here says that should be purdy close, over."

"Ro-ger Six Ac-tual, this is Peeper One head-ing in tha-at di-rection, I'll let you know, over."

"This is Echo Six Actual. Roger out."

King dropped the mike on the work bench. "He didn't give me no shit. Knew better'n that. Nothin more ta do now but wait. Do we still have some coffee?"

Jake looked up, "Excuse me Dick. I know I'm new around here, but shouldn't we inform Da Nang about this? They'll be waiting for a patrol report and wondering why we haven't sent it in to them."

King, on his way to the coffee pot, stopped in his tracks. "Yeah, we should." He nodded approvingly at Jake and turned to Clayborne. "Bill, call Da Nang and let um know what we think happened."

Clayborne picked up the microphone of one of the other seven radios in the tactical operations center. This radio, Jake noticed, was one of two equipped with a scrambler, enabling conversation in the clear, without the necessity of using code. "Papa Three this is Bravo Three, over."

Jake smiled to himself as he remembered the experiences of his first tour, before the emphasis on radio security. Back then, he thought, we kept the same call sign regardless of what net we were on. Now we have a different call sign for every net.

The radio growled back. "Bravo Three this is Papa Three, over."

"This is Bravo Three. Roger. As you know, we sent a twenty man recon patrol out beyond Hau Duc last night to check out the G2 tip about an enemy unit there. Patrol was from our province reserve. They evidently stepped into it about 0400 this morning. We lost contact by 0410. Hau Duc reported large fire fight at that time, approximately two clicks west of their CP. We called up a loach and two cobras from Chu Lai about thirty ago. They're over the area now, but so far no sightings. Over."

A short silence from the radio, then: "Roger Bravo Three. Any indications of what it was they ran into? Was it Victor Charlie or an NVA unit? Over."

"Negative Papa Three. My counterpart says our guys here asked that question several times during the contact, but it was dark. They either didn't know, or didn't have time to say. Over."

"Roger Bravo Three. Anything further? Over."

"One thing that might be significant Papa Three. The way we get it, we don't think it was a meeting engagement. The RTO of the patrol evidently thought it was an ambush. My counterpart tells me that the RTO kept yelling that they were waiting for um and that they just walked right into it. Over."

"Roger Bravo Three, Keep us informed; this is Papa Three. Out."

Clayborne set the mike down and walked to where his counterpart, Major Hai, sat on a chair hanging his head in desolation. Clayborne put his hand reassuringly on Hai's shoulder, and then realized his error and quickly touched Hai's other shoulder.

Jake smiled to himself in approval. He remembered that the Vietnamese have the superstition that everyone has a genie on each shoulder, and the balance must always be maintained. If a genie is accidentally dislodged, by someone else touching one shoulder for example, the remaining genie would take over and start controlling the unbalanced person's life with bad luck.

Hai did not look up at either touch.

"Don't worry Tiu Ta," Clayborne crooned. "It might not be so bad. For all we know it might just be a busted radio."

Hai looked up sadly. "Thank you my friend, but we know that not happen. Best we can hope is maybe one, maybe two escape and find way to Hau Duc. I should have ask for air cover. One of patrol my uncle; brother to my mother. Him in Army long time ago. Be wounded. Lose one eye, but he still want fight VC so join PF militia. Him be good man. Good farmer. Him field always make rice more than others. My mother be very sad. It sad day."

One of the Vietnamese TOC sergeants spoke softly in Vietnamese. Hai listened and then interpreted. "Him father on patrol. Him father carry radio. Last night, him hear voice of father with much fear." Hai turned to the sergeant and spoke in their own language. He turned back to Clayborne. "I give him day free to be with family."

The Vietnamese sergeant quietly left the TOC. There was a restless heaviness among the men in the room. Excitement and anxiety had suddenly and totally been replaced by gloom and the certainty of death. An American sergeant silently folded his fingers and bowed his head. Colonel Biet and one other Vietnamese made the sign of the cross. They were slightly out of synchronization, which added pathos to the aura of sadness.

Jake's mouth cloyed with dryness. He felt the heartache and sadness deeply, but it was almost like watching a movie or a play. I didn't know the men who were killed, he thought. I don't even know the men in this bunker yet. It makes me feel guilty at being still an outsider, as if I'm not welcome to share their grief. I do empathize, but there's nothing else I can do. Such a helpless feeling. If I could just offer my condolences and have it mean something, but I can't. He glanced at those around him. There were many moist eyes in the room but no one broke down. It was not the time. It was not the place. Jake could tell that his own eyes were damp.

His thoughts were interrupted by the province chief, who resolutely stood, revealing his exhaustion. "Colonel King," he said, "I will have a word with you please. Kindly ask Colonel Thorpe to join us; Colonel Tu will be with me outside." He marched gravely out through the poncho draped door.

The four strode silently until they were well out of earshot of anyone in the TOC. They all lit cigarettes as if it were intermission time at the theater.

Biet looked at King. "So Lieutenant Colonel King, the stars were correct. Do you now admit that there is an enemy force in our area?"

King responded as if he had expected the question. "Well Dai Ta, I still don't think there's nothin significant out there."

"What is your assessment of the situation?" Biet asked.

"They were ambushed, plain 'n simple. I think it was gorillas. They found out we were gonna be there 'n went out there fer this one fuckin job. They're all back home now with their weapons tucked away. We shouldn't react to this, cause there's still nothin out there to react to."

Biet blew two long columns of smoke from his nose. "And you Troom Ta Tu? What is your advice?"

Tu bowed politely to his commander. "I do not believe it is the work of guerrillas um Dai Ta Biet. The VC irregulars conduct their planning by a complex system of committees passing recommendations to higher level committees who approve or disapprove and then pass their decisions down to the cell or cells which are to act. This takes considerable time. You made the decision to patrol the area only yesterday. The plans were not completed until noon. Guerrillas would not have had time to act. Therefore, I believe we are facing an NVA unit of some size, or perhaps the VC Cadre battalion which operates in this general region."

Biet, deep in thought, looked down and scraped the sand with his boot. Finally, he asked, "What do you suggest we do?"

Tu bowed again, "I think we should request an American unit or ARVN force to enter the national lands west of our districts. If there is an enemy unit, they will find them. We must do this soon, for intelligence sources say that we may expect such a force to attack by the time of Tet, a short four weeks from now."

King interrupted, "Yeah, but let's not fall for that shit, Dai Ta. Those G2 types are always warnin a some big attack here or there, and ya know they never happen."

Biet nodded, "Yes, but we must always consider their reports as accurate, if we are to, how do you say it? play it safe?" Without waiting for a response from King, Biet turned to Jake. "And you Colonel Thorpe? As you mentioned to me last night, combat in Vietnam is not a total stranger to you. Do you have something for me to consider?"

"Well, I'm not sure Dai Ta." Jake also bowed to the Province Chief. "What I might add, you may have already considered."

"Do not be reticent Colonel Thorpe," Biet smiled, "I know you are still early on this tour and I will take that into consideration. Speak up."

"Well Sir, when I was a district advisor, there were no American troops to call on, and there were a lot fewer ARVN units, so we had to do a lot by ourselves."

"Do you suggest another patrol by the militia?" Biet asked gently but with a definite edge to his voice.

"No Sir, not at all," Jake said. From his previous district advisor experience, he knew Tu's remarks were accurate. Jake didn't think the VC had time enough to act either. He glanced at King who was studying him with a steely eyed "you'd better not cross me" look. The glowing birthmark gave emphatic meaning to the expression.

"I think we should plan against both threats," he continued. "Colonel King is probably right, everything points to an ambush rather than a chance engagement. That means the VC have a legal cadre spy who has access to whatever we're planning. So all we have to figure out is whether it was a regular NVA unit who was waiting for them or a rapidly mobilized VC unit. It seems to me that an NVA unit who was planning to launch a major attack soon would've just gone somewhere else and hid if they knew the patrol's route and wanted to lull us into thinking there was nothing out there. But the reaction time was exceptionally quick for the VC. Either way, we've got big problems. I think the best military action would be to plan for the worst scenario possible."

Biet smiled and nodded patronizingly. "Tell us your suggestions Colonel Thorpe. How do you propose we do this?"

Jake recognized the condescending tone but did not waver. "Right now, we've got that light observation helicopter out there buzzing around, and two cobras covering him. We've got to keep them on station as long as we can. If there's a big unit out there trying to sneak in on us, they won't give themselves away by opening up on those choppers. If they move during the daytime, with that big a unit, the choppers would spot them. If they don't want us to know who they are and how big they are, they'll have to hide from the choppers during daylight."

"So?" prodded Biet, now keenly.

"That means they're going to move only at night. If we get our two western districts, both Hau Duc and Tien Phouc, to send out one man listening posts. Walk them far out during the day and then hide themselves at night. The only real risk is if the LP happens to stumble right into their camp during the day. If they're careful, they'll be OK and should hear anything moving during the night. It should tell us a lot. How many. Maybe even who they are if we hear them talking. We used to do this a lot when I was here before, and it really works. It minimizes personnel risks because if they're well hidden, none of them should be spotted.

Once we know something about them, where they are, which way they're moving; we'll be able to get a US or ARVN unit right on top of them, plus artillery and air strikes."

"Yes, I like it," Biet said. "But we only have use of the helicopter team for two or three more hours today. How do we keep them with us?"

King jumped in, "Dai Ta, possession is nine tenths a the law in war time. I'll take care'a that. I'll order the pilot ta remain on station today and make sure he's out there first thing again tomorra. We'll keep him as long as we want him."

Biet smiled and raised his eyebrows to his deputy who nodded. "It seems sound," Tu agreed.

The province chief turned to King in what seemed to Jake an almost challenging way. "I am inclined to agree with Colonel Thorpe. It seems to me to be the best course of action at this time. Would you not also agree Lieutenant Colonel King?"

King crushed out his cigarette butt with his boot heel and looked squarely at Biet. The scowl was gone, and in its place an air of supreme authority. "I'm glad ya think so Dai Ta, cause I think so too. It never hurts ta consider all possible courses a enemy action. If I didn't...," here Jake thought he detected an almost threatening tone, "well I'd strongly suggest another plan."

Jake could tell both men were reacting to another agenda, something more important to them than the enemy. He wondered what the Hell it could be.

The four separated into pairs. Jake and King hustled back to the TOC to coordinate with the helicopter team and complete Jake's orientation.

Biet and Tu walked toward Ca Dor, and were already climbing the stone stairway before they started their conversation.

Colonel Biet began: "I am pleased with what I see in our new deputy advisor, your counterpart. His judgement seems sound, and he seems interested in our people. He has learned much about our customs."

Tu nodded. "He feels deeply and has the quality of empathy. His eyes were moist this morning as we listened for the results of the helicopter search."

It was Biet's turn to nod. "Yes, I have seen his type before. They are the best of Americans. They are the best advisors, and the best soldiers. They have the true soldier's nature, which is to sacrifice themselves for a cause. But, perhaps because of this nature, they are the ones who are invariably killed in combat. The selfish ones, the foolish ones, and the detached, uncaring ones, always seem to survive to go back to America."

Tu nodded again. "Perhaps this one is different. This one's shadow seems very strong."

"Perhaps so." Biet murmured. "We must wait to see what time has in store for him. And for us," he added. They strolled through the arched doorway with heads bowed. Both remembering former advisors. Former counterparts.

Later, as King walked back to the Castle for a late lunch with Captain Hastings, the S4 advisor, and Lieutenant George, the S1 advisor, another conversation took place. "Well guys," King began, "I got a little problem that maybe you can help me with."

"Yes Sir," both responded at once.

"It's a funny type a problem. When I got a military DPSA, I thought we'd naturally see eye to eye, so it'd be better'n havin a civvie type."

Neither subordinate spoke. They glanced at each other in a mutual warning to keep silent for now. "Instead," King continued, "I get another Lieutenant Colonel which gives that fuckin pig of a province chief the ability to needle me even more by callin him 'Colonel' alla time, and me 'Lieutenant Colonel.' But that's not his fault. Shit. That's just a temporary lil thing tween the Dai Ta 'n me." King looked up at the red and yellow Republic of Vietnam flag flying in front of Ca Dor.

"He's sharp," King continued, "and that's good. I'd hate it if I had some fuckin dud out here as my deputy. But, the thing is, he might be a little too clever for his own fuckin good." He paused in thought.

"I don't need ta worry about leavin, with him in charge a the province, er, the team, while I'm in Sydney for a cuppla days." He fell silent again for a few more steps. "But a few fuckin things bother me. He's soft. Hell, he was almost cryin when he heard that a few a those fuckin dinks bought it last night. What bothers me more'n that though, is that he might also be a fuckin kiss-ass to the dink brass. He fuckin bows to um! That worries me. It shows weakness. Here's what I want you guys ta do if you wanna do me a favor."

"What can we do Sir?" Hastings responded quickly.

"I want both a ya to watch him as close as you can while I'm away. I don't want him ta brown nose his way into my job that's for sure. You guys wouldn't want that neither would ya?"

"No Sir. Not at all Sir," George replied.

"Never Sir," said Captain Hastings.

"But how can we stop him?" asked George.

"No, I don't wantcha to try'n stop him. Just watch him. Take notes if you have to, ta help ya remember. I just wanna know everthing he does, good or bad while I'm gone. I'll do all the doin, if somethun needs doin, when I get back."

"Yes Sir," replied one.

"We'll do it Sir," echoed the other.

King smiled and looked up at the cloudless sky. "Good! God Damn it, I'm gonna enjoy Australia. I haven't had white pussy fer a long time."

It was 1800, when the Vietnamese first lieutenant approached Mark, who was standing the first duty watch of his tour. "Excuse me Sergeant, but there is someone outside who would like to speak to you."

Mark jumped to attention and saluted. "Tell him he can come in Sir. I'm not busy."

"No Sergeant. This person is a civilian. She is not allowed into the Tactical Operations Center. If you wish to speak with her, you must go outside and talk there."

"Her?" Mark was dumbfounded. "Who is it, my hooch maid?"

"No Sergeant. It is Co Let Chu Li, the secretary to the province chief."

Mark blinked, trying to recall the name. Then, with a flush of embarrassment, he remembered. "Oh, her. OH! HER! OK Sir, I'll go talk to her. I won't be far Sir. I'll be right outside. Call me if you need me Sir."

The lieutenant grinned broadly. "I will do so Sergeant. Take as much time as might be necessary."

Mark bolted out of the TOC and was surprised to find that dusk had already passed. A pale glow to the west outlined the mountain peaks. Everything else was darkness. His hand touched the sandbags around the steel walls of the double conex container which served as the briefing room for the TOC.

"Hello," he called out tentatively. He started to call her name, but he couldn't remember it. "Hello, I'm here," he called again.

"I am here Sergeant," Co Li said. She turned on a flashlight pointed at the ground between them.

Now that he was near her, Mark didn't know what to say. He felt obligated somehow, perhaps because of his failed rescue attempt, to begin the conversation. "Hi. How are you this evening? Did those guys last night hurt you in any way?"

"No Sergeant. I very grateful to you. You very brave, and very, how you say…? Gallant?"

Mark flushed in the darkness, happy that she could not see his embarrassment. "It was nothing, anybody would have done it. It's just that no one else saw it."

"That not be so Sergeant. Many saw. I know. I feel eyes on me from first time I enter club. You! You only one help me."

"Well, I'm glad everything turned out all right. They told me today what happened. Those two won't bother you anymore, Colonel King gave both of um an Article 15 and sent um to Da Nang. I really didn't help you. All I did was get my head caved in. Someone else actually rescued you."

"I don't think so," she said. "When you fall down it make big noise. Many men come then. Help us both."

"That's what I heard," he smiled, "I'm glad you weren't hurt."

"I come tonight, tell you sorry I am. About you be hurt for me. Please accept my apology that it was I who caused you this pain." This last was said tonelessly, as if she were reciting from memory.

Mark was amused by the thought that she had probably practiced saying it several times before attempting to meet him. She shined the flashlight onto Mark's white turban. "You look like wounded warrior. It pain you still?"

"No, not at all," Mark lied.

"You different for American," Co Li declared.

"I am? In what way?"

"Many friends work in American compound. They tell me. I see things. You different."

"I hope you mean nice different." Mark grinned, realizing that the beam of light on his bandage probably made his expression seem like a leer. He could just make out her face. She was smiling too!

"Yes; nice. You nice American. You first American I feel magnetic to." She aimed the light to their feet again.

"Magnetic?" Mark asked, totally puzzled. "What do you mean?"

"I use wrong word." His eyes were now becoming accustomed to the darkness. He saw her smile again. Her eyes were downcast. "I not know correct word. When two metal things pull together. It called…?"

"Magnetic is right, magnetic attraction."

"Attraction. Yes. That be correct word. You first American I feel attraction to."

"Oh, me too!" Mark blurted. "I'm attracted to you too. I couldn't keep my eyes off of you when you came in yesterday. That's a knockout of a dress you were wearing. I, uhh, I guess I should tell you I was one of those you felt staring at you when you came in." In the dim light, he could see that she was still smiling. He felt his pulse begin to race.

"Thank you. It my best au yai. Dai Ta say to wear it. I happy now I wear it. I happy it make you watch at me."

Mark nodded and grinned lamely. He again felt the loss for words. He wanted her to stay, to talk forever, but he couldn't think of anything that might keep her here, by his side. He felt the silence closing in. If he didn't say something soon, she'd think he was a dunce and leave.

"I must go now," she said. "My family wait. You for sure no pain now?"

"No. No pain." He was losing her; she'd be gone in a minute. "But; but wait," he blurted, "I'm sorry; the lieutenant told me, but I didn't catch it. I don't know your name. It's Co Let something, but...."

"It is Let Chu Li. When you talk to me, you call me by given name. You call me Li, Co Li."

"Co Li," Mark repeated, smiling broadly. "I'm very pleased to meet you Co Li. Where does the Co come from?"

"It mean young girl, all unmarried woman called Co. When get married, woman called Ba."

"Oh, I see. OK, thanks Co Li. I really think it's nice of you to come down here tonight. I'm glad I got to meet you."

"Thank you Sergeant," she murmured, "I understand you have given name of Mark. I call you Sergeant Mark, Ok? This is way of Vietnam. I learn family name also, to try call you for true by American way, but it too hard for tongue to say."

"Yeah, it probably is. But you can just call me Mark if you want to. You don't have to say Sergeant."

"That be, how you say? Awkward? We always say title. Vietnam people must say Sergeant Mark or Mister Mark. We sometimes say Mister Sergeant Mark." She laughed at the complexities of her language.

"Whatever you want to call me is OK, Co Li. May we talk again some time?"

"I think for sure Sergeant Mark. I must go now. You on duty. We talk again soon. You take care of head please."

"Sure. I will! Thanks for coming to see me. You've made my day."

"I not understand this," she giggled shyly, "but maybe you say what mean next time. I ask one more question OK?"

"Of course."

"What is name of servant who do wash clothing for you?"

"Her? Oh. It's Ba Nhur. Why?"

"Maybe talk with her." She giggled again with her hand to her mouth. "Maybe she tell me you bad man with her."

"Oh," Mark smiled, pleased with her curiosity. "Do you know her?"

"Yes. Her husband, my father, before friends. Her husband killed by V.C."

"Oh, I'm sorry."

"She strong. No sweat. Life hard now in Vietnam." Mark could sense that she was looking away, not at him, almost acting guilty for some reason or other. She continued, "I must go. We talk again. Goodbye for now Sergeant Mark. Chow um."

She reached across and gently brushed Mark's jaw with her fingertips. Not really a stroke. It wasn't sexual. Just a touch. A light, tender, sensual, connection.

It felt electric!

"Goodnight Co Li" Mark stammered. He could just see her silhouette after she switched off the flashlight, and then disappeared. He heard her faint footsteps receding.

His head still ached and throbbed.

But it was the lingering titillation of his cheek which dominated his thoughts. He grinned as he swaggered into the TOC.

SCENE 2

QUANG TIN PROVINCE

0830 Hours
Friday, 5 January 1968

As the lumbering Huey bumped gently onto the pierced steel planking of Hau Duc's helipad, Jake and Biet hopped off. Jake was careful to run low around the nose of the chopper, well under the still whooshing rotor blades. A painful memory flashed through his mind. Once before he had run like this. A visiting full colonel from Saigon was inspecting the company's positions. The huey pilot, back then, landed too far to one side of the pad which had been notched out of the side of a hill. As Jake followed, the colonel climbed the hill, walking straight up. All sound had been drowned in the whine of the spinning turbine. He didn't hear my shout of warning, Jake recalled, and the deadly blades decapitated him as easily as wind snuffs a candle. I was splattered with blood and brains. The colonel's helmet had bounced down the hill, followed by the rolling head.

It always comes back to me in slow motion, frame by frame. There's the face. Shocked eyes still staring. The mouth gaping and the tongue lolling to one side. Rolling, rolling. The teeth biting into the dirt as the back of the head comes around. A huge chunk of skull is missing; gore and a pinkish cottage cheese spewing behind in a

129

grizzled trail. The damned head hadn't been cut off. It was ripped from the neck by the force of the blow. Here's the face again with dirt on the tongue and whites of the eyes. And now the back of the head with the bloody crater. Rolling right at me!

The sight tormented Jake frequently in nightmares, and whenever he dismounted from a helicopter, like now.

But Hau Duc's helipad was on flat ground. Colonel King had departed yesterday for R & R, leaving Jake in charge of the team, and a young Vietnamese captain was saluting them. Biet shouted over the gradually dying engine, "This is Captain Doung, District Chief of Hau Duc District."

Biet and Captain Doung spoke energetically in Vietnamese while Jake shook off the haunting horror and surveyed the site with practiced eyes.

It was an excellent position. A clean line of sight for at least a click in every direction. The slope of the high ground wasn't steep, but it was enough, and the bunker complex was on the summit. The bunkers had been laid out well for mutual defense, with the four largest located in a diamond pattern. Smaller emplacements guarded the gaps, and others protected the interior. A single one-five-five howitzer, hunkered down in its sandbagged nest, marking the exact center; flanked by two smaller mortar pits.

A triple ring of concertina barbed wire, far out barricadoed the perimeter. Individual foxholes snuggled close in to the wire. Beyond the barrier, Jake knew, would be the mine fields.

"Captain Doung will brief us on his situation," Biet said. as they entered one of the four main bunkers.

They proceeded down slick, slimy wooden steps into the underground system. Jake remembered that every bunker he had seen during his first tour had been damp. Nothing changes, he thought.

The first chamber was two stories tall, with elevated, shelf-like fighting positions where a few soldiers perched and peered out the bunker apertures. The next area was larger still, an ammunition storage vault. Then a gigantic supply room, an aid station as large as the one in Camp Kronberg, a mammoth dining compartment, a kitchen, and another smaller dining room. Whew, Jake marveled, it's an underground fortress! Hallways lit with mud-crusted electric bulbs ran off in every direction.

At one tunnel juncture, a small naked toddler jumped out and clung to Jake's legs as if she were greeting her father. Two Vietnamese women, dressed Montagnard fashion with full skirts, long sleeved jackets and turbans giggled and bowed obsequiously as they reclaimed the child and scurried away in rubber thongs.

Jake, who had never been a father, smiled after them. The child had both pleased and embarrassed him.

"The soldiers live here with their families," Biet explained matter-of-factly. "We Vietnamese are very much oriented to our families."

Jake nodded. "Yes, Dai Ta, I remember from my previous tour."

They entered the large operations center, where Biet motioned for Jake to sit beside him. "Captain Doung does not speak English," he said. As we have no other translator here, I will interpret his briefing.'

He waved curtly to Doung who stood near a map-board on an easel. Doung immediately began to chatter away in the highly intoned native language, pointing often with his finger at the map.

While Doung spoke, Jake idly glanced about the operations center. He noticed the bare light bulb hanging directly over the easel. Swarms of bugs in frantic aerial combat dimmed the luster of incandescence. Jake noted the floor, cluttered with dead insects. We human beings might be a lot like insects, he mused, drawn irresistibly to danger despite our logic and fear; accomplishing nothing in our hot scramble, but unable to stop until it's too late.

Biet interrupted Jake's reverie with his first translation of the briefing: "He has informed me that all his hamlets are now protected by

Popular Self Defense Force units varying in size from one platoon of twenty to a squad of five at the smallest. It is a significant step forward. This is the first time I have heard that we have every hamlet defended."

Jake nodded although he only partially understood. The happy facts just told to him seemed to raise more questions than they answered. Why the Hell would they just be getting around to that now? he asked himself. That seems like it would be one of the first priorities of survival.

Biet had turned back and Doung chattered on.

At widespread intervals, Biet continued to stop the briefing and turning to Jake, would issue short, sometimes cryptic, but always positive condensations of the young captain's report. "His military units have good morale." "They found and disarmed five booby traps yesterday." "They killed three VC last week."

Finally the briefing ended. Biet stood and beckoned to Jake. "We go now to Tien Phouc."

"Did you ask him about the listening posts Sir? Is he sending them out? Have they heard anything?"

Biet smiled broadly, "Oh yes. He sends them out every evening. He has not lost any of them. They have not heard anything yet. Captain Doung thinks that the enemy has moved south, into Quang Ngai Province."

They proceeded back through the underground maze with Doung and Biet in cheerful conversation. Jake walked in silence. The patrol was lost last Monday night. This is Friday. The peeper team hasn't seen anything from the air; the listening posts haven't heard anything. Maybe there isn't anything out there now.

They departed the bunker system via a different stairway which led them into the center of the compound, near the howitzer pit. As they walked toward the wire in the renewed brilliance of sunlight, Jake squinted, trying to adjust from the sepulcher-like shadows of the bunkers. Pulling his ball cap lower, he glimpsed something out of the corner of his eye. He glanced in that direction.

A small white wooden cross listed from its loosely planted base to form an awkward x near the cement foundation of the flagpole. He could read the black lettering: "Kronberg."

Biet saw his glance. "The Vietnamese of this district have erected this memorial. Captain Kronberg was the last American advisor to Hau Duc. He is missed by all. He was killed by a sniper only two months ago." Biet abruptly wheeled and stalked back through the zig-zag gateway of the wire fence barrier and on to the helipad. Jake caught up just as they reached the chopper.

As they mounted the already cranking aircraft, Jake noted that one of the three unmarked crates they had carried was now gone. It must be something important to be escorted by the province chief himself, he decided. We get a province helicopter three times a week. This bird will be making supply runs all afternoon, I wonder what it is that demands this priority?

The helicopter lifted, tilted forward, and they were off to the second outer district, Tien Phouc.

"It's a good day Colonel Thorpe," shouted Biet.

Jake decided to take advantage of Biet's jovial mood. He leaned closer and shouted. "Sir, why don't we have an American advisory team at Hou Duc now?"

"I do not know, Colonel Thorpe. I believe your superiors in Da Nang feel that it is not safe for advisors. I do not agree. As I told you during the briefing, everything is going well."

Jake nodded, but resolved to poke into this issue. He knew it was US policy to have an advisory team at every district, and a special forces team in all isolated pockets of habitation throughout Vietnam.

He looked down from his side of the chopper. The triple canopy jungle was below. Uninterrupted greenness. No! Look at that! A big bright red tree all by itself. What do they call them? Fire Trees or Flame Trees I think. Such a blazing red. So alone in the jungle. But are they alone? For all I know, there might be an NVA regiment camped out right under it.

On the other side of the helicopter, Colonel Than Mak Biet watched the landscape sliding by below. He saw the clearing where the new mill was being constructed. Over there was the freshly relocated Montagnard hamlet, now able to be protected by government forces and safely out of reach of the marauding VC cadre unit. The farms are flourishing. The river is full of fish. He sat in contentment, watching the sun's reflection dance and jump from the occasional rice paddies so recently carved from the jungle. Progress, he thought. We are winning.

Captain Kronberg was an excellent advisor. One of the best I've known. He had a Vietnamese wife. I remember meeting her twice. The first time was when her husband was first assigned to Hau Duc. She wanted to go there and live with him as other Vietnamese wives lived with their soldier husbands. The Americans had refused, and she appealed to me. I had to tell her that it was an American decision, I could not interfere.

The second time was after he was killed. She came to me with the preposterous story that Lieutenant Colonel King had made indecent remarks and tried to seduce her when her husband was not yet in his grave. The story was so absurd; but now in retrospect, I wonder.

Biet suddenly bolted upright in the web sling seat. I denied her then because I could not believe her. I'm still not sure, but now that I know him…! If it is true…! Even if I could make it appear to be true…!

Biet sat back smugly and lit a cigarette by carefully shielding it with his body and hands. It is a good day as the stars foretold. The Holy Mother has given me a week's respite from the spotted American, and a chance memory has perhaps provided the key to neutralizing the arrogance of that mismarked devil. It is indeed a good day.

Tien Phouc was remarkably different from Hau Duc. Before the French had departed, Jake remembered from his orientation manual, Tien Phouc had been strongly competing with the island of Ceylon for the title of Cinnamon Capital of the World. Several large cinnamon tree plantations dominated the rolling topography of the district, and as they flew over the central village, Jake saw the French influence in a stronger way than he'd seen anywhere else. Two broad tree lined streets and clean white stucco buildings marked the village hub. The town looked almost European, as if it had been relocated from a Mediterranean hillside. It was beautiful from the air.

After landing, Biet introduced Major Ton, the District Chief, and Major Cecil Doyle, the District Senior Advisor. Doyle was a lean, craggy officer with a strong jaw and bushy down-swept moustache. In addition to the pistol at his belt, he carried a Thompson submachine gun strapped to his shoulder.

Major Ton did the briefing in Vietnamese as Jake and Doyle sat in the back of the TOC listening to Doyle's interpreter who whispered the translation in broken English. "Troop strength is Okey Dokey." "Troop morale is number one." "Big mine in road go boom; water buffalo, him killed bad; farmer in wagon, him OK." "Two ambushee kill three VC dead this week." "Friendly side: nobody hurt, nobody woundee, nobody dead, everybody number one." "Listening posts go out long time every day, but they no hear nothing."

As they returned to the helicopter, Biet swaggered beside Major Ton and Jake walked with Major Doyle. "From what I see, Sir," Major Doyle said, Everything Ton said is true. It's a little tense around here at times, but I think we have a pretty safe district here. We haven't had a major contact in months."

Jake nodded and glanced around. Large cypress trees swayed gently in the morning breeze. The white buildings glistened with fresh paint, and bright green lawns surrounded them. Flowers bloomed in multicolored gardens, in hedges and even in trees. It all looked so serene. The multiple sandbag emplacements and encircling barbed wire seemed totally out of place. It even feels peaceful, he mused. As they neared the landing pad, Jake noticed one of the other unmarked crates being off-loaded very carefully from the helicopter by two militiamen.

"What are we delivering today?" Jake asked.

"Oh, that's probably the District Chief's booze ration for the month," responded Doyle.

"Booze ration?"

"Yes Sir. He gets at least one crate a month from somewhere in Saigon. It's not illegal Sir. I know he pays for it. He buys it for the morale of his troops."

"How does he distribute it?"

"Gee, I don't know Sir. If you want me to, I'll try to find out."

"Yes, do that please," Jake said pensively, remembering that his former district chief had no such luxury. "And also, I'd like you to pay personal attention to those listening posts. I want you to tell me for sure that you've seen them going out the gate. Find out how they're selected too. Are they getting volunteers? Or is it being handed out as some kind of punishment for goofing off or something. Something is wrong! We all know there is or was *something* out there, something big; but no one hears anything. No one knows anything, and I can't buy it that they've just gone away."

"OK, Sir, but I know it's OK. Major Ton wouldn't lie to me."

"I'm glad you have that kind of relationship, but check anyway."

"Yes Sir." He saluted.

Jake returned the salute and climbed into the helicopter.

"We go to Ly Tin now," shouted Colonel Biet as the chopper lurched cumbersomely into the air.

Biet smiled with satisfaction. It was good to be a province chief. He was content with his life, and had no regrets. He felt no sorrow about immigrating from his home in Hanoi in 1954 with almost all other northern Catholics. He utilized the skills he had gained as a Viet Minh commander against the French by accepting a commission in the Republic of Vietnam's new army and had prospered. He loved his new country. He certainly did not regret his career. He had killed many VC and would kill them all again if he could, because they were Communists! No, he lamented nothing, not even what he had done to become the Province Chief of Quang Tin. The former PC, Colonel Than Dun Kanh, was old and had lost his fire and effectiveness. He had deserved to die. No, I do not regret that he was killed, Biet mused. The stars foretold it and they gave me my opportunity. It was my destiny.

And my wife was the one who made it happen. She may not have been the one who actually killed him, but she was surely involved in the plot. I made it a point to not discover the full details. It would have been distasteful, below the dignity of a province chief.

Sitting next to the open hatchway as the trees and terrain swept past only five hundred feet below gave Jake the giddy sensation of speed he knew he would soon adapt to. The height never seems to bother you, he thought; even though you don't wear a seat belt. The ground moves too fast to give an awareness of height. But the speed gets to you! The wind sucks at your jacket and pulls at your hat. It beats against your eyes. You feel that if you lean just one more inch closer to the door, you'll be gone; but it's just the newness. The newness of the same old dread, like combat. I'll get used to it again, where I can even sit on the deck with my feet hanging out, and not even think about falling out. I'll get used to a lot of things again.

As they circled Ly Tin, Jake was rewarded with a magnificent view of the ocean. Bright white-topped breakers marched in multiple skirmish lines toward the shore in a never ceasing, slow motion assault. In the distance, two lateen rigged fishing vessels lazily patrolled for their scaly prey in the bright sunlight. Two coastal islands guarded their sectors of the mainland under a camouflage of lush bamboo thickets and swaying palm trees. Their own defensive perimeters of white sandy beaches provided a barren no-man's land between them and the attacking sea.

Ly Tin was an ocean oriented district. Almost all the villages were stretched along the beach. The thatched roofs were just visible under the many broad leafed palm trees. The exact location of each hamlet was easily identifiable, however, for each had its clutter of canoe-like boats, and its tangled maze of drying nets between the trees and the sea.

South of Ly Tin City sprawled the mammoth American military base of Chu Lai. From the air it had the appearance of a gigantic populated moon crater, neatly organized with row upon row of aircraft, tanks, trucks, quonset huts and conex containers. Everything is arranged so neatly, thought Jake, like dominos standing carefully at attention. Waiting for the inspection to be completed. Waiting for the casual flick of a playful fingernail.

As they landed at the district headquarters, Jake remembered something else from the "Introduction to Quang Tin Province" folder that Sergeant Prescott had given him in his arrival packet. Both Tien Phouc and Ly Tin had, in the past, been political "hot beds" for the Viet Minh against the French. But the pacification program had seemed to work well. According to the folder, almost every hamlet in both locations was now classified as a "White" hamlet, which meant zero VC legal cadre and zero VC sympathizers.

Major Ken Wallace, the DSA and his counterpart, Major Trung, met them at the helipad.

The briefing was a duplicate of the one in Tien Phouc, as Major Trung extolled the virtues of his men and the peacefulness of the area through a highly skilled interpreter. No problems at all, and Major Wallace confirmed this with enthusiasm as they exited the district TOC.

Ly Tin City was the market hub of the district. Housewives shopped while bicycles, three wheeled vehicles and small trucks jerked and sputtered in a horn-blowing, pell-mell paced dance of "allemande left" and "allemande right" on the narrow streets. Despite this bustle, the odor of fish dominated all sensations. The dilapidated fish processing factory, less than one hundred yards from the district HQ fouled the air with industrial fervor.

As Jake and Wallace strode back to the landing pad, a bright red Vietnamese truck lumbered past, swirling a profuse plume of fine dust. Something about the truck caught Jake's eye. Something familiar. "Whose truck is that?" Jake asked, and halted to gaze at it.

Wallace, a burly, ruddy-faced officer, scratched under his dusty flak jacket. "I don't know, Sir. It's been around for a coupla months or so. Don't see many new trucks around here."

The truck was gone, leaving only its billowing consequence: but Jake could still see it in his mind's eye. Something; something; what was it? Then it struck him. It was a US Army truck! The grill had been switched, the bumper and fenders had been replaced, and a wooden box bed now overhung the cab roof. But it used to be one of ours, and someone wants to hide that fact! His heart raced with excitement at the memory of his mission. It's surely not the only stolen Army truck in Vietnam, but Wallace says it showed up about the right time, and we're sure in the right neighborhood. Finally, a possibility of helping Ray.

"Major Wallace, that truck is a US Army deuce and a half. I want you to get me its serial number, and find out who supposedly owns it now. Do it as covertly as you can, but get it."

Major Wallace blinked his bloodshot eyes in surprise. "A deuce and a half? How do you know" Are you sure Sir?"

"I'm sure," Jake muttered, still thinking about Gonzaga. It's a long shot, he thought, but I sure don't have any better leads to follow.

The last crate of whiskey was gone from the helicopter when Jake and Biet mounted. Jake was melancholy as the huey took off. He had been so busy in his new job that he had almost forgotten his task. I'm sorry Ray, he thought to himself. I owe it to you to remember. From here on, I'll keep after it. I won't neglect you again.

Jake looked at Biet, cross legged and comfortable in the webbed seat. The province chief pulled a notepad from his pocket and began writing, chewing on his pen during pauses of concentration. The act jolted Jake's memory. Mail call this morning, and I got that damned letter!

He had known it was bad news even before he had opened it. It had been a long time since he had received a letter from Dolores. They had been separated since shortly after he had returned from Vietnam the first time. He didn't understand it at first, her short temper, her heavy drinking, her sudden reliance on Darvon and other tranquilizers. She was so different from before he left. Then, slowly, the story came out:

She had an affair while he was gone, perhaps several. When he returned, so battle weary and happy to be home, she was overwhelmed with guilt. She spent a month in the psychiatric ward of the local hospital. They classified her as a "chronic depressive." She ran away for another month, returned, and then left again. he had heard from her, now and then, whenever she wanted something. He always wrote back, but he no longer complied with her requests or demands. There were no warm feelings left. Sadness, a little disgust, and even anger perhaps, but no fondness. She had become bitter and shrew-like. She even blamed him for their break up.

His stomach churned, but he pulled the crumpled envelope from his fatigue jacket pocket, and held the letter carefully against the whipping wind as he read it again:

"Dear Jacob,

I hope this letter finds you well and healthy, and I hope your luck of before holds this time too. But I am frightened for you. I had a dream the other night. My psychiatrist says I shouldn't tell you about it but I think you should know. I dreamed I was at a funeral. The coffin was open. The dead man had a long white beard. His skin was dry and dark. The mourners threw flowers into the casket; pansies mostly. I threw in a single rosemary bloom. Everyone started singing. I don't remember what the words were, but something about the dead man being gone and never coming back. Then someone told me the dead man's name. A silly name. It was Nonny. For some reason, I called to him, but nothing happened except he turned into you. The old man was gone and you were in the coffin. Does anyone there call you Nonny Jake?"

She'll never change, Jake decided. She had a dream that might mean I'm going to die, and she couldn't wait to send me the news. She wants me to suffer. Normally she'll do everything her doctor says. *He* obviously thought it wouldn't be the best thing to send that kind of message to someone in a combat theater. Of course, for all he knows, I might be as kookie as she is. Something like this might have really spooked me. But Hell, I know her. She could dream anything. She might even have made this up to get at me. He shook his head and read the final paragraph:

"Of course, Jake, it might just mean that I don't love you any more; that's what the doctor thinks. But I thought I should warn you. I had to, to clear my conscience.

As ever,

Dolores Coral Haldane"

Well, I hope the doctor's right. For all I know, she might write me next week asking me to come back to her. Hmm, she's taken her maiden name back. That could be significant. First time she's done that. Maybe she really is getting better. Trying to stand on her own feet. Hell, I don't know what to think.

The helicopter droned northward, following the beach toward the last outlying district, Thang Binh.

Well, Jake thought, as he replaced the letter into his pocket, I'm not going to let it bother me. He shuddered and realized he was lying to himself.

Biet shouted to him, "You will be warmer when we are on the ground. It is not far."

Jake smiled, partly from amusement and partly from politeness at the inaccuracy of the PC's assumption.

Biet returned the smile.

I like this American, Biet thought. He is neither arrogant nor timid. He has accepted what he has heard so far at the first three districts. Good. That means he will not send a condemning report to Da Nang.

He pulled out his sunglasses. Thang Binh will be hot. Thang Binh! My Nemesis! Biet glanced at Jake who was watching the heavy traffic along MR1 below. I should warn this new American about Major Dang. Who knows what Major Dang might say in *his* briefing? But, of course I cannot give any warning. It would appear to be and would actually be unprofessional for me to complain about Major Dang to an American. Major Dang is Vietnamese. He is a petty demagogue who takes advantage of this war to puff his own ego. Some of his past American advisors have called him a "grandstander," whatever that strange idiom might mean. But the fool is effective! The people of Thang Bien love him, and the VC hate him. They have tried to assassinate him many times. As much as I detest him, his death would be a loss to the republic! The stars tell me that today is a good day. Perhaps Major Dang will not embarrass me this time.

Thang Bien had no helipad. The helicopter settled on a flat, dry field amidst a giant mushroom of choking, eye stinging sand and dust. Jake dismounted automatically, but then had to crouch near the skids of the aircraft with his eyes closed until the hurricane around him ceased. When it did, and the rotor blades had slowed to a whispering "whish, whish" above him, he rose and noticed that Biet was still in the helicopter covered with a film of dust. He was just now opening his eyes.

Two men walked toward them from the far side of the field. One was an American officer, but Jake could see that he carried no weapon. He was the first unarmed American Jake had seen out of Saigon, and Jake's right eyebrow arched in a silent question.

Another surprise. The other man wore black pajamas! He was also unarmed, wearing sandals on his dusty feet. He wore no hat and no sign of rank. Who the Hell is he? Jake wondered. Have they captured a Viet Cong? By now, Biet was at Jake's side as the two approached. Both men saluted and Jake and Biet returned their salutes.

Biet handled the introductions. "Colonel Thorpe, this is Major Dang, the District Chief of Thang Binh; and this is Major Danby, his DSA."

Major Dang was a tall, strikingly handsome Vietnamese. His jet black hair gleamed in the sunlight, and his white teeth sparkled. But these attributes were not his most notable. He had the physique of a professional athlete! His muscles strained the muslin fabric of his peasants' black clothing.

Beside him, Major Conrad Danby looked like an accountant. He was older than Jake, with thin, almost frail limbs, and the beginning of a paunch extended the front of his fatigue jacket. His chubby face was adorned with rimless spectacles. When he removed his ball cap to mop the perspiration, he revealed a totally bald scalp.

They proceeded to the Thang Binh TOC, which surprised Jake by being not only above ground, but in a corrugated tin shack without sand bag protection.

Major Dang briefed the district situation in English, which was a pleasant and welcome change for Jake. Dang's briefing, however, did not vary much from the previous briefings. No VC activity; high troop morale; plenty of food for the villagers; rice production was high; a bridge is being built; a new aid station had opened; and plans for two new churches were being drawn, one for Catholics, and one for Cao Dais.

Major Dang paused and put down his map pointer and stepped forward as if to proceed to a new subject.

Biet cut him off angrily. "Have you finished with the analysis of your district Major Dang?"

"Yes, my Colonel," Dang replied, "but I would like to...."

"We do not have time for things of a trivial nature, nor for speculation," Biet stormed. "We must return now to Tam Ky." He heaved himself to his feet.

"The NVA regiment to the west of Hau Duc is neither trivial nor speculation um Dai Ta Biet. It is there, and its presence and purpose is a threat to all of Quang Tin."

Biet wheeled and pointed a finger at Dang's face. "That is enough Tiu Ta Dang! The security of Quang Tin is *my* responsibility! We are well aware of the enemy force which was near Hau Duc. It is no longer there. Your information is out of date. Thank you for your briefing, but it is now ended. Do you understand?"

Jake was transfixed by the exchange and the rage in Biet's face. Hmm, he mused, seems to be a little bad blood between these two.

"Yes Dai Ta," Dang said, subdued but obviously not cowed.

The two began speaking hotly in Vietnamese, and Jake drew Danby outside for the appearance of courtesy, and as the best way for them to also speak privately. Jake lit a cigarette and was not surprised to see Danby draw a small stub briar pipe from his jacket. It completed the image.

"What is this about the NVA regiment?" Jake asked.

"It's still out there Sir, and so is a line unit VC cadre battalion. We've had several confirming reports."

"How come you know here in Thang Binh and we don't know in province HQ?"

"Sir, forgive me for being blunt, but you guys at headquarters hear only what the South Vietnamese want you to hear. Everybody knows it's out there. Well, maybe the PC doesn't know, cause all he's got is yes men who are afraid to rock the boat. But everybody else knows." He puffed slowly and calmly on his pipe.

Jake scratched his chin. "How do you know? Did Major Dang tell you?"

"Well, we've talked about it, yes Sir; but I speak Vietnamese. I hear the same reports he does. I believe them too."

That answer surprised Jake. He decided to take a different tack. "Why doesn't Biet like Major Dang?" Jake was guessing.

"That's easy Sir. Dang's a character. You see how he dresses. He almost never wears a uniform. He feels it separates him from the people. He goes all around the district on a motor scooter. The people here in Thang Binh adore him. They'd make him a king if they could. He's honest. They say he's the only honest district chief in the province. The colonel probably doesn't trust him because of this. According to my sources, the good Dai Ta's making a fortune during this war. Dang respects him though. Dang thinks he's a pretty good province chief, a lot better than the one up north in Quang Nam. To answer your question though, I think it's just jealousy. I think Dang's popularity and effectiveness kinda scare him."

"If Biet thinks Major dang is a threat, why doesn't he just fire him or promote him up to the province staff, where he could keep him under his thumb.?"

"Just between you and me Sir, I think it's been threatened. The thing is, Dang's *too popular*, and *too effective!* We really don't have much of a VC threat. Dang's rooted them all out. The other districts are heavily infiltrated. I'm glad I'm here. It's safe. How many other districts have you seen today where the soldiers sleep in their homes and not in a barbed wire compound? You're new here Colonel. I've been here almost a year now. I suggest that you trust your eyes, not your ears."

The truth of that calmly spoken statement sliced into Jake's being like a sword thrust. He nodded and shook Danby's hand. Their eyes met and Jake felt a strong communication coming from this untypical officer. he could be trusted, and he was really good at his job. "It's good to know you Major Danby. Do you go by Connie or Conrad?"

"Conrad if you insist Sir," Danby smiled around his pipe. He removed his hat again and rubbed his shining pate. "But for some unknown reason Sir, all my friends call me Curly."

Jake laughed and patted him affectionately on the shoulder. "OK Curley, thanks for all the info. I'll talk to you again."

They ambled off toward the sandy field where the helicopter sat like a dragon fly waiting for its prey. Biet emerged from the tin TOC followed by Major Dang.

Jake remembered the three crates on board when they began the day. He turned to Danby. "Why didn't your counterpart get any booze this time? The other districts did. Wasn't there enough to go around, or is Major Dang being punished?"

"Booze Sir?" Curly asked. "We don't get any booze. All I ever see is Ba Mui Ba Beer. The soldiers drink it, but without refrigeration, it tastes like horse piss to me."

Jake almost stopped. He was quite surprised, but he didn't want the two Vietnamese officers behind them to realize that he might have discovered something. He kept walking. "Do you mean to tell me Curly, that your Major Dang doesn't get a monthly booze ration?" The question was almost a growl.

"If he does, Sir, I've never seen it. Do you want me to ask him about it Sir?"

"I sure do!" Jake exclaimed in a deadly monotone. "And don't tell anyone else what you find out except me."

"Will do Sir."

They were at the helicopter. Everyone saluted. Dang and Curly jog trotted to the far side of the field while the shrill turbine whined the heavy rotor blades slowly into motion. The high pitched scream rose steadily in tone and volume until it erupted into the familiar roar and repeated whomp of painfully buffeted air. The tornado of sand engulfed them again, slashing and smothering them simultaneously. The helicopter at last lunged upward to escape it.

It was a relief to be headed for home. Funny, Jake thought, four days here and already Tam Ky is home. He brushed sand from his eyebrows and blew his nose in his green handkerchief. He looked at Biet who was still wearing that self-satisfied smile. His stars told him he would have a good day, and he's making sure that happens. I wonder what my stars said about me today?

SCENE 3

BAU CON YE

0030 Hours
Sunday, 7 January, 1968

The tiny blackout beams made feeble thrusts into the darkness, but the road remained wrapped in black. Mark, riding shotgun for the trip, was continually surprised to feel the minute stings of flying dust which told him they were still on the rutted and twisting ribbon of sand which the men called "Lose-a-Leg Lane," a reference to the constant mine threat. He heard one of the two privates in the back seat mutter "Shit!" The soldier didn't explain this expletive, and nobody asked.

Before this, the four men had been silent, as they were every night during the trip. They hate this ten minutes of white knuckle hell as much as I do, Mark thought. Without a doubt, this jarring, teeth grinding dash through the dark is the one thing I hate more than anything else so far in Vietnam. Getting to work at noon isn't bad at all. The same road usually. This easy short cut between Camp Kronberg and the province headquarters is a lot faster than going the other way: Down to MR1, then through the city of Tam Ky. But at night, after work, after midnight, it's different.

We should follow the SOP, and alternate the routes. Never establish a routine. But passing through that dark dead city after curfew is almost as scary, and it takes twice as long. Ten minutes of terror every night is plenty.

Mark was exhausted. So were they all. They were always tired after twelve hours of duty. Mark's shoulders and neck had been stiff with strain when he crawled into the jeep; the same jeep that had brought their relief shift to work. If he could have closed his eyes at that time, he would have fallen instantly to sleep. But they had to drive back. Back to their compound at night. At night! Everyone knows that the night belongs to the V.C. That's why it's called the dead of night!

His spine tingled. Tonight's going to be it, he predicted. The VC are waiting for us tonight. I can feel it.

We're driving too fast. If something's in the road, we'd never see it. God, are we still on the road? We're driving way too fast! This would be a good night for an ambush. What if there's a tree across the road? That's a typical VC trick! We either hit the tree and kill ourselves in the crash, or stop and let the ambush shoot us down like turkeys. What if there's a mine in the road? That's the biggest danger of all. Hurry up, damn you! Hurry up!

The spleen shattering crash landings of the bouncing jeep forced Mark to grab the handle on the dash, provided for just that purpose. So many things to worry about, he thought. God it's scary! What am I doing here anyway? Yea, though I ride through the Valley of Death, I sure as Hell feel evil all around me! But I'm a sergeant. Gotta act calm, even on this infernal, blind, but wide-eyed ride. Jeez, I never thought I'd be afraid of the dark! What was that? Did something move up ahead?

He clutched the pistol grip of his loaded M-16 rifle even tighter. If somebody does shoot at us, he thought, there's no way I could shoot back at this speed without falling out! I should tell him to slow down. I'm the senior NCO. If we wreck, it'll be my fault. He's probably as scared as I am. I should tell him to slow down.

What's that? I don't remember that big rock being so close. Are we still on the road? We're almost there. God! God! Hurry up! Get there! Get there! Hurry up!

They were there. Never had the gates of Camp Kronberg looked so welcome. Mark sighed as he realized he always felt this buoyant feeling of thankfulness after every nocturnal dash for home.

Sandwiches and reconstituted milk would be waiting for them in the kitchen. Nobody ever wanted coffee. Twelve hours of uninterrupted caffeine was always enough. No one was sleepy or even tired anymore. The jeep ride always churned them so that even the emotional relief-surge of arrival didn't quite take the edge off. The tiredness would return, and sleep would eventually come, but not yet.

At the special watch table in the kitchen, the other three members of Mark's TOC crew tried to talk him into a few hands of penny-ante poker before they turned in, but Mark declined. He had a few more experiences he wanted to write in his journal, and this would be a good time.

Back out under the stars, Mark clumped along on the pallet board pathway. These raised wooden trails ran throughout Camp Kronberg, allowing soldiers to walk to and fro without stepping into the perpetual monsoon mud, which seemed to be the natural floor of the encampment.

He found the nearest latrine. It was just a three holer, but he didn't need to go inside. He climbed the two steps to the covered plank platform along one side where an oversized galvanized gutter hugged the latrine's outer wall at thigh level. Mark smiled as he remembered what everyone called this elevated comfort station: "The Pissing Porch."

He urinated into the tin trough; the sound resonated through the midnight stillness like a garden hose in a garbage can. But Mark didn't think about the noise. He was still trying to unwind from the jeep ride.

He zipped up and stepped back, conscious that he couldn't stray too far from the latrine wall or he might fall off the platform. In the darkness, he couldn't see the edge. He remembered the height though. In his imagination, it was higher still. He had the feeling that he was on a stage about to perform. The spotlight was about to snap on with a blinding flash, and the audience would applaud.

But a cannon boomed in the distance and reality returned. He was in a theatre all right! He was in a combat theatre.

He groped toward his quonset hut. The compound was so damned dark! Blackout curtains hung in every window. By now, though, he knew the way. One, the first door. Two, three, four, five; here's my hooch, the last one in the hut. The officers are lucky, he thought. Each one gets half a quonset for himself while ours are all partitioned for ten men, five to a side. Glad I don't have to sleep two or three men to a room though, like the privates.

He swung open the screen door, then unlocked the wooden one, and entered. Turning on the lamp, he parked his rifle against the wall and walked across the room to his tiny desk. As his left boot touched the small woven rug in the center of the floor, the hackles on his neck tickled his skin. Something—a smell? A very slight sound? A minuscule movement off to his left? Something. He was not alone! He could sense it. He glanced toward the door and his rifle, both too far away. His heart was pounding. He could feel it hammering in his chest. He could even hear it. Casually, he took another step while unsnapping the bayonet at his hip. He pulled it, wheeled and crouched, the way he'd been taught in AIT. His blade pointing wickedly toward the felt presence of the unknown intruder.

"Hello Sergeant Mark, long time no see," Co Li giggled. Her tone ignored his murderous attack stance. She was sitting in the one chair in the room. It was supposed to be under the small desk, but she had pulled it next to the far wall where it faced the door. Mark could see that she wore the black pajama uniform of the vietnamese peasant. A conical straw hat lay at her feet.

"How did you get in here?" Mark stammered as he awkwardly relaxed. Sheathing the bayonet, he struggled to make sense of his conflicting thoughts. *She's a VC here to kill me. She's here for sex. Maybe she got locked in here by accident. Don't let my guard down for a minute! Smile at her and calm down, you idiot, it's going to be your lucky night!*

Often told war stories of VC slipping into compounds at night flashed through his mind. He glanced around looking for suspicious boxes or hand grenades lying with pins half pulled. He smiled stupidly and self-consciously.

"I come in morning same time all Vietnam people. Guards let all in together. Ba Nhur, your housemaid, she work for other men in morning. You still sleep. I help her. We talk about you. We watch you go away in jeep. Then we work here. Clean bed. Wash clothes. Ba Nhur teach me iron your pants. Ba Nhur lock door when she leave. She go out with all housemaids. I stay here, wait for you."

"But the guards count the workers coming in and going out. If they don't all go out, they have a search," Mark gasped. He imagined his embarrassment if the MPs pounded on his door now and found her in his room. He reached over and turned on the desk lamp, the brighter light easing his tension and apprehension. He took another furtive glance around, now feeling guilty. He could never suspect this sweet young girl of being an actual terrorist.

Her smile was indulgent. "Yes, should be so, but they never tell when number not right. Ba Nhur tell me. Many times, other house maids stay with GI. Sometimes maybe two, maybe three stay. Guards not search. Never do nothing. They think maybe mistake in morning. They no want to make trouble, find nothing, look bad. Everybody know. No sweat. Nobody come!" She was obviously proud of her superior knowledge about camp security.

Holy Cow! I'd better tell First Sergeant Prescott about this in the morning, he thought.

"You not happy to see me?" Co Li asked coyly.

"Of course I am, I'm delighted," he grinned. "It's just that I'm surprised."

"I think maybe I surprise you," she smiled, her even white teeth flashing.

Mark returned the smile. Astonished would be a better description of what he felt. He had only spoken to her three times since getting himself bopped on the head. Let's see, he thought, first was last Tuesday on duty. It seems like a month ago; yet it seems like yesterday. I saw her again on Thursday, when I went around and rapped on her window. She was nervous at first. Acted like she expected someone else, but then we got along pretty well. Let's see, I saw her again on Wednesday, when I delivered a message to the Province Chief. I know she likes me; I can tell that, and God, I can't get her out of my mind ever since she touched me on the face that night.

For lack of something else to do, Mark took off his web gear and laid it across his desk, across the journal. A question crossed his mind. "Do you read English Co Li?"

"No Sergeant Mark, nobody teach me," she said innocently.

Thank God, he thought. It'd sure be embarrassing if she read what I wrote about her; how I've dreamed about her. I really made some hot comments in there.

He frowned in sudden confusion. Why is she here? I know why an American girl would come to a man's room after midnight, but she's Vietnamese. Is it the same? Sure it is. It must be. Why else would she do it? But, he remembered, I haven't even kissed her yet. He decided a blunt question was better than cross examining himself for her motivation. He turned to face her. "Co Li:" He paused, losing his courage.

"Yes Sergeant Mark?"

"Co Li, why are you here tonight?"

Her eyebrows arched in surprise. She seemed to not know how to answer. Then her mouth slowly widened into a tolerant smile, her tone was that of a teacher answering the silly question of a first grader. "I come to be with you Sergeant Mark."

Their eyes caught each other's gaze and held it. It was a long moment of silent searching. Mark knew for a certainty they were going to kiss tonight.

He crossed the room and sat on the bed, closer to her. "I really am glad you came."

"I stay all day and wait for you," she smiled proudly.

He reached out his hand, just to hold hers, nothing more, but she responded by springing out of the chair to sit beside him on the bed.

"I wait long time for you," she purred, leaning her face toward his.

Still holding her hand, he kissed her gently. Her kiss was warm, inviting. He inhaled her aroma. A clean, springlike fragrance. It wasn't perfume. It was her.

Their lips disengaged but she held her face close. They were both smiling. Her eyes twinkled, mischievous yet affectionate.

He ran his fingers along her cheek, her ear, and then to her raven hair. "You've fixed you hair differently," he murmured. She had pulled her hair into a single ebony braid down her back.

"Fix hair for work; come in gate this way. You want me to take out?" she asked eagerly.

"No, your hair's fine", he reassured her. He kissed her again, his hand behind her head pressing her face to his. She was willing, pliant, eager.

She reached up and caressed his cheek, the way she had done in the darkness outside the TOC. It brought the same tingle. She's magic, he thought.

He kissed her once more, and then again.

His hand caressed her neck, and then her shoulder through the rough muslin fabric.

Slowly, his fingers found the large top button. She smiled her acceptance. He kissed her again as the disk popped free. The other buttons also loosened easily and quickly.

Hesitantly, tentatively, he reached inside and cupped her naked breast. He squeezed softly. Finding the nipple, he gently tweaked it in his fingers. Her breath was warm on his cheek.

Their lips parted once more and they again gazed into each other's eyes as he massaged with tender, rising passion.

He pulled his hand away abruptly. "I'll turn the lights out," he announced, and stood up to do so. He was conscious that his erection caused a horizontal tent in his baggy fatigues.

"Why?" she asked in total innocence.

He turned to look at her in puzzlement. "Why what? What do you mean why?"

"Why turn out lights? You not want to see me?"

"Well, I, er, sure I do; but, but, don't you turn out the lights to make love?"

"No," she responded. It was her turn to be puzzled. "When we make love, we make love. If light off, we leave off. When light on, we leave on. Light nothing to do with make love. American people turn light out always?"

Mark sat down on the bed again. The interruption had caused the trouser tent to collapse. "Well, no. Ahh, not always. I guess usually. At least sometimes."

Co Li now showed embarrassment. "I sorry Sergeant Mark. Sin loy please. I sorry. No sweat. You turn off if you want. Is OK."

Mark was in a quandary. Should I walk across the room and turn the damn light off, making her think I can't do it with it on? Or should I just barge ahead? Hell! After all this talk, I'll be so damned aware of it, I really will feel like I'm doing it in front of an audience or something.

Co Li broke into his ambivalence. "You want me to turn off light for you Sergeant Mark?"

He pulled her to him and kissed her again, fiercely but briefly. He held her at arm's length. "Co Li, this is our first time together. The first time we'll make love. I want it to be special."

She nodded eagerly.

"I didn't think before, about the light. I forgot that we might have different ways. But that doesn't matter. After tonight, I'll never think about the light again. But just this time, I'd like to turn it off, if it's OK with you."

Co Li grinned radiantly. The mischief sparkling from her eyes. "We do what you want, Sergeant Mark. Tonight we touch, but,..." she reached one hand to her shirt front and pulled it to one side, revealing one perfect conical breast with its large brownish nipple. "Tonight, you not see what you touch. You miss something."

Mark laughed, jumped up and switched off the light. Expecting darkness, he was surprised to find the desk lamp still on. He could hear Co Li stirring on the bunk as he sped across the room to flip the final switch. The room, the world, plunged into blackness. He crept back toward the softly rustling noise. He barked his shin painfully on the metal bed frame and hopped on one foot for a few seconds until the agony decreased. He sat down and reached for her. She wasn't there.

Her hand caught his arm. "I am here Sergeant Mark." She was giggling again. She guided his hand to her breast. She was on her back, naked.

"So Sergeant Mark, I surprise you again, no?"

"You sure did," Mark laughed, as he bent to kiss her nipple.

"No, no," she said softly, gently pulling at his jacket. "Take off first. Do now. Better now than stop in middle."

"OK," he agreed; but it seemed forever before boots, socks, uniform and skivvies were somewhere on the floor.

All the while he undressed, Co Li ran her fingers playfully along his neck in leisurely, tempting strokes.

At last he turned to her. He leaned down to find her face under his; his hands groping her slim body.

But this time, she pushed him away. "Sin loy Sergeant Mark. The metal around your neck," She giggled again. "It tickle."

Laughing silently in the dark, and thinking the interruptions would never cease, Mark spun his dog tags to his back, leaving the chain around his neck. He cupped her breast again. "Is everything OK now?" he asked teasingly.

"Mmmmm, I think for sure Sergeant Mark." The mocking laughter in her voice was unmistakable.

He stretched out beside her, kissing and fondling her body. She circled his neck with her arms, holding him loosely but warmly. Their lips crushed and clung together. Mark could feel her lithe nakedness next to his. So smooth. So alive. So yielding.

For long, gentle moments, they caressed and petted. Neither now felt the need to hurry. They recognized each other's passion and willed it to linger and last. They bathed in the shared tenderness, in the warmth of togetherness.

As they neared the zenith, where containment would be left behind, Mark suddenly realized how small she was. As they kissed, he could feel her bare feet against his knees. But the thought was fleeting, and melted away in the fervor of desire.

He recalled it however, at the crucial time of connection, when, despite his gymnastic endeavors, he couldn't make the primal merger while still nibbling at her breast.

But function prevailed over form, and union was accomplished.

And then it was over! The extension of ardor had been too much. Mark lost control almost immediately. His face grimaced. He halted his hungry thrusting and tensed with strain, but he couldn't hold back. His body shuddered deliciously.

Co Li continued writhing for a few more seconds before she realized he had stopped. She lay quietly, her heavy breathing still audible. "You finish already?" she asked innocently from beneath his chest.

Mark sensed her disappointment even though he could tell she was trying hard not to show it. He raised to his elbows and backed out of her with a flaccid and disillusioning plop. He lay down by her side. He began to nibble at her breast and massage her groin.

Slowly at first, and then rapidly, her passion reawakened. Mark continued to administer to her as a loving duty, and she responded. She twisted and bounced. She writhed and moaned. The iron bed legs grated on the concrete floor as the bunk bounced away from the wall. Mark was forced to divide his attention between serving Co Li's needs, and hanging on, as the single sized bed suddenly seemed far too small. But the crescendo was reached and the hot tropical night was quiet once more.

Co Li did not move or speak. At first, Mark thought she had gone to sleep; she was so still. But she reached up, cupped her hand around his shoulder and caressed his arm, "You are nice man," she said softly.

Mark leaned down and their lips met softly. The inferno became a glow as they both basked in tenderness and warmth.

Finally, Co Li pushed Mark away playfully. "Let me up now Sergeant Mark, I must go toilet room."

"Toilet room?" Mark asked. "I don't have a toilet in here."

He could sense her surprise. "For sure Sergeant Mark. There. I see before you come." He could just see her pointing to the small half wall enclosure in one corner where a steel wash basin with hot and cold water had only recently been installed.

"That's not a toilet," Mark said incredulously. "That's only a sink for shaving and washing up."

"For sure Sergeant Mark. That be toilet." Her tone was that of a patient mother instructing a ten year old child. "What else toilet be for?"

Mark remained silent. Despite their love making, he felt he didn't know her well enough yet to be able to tell her what he thought a toilet was. He got out of her way, half wondering if, in spite of what she said, she might be planning to use the sink for a bodily function.

His eyes, now adjusted to the darkness, watched her rise from the bed. She cupped one hand in front of her in a maidenlike gesture and padded softly toward the sink. Mark's eyes were focused on her doll sized buttocks as she vanished through the doorway. The washroom light, a single bulb hanging from a drop cord, switched on.

She was in here by herself long enough to find out where everything is, he thought. He heard the sink faucet being turned on and noticed that her nude shadow on the floor was bending over the sink. He watched as the long shadow mopped its face with a towel, then lifted each arm and wiped its upper torso. It crouched and disappeared, but he could hear the rag being rustled busily. The shadow rose again and formed a perfect nude silhouette in profile, standing erect and poised as it washed the towel in the sink.

What the heck is she doing in there? Mark thought. Looks like she's taking a spits bath.

Her head popped around the corner of the wall panel. "You have pot or bucket?" she asked. "I need to put water in."

"No, but you can use my helmet. Its right there beside you on the floor. Just pull the inside liner out and take off the cover."

She made more sloshing noises and soon appeared again with the helmet half full of water. One of Mark's Army green towels draped over her arm. "Why soldiers put cloth on top of helmet?" she asked as she knelt beside him. She dipped the towel in the warm water and after wringing, began to softly rub Mark's shoulders, arms and chest. The warmth of the towel soothed his skin, still slightly sensitive after sex, and the moisture left behind cooled him instantly, even in the sweltering heat of the room. It was an exquisite sensation. "Cloth not help to stop bullet," she said. "Why wear?"

"It's just a helmet cover," Mark answered. "It helps with camouflage." He wondered if she needed a more detailed explanation.

"Oh," she nodded. "I understand." She continued to lightly brush and wipe his stomach and legs. Mark was in such ecstasy, his eyes tended to roll back into his head.

With the gentleness of a nurse, Co Li brought her fingers and the pleasure bringing towel to Mark's groin. She lifted, stroked, and bathed him. It was not erotic; it was sensual rapture.

Suddenly she stopped. Her head snapped forward alertly and she peered intently at Mark's genitals. Mark was alarmed. "What's the matter?" he asked, raising his head.

Without speaking, she bolted upright, tossed the towel to the floor, and darted to turn on the desk lamp. She hurried back to stand over him, using the brighter light to inspect the part of his anatomy she had just cleaned.

"What's the matter?" Mark repeated, tearing his eyes from the sight of her delightful nakedness to his own area of concern.

She dropped to her knees for a closer look. She was obviously puzzled. "Americans different from Vietnamese men." She stated simply.

"Different? How?" asked Mark, glancing self consciously at his limp member. "We're not different!"

"Yes, different," she said matter of factly. "Vietnamese men hide top with skin, like priest. Wear hood over bald head. You no have."

Mark couldn't help the burst of laughter that erupted. Co Li looked up at him, then down in embarrassment. She knew she had made some kind of error.

"We're not different," Mark finally gasped, his chest still convulsing with mirth. "American men, all men, are born the same, but many boys get the foreskin cut off when they're babies."

"Why?" She stammered, her eyes wide with shock and horror.

"Well, it's a long story, it's just a custom now."

"American custom to hurt babies? To cut babies?" Her astonishment was even greater now. "It for sure true what many Vietnam people say. American very bad. Very mean. Vietnam people not hurt babies!" This last was said with emphasis, pronouncing the superior wisdom and greater benevolence of her race.

"We don't hurt babies either!" Mark felt compelled to defend his own culture.

"Have to hurt! You cut! You cut with knife?"

"Well yeah, I guess so, but they don't remember it. I don't remember it."

"If do to Vietnam baby, he remember!" She stood and crossed her arms under her pointed breasts. Her hips jiggled with defiance and outrage.

Mark held his tongue. He wanted to tell her about the Jews and the Bible; about how it all started. He wanted to tell her that many cultures practiced circumcision, not just the United States. He wanted to persuade her that Americans are not cruel beasts who mutilate infants, but he knew that here, tonight, he would never convince her. He would not win this argument.

"Co Li," he pleaded, "I can't explain our customs. I can't help who I am or where I come from anymore than you can. Can't we just forget about this until some other time?"

Her arms were still folded angrily in front of her.

"Did you ever hurt babies?" she asked finally, her lower lip quivering slightly.

Mark swung his feet to the floor and stood up to look down at her face. "Co Li, I've never cut a baby. I've never even spanked one."

She softened. "You promise?" she asked hopefully but petulantly.

Thinking the fight was at last over, Mark relaxed and answered flippantly, "Yes I do. I cross my heart and hope to die."

"You hope what?" Her eyes widened again and she stepped away from him in renewed shock.

"Forget it, forget it. It doesn't mean anything. It's just an expression." He followed after her reassuringly. Their nude shadows on the wall performing a tragi-comic dance of reconciliation.

She was calmed but still wary. She allowed him to catch her in the center of the room. He pulled her close, her face nuzzled against his lower chest. She glanced up at him as he held her close. "I never understand Americans," she finally murmured. "But maybe you different. Everybody say so." She looked up into his face and smiled. She had reached her decision. "OK," she said, "We go make love again."

They did. Twice more. And after each frenzied, sweltering session, Co Li bathed them both with the warm, wet towel. Then they talked, learning more about their differences, and their similarities.

In the early morning hours, Co Li looked happily around the room. "This be special place for us. Need special name."

"It's my hooch," mumbled Mark sleepily. "Sure isn't anything special."

"Oh yes. Here, we make love first time. We call it Bau Con Ye."

"Sounds nice," responded Mark around a yawn he couldn't stifle. He wanted to stay awake, but his eyelids drooped.

"It have special meaning for us, just for us," she giggled. "Do you want to know what words mean?"

While waiting for him to respond, Co Li glanced with happiness at the walls, the ceiling, everything; trying to memorize every detail. "Do you want to know what words mean?" she asked again.

He did not answer; he was asleep.

She kissed his chest. He didn't move. Her hand crept to his pubic hair and lower. She fondled the little sleeping soldier whose helmet had no cover.

Still Mark slept.

She brought her hair braid around in front to tickle his nose. His eyes opened and he rubbed his face wildly.

She leaned across him and kissed him playfully on the cheek. "I no can sleep yet," she giggled.

Mark fell asleep again at about five in the morning. Co Li had propped a pillow against the headboard and sat resting against it. Mark lay on his side with his head on her curved belly. Both arms holding her as he might hold a pillow or a person trying to escape. One leg was drawn up and draped over her ankles. The desk lamp was still on.

Co Li ran her fingertips lightly along his face, soothing him into deeper sleep. She could not move without disturbing him, but she had no desire to move.

She knew she looked the picture of oriental femininity: loving; caring for her man; sacrificing her own comfort and night's rest for him. But she was not thinking about comfort. She was remembering her brother's words.

I have done what he asked, she thought. I have employed the wiles of my gender to draw close to an enemy of the people. Yet I know he will not be pleased.

He wished me to seduce either Dai Ta Biet or an American officer, but I could not do that. The Dai Ta is old and fat. His teeth are brown and his skin is as dry and wrinkled as crumpled paper. The American officers are haughty and ugly. Their long noses forever stick into the air as if they smell the sewer canals of Saigon.

My brother has commanded that I do this, and so I will; but I will choose with whom I do it. Sergeant Mark is different. He is not like the others. If I must use my body in the service of our country, it will be with him.

Co Li smiled as she continued to stroke Mark's face. It was not as bad as I expected, she thought. The wise ones say that to do one's duty well, one must enjoy doing it. Tonight, I must confess, I did my duty very well.

SCENE 4

THE STOCKADE

0900 Hours
Monday, 8 January, 1968

Jake shook his head in bewilderment. On every map, the Quang Tin stockade appeared as a precise black dot in the crotch of a neat blue Y where two fresh water rivers emptied into a salt water inlet. But as he approached it along the raised dirt road from Tam Ky, the prison's only ground access, he realized the map's symbolism was far too flattering and very misleading.

A giant, mud-colored, gruesome building squatted behind a tall chain-link fence on the only dry ground within miles. The knee deep brackish tidal swamp which surrounded the area prohibited farming, fishing and escape. A few thin clumps of starving reeds punctured the murky brown surface as the only surviving vegetation in this continuous war of waters.

The flora was not the only endangered species either, Jake knew, for the salty swamp had been peppered with government placed punji stakes, spring loaded spear traps and anti-personnel mines.

Lieutenant Colonel Tu met Jake at the well guarded gate. Tu was accompanied by a burly American dressed as if he were on an African safari. He wore a khaki colored bush jacket, shorts, and a snakeskin banded felt hat. A bright blue scarf was just visible under his full silvery beard, where a few streaks of charcoal revealed the hair color of flamboyant youth. A turkey feather, fastened to the hat band at a rakish angle by a gold police badge, implied that zest and energy had not been left behind by advancing years.

Race Haldane, the National Police advisor, one of the four State Department civilians on Team Two, waved lethargically in greeting. Jake had met him before, when they had been introduced, and he had seemed surly and withdrawn even then. He's making sure I know he doesn't have to salute, Jake thought.

The three men sauntered toward the ugly stockade. Jake's eyes were caught by the highly polished, black pistol belt and waist high holster worn by the civilian. The long barreled .357 Magnum gleamed from its nest.

Haldane spoke first. "We got a Chu Hoi in today Colonel. First one in a long time. I just happened to be here at the stockade this mornin when they brought him in. Otherwise I might not'a heard about it for a week." His deep, booming voice echoed from the walls of the disfigured dungeon.

"What's a Chu Hoi?" asked Jake.

Tu and Haldane both stopped. Their heads swiveled toward him in startled surprise. It's obviously something I should've known, Jake thought. He smiled apologetically and shrugged.

"Sorry to sound stupid," he said. "But I'm still a newby remember?" He looked at his new Sieko watch. "I've only been here a week." He looked up again at them. "A week today as a matter of fact."

Tu bowed in apology. "I regret my surprise Troom Ta Thorpe. You have assimilated into our province so quickly and are already so knowledgeable in our ways, I forget that you have been here such a short time."

Race Haldane opened his mouth to speak, perhaps to also apologize, but perhaps not. Jake had heard of Haldane's reputation, that he normally didn't care whether he embarrassed anyone or not, and that he disliked anything military. Tu continued speaking:

"Chu Hoi means open arms. It is a government program which encourages the enemy to defect to our side. We drop many leaflets throughout the jungle, even on the Ho Chi Minh trail in Cambodia and Laos. We also distribute them throughout the cities and villages. The leaflets proclaim that if any enemy rallies to our side, we will welcome them with chu hoi."

"Good idea," agreed Jake. "We should have had it when I was here before. When our guys captured one of the bad guys back then, they usually didn't give him much of a chance to switch sides. When a real flesh and blood enemy fell into the hands of my district militia, they just vented their frustrations on him. Or her," he added as an afterthought.

"Hasn't changed none Colonel." Haldane interjected. Callously indifferent to Tu's race or rank. He went on. "That's why we don't get many Chu Hois. Some poor VC snuffy gets his belly fulla duckin arclights, napalm and artillery shells, so he gives up and walks into some village with his arms raised and a smile on his puss, holdin a God Damned chu hoi pass over his head like it's a ticket to the fuckin world series, and what happens? The ruff puffs shoot him down like a mad dog; or, if some miracle happens and he gets back here to the stockade with only a few lumps on his head, like this one today, the NPFF usually finish him off. Shit, the National Police Field Forces are just as tough on the chu hois as they are on a captured sapper." He paused, glaring challengingly at Tu in unmasked accusation.

Still looking at Jake, Tu corrected Haldane tonelessly: "An enemy who participates in the Chu Hoi program is properly called a Hoi Chanh. Unfortunately, however, your police advisor is more accurate than not. We Vietnamese of the Republic did not start this war. We did not want this war. The Communists have brought it to us.

There is no one in South Vietnam who has not lost a family member; perhaps many relatives and many friends.

Modern warfare with rifles, bombs and artillery, often gives us victory in battles. But the victories are somehow empty, as we hardly ever see our enemies die. They are usually already dead when we do see them. The only people we watch die are loved ones and comrades-in-arms. The need for revenge is still inside.

We who are leaders, the officers and government officials; we recognize, as we plan our future course, that we must not only win the war, but we must also turn the thoughts of all who have been swayed by enemy propaganda. Americans call it 'win them over,' and 'winning their hearts and minds.' We leaders understand this, but these words are latrine jokes to our soldiers."

Tu's voice was hoarse, but it was far from toneless now. "We leaders understand that peace will not come until the people of the south are united, but our men fight only for a little personal freedom and much vengeance. We officers sometimes fall victim to the same emotion, and therefore understand why our men do as they do.

I, myself, when I was a dai wi, a captain, once lost my control, and allowed my hatred, anger and frustration to come forth. I shot a terrorist who had just thrown a satchel charge into the sleeping quarters of my men. I shot him as he was kneeling at my feet begging for his life. I shot him for my men who were dead by his hand, and I shot him for my mother and my uncle. I was thinking of them when I pulled the trigger."

Tu paused and lit a cigarette with slightly trembling hands. He exhaled a burst of smoke as an exclamation point to his memories. He continued:

"But we who are the leaders, must work harder to educate our people. We must teach them why the Chu Hoi program must be allowed to work. Winning the war must take priority over personal hatred."

Race Haldane's eyes had burned into Tu's face when the Deputy Province Chief had begun his monologue, but as the explanation registered, Haldane's expression softened in sympathy and understanding.

"I never thought about it like that Colonel. I guess I just thought no one knew what they were doing. I just figured all the Vietnamese were alike, just naturally mean. I didn't see much difference between the VC assinatin a government village chief and our guys kickin hell outta some Chu Hoi."

Tu relaxed and focused on Haldane's rugged face. "I cannot defend the VC's motives Mr. Haldane, and I will agree that a single life is not valued as highly in the Orient as it seems to be in what you call Western Civilization. But if we were all just naturally mean, as you say, we would be better soldiers. As you may know, our major problem is to teach young men that they must fight. If we were savage, and therefore better soldiers, we would not need American advisors."

Tu chuckled with glee at what he apparently thought was a joke he had made. Jake and Race glanced at each other in confusion and laughed also, but their's was a forced laugh. The tension was broken, however, and they all relaxed.

"Well, anyway," Haldane announced, "let's go talk to our new boy. I got him separated in a private cell, and I told the warden I'd do to him anything that was done to the prisoner, so I doubt if he's any worse'n when he came in."

The three marched off again toward the ominous, menacing prison. Jake noticed that there were windows in the grotesque structure after all. Two of them. Both barred, one on either side of the black double doorway. They were like evil eyes on either side of a trap about to be sprung. From this viewpoint, the stockade resembled a great, lurking toad.

With an apprehensive and involuntary shudder, Jake entered the now gaping jaws of the stockade with the others. An NPFF captain, with one sleeve of his white shirt hanging empty, jumped to his feet and saluted. Tu gave him a curt command in Vietnamese, and the young officer led the way down a dimly lit corridor. The air reeked with the stench of sweat, vomit, urine and human feces.

Race, who walked with his hands ponderously swinging at his hips, smiled. "The perfume of the Orient." He took a deep breath. "Not bad today; usually smells fishier. They don't have no johns in the cells, don't even allow none of um to go outside to piss or shit! About once a week or so, if they think about it, they give each prisoner a bucket a cold water and a broom, but some of um are too weak or broken spirited to use um. Guards don't care if they clean their cells or not, no skin off their ass. Smell don't seem to bother them none."

They turned a corner and began to pass rows of cells.

Haggard, tired eyes followed them. One occupant per closet sized cell. Each had a thin, rough sleeping pad occupying over half the floor space. Most were dressed in filthy, shredded black pajamas, but some wore only a white loincloth, or something that evidently used to be white. Grime smudged their faces. Their fingernails, as they clutched the bars for balance, were long and caked with dirt.

"We don't treat child rapists this way," Race grumbled. "They're worse off than caged animals. I couldn't live like this. I'd die first. I'd just will myself to die, any American would."

"No you wouldn't," corrected Jake. "Americans are no different. Man is an adaptive animal." He saw Race turn his head in disbelief but continued. "I think people are the same everywhere, and people tend to find a way to survive regardless of the conditions; whether it's in a jungle, a ghetto, a desert or an unsanitary prison."

Jake glanced into the cells they were passing. The lifeless eyes which peered back; the slumped, stooped shoulders; the brownish yellow teeth behind cracked lips; and the absolute absence of hope, silently denounced his philosophy.

The Hoi Chanh sat sullenly in the corner of his cell, his arms folded across the tops of his knees, his eyes staring into space. He wore canvas footwear, the olive drab uniform of the NVA, a still bleeding cut somewhere above his hair line and a huge purple mouse on one cheekbone.

The one armed police captain turned the lock of the cell door with a key from a large jangling ring of siblings, and, with the metallic grating of unoiled hinges, swung the jail door open.

The defector did not look up, but Jake noticed him take a deep breath, of hope perhaps; or maybe only of stoic acceptance of whatever was to come.

Jake, Race and Tu filed into the cell, which, because of its small size, forced them to stand in a semi circle, looming over the huddled mass who was once an enemy soldier.

The police captain remained in the hallway. He started to swing the cell door closed behind them, but Tu barked at him in sharp toned Vietnamese, and it remained ajar.

Tu squatted flat footed in front of the prisoner and spoke softly in their native tongue. The Hoi Chanh did not respond.

Tu glanced up at the Americans. "I have tried to reassure him that he is now safe and will no longer be beaten." The tone of his voice showed disappointment. "But it is obvious that we are already too late; he does not believe me."

Race Haldane laughed. "Hell, I wouldn't neither. He rallies to our side expectin to be treated like a lost brother, 'n the first ones who see him beat the shit outta him 'n throw him into this hell hole. An hour later, a smooth talkin brass shows up with two long noses and says you can trust us, cause we're the good guys."

Tu's eyes became thin horizontal lines and his voice revealed the strain of anger control as he replied "And do you, Mr. Haldane, have a suggestion as to how we might loosen his tongue and gain his trust?"

"Sure I do," Race boomed combatively, "but you won't do it."

"Tell me."

"Let him go! Let's take 'im out for some breakfast. Let's take care a his face and give 'im a bath. Hell. We didn't capture him, he defected. He came over willingly. But you're still treatin him like a God Damned POW!"

"There are documented cases, Mr. Haldane, of Chu Hoi ralliers who have claimed to know the location of ammunition dumps or rice caches only to lead their escorts into an ambush. We must treat him in a friendly manner, but we must remember that he may only be an enemy acting under orders."

"Well Colonel, that's not what your Chu Hoi passes say. They say come on over. You'll be one of us. We'll welcome you with open arms as a hero. They don't say come on over and we'll give you a nice rotten jail cell and we promise not to beat you after the first day."

The two fell silent. Both looked to Jake for support of their particular viewpoints. Jake thought of relieving the tension with a joke. Maybe he'd suggest that they flip a coin or something, but he realized neither was in a mood for humor. He recognized the validity of Tu's argument and knew that as the Deputy Province Chief, Tu's primary responsibilities included the security and safety of the people of Quang Tin.

Yet he also knew that Race was correct. Supposedly there's an NVA regiment in the province, and here's an NVA soldier, in our hands willingly. One plus one equals two. This guy has to know where they are and probably when and where they're going to hit us.

Jake inclined his head toward Tu. "Troom Ta Tu, forgive me, but I believe the civilian is right. The soldier will not talk to us here in this jail cell. He has no reason to trust us. Let's take a shot at true hospitality. We've got to learn where his unit is and what it's up to.

"What if he escapes?" Tu asked, still squatting.

"Well, we'll try to not let that happen. After all, we're armed and he isn't. I also think the rewards of success against the penalties for failure put the odds in our favor. If he escapes, it'll mean the enemy strength has gone up by only one man."

"One man who will probably see much of our defenses, our weapons and our procedures. Such information would be highly prized by an attacking force." Tu stated this almost off handedly, totally preoccupied with his thoughts, staring into the cell wall for some moments. The others waited. Finally he turned upward again and caught Jake's eyes with his own in a calm, steady, deadly gaze. "You Troom Ta Thorpe, must accept total responsibility for his actions and his security. I will be your interpreter and help you as I can. But my hands are clean. If anything goes wrong, it will be on your head."

"I accept the responsibility Troom Ta," Jake replied unblinkingly.

"Fanfuckintastic!" cheered Race. "Lets get this show on the road!"

Tu rose to his feet, hooking the reluctant NVA soldier by his armpits to pull him also to a standing position.

"Tell him where we're going and what we're going to do," Jake dictated to Tu, automatically assuming the mantle of leadership with the yoke of responsibility.

Tu chattered away in a sing-song monologue as they surged down the hallway to the sunlight and to breathable air.

They took him to Camp Kronberg first, to the open air shower facility.

While the Hoi Chanh bathed, the two officers and the bearded civilian watched. They did not observe him for security reasons, for inside the American compound, there was no place for him to run. But they watched with amusement and pathos, as the former jungle creature relished the forgotten luxury of soap and warm water.

Now dressed and looking absurd in a borrowed, but oversized outfit of Race's and a new pair of thongs; the defector looked like a child who was being swallowed by his father's Sunday suit.

At the cupboard sized camp PX, Jake picked up a comb, toothbrush, toothpaste, a stick of deodorant, mosquito repellant, cigarettes, more soap and a few candy bars, which the dazzled newcomer accepted with only a mild expression of pleasure.

Doc Usher, the Team Two medic, who was a junior NCO and certainly not a doctor, was the next stop. Usher was a medic because of his refusal to bear arms rather than because of any penchant or aptitude for medicine, but he spread a dab of greasy astringent over the cut in the injured man's scalp, and gave him a small bag of ice to hold against the purple lump under his eye.

At the kitchen table in Jake's trailer, Haldane and the two officers drank coffee as the hoi chanh received a special midmorning breakfast of soft boiled eggs, bacon and a glob of mashed potatoes left over from last night's supper. There was an awkward moment when he first saw the meal. He and Tu exchanged a few quick phrases which resulted in a dash to the kitchen by Race, who returned with a bottle of nouc mam, the acrid, foul-smelling, fish oil every Vietnamese uses to flavor his food. After the bacon, potatoes and eggs had been drowned in this, the food disappeared quickly.

The four smoked after the meal talking calmly and easily. His name, they learned, was Kor Uz Minh, and he was a combatant, equal to the rank of private. He said he had been sick and separated from his unit. To almost every question, he replied "Da cum bik," which the inquisitors knew to mean "I don't know Sir." All three knew he was lying.

Evidently, a shower and a meal weren't enough, when they only shortly followed a rifle butt to the face.

After an hour, Tu departed to see to provincial matters. As other duties required Jake's attention, Private Minh was finally entrusted to Race Haldane, who voluntarily assumed the triple role of jailer, protector and companion. Race was not fluent in Vietnamese, but he could get by. He was sure that he could win the defector over. During their time together, he made many promises and reassurances.

There were three days of promises and reassurances. Three days of banquet type meals, American cigarettes and warm showers. Three nights of sleeping in an Army canvas cot beside Race Haldane's bed. It even took Race's expensive wristwatch which Minh had admired in an obvious way, before Race admitted defeat, and before Jake conceded that the gamble had been lost.

Wednesday, January tenth, dawned under a gloomy overcast sky. Lieutenant Colonel King was due back from Australia tomorrow. The pink team had still not located any sign of the NVA regiment. An infra-red heat seeking, night flying, "Snifter" helicopter had not located more than a few isolated blips on the dark film representing western Quang Tin. Isolated reports of movement received from the listening posts of Hau Duc and Tien Phouc were both vague and contradictory, but Curly still claimed that an NVA regiment was poised for an attack somewhere near Hau Duc. G2 reports from Da Nang continued to claim that the enemy was preparing for large scale attacks in many areas.

And Private Kor Uz Minh, in the meanwhile, gained weight and remained silent.

When Jake confessed to his counterpart the failure of the friendship ploy, Tu nodded in a more understanding way than Jake had expected.

"It has not failed my friend," Tu began; "Time, as it normally does, has enabled us to find the solution. I have given the matter considerable thought. A plan has occurred to me. Time has allowed me to recognize your overtures of friendship as the key which unfastens the lock. We now only lack a gentle push to open the door."

"And who's going to do the shoving?" Jake's eyebrow arched with a tinge of suspicion.

Tu pushed a handbill, printed in Vietnamese, across his desk toward Jake. "We will circulate this leaflet, and we will tell the defector that we have done so. We will also inform him that he will be released from our custody."

Jake was puzzled. "What does it say?"

Tu picked it up and translated. "It says that an NVA soldier named Kor Uz Minh, from the unit that now hides in the western area of our province, has come over to our side. It is cause for much celebration and congratulations to him for his courageous act; for the information he has given us will save the lives of many South Vietnamese people and will give us much preparation for the coming battle. He is now recognized as a hero and his actions will speed the approach of peace to our land."

"But he hasn't given us any information," Jake stammered.

"The VC legal cadre who read this notice will not know what he has told us and what he has not. The letter speaks of a forthcoming battle, which if planned, is surely considered a secret by our enemies. They will assume that their plans have been compromised. Private Minh will be immediately marked for assassination."

"You mean you're going to bluff, hoping the NVA will change their minds and not attack. And, in the meanwhile, turn poor Minh out, knowing he'll be killed?"

"No, Troom Ta Thorpe, it is easier than that. Private Minh will understand. We are, what you Americans call, burning his bridges behind him. It will eliminate all motivation for him to remain silent. After he reads this letter, and is convinced that we have distributed it, the door will open. He will talk."

That afternoon, Kor Uz Minh, who turned out to be Sergeant Kor Uz Minh, of the Reconnaissance Platoon, of the 21st Independent Regiment of the People's Army of Vietnam, read the leaflet and talked.

Scene 5

IN FRONT OF THE ALTER

1800 Hours
Wednesday, 10 January, 1968

Co Li carefully washed the three stones of the open hearth stove. She could not move or jostle them as their exact positions had been dictated by the soothsayer to appease the spirits at the time the kitchen was constructed. Satisfied that the stones remained undisturbed yet were now spotless, she draped the cloth on the wall hook and inhaled deeply. Her brother wanted to talk to her.

Since her mother had been killed accidentally in a Viet Minh terrorist attack against the French, Co Li had assumed all domestic duties of the household. Because she had been a good student, and had done well on her examinations, she had qualified for the prestigious job of Secretary to the Province Chief of Quang Tin; but that honor, and that job did not mitigate her position as the only female member of the Let household. She had to obey her brother.

Perhaps he knows already, she thought. Ba Nhur might have told someone; if so, he knows too, for news of sex is quick to travel far. If he has not heard, he wishes to berate me for not obeying. If so, I will surprise him with my success. She smiled at this irony, for she knew he would be disappointed with her choice. Nevertheless, she thought, I have done his bidding, he cannot be too upset.

My brother was careful to wait until after our father departed for the municipal council meeting in the city before mentioning that there was to be a talk. Anh Ty takes his role as leader of the people seriously. But he respects our family honor, and he would not want our father to know what I have been asked to do.

She parted the many stringed beaded curtain which hung in the doorway to discourage flies, and entered the parlor. The swaying wooden beads clicked behind her like a hundred crickets. Her brother was kneeling at the altar that dominated the central room of the house. He was completing his family duty of paying daily homage to their ancestors, all of whom were represented by carved tablets. He had already offered to them a small portion of each dish from the evening meal. The bowls nestled on the altar amidst the tablets, candles, photographs and prayer sticks. The burning incense filled the air with the familiar spicy aroma. She waited in respect while he fulfilled the required worship time.

He stood, bowed to their ancestors, and then turned to face her. His tongue moistened his lips. She remembered that he had been very quiet and solemn during the meal. He knows, she thought. She waited for him to speak first.

"In three week's time," he said, "the people will rise up and cast off the chains of the Americans. In three week's time Vietnam will be united as one country." He spoke thoughtfully, calmly. Co Li knew, however, that the forthcoming victory was not the subject her brother wished to talk about. The attack had been planned and discussed for several months, but it was not the way of her people to come directly to the point. Her breath caught in her throat as she waited.

"History will repeat itself," he continued. "One hundred and seventy nine years ago, the illustrious Tay Son led our people to a glorious victory over the Chinese invaders by attacking Hanoi during the holiday period of Tet. Our uprising against the cities throughout the country this time will achieve the same surprise and the same success. Even now the generals of the lackey ARVN forces are granting leave time to their soldiers for the holidays. They look forward to the traditional cease fire as a time of rest. They will be totally unprepared for the attacks."

Co Li nodded. She had heard it all before. She also fervently wanted peace. It was exciting to know that the end was so near; the victory so close.

Ty went on: "We will win! And when our people see that we are victorious in the cities, they will throng to us and welcome us as liberators. The Provisional Revolutionary Government will assume the rightful leadership of the land."

She smiled proudly. She knew he was still skirting the actual subject, but he could always sway her with his passion.

Ty continued, "Our father will be the new Province Chief, and I will become the political leader of Tam Ky City."

"It is an honor you deserve my brother. The people know that you are loyal and fair. You have earned this right, and our father's glory will shine like the sun."

"Yes, my sister, our time is almost here. But the provincial government announced today that a hoi chanh has informed them of our plans and they will now be prepared for the attack. They are so stupid! They should have said nothing. They are probably guessing, thinking that if we are planning an attack, this bluff would cause us to halt it. The militia has not been told to be at strength during Tet. Neither the ARVN nor the Americans have been summoned, and they did not announce that we were planning to violate the holiday peace period, which they surely would have done had they known for sure. The odds are high, therefore, that this is indeed only a bluff. But they have heard something. We have three weeks to alter our timing, our attack routes and even our targets if we learn what they have discovered."

Co Li was puzzled. Perhaps this was what he wanted to talk about. Perhaps he is worried about enemy intelligence.

"But the people have been betrayed. And because of this disloyalty, the entire plan may be in jeopardy. What shall I, as a leader of the people, do about such treachery?"

"But Anh Ty, you do not know who the traitor is. You implied that the government might be lying; perhaps they do not have a hoi chanh."

Ty's eyes grew hard as he looked at her. "Oh, the government named him. I have never heard of him, but it matters not whether he is real, for I do not speak of the hoi chanh. If there is such a cowardly worm, he does not know which of his ends is mouth, and which is rectum; and therefore he is too stupid to know which end to follow for nourishment! No! I speak of one who claims to be a patriot, but refuses to follow the commands of a leader of the people. One who shirks her duties as the obedient thi of her family."

Panic stabbed into Co Li's throat. Shock numbed her frame. Her breath came in short rapid whispers. He is so clever, she thought, catching me by surprise even when I was expecting it. She could feel pain in her jaws as she gritted her teeth.

"I have not been disobedient My Anh." She could hear the tremor in her voice.

"If you had done as I asked; if you had used the ways of a woman on that pig you work for each day, you would have him drooling over your body by now. We would have the information about the hoi chanh. But you balk at the task. You have been disloyal to the people of Viet Nam."

Co Li squared her shoulders. The shock was over. This was the argument she had expected. This was the scene she had rehearsed. "You did not say it had to be the Dai Ta, my brother, he is too old and fat."

"What difference does that make woman! I do not ask you to marry him. Merely to seduce him. A man such as he, with no self discipline, would be easy prey for you with your youth and beauty."

"But Anh Ty, you said I could pick an American."

"Of course I did. An American would be even better, for they are the true power in South Vietnam. Biet and the Republic are only puppets of the colonial powers. But you surely would want a Vietnamese rather than a long nose. Even an old man like Biet would be preferable."

"If an American would be best, then you may rest easy my brother, for I have selected one of those."

Ty gazed at her for a long minute. The flicker of a smile touched the corners of his mouth. He sat down on the polished bench against the wall and lit a cigarette. "So who is it to be?" he asked. "The new Troom Ta who pretends to know our ways? The major with the brown stained teeth? I would like to hear your choice, and then your plan to lure him to your bed."

"I have already been to bed with him my brother."

Ty's eyes brightened. "You have? I am surprised, my sister. I apologize for my hasty words of before. You are indeed a daughter of the people. You are truly a dutiful soldier to our cause."

Co Li hung her head to avoid looking into his eyes. "Thank you my anh."

"Well who is it?"

Taking a deep breath, she raised her head. "Anh Ty, I have done as you requested. I have offered my body in the service of our country. But I cannot be proud of what I have done; of what I am doing. I sacrifice my scruples for the cause that is greater, but I feel the loss of my honor and the rent in my reputation. Must I announce aloud the name of the enemy who has besmirched me?"

Her brother's eyes narrowed. "You are doing this thing for your country; and because I have asked it of you. There is no dishonor. Who is he?"

She lowered her eyes again. A knot of anxiety churned in her stomach. Why am I so troubled? she thought. I did as he asked. "His name is Fellogese," she said. "He works in the command bunker."

"A name so unpronounceable I would remember; I have not heard of him. What is his rank, a captain?"

"He is a sergeant, Anh Ty."

"A sergeant! By grandfather's ghost, why a sergeant? You could have had anyone you wanted, and you chose a sergeant?"

"He was nice to me Anh Ty."

Ty jumped up from the bench and faced her. "Nice to you? Nice to you? I wanted you to seduce someone for information, someone important who knows what is happening. I give you a job to do, and you pick a buffalo dung sergeant because he was nice to you? By all the spirits in Hell woman, is your brain made of rotting fish?"

"He works in the command center, Anh Ty. And a sergeant is not so lowly."

Ty wheeled about and walked to the alter. He stared at the flickering candles with his hands stuffed into his pockets. Without turning, he spoke again. "What is the real reason you chose this sergeant of yours; what's his name again?"

"Fellogese, Anh Ty. Sergeant Mark Fellogese. I chose him because you told me to have sex with an American. He was—there."

He turned to look at her. "I asked you to do this over a month ago, you have seen many Americans since then. Do not try to tell me you jumped at the first opportunity. Tell me the truth, why him?"

Her stomach tightened again. It was going to be even more difficult than she thought. "He is different from the others, Anh Ty."

"How is he different?"

"I don't really know; he was—nice to me."

"Are you attracted to this sergeant with the long name?"

Li started to nod her head affirmatively, but caught herself. "Of course not Anh Ty, he is an American. But—well, he is different."

"You *are* attracted to him then?" Ty was triumphant. His jaw thrust forward fiercely. He had seen her hesitation.

Tears leaped into her eyes. "You were the one who asked me to sleep with one of them." She stamped her foot on the planked floor. She could hear herself screaming. "How could I do that with any credibility at all if I did not at least like the one I chose? I am not a common whore who can pretend to love whoever gives her money. You told me to do it! You are my brother and I am a patriot, so I had to do as I was told. I have done it. I will continue to do it as you would require. But if I must lie next to a naked man and allow that man to enter my body, I will be the one to choose who that man will be!"

Ty shook his head sadly. "I have heard our father truthfully say that, in this matter, the French occupation has done our culture the most harm. Before them, there was no talk of necessary emotion for a woman to lie with a man. There was only marriage, family and duty. But the French told our women about a myth called love. Now all women expect to swoon and feel a fluttering heart, as if they had too much wine, before they have sex or become a wife. Phoo! You are caught up in that foolish fantasy. The old ways are better. In the rural areas many parents still choose the best wife for their son."

"I did not swoon nor feel a fluttering heart, my brother." Co Li was again in control of her emotions. "Nor do I expect to. It is merely a matter of practicality. If I am to play well the part of a lover, I must pretend to love. I cannot do this if the man I lie next to is a detestable pig."

"Can I assume therefore, that the time you spent in his bed was not an unpleasant experience?"

The knot in her stomach twisted and hardened. She knew he would see through a lie. "Anh Ty, when a feather brushes my arm, I cannot stop the tickle I would feel it even if I hated the goose from which it was plucked. The sensations I experienced with the American had nothing to do with the duty which caused me to experience them."

"Perhaps not," Ty grinned sarcastically as he snuffed his cigarette in a blue ceramic bowl. "But by your own admission, they would have been different if you had been with a detestable pig."

Li folded her arms across her chest. "You are implying that I have romantic feelings for this American." She inhaled deeply. She hated to say the next words, but it was the only thing that would convince him. She felt somehow that she was betraying Sergeant Mark. Don't be silly, she said to herself, it is true so say it. "That is absurd. He is an enemy!" she said aloud.

"An enemy who is different."

"Yes. So what?"

"An enemy who is not a detestable pig."

"No he isn't. So what?"

"A sergeant who probably doesn't know anything about American decisions in the war."

"He might, I haven't asked him yet."

They glared at each other, and then he relaxed, a little of the old affection returning to his eyes. "You should hear yourself. You have chosen a man for the purpose of espionage, yet your qualifications for this choice had nothing to do with this purpose. Don't you see how ridiculous it sounds?"

"Anh Ty, you keep forgetting that he works in the command center. He surely knows some secrets."

"I doubt if he knows anything. I should order you to stop seeing this sergeant and select an officer as your target." He paused and looked into her eyes. "But I cannot stop the rain. I cannot forbid the wind to come. I have authority, but I know the spirit of my sister. Independence is in the blood of our people, but it is in you more perversely than most. What am I to do with you?"

"I will not sleep with any of the others!" "None of them! They are pigs. They are worse than pigs! You can't make me do it." She said it emphatically, but it sounded to her as if she were whining. She knew she had won. Why was she so upset?

Ty lit another cigarette and paused as he exhaled the smoke in a long stream. "I must ask you one question. Are you still one of us?"

"Of course I am. I am still of this family my anh; I still wish the union of our people and the independence of our country." Her voice was steady and resolute now.

"Then prove it little sister of the people!" He leaned his suddenly hard face within inches of hers. His voice growled from his throat like a panther. "He must know some things which might be of interest. I order you now to discover information that will help our people. I challenge you to change my low opinion of your judgement. If you must be more woman than soldier, then be a woman who works effectively for our cause. This is the only way to atone for your silliness. I speak as your leader, not as your brother. Do you understand me?"

Co Li nodded stiffly. Fear clutched at her throat. She could not speak. Her brother had never shouted at her before. She had never seen him so fierce.

Ty wheeled about and relaxed. He again seemed to be addressing the alter. "In the meanwhile, I will say to the comrades that you do this reluctantly at my command. I will claim that you are a hero to our cause. This will stop any evil rumors. But we must not tell father. He would wither and die to learn of your conduct even if we both told him that you did it as an obedient servant to our cause, for I'm not sure either of us could be convincing."

Li bowed low to her brother. "Thank you my anh, as ever, you prove you are wise as well as loyal."

He looked at her with sorrow. "I will always be loyal to our family as I am loyal to our country. I do not feel wise in my acceptance of your lack of judgement. But when the river cannot be damned, we make it turn the wheel. Tet comes soon. The Vietnamese year 4605. It will be the year of the monkey, and the element for the new year is earth. The monkey is clever and quick; the earth must return to its rightful owners. Bring me information from your sergeant. I need to know what they have discovered from this hoi chanh traitor, if anything; so that this sham government may die with the year of the goat."

"I will try my anh. You have made me happy."

Ty raised an eyebrow. "So I have made you happy by allowing you to continue with your sergeant?" He shook his head sadly. "Well, no matter. It is a temporary happiness. Three weeks only. If it were longer, I would tell father myself. When the year of the goat dies, this relationship, regardless of how you actually feel, must also die, in one way or another." His tone was ominous, almost threatening.

"Yes my anh," she said, and she knew he spoke the truth.

Ty turned and stalked from the house, leaving Li to ponder other truths. Facts about her feelings, which they both had just discovered.

SCENE 6

THE CONFERENCE ROOM

1800 Hours
Wednesday, 10 January, 1968

Kor Uz Minh, decked out in blue jeans and a colorful California style, short sleeved shirt, sat in the arm chair at the head of the polished conference table as if the meeting had been called at his beckoning. He held his head erect and his ebony eyes were clear. The bruise on his face had mellowed to a mild light blue. Race Haldane's gold watch glittered from his wrist. Jake marveled, for the former NVA soldier in no way resembled the vanquished hulk of three days before.

Jake and Haldane sat on one side of the long table, Lieutenant Colonel Tu on the other. Tu studiously flipped through a stack of papers. Race Haldane scratched his chin through his mottled gray beard. A bead of sweat dripped into his eye and he pawed at it angrily.

Jake felt an air of expectancy hanging over the room like a ticking bomb. He lit a cigarette, causing a chain reaction as the other three were reminded of their own nicotine needs. Pockets rustled, match heads scraped, fingers flicked metal cogs against flint, everyone inhaled in turn; and the room cloaked itself with slowly drifting haze.

Race leaned toward Jake with an absurdly loud attempt at a whisper: "He's ready to talk, Colonel, but only to the three of us first. He says he'll talk to the military intelligence types later, as much as we want, but there's somethun he wants only us to hear first." His stage whisper reverberated around the room like a foghorn.

Jake nodded. "Well let's start by finding out where the Hell that regiment is. Would you ask him that Troom Ta?"

Tu curtly asked the question in Vietnamese, pointing to the large province map embed-ded behind clear plexiglass at the far end of the room.

As Minh answered, Jake watched his face intently for signs of evasion or deception. This time, Jake was convinced he spoke the truth.

Tu translated the answer. "He doesn't know. They move almost every night. There are many tunnel systems in the jungle which have been constructed by the local VC. These systems are about three or four miles apart, and he doesn't know how many there are. They move either at dusk or at dawn from one to another. It appears that their regimental political officer believes that you Americans have airplanes which can smell exposed skin and detect even the slightest movement. For this reason, they move quickly and remain in the tunnels the rest of the day. They do not stay in one location for fear a traitor will reveal where they are."

Jake and Race exchanged glances. Tu went on:

"He says the morale is getting lower each day as the tunnels are unbearable. The tunnels are not made for permanent occupancy. They are merely holes in the ground. It is cooler than outside, but mud, beetles, spiders and snakes cause them much discomfort. The inside latrines fill up quickly, and they are beaten if they so much as stick their faces outside for a breath of fresh air."

Jake clasped his hands together, making a steeple with his index fingers. He rested his chin on this structure thoughtfully. So that's why we haven't spotted them, he thought. They've got poor information but because of it, they're doing the right things. We'll never spot them from the air, and the IR birds, which fly at night, won't pick up anything either. The only time they move is when our listening posts are changing shifts.

While Jake pondered, Tu peppered Minh with more questions.

Then he turned to the two Americans. "His unit is the 21st Independent NVA Regiment. In October and early November it was in action near Dak To. They were evidently mauled quite badly, especially by artillery and B-52 strikes. They withdrew to a base camp in Laos, where they received resupply and replacements to full strength. A new colonel assumed command of the regiment there and, according to Minh, was eager to prove his combat mettle, so they departed the safe area three weeks earlier than required. The regimental political officer first objected that the early arrival in the attack zone would give away their offensive intentions, but later agreed that the new anti-detection tactics should be tested."

Jake interjected: "Was Minh at Dak To, or did he join the unit as a replacement?"

Jake watched Minh again as the question was translated. Minh began his answer calmly, but a look of fear, then terror crossed his features. His voice was animated and his hands gestured wildly. When he finished, his hands still trembled.

"He is a veteran of the Dak To action. He describes it as a total defeat. He says they were constantly on the defensive. The officers of their unit were demoralized by the swiftness with which the Americans reacted to their every movement. He says that, at first, they suspected spies with radios in their own ranks. He uses a word which I do not think has an equivalent in English. It means to be frightened by supernatural causes. The closest word I can think of is eerie or uncanny perhaps. He felt it was foolish to leave base camp early and chance the same fate just to test a new avoidance technique."

"Why'd he go along then?" asked Race. "Why didn't he just chu hoi right off the bat?"

Tu asked the question, and this time, Minh ducked his head and stared at his reflection in the polished surface of the table as he answered. Jake and Race exchanged glances. Here it comes, Jake thought, a bald faced lie! No way is this news to be believed. He wondered if that was what Race thought also.

Tu translated the reply: "He says there were four reasons. First, he is a soldier, and a soldier does what he is told. Second, even though he was skeptical, the new tactic might actually work. If the Americans could not detect them, his fear would be for nothing. The third reason he gives is, I think the most important for us to consider: He says that they were told that the battle they were to fight would be the last battle of the war. They were promised that, after this battle, the war would end and the Americans would go away!"

Tu paused, looking at the two Americans, evidently making sure they understood the importance of what he had just said.

Jake did, but he remembered the way Minh had answered. This was merely the lie I detected, he thought.

"What was the fourth reason?" he asked.

"Before I give you this answer, I think I should remind you that I am acting at this point as an interpreter only. I am trying to convey his exact words when I can, although I might sometimes shorten his response to save time."

"I know that Troom Ta," Jake said. "I won't hold his answers against you."

Tu nodded. "I have had many unpleasant experiences in the past when acting as a translator. Many Americans tend to be suspicious when they do not understand what is being said. They forget that we are fighting on the same side, for the same goals. They feel that I will somehow mistranslate either the question or the response in order to mislead them. The French were the same. The point I must be certain you understand is that we are allies. The enemy, or at least the former enemy is at the head of the table."

"Oh, for Christ's sake Colonel, we're not that stupid," Haldane blurted. "Besides," he grinned proudly at Jake, "my Vietnamese ain't perfect but I heard what he said too. I don't believe it, but I was able to follow most'a it."

Tu nodded, smiled, and inhaled deeply. "The fourth reason he gives is that he was and to some extent still is a believer in the cause for which he was fighting. He hated all Americans and felt he must do everything, even lose his life if necessary, to rid his motherland from the boot heels of your colonial forces." Tu's lips twitched as if he were suppressing a smile as he continued. "He does say he has altered his opinion somewhat after making Mr. Haldane's acquaintance."

"Shit! I shouldn'a givin him that fuckin watch, that's for sure," Race snorted.

Jake lit another cigarette, his thoughts whirling. That might be why Minh acted so guilty. Telling us to out faces that he hated us, perhaps still hates us, even after we treated him so well. Hell, I'd duck my head too if I said that in this room. The Vietnamese don't like to look at anyone directly in the eyes anyway. God! If he is a liar, he's the best I've ever seen.

"What do you think?" He asked Tu. "Is he lying or is he telling the truth?"

"He's lyin through his fuckin teeth!" Race broke in. "He never acted like no Commie while he stayed with me. He was either connin me then or lyin to all of us now. I say it's now."

"Perhaps," said Tu, with an air of superior knowledge. There are a few inconsistences I have noticed, but I will await my turn. I suggest we hear him out before we challenge details or form opinions."

Jake nodded and relaxed. "Ask him what the political officer meant about this being the last battle. And then ask him why he believed him."

The question was asked and answered at length. Finally, Tu turned and spoke in English. "He says that all the political officers at every level: regiment, battalion, company and platoon are saying the same thing. America is already losing the war. It has agreed to a bombing halt in North Vietnam and has even agreed to meet for peace talks in Paris. They say that these facts show that America does not have the strategic staying power to maintain the war. 'If they are not losing,' the political officers say, 'then why else would America make these concessions?'"

Tu bobbed his head in a nervous, almost continual series of genu-flections as he repeated the hoi chanh's comments. Jake recognized the meaning. My God, he thought, Tu thinks the same thing those NVA political officers do. I'm going to have to talk with him; assure him that we're here to stay; that we've made a commitment.

Tu continued: "Additionally, he says that the political officers explained what happened at Dak To. They claimed that the 21st and two other NVA regiments had gone there not to fight, but as a feint to draw the Americans away from the populated cities. He says that as the result of that feint and others like it, all American units are now widely scattered throughout the jungles of South Vietnam and away from the populated cities."

Tu paused, apparently remembering something. "I might also men-tion that he, himself is doubtful of this explanation. He confessed to me that he and some of the other Dak To survivors sometimes joked to themselves, when they were out of the hearing of the political officers, that if they lost so many men in a sham battle, when they were supposed to be avoiding combat, how many more would they lose in a real fight with the Americans? However, he also claims that the persistence of the political officers' arguments was convinc-ing. He says that even the veterans of his unit began to believe them totally, and their success in avoiding detection while this time in the jungle gave credibility to the claims."

Tu swallowed and licked his lips. Taking a deep breath, he began again. "He says the main attack is planned for the time of Tet, during the traditional holiday cease fire. The political officers said that the ARVN and militia units would rise up and join the revolutionary movement along with all of what they call the enslaved people of South Vietnam."

Tu's voice dripped with sarcasm and scorn as he parroted these words. He was smiling, but he did not appear to be amused.

"The political officers said the NVA soldiers will be welcomed, sheltered and supported by the people as soon as the combat is completed and they have control of the villages and cities. They feel that the American advisors will provide the only real resistance, but since they will be outnumbered thirty to one by the NVA. Victory will be certain. I really do believe that he thinks it will be the final battle of the war."

"Well, then let's hear it," said Jake. "What's the target that's going to win them the war?"

Tu nodded his agreement as to the appropriateness of the question and fired a salvo of rapid-fire Vietnamese. Minh answered them all, some in great length, some with only a few words. Tu jotted notes in a scrawl on the pad in front of him. Jake was aware of a clock ticking somewhere nearby and of Race's exhaled explosions of emotion which indicated that he was understanding all or parts of what was being said. Jake felt isolated. He was the only one in the room who didn't know what was going on. His knee itched. He scratched it. His mouth was dry. He glanced around the room. No coffee and no water. He lit another cigarette and smoked it. He lit another. This one was half consumed by the time Tu turned toward him.

"He has given me a detailed plan of attack, which I will share with you later. The main local targets are Province Headquarters and your American camp here in Tam Ky. The 123rd VC Cadre Battalion is to attack, Tang Binh. There will be a small diversionary attack against the American base at Chu Lai to ensure that the forces there do not reinforce us here in the city."

Jake swallowed hard and nodded. That solves that problem, he thought. We thought the reports were contradictory when some said we were facing an NVA regiment and some said a VC main line unit. Now we know. They're both out there!

Tu continued: "All units which are to attack South Vietnamese targets have been issued, what do you call them? Machines that make the voice more loud?"

"Voice amplifiers," said Jake.

"Bullhorns," said Race.

"Yes, those," Tu said, his eyes shifting back and forth between the two. "Their political officers have been very persuasive. I feel that he really believes most South Vietnamese will rally to their cause when asked to do so by these machines."

Do you think there's any chance of that?" Jake asked. "Even if only twenty-five percent did, it would mean a major victory for them. You know your people better than we do Troom Ta. Is there any basis for their belief?"

Tu gave a glottal cough followed by a lip flapping "hummphhh" of out-rushing air. "Impossible! It is pure propaganda to pump up their courage. The entire story is pure nonsense."

He set his ball point pen down carefully and interlaced the fingers of both hands into a ball over his notepad. "You will pardon my interruption of this interrogation please Colonel Thorpe, but you seem to be taking this man's story far too seriously. The prisoner seems sincere, I admit this. If his story were believable, even I would be tempted to feel he is speaking truthfully. But this is not so. His information is—, what is the word? Far fetched I think. Yes, far fetched. Stretched too far. There are too many inconsistences do you see?"

"Not yet, Troom Ta, but I'd like to hear them."

"He's a chu hoi rallier, not a prisoner," Race blurted.

Tu went on without even looking at Race. "First of all, he claims to be from the north, but he speaks with a South Vietnamese dialect. In fact, he speaks with a local dialect. He does not even attempt to disguise it. He is from Quang Tin Province!"

"Well, well, well!" Jake sighed. He was relieved, yet not as relieved as he wanted to be. The story somehow still had the ring of truth. "That does seem to throw a bit of cold water on the fire. What else?"

"Second, it is absurd to think that the people of the south think favorably toward the Communist revolution. We fight for freedom, not further enslavement. That is what this war is all about."

"OK, I'll accept that. It certainly has always seemed that way to me. What else?"

"Third, how could he or any Moscow trained political officer think that this battle he speaks of will win the war for the north? Tam Ky is such a small city. Quang Tin is such an unimportant province. Why would the seizure of this entire province, even if it one hundred percent effective, win the war for them?"

"Yes, I have to admit that that crossed my mind also. Have you asked him about any of these?"

"Not yet," said Tu, glancing with hostility at Minh. "I have been waiting to see what other lies he tells to trap himself even more."

"Ask him your last question first. Ask him about winning the war. I'd like to hear that first."

Tu nodded and aimed a blast of staccato Vietnamese at Minh.

Minh answered without hesitation while Tu took rapid notes.

"It is too preposterous to be believed," Tu reported. "He says that at the time of Tet, there will be battles in almost *every city in South Vietnam!* He includes Hue and Saigon! He says it will be the first time all South Vietnamese legal VC cadre will be called to mobilization at the same time. Our battle here in this province is supposedly only a small bite of the elephant. He says all of the Laos and Cambodian base camps will be emptied of reserves and fighting troops. This is not to be one battle, but many at the same time. He says thousands, but of course that could not be true."

"You do know, Troom Ta, that American intelligence has been predicting some kind of general offensive on a major scale, perhaps nation-wide, around the time of Tet?" Jake asked.

Yes, the South Vietnamese intelligence also. But every city? This is too massive to be believed."

"Perhaps, but it does explain why he believes it's going to be the one that turns the tide. The final battle of the war."

Tu nodded and broke into more Vietnamese questions. Minh still seemed, to Jake's eyes, sincere.

"I have asked him what his orders were after the battle. What they were to do after overrunning our positions." Jake nodded his appreciation of a well timed query.

"He says there were no withdrawal orders. His unit is to regroup and dispatch any pockets of resistance and then assemble in the city of Tam Ky. The city itself is to be spared, as it is expected that all the people will seize the opportunity to throw off the American chains and join them in victory." Tu could not resist a disgusted shake of his head before going on.

"By mixing with the happy, liberated people in the city, the unit gains three objectives. They consolidate the psychological advantage obtained in the victory. They eliminate all civilians who are known or acknowledged American sympathizers, and they effectively mask the regiment from retaliation as it is well understood by all that Americans will not attack with artillery or air power when civilians are in the target area. His unit is to remain in Tam Ky until the end of the war has been announced, which, so he has been told, should be only a matter of a few days or perhaps a few hours. Since literally every other city in South Vietnam is supposed to be occupied in the same manner, the American units will not come out of the jungle to attack. They will recognize the hopelessness of the effort and sue for peace. They will go home."

Jake noticed a change in Tu's posture. He didn't seem to be as angry. That answer hit home, Jake thought. An attack with no withdrawal plan really does sound like they expect to win. Even Tu's beginning to believe Minh now.

"Well I wanna know what's ta happen in the other districts: Ly Tin, Tien Phouc and How Duc," Race rumbled. "That's almost half the population of the whole province, but they're not attackin those cities. Whatta they gonna do just ignore um and expect um to surrender without a shot fired? Ask him that."

Tu's face indicated his irritation at the lack of respect which the underling American should have shown, but he translated the question without a side comment. His shoulders sagged as he listened to the answer. He turned and responded directly to Race. Tu's face was expressionless, but his voice carried the sound of death.

"He says there is no need for regular forces to attack these districts. The revolutionary governments already control the people. There will simply be a quiet coup on new year's eve. The few loyalist troops who might foolishly try to resist, and all American advisors will be assassinated."

Jake, Tu and Race all exchanged meaningful, worried glances. This answer was the only one that could have made sense of the total concentration of power elsewhere. Jake remembered his trip around the province and Curly's words of warning in regard to the other districts. Of everything they had heard so far in this meeting, this was the most frightening, because if it were true, or even half true, the province of Quang Tin was lost. Even if they were able to somehow defend Tam Ky against the planned attack, they were still beaten if three of the four districts needed no attack to fall. And the horror was, it might be true. Even Tu thinks so!

Act 3

SCENE 1

THE CONFERENCE ROOM

1930 Hours
Wednesday, 10 January, 1968

Jake sat in stunned silence. *Are the Viet Cong so strong in three of Quang Tin's five districts that they can take over the local government, overrun the militia forces and kill all the American advisors without any outside help? If so, we've lost this province already. We've just been kidding ourselves that we're being effective over here!* He saw Race shudder involuntarily. Tu was trying to swallow, but he seemed to lack the necessary saliva.

The NVA are going to attack Tam Ky and Tang Binh. Unless we can get a large American or ARVN unit in here to help, all our provincial military forces will have to be in those two places to meet these attacks. Ly Tin, Tien Phouc and Hau Duc must stand alone, undefended except for their own territorial units and advisors. He glanced at the hoi chanh sitting at the head of the table. *At least that's what this guy says.*

The former NVA sergeant's composure was totally intact. *Is his story true, or is it a titanic misinformation attempt?*

Jake decided to find out. He looked at Tu. "Ask him why he defected if he feels so certain of victory for the NVA."

Minh pulled another cigarette from his neon colored shirt and lit it as he listened to the question in Vietnamese. He looked at the ceiling and blew a long stemmed mushroom of smoke toward the ceiling. His eyes revealed sadness and his voice choked as he gave a lengthy answer. Tu nodded but paused before translating.

Race couldn't wait. "I didn't get that Colonel. Wha'd he say?"

Tu glanced at Haldane and then back to Minh as he answered. "He says his family was originally from here, from the district of Tien Phouc actually. His father was a senior Viet Minh officer. When he was twelve, they moved north to Hanoi in 1954 with the temporary peace accords, because his father did not trust the French to leave as they promised. His father has since died of a lung disease in a poorly equipped hospital in the north. His mother begs for food in the streets of Hanoi.

Four days ago, he and his platoon crept out of the jungle at night to plan the various attack routes. As he passed through Phouc Loc, his childhood village, he was challenged by a member of the hamlet PSDF security. Through Minh's superior training, he was able to overpower the youth and kill him before the young sentry could sound the alarm. In searching his pockets for information and valuables, he found that he had killed his own cousin.

Later that night, his squad met with the VC District Chief to coordinate plans. That leader boasted of his ability to rise out of his undercover role and assume total control of the district. He did not recognize Minh, but Minh remembered him as a person whom his father despised as a coward during the anti-French war. The shadow government VC leader stated that several loyalist traiters would be executed as soon as he assumed control of the district. He named some of them. Many were Minh's relatives.

Upon leaving the meeting, Minh vowed that no more of his family would die in this war by his actions. He also felt the need for an act of repentance according to the religion of Confucius, as he had personally disrupted the social harmony of his family. He knew of the Chu Hoi program and decided to surrender. He thought he could just name the VC District Chief and provide no more information to our side. He felt we would kill that VC before the battle, saving his family, but without an impact on the battle itself. He planned to be a passive member of our government for three weeks, and then would be liberated by the victory. Now, he says, he will surely be shot by the communists.

He says he surrendered himself at dawn of that same day to the militia of Ky Long Village. Where, as you know, he was badly treated. He told his capters of the District Chief, but they did not listen. This is why he asked to be interviewed by the three of us first. He trusts us to listen and take action."

"What's his name?" growled Race, "Me and my guys'll go get im tomorrow!"

Minh smiled vindictively as he pronounced the VC's name. Race spoke a curt phrase in Vietnamese and Minh bowed appreciatively, replying, "Cam on um," which Jake recognized as "Thank you Sir."

"Well, that answers the question of why he speaks with a Quang Tin accent," murmured Jake, "but I'm with him. I doubt if locking up one VC leader will have much of an effect on the overall plan." He nodded to Tu. "Ask him if he knows anything else about our province that might be useful."

Tu asked and Minh responded.

"He says two members of his reconnaissance platoon are from Ly Tin. They joined the unit in Laos with the other replacements. They are brothers and former loyalists. They are sons of the late police chief of Ly Tin."

"You mean the sons of Nguyen Van Qou?" Race exploded. "Fuck! I wondered what happened ta them. I know um. They're nice kids. Or were at least," He dropped his head pensively.

Minh continued speaking, with Tu acting as his English echo. "He says they rallied to the Viet Cong after their father was murdered by our Province Chief, Colonel Biet. I have already informed him

that an American, the senior advisor before Colonel King is suspected of the murder, but he says that the brothers say the American was made to look guilty to shift blame. They say their father left
their house to visit Colonel Biet and was never seen alive again." Tu
shook his head vehemently. "This cannot be true. Do not misunder-
stand me; I am not doubting Sergeant Minh. I believe he has indeed
heard this story from the two traitorous sons, but it is unthinkable
that Colonel Biet had a hand in this murder. Nguyen Van Quo was
his close friend."

Jake leaned forward in his chair, his pulse racing with excitement
that this might be something that could help clear Ray Gonzaga.
"Troom Ta, you acted like you believed at least part of his story a
while ago; what do you think now? Do you still believe him? Or,
because of this, are you again suspicious about the attack plan?"

Tu didn't hesitate. "He has explained why he has a local dialect. I
believe this about him. I also know of the boy's murder in the village of Phouc Loc four days ago. For these reasons, I have less incli-
nation to doubt all his information. Nevertheless, we must not be
too quick, like the fish, to grab and swallow what flashes before our
face. I know my people. I cannot believe the South Vietnamese will
rise up against us as he indicates."

Jake nodded, wondering if his agreement was more wish than
logic. "I agree. How are we going to handle this information about
Colonel Biet? It's not Minh's testimony after all; it's what we call
hear-say information. Interesting, but not admissible in a court of
law. Of course, we're not in a court of law, and not in the states.
That's why I ask the question."

Tu responded slowly. "I do not plan to tell Colonel Biet about this. I
do not believe it, and no good would purpose would be served in
upsetting the province chief needlessly. I cannot tell you what to
say or do, but if it is your report, there will be no confirmation from
our side."

Race held his hand to his brow, smoothing the wild tangle over one
eye as he sneaked a look at Jake. Jake glanced his way and received

a surreptitious wink, hidden from Tu behind the hand. Race dropped his arm. "Well," he said, "you're probably right Colonel. No skin off our ass anyway. Does our guest have other information?"

Minh scratched his ear thoughtfully when he heard this question. Hesitantly, he responded. Tu shook his head unbelievingly again before he translated: "He says there is something very odd being discussed by all local VC. He heard it first from the two sons of Nguyen Van Quo, but heard it again from the Tien Phouc District Chief. It appears that two very low level Viet Cong supply runners were captured by our side after an ambush. While in captivity, they confessed to having seen an American code book. They even described it accurately. Hearing about this through their intelligence network, the VC are questioning all units as to where this book could be. It would be, of course, of great value, but they cannot find it. The porters saw it but did not have it when captured, and no guerilla unit claims to have it or to have seen it. The VC are calling it the ghost code book. The VC officers cannot understand how such an important document was seen by lowly porters and not seen by those who might utilize this intelligence discovery."

"He's talkin bout the code book that Ray Gonzaga was sposed to'uv sold to um," boomed Race.

"It would appear so," said Tu.

Jake smiled furtively. He could feel his temples throbbing. Bingo, he thought. Another piece of the puzzle is now on the board. But what does it mean? Either those porters got it from someone else and then lost it or hid it; or they lied about seeing it. Why would they do that? This, at least gives me somewhere to start.

Tu stood as if to leave.

"Whad'da we gonna do with our prize package now?" asked Race, indicating Minh with his thumb.

"We have no more need for his services," droned Tu. "I propose to send him to the Armed Propaganda Team. "This, as you know, is a small unit consisting of former VC. They are sent on many worthwhile missions where their former contacts and training allow them to be effective, yet never a danger to our people."

"Yeah, they get sent on suicide missions and other shit details," Race smirked sarcastically. "He told me he wants ta do somethun else."

"I am not inclined to allow any former enemy of my country to do, as you put it, what he wants to do, just because he wants to do it. We are at war. We must place him where he can help most and where he can injure us little," replied Tu. His bowing head and smiling face belied the edge to his voice.

They both looked to Jake again to resolve the deadlock.

"I'd like to know what it is we're talking about before I give an opinion," Jake said. "What is it he wants to do?"

"The way I get it," Race smiled, "he wants ta be a dancer or somethun. He says he's checked and knows we don't have none, and that he can do beaucoup good by kickin up his heels. I didn't get it all the way, just the jist of it. I don't see how dancin can hurt us none." He glanced up antagonistically at Tu and back again at Jake. "Course, I don't see how it can help us none neither."

Tu turned and exchanged a rapid fire dialogue with Minh, who became very animated. His face became alive. His eyes sparkled as his hands made dramatic, graceful swoops.

Tu smiled in genuine amusement. "In the north, before he was conscripted to the military, he was a member of a very popular touring theater group. It is a well known group and has been in existence for many years. Although I have never seen one of their productions, I remember hearing of it before I came to the south in 1954. His group was famous for the hat boi style of theater, which is what you would say in English, the classical or traditional style. It is quite colorful and exciting, much like your opera; although I think Americans would not understand. There is much crying out from the actors and much noise from gongs and drums."

"He's not a dancer then?" asked Race. "I thought he told me he was a dancer."

"Well, in a way, he is. Hat boi makes much use of music, and the actors move in rhythmic movements which Americans would call dancing. It requires much skill and training. He is even more accomplished however. He tells me he is also trained in the cai luong form of theater. This is more contemporary; more like your American stage plays."

"I don't get it," growled Race. "Whad'd he mean when he said he could help our side by dancin? I know that's what he said yesterday when we were talkin."

"Yes," Tu was still smiling. It is something I hadn't considered, but the concept seems worthwhile. As you know, we Vietnamese now have government television stations in the larger cities, and radio stations such as the one here in Tam Ky. We use these as a primary method of informing the people of news and items they should know."

"Propaganda!" snorted Race.

"We are at war," Tu scolded. "We do what we must to win; as you would do if this were your country."

"OK, OK, go ahead," Race conceded. "What's this got ta do with dancin?"

"We have not been a modernized country for long. Before the electronic news media, the government relied upon printed leaflets and posters, a method we still use today." He paused, pulling one of the posters about Minh out of his briefcase. "As you have seen in this case, such a method is still effective. However, a historic manner of instructing our people is by sending forth a group of touring actors who portray our government message in drama performances which are intermixed with skits, as I think you call them, of a nonpolitical nature. This type of information spreading has always been popular with the people because it is entertainment, and with governments because the people actually listen to the messages.

Both sides used this tactic extensively in 1954 when the north was trying to attract people away from South Vietnam, and the South was trying to attract people away from Communism. Sergeant Minh has suggested that he be allowed to form such a touring group. It will perform hat boi, cai luong, comedy acts, dances and government sponsored drama scenes which will recreate our victories over the VC and the dangers of life under Communism." Tu smiled broadly. "Even as I describe this this concept, I envision its possibilities. Such a diversion will be welcomed by the people. They will see that the Quang Tin government seeks to make them happy and safe."

"Well I've got a question," interjected Jake. "If he thinks the NVA is going to win and he's going to die in three weeks, why does he want to take on a stage career? Seems to me he would want to get behind the biggest gun he could find and fight like hell."

Tu was still standing. He turned and rebounded the question in Vietnamese. Minh answered, smiling coyly and lowering his eyes to the floor.

"He says he feels he can make a larger impact doing this. He is only one soldier, but he might persuade hundreds to fight on rather than to join the Communists. He also admits that in case they do still win, he can claim that he was a non-combatant because we did not trust him with a weapon. Therefore he may survive. I will add to this something he did not say. The Vietnamese have great respect for actors and artists of any kind. Since he is an actor, his life has more value to both sides. I must confess to you that I feel more—well, respect for him now that I know he is talented. But also, I am more wary of his information, as he is now a confessed role player."

"Bein an actor don't make me respect him none," Race noted.

Tu turned back to Minh and rattled in rapid Vietnamese. Minh stood obediently. "I have told him to come with me," Tu stated. I will provide a bodyguard to protect him from assassination. He will eat and sleep with the militia. During daylight periods, he will be allowed to travel anywhere in the province to,… how do you say? To listen the first time to actors who want to perform?"

"Audition," Jake said.

"Yes, to audition people for his new acting group. I have given him ten days to select his group and practice. At that time, he will have his opening night. It will be a command performance. The Province Chief, myself, and our families will be there. Both of you are of course invited, as will be Colonel King when he returns from his vacation."

"Ten days! Holy shit!" blurted Race.

"Ten days does seem to be a short time to get a performance ready; one like you describe, Jake agreed.

"Today is the tenth day of your calendar year. Our New Year's Day falls on the thirtieth day of your month. War has a way of condensing the time required to do necessary tasks. If we are to receive a beneficial effect from this government theater group, we must have them perform as soon and as often as possible in the ten days after their first show. I will go now to Colonel Biet. I will tell him what we have been told today. I will also seek to extract from him an adequate stipend to support this new government information tool."

"Before you go Troom Ta," Jake stopped them as they headed out the door. "There is one other thing. We have the key information we needed from him, but he still has more to give us. I recommend that our S2 types be allowed to interrogate him further to get such things as order of battle, routes they plan to take, and other details that we haven't asked him about, but which are really just as important in the military intelligence game."

"Yes, you are right," responded Tu thoughtfully. "I will arrange a combined intelligence interrogation in one hour. They may question him for the rest of the evening and perhaps most of the night. After that, I will make him available for specific questions for ten minutes each day. We must give our new entertainment star the time he needs for his new duties, because,…" he paused for effect, "the show must go on!" He snapped his fingers dramatically while laughing at his own joke; and Minh, whose puzzled face showed that he didn't understand, jumped to follow him.

"Where did he learn that expression?" asked Jake, grinning. "Has he been watching American movies?"

"Well, probably," smiled Race. "As I understand it, Tu's been in the US twice. He went ta the Army C&GS School about five years ago. Then, just before his assignment here, he attended the Army War College in Kansas. That's why he speaks English so well. Biet's been ta both schools too."

Jake nodded, but was only half listening. He dialed the telephone in the corner of the room. "Put Major Clayborne on," he said. He waited. "Bill, Colonel Thorpe. I'm in the conference room. Come over on the double and bring your notebook. I'm going to give you a flash message for Da Nang. It's hot and I want to get it on the scrambler ASAP. So double time, OK?"

He replaced the receiver as Clayborne's "Yes Sir" was still in progress. "Race, I want you to stick around. Help me make sure I don't leave out anything important in kicking this report upstairs. Hell, so much to think about. Glad Colonel King's back in here tomorrow."

"Sure Colonel," boomed Race. He smiled fatherly. "Don't worry Colonel. You're damned good at your job. You're willin ta take responsibility, which a lotta brass are afraid ta do. Specially these guys we're sposed ta be helpin. You got common sense too. That Troom Ta what just left, he would'a'na thought about givin the MI a crack at our fairy queen. Shit! Can you imagine that? Our little NVA snuffy turns out ta be a God Damned recon sergeant. Hell, they're all sposed ta be tough mother fuckers. But ours turns out ta be some wimp dancer! It don't figger!"

"Well a lot of things puzzle me Race. For example, why'd you wink at me during the session? I think it was when the Hoi Chanh was talking about the two brothers."

"Yeah. Glad you brought it up. I heard the same story our limp wristed Commie just told, almost, from the police station at Ly Tin. The new police captain down there don't want ta be quoted, so he kinda talked in circles, but the way I got it is he thinks Captain Quo was investigatin' a high rankin' province officer for sellin US black market stuff to some big wig civilians in Ly Tin. He wouldn't give any names, but if Quo's own boys think it was Biet what did the hatchet job, it kinda fits. I was pretty close ta Ray Gonzaga. Hell, all us civilians were. He was one of us. I sure don't think he knocked off Quo."

Jake made a mental note that Race Haldane was someone he might trust in the future. But no need to tip my hand just yet, he thought.

Three distinct explosions sounded in the distance. Both Race and Jake recognized the sound.

"That's incomin" said Race.

Jake nodded. If the incoming rounds were accompanied by a serious ground attack, there would be a siren. They waited.

"What made you come over here Race? From that police badge on your hat, it looks like you didn't need excitement."

"Nope. Had my share. I'm from St. Paul, Minnesota. Twenty-five years on the force there. Made captain and had a shot at makin chief. But then I took a look at the poor bastard who had the job and saw how much ass kissin and public speakin he had ta do as part of it. I just decided ta retire and take it easy for awhile. Hell! Hadn't been home a week before the God Damned State department called me. Offered me more money in eighteen months over here than I'd made in the last five years."

Jake nodded in silence. "Do you like the job?"

"Lot more'n I thought I would. I like the Viets. They're OK. I get cross-wise with you Army types every once in a while. You're OK, like I said, but your boss,... well, forget I said this, but he's an asshole!"

Jake didn't know how to respond, so he remained silent. Race got up to leave.

"Don't go yet Race. I still want your help when we dictate that message to Da Nang."

Race sat down again. "OK," he bellowed, his voice back to its usual volume. "Wonder where the fuck that ass kissin major is? It's not that far over here."

Jake suddenly remembered Ray. "One more thing before he gets here Race. I'd like you to find out where those two VC porters are. The ones who gave that info about Mr. Gonzaga's code book. We both know there's something fishy there. Let's try to find out what it is."

"Gotcha Colonel. Anythin else?"

The telephone rang before Jake could respond. He picked it up. "Colonel Thorpe!"

"Colonel, this is First Sergeant Prescott over at the camp. You'd better get over here Sir. Right away. The VC just lobbed some mortar shells on us. We got three wounded and one KIA."

They bolted for the door. The flash message to Da Nang could wait!

SCENE 2

THE HOUSE TRAILER

1100 Hours
13 January, 1968

"Ughh!" "Hit the fuckin thing John!" "Get it over; get it over!"
"Ouww! That hurt, you shithead!"

The clamor from the game outside tumbled into the house trailer. Grunts, bellowed threats and screams of pain from the players; catcalls and more profanity from the spectators; and sporadic, flat whacks as open palms slapped the ball in clumsy, gentle arcs over the net and back again.

Jake smiled as he recalled the different sounds of a stateside volleyball contest. A real world game produced rubber-soled squeaks on hardwood floors; "ooohs" and "aaahs" from observers who applauded after every point; and "thuck, thuck THUNK" during play, as the snow white ball was passed and set by fingertips and then smashed with a fist into the enemy court. This last hit, Jake remembered, was called a "kill" by most. The savage "THUNK" of the kill was usually followed by the referee's whistle signifying a side out or a point scored.

But the sounds aren't the only differences, Jake realized. Here, the game is played outside in the tropical heat. The shirtless competitors wear baggy fatigue trousers and jungle boots. The net sags slovenly and the court boundaries scraped into the ankle deep sand are obscured by boot prints.

Jake winced as he watched a Thang Binh athlete stumble into the net trying to reach the ball. A Kronberg player kicked him viciously in the shins and a teammate threw sand into the entangled player's face. The Thang Binh team, however, managed to spank the scruffy ball into a lazy, graceful arc back over the net. It was Kronberg's turn to shout "Get it over; get it over," as each team member fought each other to be the one to slap the ball back to the other side. Sweat flew from gyrating torsos, and the sun sparkled from flying dog-tags.

The Vietnam version of volleyball is played, appropriately, Jake thought with a wry smile, according to 'jungle rules;' which meant no rules. The kicking, sand throwing, net grabbing and palm slap-ping are all legal here. Anything's legal. There's no referee. Yet the game is almost a child's pitty-pat play. The ball is always returned so softly, so peacefully. There are never any kills in Vietnam volley-ball.

Curly Danby stood at Jake's side in the house trailer, watching the game intently from the large window in Jake's kitchen. He cheered loudly when Thang Binh scored. He had been trying to entice Jake into a wager on the game.

"You're just pulling my leg Colonel. You really don't wanna bet cause you think our team'll kick your team's butt."

"No, Curly, that's not it."

"What is it then?"

Jake considered his answer. "Well, let's call it a matter of profes-sional principle. I'm your boss just like I'm Claiborne's boss. I don't want you or any of your guys thinking that I feel you're not part of Team Two. I'm as much a part of your team as I am the Kronberg team."

"Well Sir," grinned Curly, "I think that sounds like professional bullshit. You live with these guys; you have to feel closer to them. What if I spot you five points a game? Would you go for that?" He smiled as if he had scored a point himself.

Jake chuckled. "Of course not. That would be the worst thing I could do. I'd still be showing partiality for one side, alienating the other side. Yet simultaneous, I'd show the team I'm betting on that I don't have confidence in them."

Curly smiled mischievously and glanced back at the game. "I still think you're shitting me Sir. Everybody's rooting for one side or the other."

"Well, there's a practical reason also," replied Jake, returning his gaze also to the frenzy outside. "We've got a war going on; a real war. I need every one of these guys to be ready to fight the NVA. It bothers the Hell out of me that they're trying to kill each other just for fun; I'm sure not going to add any motivation to their blood lust."

Curly grinned triumphantly as he wheeled to face him. "Now I gotcha Colonel. I almost bought that professional principles crap. Your position here and all. But now you change it to—" he paused for dramatic effect, —"practicality." He laughed a cheerful cackle. "They all start with the letter p: professional principles, position, practicality. Let's face it Colonel. You've given yourself away. I think you won't bet because you're pessimistic, prudent and maybe even parsimonious!" He guffawed. "You're a penny pincher!" He doubled over with laughter at his own wit.

Jake shook his head, but couldn't help but grin.

"What about the odds Sir? I'll make it my three to your one."

"No Curly, and that's final," Jake laughed. "How about some coffee? I brought some over from the kitchen. It's already made."

"That's great Sir. Sure I'll take some." Curly pulled a stubby corn-cob pipe from his pocket and patted his trousers for tobacco and fire.

Jake poured two mugs of the black liquid, noting the similarity in texture to molten lava. He pondered Curley's teasing remarks. It is my job to be neutral, he thought. But Curly obviously wouldn't feel this way if he were in my shoes, and they say that Colonel King openly supported the Kronberg team from the start of the tournament three weeks ago. Maybe I'm different. Or maybe it's something else and I've just alibied it with high-toned rationalization. I am a newcomer here. Maybe I feel I still don't fit in here at Camp Kronberg. Maybe I really don't belong.

From the window, Curly interrupted Jake's introspection. "Hey Colonel. Did you know Colonel King's here in the compound? I thought he'd gone up to Da Nang to hash over some new intelligence info."

"He did!" Jake exclaimed with surprise. "He left this morning; said he'd be gone all day."

"Well he's here Sir. I just saw him walk into that hooch over there across the volleyball court."

"Where? Which one?"

"Over there Sir. Second door from the left. Can't see him now because he's inside. I know it was him though. He had on that new Aussie bush hat I've heard we're all supposed to buy."

"Hmm," Jake murmured. "That's Sergeant Lentz's old hooch, the NCO who was killed day before yesterday in the mortar attack."

"Yes Sir. Heard about it. Too bad! How're the other guys?"

"No problem. They're all three back on the job. Superficial wounds only. The worst one got his face all cut up. Took a few stitches, but the doctors at China Beach say he won't even scar."

"Pretty good way to earn the purple heart if you ask me."

Jake smiled at the caustic military humor. "I'm still not convinced there's a good way to earn a purple heart, but if you're going to get one, I guess this is as good a way as any." He continued smiling as he remembered his first tour where one of his squad leaders cut his finger slightly because the semi-distant detonation of an incoming mortar had caused him to jump while opening a C-Ration can of peanut butter. He had earned the purple heart! Jake also remembered his battalion commander who fell during a fire fight with the NVA, lacerating a knee; but who refused to see the medic about it because he didn't want to earn his purple heart in "such a chicken shit way as this."

"By the way Sir," Curly broke into his thoughts. "Before I forget it, I found out about that booze ration for the district chiefs. It took some doing. As close to Major Dang and I are, when he understood what I was asking him, he really backed off. I hope you don't mind Sir, but I used your name in vain. I told him you were the one who wanted to know and that I had to tell you. He started to tell me some cock and bull story, but I could tell he was making it up as he went, so I told him I wanted the straight skinny and no bullshit. He finally told me, but he, ahhh, made it a point that I didn't hear it from him; if you know what I mean."

"I gotcha; go ahead."

"Well it seems like it's one of our Province Chief's little profit ventures Sir. It's American booze; good labels; and he comes up with it every month. He more or less cons most of his officers to buy it from him. Sells it pretty cheap though, because the other district chiefs and several of Biet's staff re-sell it to their flunkies, and they make a profit too."

"I thought it must be something like that," mused Jake. "Any ideas at all where the booze is coming from?"

"No Sir. It has to be black market though. It's from somewhere in Da Nang what I'm guessing.

"Why was Major Dang so guarded? I thought he didn't like Biet."

"No Sir, he doesn't. But Dang's real loyal. He feels Biet has his faults. Shouldn't skim money out of the province funds and shit like that, but he still thinks Biet's not that bad. So many others are evidently worse. I think Dang's afraid of who might be chosen as Province Chief if Biet goes down."

"Your Major Dang has a lot of principles but a side of practicality too."

"Yes Sir, he does. But so do most Vietnamese." Curly pulled a green handkerchief from somewhere, mopped his shining scalp, and returned his attention to the game.

Jake watched the game too, but his thoughts were not on the activity outside. The pieces are coming together, he realized. This fits with the news I got yesterday from Doyle. I'm getting close. That stolen Army truck's serial number matches the one Ray's accused of selling, and the owner is the Ly Tin Fish Processing Company. That's the closest thing to big business in Quang Tin, and the best thing is the manager down there says he thinks it came from the Quang Tin government. It sure ties in with the booze. Our good Province Chief seems to have his fingers in a lot of pies, and they seem like the same pies that have hit Ray Gonzaga in the face. But the code book's still missing. That looks like the final piece of the puzzle. I hope Race gets me news on that soon.

The two men watched the color and fury of the competitive combat event. Bright red had been added to the pastels of sand tan and olive green. Blood oozed from scraped elbows and torn knees.

The cheers and catcalls of the mob surrounding the court still whipped around the compound in opposing waves to collide and blend into a cacophonous tornado-like background of sound.

Jake observed two Red Cross doughnut dollies circulating through the masculine turmoil. They arrived every other Saturday from Da Nang, usually wearing Army fatigues and Red Cross arm bands. Today, however, for some reason, they wore their traditional faded blue smocks. Both women were coarse, ill favored, awkward examples of American womanhood, just barely feminine. Jake knew that for approximately half his men, white skin and round eyes were the only criteria for beauty here, and for this half, the women were stunningly attractive. For the other men, race was not a requirement, so the lithe and grace of the more numerous Vietnamese distaff side prevailed. Jake smiled. No one on one side could understand the other side's taste in women.

The doughnut dollies flounced through the screaming multitude dispensing cookies, library books, winks and innuendos, while receiving overt pinches, covert grabs, obscene suggestions and accidental shoves. Everyone seemed to be in a good mood.

Across the playing field, Colonel King appeared, stepping through the screen door of Sergeant Lentz's former hooch. He idly watched the mayhem of the volleyball game for a few moments. Jake saw him look up at the trailer window and see the two of them standing in the air conditioned comfort. He began to weave his way through the jostling throng toward them.

"Here comes Colonel King," said Curly beside him.

"Yes," responded Jake thoughtfully.

"Can I ask a question just out of curiosity Sir?"

"Sure."

"Did Colonel King take his wife to Sydney with him, or did he leave her in Bangkok?"

Jake paused before answering. It was none of Curly's business. Nor was it any of his own. If he didn't answer, or shrugged off the question, it would be the same as an answer. Only a "Yes he took her," would quell the rumors. But he couldn't lie.

"His wife couldn't make it for some reason," he said without turning from the window.

"That's what all the NCOs are saying too," smirked Curly. He has FAST privilege which allow his wife to be close and he can visit her once a month, but when R&R comes around, he goes to Australia without her. Lots of tongues are wagging."

"Just make sure one of them is not yours," snapped Jake, smiling to soften the warning. "Take a lesson from Major Dang."

Curly nodded, but with a slight smirk.

The two faced about and saluted casually as King strode through the doorway without knocking.

"Shiiit!" King hailed in drawled exasperation. "I sure as Hell hope Charlie don't mortar us today. We'd never hear the pops'n whistles, an we'd have a hunnert bodies out there. I knew today was the championship game, but I forgot about it till I got over here. Too late now. If it happens when I'm here, I'm fuckin responsible. How close is it ta bein over? What's the score?"

Jake and Curly glanced at each other. Neither knew, and they laughed.

"Looks like your guess is as good as ours Dick," smiled Jake.

"Shit Curly, you should know at least," blurted King. "That's your team out there. This is for the Goddamn Team Two championship. It'll be a big fuckin deal ta be the number one team from the number one team; and Team Two is number one, right guys?"

"Yes Sir," they both chorused. This was tradition. This was expected. The two men answered automatically, unthinkingly. Neither man even remotely considered whether or not truth was a factor.

"Have you guys bought your new Team Two hats yet?" growled King, stroking his olive green Australian bush hat. "I bought two hunnert a these fuckers. One fer everone on the team and a few extra in case someone wants ta send one home or keep a souvenir or somethin."

"You bought them Dick?" asked Jake. "I thought you just ordered them through the PX system."

"Nah! That's the story I gave out. I bought um in Sydney. Brought um back with me. Makes it faster and cheaper. I put um in our PX here in the camp ta let them sell um fer me. I'm not makin a profit. Sellin um fer the same price I paid fer um. Three fifty each. That's a fuckin bargain. Shit. This hat'd go fer five bucks at least in the PX and it'd be at least ten bucks back in the world." He held it aloft for them to admire.

"Not bad at all," mumbled Jake without conviction.

"Looks good Sir," said Curly, with an equal lack of enthusiasm.

"Glad ya both feel that way, cause I want you two ta help set the example; be one'a the first ones. This hat's gonna become our symbol. We're gonna be special. The advisory team that wears the bush hats. Ever swingin dick is gonna hear about us and look up ta us. This fuckin hat's gonna be the symbol of professionalism in the whole Goddamn advisor business! I want everone on the team ta start wearin um. No exceptions!"

Jake and Curly exchanged a quick glance and both nodded in acquiescence to their commander. "Yes Sir," they said solemnly.

Jake silently wondered how this breech of uniform regulations would go over with the higher echelons of their command chain, but decided that it probably would. This was a war zone. All uniform regulations were relaxed. Men went shirtless during the day, some wore bandannas or head scarves rather than hats or helmets. This hat might look a bit foreign, but it was no more foreign than the beret and definitely more military than a head scarf. He decided to change the subject. "How was your R&R Dick? How was Australia?"

"Hey it was fantastic! Those Aussie women are really somethin. They couldn't keep their hands offa me. I got laid ever fuckin night I was there. Four different broads in six nights. I'm exhausted. God do they love ta fuck!"

Jake felt his eyes rolling upward. Shit, he thought. Why should I try so hard to guard King's reputation when he's so willing to destroy it himself?

"Is this something that happens to all GIs who go there Sir? Or were you just lucky?" grinned Curly with a sidelong glance of pure enjoyment at Jake.

"Shit! It's available over there fer almost everbody. I even saw some black dudes in Sydney with good lookin Aussie bimbos. Course I always do OK. Shit. I've got a tradition ta uphold."

"What kind of tradition would that be?" chuckled Jake, deciding to join in jovial mood.

"Ya have ta think about it. I have ta live upta my name. My name isn't just my name either. It means somethun else besides. Think about it. I'm the one and only Dick King. I'm the biggest fuckin prick around, an I always get more ass than anyone else."

Jake and Curly laughed. "I heard you have a Junior at the end of your name," Jake said. "Does that mean you're just the king of undersized winkies?"

Curly guffawed, but King only smiled. "No way," he said, almost seriously. "If ya really wanna know the truth, my birth certificate reads 'Richard Cain King, roman numeral three! My father was king 'a cocks before me, an my grandfather before him. You might say I came from a long line 'a regal Dicks!"

"Well Sir," Curly chortled. "Since Colonel Thorp here is the number two man in this outfit, and your title is King as well as your name, that must make him the Prince." He turned to Jake, his eyes twinkling with mirth, his mouth smiling cynically. "How bout it Sir? Are you the Prick Prince of Team Two?"

"If I had a head as bald as yours, I'd be kind of careful who I called a prick around here."

"According to Freud Sir, I'm a symbol; just like the colonel's new hat. I'm a walking talking phallic symbol. That's something to be proud of, bein a symbol I mean." He looked back at King. "Hell, we're all symbols of something over here aren't we Sir? Democracy? Freedom? The American way of life?"

"Fuck!" said King. "I'll tell ya one thing. I'm the fuckin symbol of authority around here, and as such, I say I've had enough a this shit. Why don'tcha get outta here now Curly and go root for yer raggedy ass team. I've got some private business with Colonel Thorpe."

"Yes Sir. On my way Sir." Curly saluted and sauntered out cheerfully, reaching for his pipe as the screen door swung shut.

King turned to Jake. "That fucker's a real smart ass. I hope we really kick his team's ass today. He's gonna make our lives miserable if he wins."

Jake arched an eyebrow at King's partiality, but decided to sidetrack the issue. "I'll tell you how we can change that, Dick. In fact, I was going to recommend it anyway."

"What's that?"

"I think we ought to consider transferring Curly up here to the province headquarters. He's done a good job at district level. Been there over six months, and we sure could use his language skills and moxie up here."

"Are you shittin me? That bald headed wimp! No fuckin way I'd have him around me. Bad enough he's on my team. Look at that fuckin gut on him. Shit Jake, I thought you had better judgement than that. It's outta the question."

Jake was stunned. How could King be so narrow minded? Danby is an excellent officer: keen, intelligent, effective, with a well placed sense of priorities. Yet King is judging him on appearance alone. Too bad. The team would be stronger if Danby could be up here giving us his insights and experience on a daily basis. Better drop the subject now though. No need to beat a dead horse.

King stomped over to the hot plate and poured himself a cup of black coffee. "Speakin a yer judgement, by the way," he spoke to the cup he was holding rather than to Jake. "I hear ya took full responsibility fer the security a that Chu Hoi who spilled his fuckin guts."

"Yes I did. Good thing too. We'd've never gotten the info we did if I hadn't."

"Well Jake, it worked out fer ya this time, but it was too big a risk ta take. You fell inta the shitter and came up smellin like a rose. I gotta tell ya, and this is an official warnin, it was poor fuckin judgement no matter what happened."

"Poor judgement?" Jake showed his surprise again.

"God Damned right it was poor judgement. We're not over here ta do these fuckin dinks' job fer um. We're over here as advisors, not doers. If these nut scratchers have their way, we'd be doin all the fightin; takin all the responsibility and makin all the decisions in this God Damned war! It's our job ta kick um in the ass ta make um do their fuckin jobs. Shit! They're not tryin ta win this war. They want us ta win it for um."

"But that is the idea isn't it Dick? To win? I just did what I felt I had to do. As an officer, I'm supposed to accept responsibility."

"Shit! Now I'm really worried about yer judgement Jake. You don't know what's yer responsibility an what's theirs. Lemme tell ya how they look at responsibility. In our army, the higher the rank the more responsibility, right? We may get a few perks, but if there's a no sweat job somewhere, we send our duds to it, right? We send our best officers to the fuckin tough jobs, right?"

Jake nodded to all three questions.

"Well it's just the fuckin opposite over here. Look at the province chiefs. There's a total a forty eight provinces. Some are easy, like Gia Dinh and Vung Tau. Almost no VC threat atall. You know what the province chief's rank is in those plush jobs?" He didn't wait for the shake of Jake's head. "Brigadier fuckin General, that's what! Hell! They even have a two star as the City Chief a Saigon. Then they put a colonel in the mid-threat provinces, like this one. But in the really tough ones, like Quang Tri, Quang Ngai and Hau Nghia, that's next ta the Parrot's Beak, they put a lieutenant colonel in as chief, cause there's more danger an' they can afford ta lose one'a them better."

Jake sat silently, listening intently.

"Fuck!" King continued. "Biet does the same Goddamn thing here. What's the most dangerous district? Hau Duc, right? And who's out there? A fuckin junior Dai Wi. Shit! They don't wanna win. They just wanna get by the easy way."

"Why don't we have an advisor in Hau Duc?" asked Jake, interrupting King's tirade.

"Shit. Don't play a Ray Gonzaga on me Jake. You know what we're supposed ta do over here. Do the fuckin job but don't get anybody killed if ya don't have to. Gonzaga kept wantin ta put advisors out there too, but after Kronberg bought it, I said no. Even before Gonzaga got his ass in a sling! I was the senior military mother fucker, an I put my foot down. If Biet thinks it's too dangerous out there fer an ARVN major, then it's too God Damned dangerous fer an American officer. I'm not gonna get my ass chewed out fer losin any troops that I don't have to."

Both men's eyes bored intently into the other's. Neither man flinched. The muffled shouts of the volleyball game wafted around them. As if on signal, they both looked away.

"Wonder who's winnin," King mumbled.

Jake shook his head without answering. They both lit cigarettes.

"What did Da Nang say? Are they going to give us any additional troops for Tet?" asked Jake.

"Nah. They're treatin it like it's all hot air. Course, I think it's mostly hot air too. They think that fuckin dink Chu Hoi is a plant. Sent in here with bum info as a decoy. They're not totally discountin it, cause they've evidently got some other intel from somewhere that pretty much confirms somma what your Sonuvvabitch said. But it looks like mosta their stuff points ta a big operation up north against the fuckin marines. They think maybe Khe Sanh; a little base on the DMZ."

"Dick, I'm telling you, I was there at the interrogation. That guy was telling the truth. Man, we're going to be hit hard on the Tet holidays!"

"Fuck Jake! You worry too much. We been kickin the shit outta the NVA ever since we got here. They can gin up a major operation once in a while, here an there. But we got um on the fuckin run. No way they can mount an all-out offensive like he's talkin about. It's outta the question. That's what I believe, 'n I said the same thing ta Lamar this mornin when he asked me."

"Well you're the boss, but I'm takin this thing seriously. I'm going to do all I can to get ready just in case."

"Shit, go ahead. No skin offa my ass. But remember! Don't do it yerself. Get the nut scratchers ta do it fer themselves. It's their fuckin country and their fuckin war."

"Is it OK if I get some arclights or air strikes out there where that regiment might be?"

"Sure. That's parta our job as long as the dinks want um too."

"I'm also still going to try to get that Major Forrester over here from Chu Lai to get better coordination between us and the fly boys."

"Fine with me. Just remember ta don't do mor'n yer sposed to!"

"OK. I'll watch it Dick."

"I'm gonna get outta here now. Go down ta the game. I probably should be there at the final point ta congratulate the champs an give um the trophy. Hell. It probably wouldn't mean much to um ta be the Team Two champions unless the Old Man himself gave um the trophy would it?"

Jake smiled laconically and saluted casually. King waved and banged out through the screen door.

Jake watched him go. As prejudiced as he is, Jake thought, I have to confess that he's more right than wrong about this advisory business. I've got to do the right thing and not do it all myself. And that, he realized, will be a tougher job than it would be if I could do it myself.

The game ended. Thang Binh won. Colonel King praised the winners with gusto and seemed to display real enthusiasm as he handed the trophy to a delighted Major Danby.

Jake watched the ceremony from his window, knowing the friendly smiles on each man's face hid thoughts of antagonism. His own thoughts were still troubled. It's almost like not being in the American Army over here. The right thing to do is not always right. I've always done well in the Army by just getting the job done. But here I get chewed out for it.

He heard a slight tapping on his door. He opened it to find a withered Vietnamese crone standing on his doorstep with her conical straw hat in her wrinkled hands.

"Yes?" he said.

"Sin loi Troom Ta. Me Ba Nhur, housemaid for hooch. That hooch." She bowed respectfully and pointed across the playing field.

"Yes?"

"Me Sergeant Lentz housemaid. Washee him clothes. Clean him room. Do for five GI."

"Did he owe you money?"

"No. No Troom Ta. Him pay number one. I clean him room hom qua—yesday. Clean for last time. Very bad. VC number ten"

"Yes they are," smiled Jake, waiting for her to come to the point of her visit.

"Sergeant Lentz, him clothes; him stuff. Put all box hom qua—yesday. Box go stateside. Box go Sergeant Lentz' mamasan hom qua, yesday."

"Yes, Ba Nhur. Thank you for your help. I'm sure you did a good job, and I'll make sure you get assigned to the next person who comes in here."

She acted like she hadn't heard him. "Hom qua, yesday, I clean him room. Big box go stateside. I find little book. Not good send mamasan. Big box go stateside; I give little book you. You maybe keep; maybe throw away; no sweat. No give Sergeant Lentz' mamasan!"

"Oh! I understand. Where is this book you found?

From the inside of her straw hat, she produced a pocket sized hard backed book. A thick rubber band held the book closed. "I find hom qua. Number ten bad. Me no send mamasan! Me no keep!" She handed him the book. "No belong me. Bad for mamasan. Bad for other GI." She pointed a bony finger at his face. "No send mamasan. You keep; you throw away. You say."

"OK Ba Nhur, I'll look at it and decide what to do." He bowed his appreciation. "Cam on Ba." He thanked her in her language.

"Cam on Troom Ta." She bowed again with a fierce but satisfied smile as she backed down the stairs and away from his doorstep.

He watched as she flipped on her yellow conical hat and set off at a jogging pace toward the gate of the camp. He glanced down at the non-descript, untitled little volume in his hand. Probably pornography, he thought. She sure doesn't want me to send it to Sergeant Lentz's mother.

With the sad heaviness that always accompanies the handling of a dead person's property, he slipped the rubber band and opened the cover.

Ba Nhur was right! Each page was a lurid black and white photo with captions in French. It wasn't just pornography, it was the most savage and vicious pornography Jake had ever seen, and the pictures made him feel ill. Children being hurt, and women being tortured. Shuddering, he threw the book across the room. He had aimed at the waste paper basket, but it missed, hit the wall and landed on the floor.

Disgusted that he had to touch it again, he walked over to do the job right. He picked up the book by the back cover as if it were lice infested, and that's when he noticed the bulge. He looked closer. The back cover was unnaturally thick. Intrigued, but wary that it might be something even worse that the contents of the book, he peeled off the surface paper.

Three identical photographs fell into his hand. He recognized the Province Chief. Why the Hell would Lentz hide these in here? Jake thought. Then he noticed the words on the book Biet and the other Vietnamese soldier were looking at. "Secret;" "Gonzaga;" and "November." Jake knew at once what he was viewing!

SCENE 3

TAM KY

0820 Hours
Sunday, 14 January, 1968

"Just coffee and toast please," Mark said to the young waiter who had bowed three times in welcome. The boy stood across the little sidewalk table directly in front of Mark, but made no move in response. He bowed again.

"Just coffee and toast. You know! Coffee and toast." Mark pronounced the words distinctly.

Smiling broadly, the boy scratched his chest through his bright red jacket. He bowed yet again. When he straightened, his helpful, willing gaze probed and beseeched Mark's eyes. His tense posture signalled his eagerness to please; but his feet seemed planted in the sidewalk cement.

"Coffee and toast dammit. Coffee and toast!" This time Mark accompanied his raised voice with an exaggerated pantomime of an actor drinking a hot liquid from an invisible cup while pretending to hold a saucer in the other hand.

The boy's eyes enlarged and danced. "OK GI, OK." His white teeth gleamed in a grimace of delight. He bowed one more time and bolted for the kitchen.

Hell, Mark thought. I won't get any toast. I'm glad I did the coffee first. I guess I haven't lost my acting skills. I wonder what routine I would have done for toast?

He lit a cigarette and glanced around. The sidewalk café was almost in the center of the city. Trucks, motor scooters and bicycles on MR1 passed within three feet of his outstretched leg as it disected the city. The large yellow umbrella over his table only partially shaded his wrought iron chair from the morning sun. He looked down the walk-way and then to the shops across MR1, the main drag through town. This was the only sidewalk café in sight. It had to be the right one.

He glanced at his bare wrist and noticed again the raw, red rash where his watch had been. Damn tropics! He shrugged inwardly and stretched the watch, now looped through his lapel buttonhole, so he could see its face. Ten more minutes before she was due. He dropped the watch and it fell to its new position, hanging upside down on his chest. Everyone says the Vietnamese are never on time, he thought. But she will be. God what a girl!

An old man, proudly flaunting a chest full of French medals, limped past on a pair of battered crutches. The right trouser leg of his black pajamas swinging empty. A child of about seven years padded in the opposite direction on bare feet, carrying a naked, contented infant cradled against her shoulder. An American column of M-48 tanks rumbled through the city headed north. The long line of lumbering war monsters spewed a dense, acrid smelling diesel fog which hung over the city. Despite the thunderous rumble of the massive engines and the clatter and squeal of metal treads on pavement, the shouts of the marines sitting or lounging on the tanks were painfully audible:

"Hey Cunt! Ever had it up your ass?" "Hey Granny! You with no teeth. I gotta tube steak you can chew on!" The column seemed endless. The shouting and loud chortles continuous. The people of Tam Ky paid no heed.

But Mark shrunk in his chair, hoping no one would notice he was an American. He wouldn't look at the marines, but he couldn't face the Asians. The tops of his ears burned. He could feel the pulse in his temples. He had never before been ashamed of his nationality.

The red coated waiter appeared again carrying a tray, an ornate china teapot, and a porcelain cup without a handle. He placed the cup in front of Mark and poured it full of greenish tea. It looked terrible and smelled worse. Brown, soggy leaves swirled in the faded jade liquid and bundled into a blob at the bottom. Mark started to complain, but decided it wasn't worth it. He sipped at the hot tea. It wasn't quite as bad as it looked, but it sure wasn't coffee!

He glanced again at his watch, hanging like a medal from his shirt. Just a few more minutes to go before Co Li arrives. He smiled inwardly at the thought of her. She was so vivacious. So like a prize, yet loving and giving. Her perky breasts were so silky and firm; her thighs so alive. They had had sex three times so far. No! They had not had sex. They had made love! But if he was truly in love, why were his thoughts of her so dominated by lust?

He concentrated on the street shops to take his mind off his struggling emotions. I'll make some mental notes and write them down tonight in my journal, he thought. I don't want to forget anything from my first trip to the city.

A bicycle repair shop was next door. Sparks flew from a grinder. And a welding arc illuminated the dark interior with an eerie blue intermittent glow.

The next building over was a two storied apartment type structure panted chartreuse. The large sign above the door was in English. It read: "MAGIC FINGERS MASSAGE PARLOR." A nude oriental woman, painted so that only her back and buttocks were exposed, occupied one side of the sign. Her face turned back over her shoulder staring into the street. Her mouth was shaped in a provocative "o." She wore a perpetual wink, and her hand curled around one of the two phallus shaped knobs of a chair-back.

Wow, Mark thought. Sure doesn't leave much room for imagination! He glanced in the other direction.

Next to the restaurant on this side was a small shack, just barely standing. The sign read "Tuong So; Coi Boi; Tu Vi." The blue background was spangled with stars. Hanging from this sign, so that it swung just over the low doorway was a grotesque paper mache hand. The up-lifted fingers splayed in the minute street breezes as if it were beckoning, or waving goodbye.

Next to the astrologer's shack loomed a neon outlined brick facade with the English word "Bar" in brilliant scarlet over a narrow beaded doorway.

Mark's eyes flicked to the adjacent building. Another massage parlor with another explicitly painted nude female. This shop was named "THE PLEASURE PALACE."

His gaze swept across the street. Three more bars, one fresh vegetable vendor, and two more massage parlors were in sight. The signs in gaudy, clashing colors shouting almost audibly into the city: "AMERICANS COME HERE MASSAGE PARLOR," and "THE BLACK PUSSY—cat MASSAGE PARLOR," with the "cat" in such small letters that Mark didn't notice it at first.

"Damn," he said under his breath. "You'd think by looking at the business signs that the only things US soldiers think about over here is booze and sex." He shook his head in disgust.

Just at that moment, Co Li came into view. She wore a lavender au yi over white trousers. The au yi transformed her walk into a graceful ballet as she glided toward him. Her conical hat was at the back of her neck held by a bright white satin ribbon around her throat. Her face, framed like a halo by the hat, radiated happiness and sensuality. Mark again felt his pulse hammering. He couldn't wait to touch her, to stroke her.

She beamed in greeting. Re-tilting the straw hat onto her head, she sat down swiftly in the other chair at his table.

"Hello, Sergeant Mark, long time no see." Her voice was soft yet bubbling, and Mark's throat was suddenly constricted. He tried to swallow. Co Li glanced nervously from side to side.

"Chow Co Li," Mark finally blurted. "You look wonderful."

"This au yi is present from Ty, my brother. You like?"

"It's gorgeous. Would you like some tea or something?"

She smiled happily. "No. I sit with you. You drink tea." She glanced at the teapot on the table and his half empty cup. "You drink Vietnam tea?" Her former radiant face brightened even more. "Oh Sergeant Mark, I know before you different from other American. You different for sure. You very special man!"

Mark could not hold his eyes steady. His gaze dropped to the teacup. "It's not bad," he said guiltily.

Something in his tone must have aroused Li's suspicion. "You sure you like Vietnam tea? You drink now. I watch face. Face tell me if true you like or no."

Challenged now, and determined to meet her expectations, Mark's masculine bravado rose to the occasion. He emptied the small cup in one gulp. He choked and coughed as he felt the clump of slimy, evil tasting tea leaves slide into his throat.

Li ducked her head and hid her smile behind her flattened palm, the way all women of the Orient are taught to do. The gesture was totally ineffective in disguising her amusement though, as her eyes sparked with mirth.

Mark was still coughing and clearing his throat. He pulled out his green handkerchief to spit the leaves into it, but he couldn't cough them out. They clung to his teeth and to the inside of his throat like wallpaper. The acid taste almost made him retch. In desperation, he poured himself another full cup, this time straining the tea through his handkerchief. Tears streamed down his face. He gulped the fluid down, but fresh from the pot, it scalded his mouth and tongue. He gasped in pain. More tears flowed. Co Li doubled over with laughter. However, Mark suddenly realized that it had almost cleared his throat of the wilted weeds. He repeated the process, more carefully this time, and felt better. He wiped his eyes with the heel of his hand.

Li's fingers were still flattened in front of her face. Her shoulders rocked with silent laughter. She stoped, lowered her hand in between partially subdued giggles said, "Can tell you like Vietnam tea very much. You very thirsty for sure. But before, I not know you hungry too." She giggled again and pointed to his soggy handkerchief with the neat pile of brown leaves in the sodden center. "You save for later?"

This time, both hands went to her mouth, but the charming feminine mannerism could not muffle her peals of laughter which spilled over the nearby tables.

Just as Li brought her spasms of hilarity to a hiccupping measure of control, a group of three matronly women moved through the sidewalk café in a cluster, all dressed in black pajamas. The tallest of the three, a reed thin and spry old crone, shouted something, apparently to someone far away, and the other two guffawed as they made their way past Mark and Li.

Co Li's laughter stopped abruptly. Her eyes welled with tears. Her hands were still near her mouth, but they were now frozen there. She sat rigidly, staring straight ahead.

"Co Li! What is the matter?" Mark reached across the table to touch his arm, but she avoided his hand, placing hers in her lap. Her lips twitched upward in a forced smile although her eyes still showed pain and sadness.

"What's the matter? Did I do something wrong?"

"No. You do nothing. No sweat. It nothing."

Well something happened. Was it the old woman?"

Li's eyes dropped to look at her lap. She smiled again and then emitted a small grunt of forced humor. "It funny. She make a joke."

"It must have been some joke for you to react like that. What did she say? Was it about me?"

"She make joke to me. It secret joke."

"Secret? Hell, she shouted it, whatever it was! That was no secret. Everybody in town heard her. What did she say?"

Li looked intently at Mark, evidently trying to decide whether or not to tell him. She took a deep breath, smiled again and nodded. "She ask me if maybe something wrong. Maybe Vietnam man too small to fill me up. She say she have buffalo at house even bigger than GI." Her eyes were sad, but the flicker of a smile was present. She could see the humor even though the rude remark had sorely wounded her.

Mark couldn't see any humor at all. He started to rise. "That old bitch! That's a terrible thing to say." He sat down again swiftly as his quick anger was overcome by compassion. "Oh Li. I'm sorry! We won't meet in public any more. Perhaps we should stop seeing each other." He heard himself say it, but even he heard the insincerity in his voice. He couldn't bear not being with her again; not touching her again.

She shook her head with defiance. "No. I not want you go somewhere else; love someone else. I not want love someone else, only you. Forgive please. I forget this might happen. I before want you see my city; want you understand my people. I before think this make you happy; think maybe I do this, be happy also. Her eyes brimmed with tears, but she fought them back with the knuckles of one hand.

Mark's thoughts were in tumult. She said she loves me. God that's great! Poor thing though, to be insulted by her own people. What if someone else does the same thing? I can't leave her now, feeling like this. She might decide it's not worth it. I can't lose her now. "Maybe we could go somewhere else?" he stammered.

She shook her head, but as she did so, her eyes seemed to catch sight of something far down the street. She paused. "You have one thousand dong?"

Mark remembered that he had changed a twenty into dong only yesterday. "Yes, I have over two thousand dong."

"OK." She squared her shoulders and beamed again. "We no can go my house. We no can go US camp. Guards now count everybody for sure. Even hooch maids no more can stay. Get caught. Lose pass."

Mark blinked guiltily. He knew why the changes had been made. The first sergeant had acted immediately after Mark had told him of a 'rumor going around.'

Li continued: "We go hotel. They not know me. You see big building there?" She pointed. "Big house have many windows. House color of this." She stuck out her tongue and touched her finger to it. The comic nature of the gesture made her giggle, but she cut it off sharply even though her eyes still daanced with inspiration. "Big house be hotel. You give me money and I go first. Pay for room. I say I wife. You come later. In room we talk. Maybe do other things." Her eyes sparked with romantic mischief.

"Why can't I just go in with you?"

"Then they know we not man and wife. They think bad about me."

"Ok," Mark smiled. "I'll wait ten minutes and follow you."

Li's face hardened. "Ten minute? Ten minute no good. Everybody know what we do. You wait one hour. Then come. Nobody think bad thing.

"An hour!?" Mark almost shouted. He glanced at his upside down watch. "It's after eight thirty already. I have to be back at work by noon. Hell, I want to spend whatever time we have together."

Li crossed her arms across her small chest. "We maybe sit here, have more tea. We maybe walk, meet same same woman again?"

"What should I do while I'm waiting? Mark relented, feeling cheated at this sudden change of plans.

She thought for a moment and then grinned. "You take Vietnam haircut before?"

"Sure. I get one every week at the camp. I got one yesterday."

"Not same. You go Vietnam haircut place. I think maybe you like. Then come hotel."

Mark was delighted. Hell, a haircut would take only ten or fifteen minutes at the most unless he had to wait. She must have changed her mind about the time. He rose to his feet. They stood facing each other across the table.

"You go other way. People think we say goodbye. Many haircut place in city. Go any haircut place." The impish smile still lingered. "Then you come for me."

Mark paid for the tea and they left the café. Li strolled north without looking back, and Mark resolutely marched south looking for the nearest barbershop.

He found one easily. The striped barber pole looked almost the same as in the states, except most such symbols there twirled with illuminated electric energy. This one was painted and immobile.

One hour and ten minutes later, he almost staggered back onto the sidewalk. It had been a haircut he would never forget. Even before going in, his hair had been well within military limits. But today, it had been trimmed, washed, blown dry and brushed neatly after a thorough scalp massage. His face had been shaved, cologned and lovingly kneaded until his skin tingled. His shoulders had been rubbed; his boots had been polished and his fingernails manicured.

He had not been serviced by a single barber, but by a team of three busy, au yi clad beauties who had giggled and cooed over him as if he were a baby. He felt as if he had been in one of those new automatic car wash places he had seen in New York just before he had come to Vietnam. Everything seemed to happen at the same time. It was a blur, a whirlwind, an explosion of sensation. There had been the rows of colored bottles and the blend of au yi hues, all duplicated and multiplied by the mirrored walls and ceiling. The scents of oils, balms and perfumes accented the soft radio music and the bird sound tittering of the courtesan-like workers. This, along with the stimulation to his head, shoulders, face, fingers and feet had been both relaxing and invigorating. There had not been a hint of sexuality, or had there? Mark wasn't really sure. At times, now that he thought about it, the women might have been suggesting, implying, maybe even blatantly inviting. But then they would change the mood. And all that giggling! It had been confusing. It had also been one of the most sensual and sensuous experiences of his young life. His entire body throbbed with life. The cost had been one hundred dong, slightly less than one US dollar!

Outside, Mark took a deep breath. Li was waiting, but he stopped to buy flowers from one of the many street vendors. I know she'll like flowers, he thought, even if we are supposed to be married.

Mark entered the hotel. The lobby was small, cluttered and appointed with old but formerly elegant overstuffed chairs. A musty, mildewed aroma hung in the air. Mark squared his shoulders and tried to look confident as he nonchalantly strode to the desk. "Fellogese," he announced to the stooped, ancient veteran behind the counter. "My wife should be here already."

The wrinkled graybeard smiled enigmatically and handed Mark a key. Was the old buzzard suspicious? Was it a smile of lechery? Why do I need a key? Isn't she in the room? He glanced inquisitively from the key to the still smiling gargoyle.

"Your wife, she pay already. She in room now. You no pay. No sweat GI."

Mollified, but still puzzled by the extra key, Mark stumbled upstairs, one flight up. He knocked tentatively, then turned the key in the lock and entered.

Li sat upright in the bed smiling radiantly. A shaft of sunlight from the window, like a stage spotlight, illuminated the bed and her naked torso. The bedclothes were pulled to her waist. Her arms stretched to welcome him. He rushed to her side and kissed her. The unnoticed flowers lay at the foot of the bed.

Their lips slowly, reluctantly pulled apart. Mark's hands were on her back and breasts. His mind told him to break away now and strip off his own clothing, but his hands couldn't leave her.

Co Li stroked his chin. "You smell good Sergeant Mark. You like Vietnam haircut?"

"Yeah; yeah, I did," he nodded, his hands still busy, his lips now on her neck. "But all I could think about was you. I couldn't wait to get here."

"In old days, we have hat a dau where man get massage. Get drink of alcohol. Maybe smoke from pipe of good dreams. Feel good. Women do for man; then he go home to wife. Make much love with wife. No have now. Haircut place not same, but almost same."

"You mean they had geisha houses in Vietnam?"

"Not know geisha. Hat a dau for man. Make men feel good. Make man feel good. Cost much money. Hat a dau only for man who have money. Haircut place not much money. Many wife send man go haircut place now. Have happy time when him come home."

"You mean you sent me there deliberately to turn me on? Hell, I was feeling guilty about what I was thinking, and you did it on purpose."

She giggled and reached for his zipper. "Did haircut place do good job? You ready for Co Li now?"

He stood and began to shed his uniform. "I'll show you how ready I am."

As his jacket, boots, trousers, and skivvies were tossed to a crumpled pile, Mark thought about the massage parlors of the street, the barber shops and their obvious forerunner, the "hat a dau." This new knowledge somehow gave him a sense of relief. It's not just that GI's are sex starved, he thought. It's that one culture is accustomed to openly provide those services and the other culture is all to happy to pay for them.

Co Li was giggling again. "Oh, Sergeant Mark! Haircut place do good job!"

Mark leaned out of bed and reached for his fatigue jacket. He fumbled for his cigarettes, found the pack, extracted one, and lit it while still half in and half out of bed. He noticed that his watch read ten thirty five. He should be heading for work by eleven thirty or so. He felt Li's hand on his back and then a sharp pain on his buttocks. She had pinched him.

"Hey. You want me to do that to you?" He rolled up to a propped sitting position, the pillow and headboard behind him. He put his arm around her and she snuggled against him like a sleepy kitten. She mumbled something against his chest.

"What'd you say?"

"I call you 'Anh.' It mean big brother. It what woman in love call her man."

"And what do I call you? Sister?"

"If you love me, you call me 'Em.' That mean little sister."

"You mean lovers call each other brother and sister? Wow. That's different. What do you call your brother then?"

"Same same, Sergeant Mark. Anh. If we make love, we like family. Is best kind of love. You not think so?"

"If you say so—Em."

She snuggled again into his chest and said something else unintelligible as her mouth was muffled by his skin.

"What'd you say now?'

She turned her head. "I say Tet come soon. You know Tet?"

"Well, I've heard of it. I know it's supposed to be a big deal here in Vietnam."

"Yes. It our most important holiday. It beginning of new year. Old things go away. Everything start new."

Mark hugged her closer, affectionately. "Do you stay up late at night, drink till you fall down, wear silly hats and throw rolls of colored ribbon into the air like we do on New Year's Eve?"

Li smothered he smile against his chest. "No. I see American movie one time where American people do this. I know you speak true. All very funny. Tet very serious time for all Vietnam people. Everybody buy new clothes for Tet. Brother buy me au yi for Tet, but I do bad; wear today for you.

Always we remember what we wear when we have bad luck. These clothes we throw away at Tet if we have money for new. One week before Tet begin, everybody put up cay neu: big bamboo pole in front of house to keep evil spirits away from house at time of Tet. If bad spirits come in, family will have bad luck all year. Tet have many celebration. Some men drink, get drunk; but Tet be family holiday. Have special, important meaning for family. All family must be together for Tet."

"Well, it's kind of a family day back home for us too," Mark said as he flicked his ash into a nearby clam-shell ashtray. "We all gather round the television and watch parades and football games. At least the men do. The women usually are in the kitchen cooking a big dinner."

"We have parade also; only more like dance in street through city. First day is dance of horned horse for good luck. Next day is dance of dragon to chase away bad spirits."

"Horned horse? You mean a unicorn?"

"Not know English word. White horse with one horn here." She smilingly pointed to her forehead. "Horned horse have special meaning for Vietnam people. Bring good luck. Since war come, many people not ask horned horse for luck. War not good luck. Horned horse cannot stop war. Many people no more believe in horned horse, but people of Tam Ky still believe. People hang money from windows; high windows along street. Horned horse must find, eat money. Bring good luck to people who give money."

"How do the people who give the money know it's the horned horse who gets it?" Mark's confusion was sincere. He wasn't really sure what they were talking about.

"They see him eat, you funny man. Two, maybe three men inside horned horse for street dance. They see money; climb up wall to window. Take money for horned horse to eat." She laughed and shook her head as if she were instructing a small child. "Dragon strong. Dragon not eat. Chase away all bad spirits." She glanced around the room as if she were about to betray a national secret. "But same same men inside dragon on second day as dance inside horned horse on first day." She giggled softly again. "Only more. Dragon much more long. Many men make dragon dance. One man in head make eyes roll; make mouth open like bite something. Make smoke come from mouth."

Mark smiled, "Sounds better than our Rose Parade."

Li propped herself on her elbows and peered into his face intently, then looked away. "What you name mean?" she asked.

"Say again? I don't get you. What do you mean?"

"You name." She closed her eyes and recited from memory. "Mark Amory Fellogese. It mean something. What mean?"

"It means me. American names don't have meanings; they're just names."

"All name mean something in all language. I learn this from school. Name very important to Vietnam people. Very important at time of Tet. First man to house in new year very special. Everybody try to get man come first. Not woman. Man should be white, like horned horse. More white first man, more good luck. Vietnam people always ask American come first on first day. Man with name like 'Cho,' that mean dog, never get ask on first day even if he good friend."

"Well I'm sorry, Co Li, I don't know what my name means. It probably is just a name like everybody else."

"You nice man. Have almost white skin. But you have black hair like Vietnam people. Maybe you name bad. Maybe you sick and weak when come out from mother. Maybe she give you ugly name. Bad name like 'Cho," so all evil spirit not want you. Then not tell you what you name mean. You maybe come my house before Tet start. Go back GI camp before Tet begin."

She spoke lightly, almost jokingly, but her eyes flicked from side to side, then to the floor, to Mark, and back again to the floor. Mark remembered that shifty eyes were normal for the Vietnamese as, for them, staring was very impolite. Most went out of their way to avoid any semblance of a steady gaze. But this time, Li actually seemed nervous. He brushed the thought aside. She's just embarrassed about thinking that I might bring her family bad luck, he thought.

"Don't worry Co Li, my little em. I won't be the first visitor. Besides, I have to work. It's my regular shift and we've already been told that nobody's getting off that day. I doubt if any GI will be able to come. We'll all be working."

Li started. She glanced up quickly then down again. She is nervous, Mark thought.

"Do all GI work on first day of Tet?" she asked. She wouldn't look at him. She even seemed to be ashamed of something.

"I think so. I don't know what's up, but evidently something is. I hear they've canceled all leaves and R & Rs for that time. They haven't told us anything yet. Only that we've all got to be here."

She swallowed, then straightened her head and brightened.

"Maybe you come on second day. Tet be for seven day. Maybe you come on other day also. Eat banh chung—cake for Tet. You like. Taste good."

Mark smiled. "I'll try."

Li's fingers began to play with the few hairs on his chest. She continued to talk about the traditions of the Tet festival. She told him of the family gathering on the day before Tet to light candles and joss sticks at the family altar. This was to invite the souls of their ancestors back into the house to share in the celebrations. She told him of the bright colors and decorations. She told him of the traditional firecrackers which were forbidden this year because of the war. The firecrackers sounded too much like gunfire, but they would hear much other noise to frighten away bad spirits. There would be gongs, bells, drums and cymbals. She told him about the special mirrors hung at the entrances of family homes so that any evil spirit that might get through the noise and get past the cay neu would then see itself and thus frighten itself away. She said that some people left these mirrors up all year, but most only put them up for the holidays.

Mark was amused. It was all so different, so fascinating. Co Li was so open about her beliefs and the beliefs of her people. So willing to please him. So eager for his approval.

He clutched her closer and she touched his nose and mouth with her finger.

"I no think I ever love GI with big nose. Face like dead man—so white. It maybe bring good luck at time of Tet, but white face not good other times. But now, I like. When we together, I more happy than ever before in life. When we not together, I want be together. With you; only you. Father die if he know I love you, but he not know."

"What about your brother, does he know?"

"Brother know. Not like much. He never like GI, but he not tell father."

"You know, Co Li, that we can't keep our relationship a secret always. Someone will find out. What will happen then?"

Li lowered her eyes and looked away. "Not good to worry about long time to come. Only worry about today. Gods and spirits say what will happen. We only think what happen now." She lunged forward and kissed him passionately.

At eleven fifteen, Mark walked out of the hotel. He had departed early despite Li's clinging and his own yearning. A natural pause had come in their lovemaking and conversation. When it occurred, Mark decided he had to break away at that opportunity. If they had started to talk again, or started something else, anything else, he would not have been able to leave in time.

He strolled casually along the sidewalk toward the province capital. I wonder why she got so nervous when she talked about me coming to her house at Tet? He shrugged and continued walking.

SCENE 4

THE HOTEL ROOM

1245 Hours
Monday, 15 January, 1968

Colonel Than Mak Biet waived casually to the three youths on the sidewalk who whooped and swirled their arms. He enjoyed riding through Tam Ky. The people of the city always waved and cheered. At least some of them did. Others would be too preoccupied with their own chores or their own miseries to bother looking up to see who might be riding down MR-1 wearing a starched and pressed fatigue uniform, French style sunglasses and a silver and gold Dai Ta's rank. They could be excused. But some, he knew, were either VC, or VC sympathizers; and these would not cheer because they might be reported to the local force VC commander for being disloyal.

Some day, he thought, I'll ride through town with movie cameras trained on the crowd. Then, after the deliberate non-wavers are identified by the Phoenix cadre and the national police, I will arrest them. It should break the back of the local VC cell. The Americans would object of course. They would think that not waving would be insufficient evidence for an arrest. But it is our country. It is my province. I am better able to tell who of our people is my enemy and who is not. This is war. The long noses are more interested in doing things legally, or doing things their way, than they are in winning the war.

The jeep slowed to a walking pace behind three Lambretta motor scooters which were slowed by a U.S. Army truck lumbering south toward Chu Lai. Biet squirmed in the green leather seat and leaned out to see why the truck did not move faster. "Sound your horn," he demanded of his driver.

The tinny, nasal beep added its strident din to the cacophony of the city street.

I hate this delay, he thought. I know he will wait for me, but I am impatient to see him. What an opportunity! What a splendid stroke of luck! All the way from Saigon, and he's here! Here in Tam Ky. He didn't come to see me, but the stars have intervened and have given me this opportunity. He closed his eyes and made the sign of the cross in a jerky, covert motion so as to not advertise the fact that he was praying. "Mother of Jesus, help him to see clearly, and let me hear only good news." The jeep slowed even more as the nearest Lambretta teetered inches in front of the bumper.

An old woman in black pajamas and a red, polka dot bandanna ran to his jeep. "Dai Ta, Dai Ta," she screamed. "Buy my charms. Tiger teeth to ward off evil, and tiger talons to overcome your foes. Only twenty five dong for each." She ran at an easy jog to keep abreast, displaying the polished trinkets in a flat basket.

Biet looked at her weathered face and saw that she shouted through almost toothless gums.

"Away. Away," he shouted over the noise of the city.

"Dai Ta, you are rich and I am poor. You can afford these charms. You are a man of stature; your hands are soft. You have many enemies, and the evil spirits are jealous of your power. You need my charms. Please Dai Ta! I give them to you for special price, only ten dong for each."

"I wouldn't buy a single charm from you if they were only one piaster each, you repulsive hag. Now get away from my jeep before your ugliness brings me bad luck." He turned away from her and settled back in his seat, still mentally urging the traffic to speed faster.

The old woman stopped jogging and fell behind. Reaching into her basket, she selected three tiger claws and positioned them carefully between her fingers. She made a fist so the claws protruded maliciously outward.

Silently, defiantly, oblivious to the cycles and traffic around her, she waved her fist and the curved, cruel looking talons in a clawing motion toward the diminishing back of the Province Chief's head.

"What time is it?" Biet shouted at his driver.

"I do not know, my Dai Ta. I think it was some time after mid-day when we were preparing to leave Ca Dor."

Biet glanced at the sun, as if he were trained to tell time by its position. But he wasn't. Its brilliance hurt his eyes, even through the dark tint of his glasses. He didn't know how late he was. He might even be early. He wore a wristwatch, but he didn't look at it. He never looked at it. That was an American trait. Vietnamese wear watches as jewelry. Masculine bracelets. He was Vietnamese, and the man he was to meet was Vietnamese. He will understand if I am late, but I wish the traffic were not so slow.

The jeep pulled up to the only hotel in Tam Ky, a four story box created with absolutely no ornamentation nor architectural imagination. Its freshly painted, pastel pink exterior with black trim reminded Biet of a still life by Salvador Dali.

Biet's feet hit the gravel parking area before the wheels stopped turning. "Wait here," he commanded. He hurried inside. With imperious disdain, he stomped up the uncarpeted stairway, forcing himself to climb slowly so he wouldn't arrive out of breath.

At the top of the third landing, he glanced along the short hallway. The numbers were clearly visible. Number 307 stood only two rooms away. It is a good number, he thought. I wonder if he chose it deliberately. I'm sure he did. It's probably the most popular room in every hotel in Vietnam. He took a deep breath and marched purposefully to the door. He knocked.

"Please to enter," said a voice from inside.

Biet trudged into the room. His hands were trembling. He must keep control. This man is a stranger in Quang Tin. I am the Province Chief here. I have nothing to fear from him; he must show me respect. But it is what he might say which causes me to tremble.

A small, frail man with a severely stooped back, sat cross legged on the floor of the single room apartment. Biet guessed his age to be about fifty five or sixty. Or perhaps eighty. He wore a bright yellow silk robe with black Chinese characters on the lapels. Beneath the robe, Biet could see that he wore a white business shirt and a solid black necktie. The man did not rise.

"I am Dai Ta Than Mak Biet, Province Chief of Quang Tin. Are you Khanh-Son, the astrologer from Saigon? He asked.

"I am Khanh-Son; astrologer—palmist and—foreteller of—destinies. I live and practice in—Saigon." The halting speech, surprised Biet. Was this an affectation? Or does he so carefully control his speech that he thinks of each phrase before he utters it?

"It is said," Biet mumbled, "that you are General Ye's astrologer, is this so?"

"General Ye—is one of my clients—yes—that is so."

"Are you the astrologer who predicted that one of General Ye's household servants would attempt to assassinate him?"

"I—advised him—that the stars indicated—treachery—within his household—yes—that is so."

Biet paused, breathing hard despite his former calming efforts. "I wish to know my future," he blurted.

"Is there no one—in Quang Tin—who reads the stars—for you now?"

"Yes, of course there is. But he has been wrong too often. The one before him was even worse."

Khanh-Son nodded. "Have you—been given a prediction—which you—do not trust?—A warning perhaps?—Or—something—even—more—serious?"

The old man's deliberate manner of speech was maddening. He is as shrewd as a snake, Biet thought. "Perhaps," he said. "This warning, if it is a warning, did not come from an astrologer. My astrologer's advice was confusing, as it often is. I do not trust him. I feel that he predicts events which do not happen, and then always refers to other items of his prediction which, according to him, makes his prediction truthful. I admit that sometimes he is wise and correct, but he does not have your reputation. It is said that, in Vietnam, you see the future with more clarity than anyone. I hear that you use something called the British system of Astrology."

"I was originally trained—in the Chinese technique,—but I found—it to be—less scientific—Are you familiar—with the British system?"

"No. My stars have always been read by those who practice the traditional ways."

"The twelve animal symbols—of the traditional system—have no relationship—to the stars.—The British system—is based upon—the Zodiac,—which are twelve constellations—of the stars themselves.—It is the stars—which govern the destinies—of mankind. It is logical—therefore,—to base our studies on these—rather than earthly animals."

Biet blinked and nodded. "You find it more accurate then?"

"The Zodiac characteristics—define a monthly—or lunar cycle—rather than the twelve year cycle—we orientals are—accustomed to. This gives more—precision."

"Then please read my destiny" Biet pleaded.

Khan-Son nodded again. "In Saigon,—the inflation rate—is surely much higher,—costs of all things—are higher,—my usual fee—would most assuredly seem to you—to be usurious...and unacceptable—here in Tam Ky."

"I will pay your fee. Name your figure. I can pay it."

"My usual compensation—is—three thousand dong per visit, but..."

Biet interrupted, "I'll pay you this amount."

The old man continued as if Biet had not spoken: "It is necessary—to charge—five thousand dong—on the first—visit—because of the time required—to obtain the initial data...of natal date, hour of birth—and other basics needed—to establish your personal celestial chart."

Biet cursed under his breath. He had been too eager, too quick to agree to the first preposterous fee. He must not answer too quickly this time or this grey topped old turtle would find reasons for additional charges. He rubbed his chin as if in thought. "Very well, I will pay this amount. However, I must receive a full reading today, in this one sitting. I will not be told that my chart is too complex to interpret in one day and I must therefore pay for another visit tomorrow. Five thousand dong is the payment for all services."

Khan-Son raised his wrinkled face slowly to the still standing Province Chief. "If I am to—predict your—future,—it will be useless,—if you do not—trust what I say.—If you do not—trust me,—it would be—unwise of you—to pay a single dong—to hear my words."

Biet bowed to him. "Do not take offence to my statement, Master of the Heavens." He smiled, "I come to you because you are wise in the art of seeing what others cannot see. It is only natural to find that you are also wise in the art of business matters. But in business matters, I do not trust my own mother."

Khan-Son's brittle face seemed to break in half as he also smiled. He extended his arm in an invitation to join him on the floor. "You will have—your full reading—at this sitting. A hotel room—is not as—professional—as my office,—but the floor is—comfortable—to all Vietnamese. Let us begin—At what hour—and date—were you born?"

Biet grunted into an uncomfortable cross legged position opposite the old man and answered him automatically. "On the sixth day of the fifth month of the year of the Dragon."

"No,—I need your—natal date according to—the western calendar."

Biet's eyes rolled upward as he made the mental calculation. This is 1968, forty years ago would be 1928. Then one needs to add a month for the western way, so it would be the sixth month, and not the fifth. The sixth month is June. "The sixth day of June, 1928, at exactly six o:clock in the evening."

The old man pulled a low elbow table, laden with books and charts, to his side. He deftly turned the pages of a large book until he found the page he was looking for, marked it, and set it aside. He did the same with three other, smaller books, and unrolled a large chart to the appropriate section. He turned to his visitor. "May I—see your—palm—please?"

"Yes, of course," Biet responded. "But first, I must ask a question. I know from your reputation that you are indeed a seer. Therefore, my question is curiosity only and not meant to express doubt on my part." He paused and the old man nodded for him to continue. "Why is it, Exalted Sir, that you consult books to read my palm? All others whose assistance I have sought, consulted books and charts for the stars, but they read my palm without the need of references."

The wrinkled face cracked again into a tired smile. "You—are perceptive as to procedures—my noted client,—but not as to—detail. These books are—astrological references.—I asked for your nativity date—and have prepared the books—for rapid analysis and review. The lines of your palm—are revealing—and necessary for full—perspective and accurate—understanding—of your destiny. The palm alone—is only part of the picture. One must not view—the palm as a separate—indicator—from the stars. It must be read—in conjunction—with your star charts. Both must be—reviewed together. It is the composite—complete picture...which foretells the future."

Biet nodded, ashamed now about his naivete, and the provinciality of the rustic, rural astrologers whom he had been seeing before. No wonder they were wrong so often. He extended his left hand, palm upward, somewhat hesitantly. In Quang Tin, even in the larger city of Da Nang, only the left hands of men were read. The left hand is masculine; the right hand is feminine. Women always had their right hands read. But was this rural superstition? Was it the same in Saigon? Saigon, now, seemed so remote, so superior in culture, so advanced in technology.

Biet sighed inwardly in relief as the old man accepted his flattened palm and scrutinized it carefully. The astrologer made short, hasty notes into a schoolboy type notebook which he pulled from the table.

Biet churned with anxiety and eagerness, but he refused to yield to the burning temptation to ask "What do you see? What does it say?" He would not expose his unworldliness again. He would be patient.

Finally, Khan-Son released the Province Chief's hand and studied the pages of the previously marked books, making quick, short notes into his notebook from time to time. And time passed slowly.

A lizard ran across the wall behind the intent, stooped old man. Biet watched the reptile closely, as if it were important. It was common, of course, to see a lizard on any interior wall. But, absurdly, Biet could not help but think of this particular lizard as the second self of the ancient astrologer who now sat across from him. The same wrinkled skin, he thought. The same hooded eyes. Biet could see the lizard's pulse throbbing in its profiled throat. He is waiting to see if I have the patience to wait for the reading to be completed. He sets his other self on the wall to watch me while he reads. I will not yield. I will wait him out. What am I thinking? This is truly absurd. Of course it is not true. Why am I thinking like a Buddhist? I am a Catholic! Still, however, he watched the greenish black reptile until it finally jerked and high-stepped across the wall to the top of a large bookshelf, where it ducked out of sight.

The old man coughed, and rerolled his last chart. He made several more notes or calculations in his notebook and set down his ball point pen. Laying his notes in his lap, he examined them for some moments with the bony fingers of both hands entwined at his chest. At last, he appeared to give a painful or sorrowful sigh and looked up.

"You are Gemini with moon in Capricorn and therefore have a great need for power and capital. Your chart and your hands tell me that you have overcome great obstacles, at the expense of many others, to achieve these goals. Your uniform and title tell me that you have been, thus far, successful. Some have thought of you as ruthless, and it is a term you do not object to, nor deny." There was no trace, now, of the halting, hesitant, speech pattern.

Biet nodded, "It is wartime. War requires strong men and strong action."

"Yes," the old man almost winked. "But you would be equally strong, using your word, if there were no war. It is your nature, not the circumstance. And it is dictated by the stars."

Biet shrugged. Other astrologers, using the traditional methods, had told him the same. He was, after all, born in the year of the Dragon, in the month of the Dragon and on the exact hour of the snake. This new British system used terms he had never heard before, but the readings were the same. Old news.

Khan-Son continued. "I will not give you more information from your natal chart, for this is surely known to you. Any astrologer can read a natal chart for you. It will be the same in every system. You pay me to predict what will come, and I have seen something. I have found, I think, the event you are worried about. It will come on the eve of the new year, the night before Tet!"

Biet was astounded. The man was remarkable. How did he know?

The old man droned on in a voice filled with ominous foreboding. "On the night before the new year begins, your moon, a new moon, transits the seventh house. The seventh house, among other things, is the house of declared enemies. A new moon here is always dangerous for one with many foes, and, of course, it happens once every month. On this night, however, your Saturn is transiting Gemini. Even though this is your birth sign, we must not forget that it sends a strong signal of perversity and the tendency for self undoing. Uranus, the planet of fire and explosion, is in Leo, a fire sign. Worse yet, Uranus is in unfavorable aspect to Saturn; a condition which often brings riots and destruction even when Uranus is not in Leo."

He paused, looking up from his notes to his client, who sat wide eyed and silent, listening.

Jupiter is in Scorpio, the eighth house. This usually portends good fortune in love and finance. But on that day, Jupiter is opposed to Neptune which tends to reverse the sign from positive to negative. All I have read to this point auger violence, misfortune, evil and pain. But the worst is yet to come. For Mars, the planet of war is in direct conjunction with Jupiter. This doubles Jupiter's evil foreboding, especially as both are in the eighth house, the house of death."

"Am I to die on that night?" gasped Biet breathlessly.

The wrinkled eyelids closed thoughtfully. "It is certain that on the eve before the new year, there will be fire and great violence about your person. You will also feel pain. The date, of course, does not surprise you. It is about this date that you came to see me."

"Yes. That is the date which worries me."

"It is worthy of worry. My advice is to protect yourself well on that night. Make plans for defense and see to the details of those plans. Take no unnecessary risks."

"Should I go away? Perhaps to Da Nang or even Saigon?"

"Your stars say this will happen to you. It will happen wherever you are. However, with forewarning, your intellect and energy should allow you to survive. Your palm's lifeline is interrupted there."

He reached out and snatched Biet's hand as if catching a butterfly on a twig. He pointed to the heel of the Province Chief's palm, where an almost imperceptible but evil looking gap appeared in the central line dissecting the palm. "But then it continues."

"What does this mean?" asked Biet, staring stupidly at his palm as if he had never seen it before.

"It could mean a serious injury, or a close brush with death. It could mean the near miss of a bullet aimed at your head. It could mean a period of unconsciousness or even a time of extreme fear, where death seems to be imminent. The important fact, however, is that the line continues, and the charts indicate power and glory will continue to flow to your name."

Biet nodded solemnly. "With your foresight, I will endure. I will take no unnecessary risks and will remain calm. I will not panic as I have no reason. I will use common sense, and will show courage." He smiled woodenly. And I will pray fervently to Jesus and to Mother Mary also, he thought.

The two men both rose as if on cue. They exchanged bows and then shook hands in the western tradition. Biet silently peeled five thousand dong from a wad of bills which was still thick when he returned it to his pocket. He felt that this was the wisest investment he had ever made. Khan-Son accepted the fee without words, and neither spoke as Biet closed the door behind him.

Khan-Son walked to his notes and the charts and peered down at them. His back was bent as if he were trying to form a living question mark. He glanced up at the wall where the lizard had found a shaft of afternoon sun. It squatted in the center of this illuminated spot like an actor about to deliver a stage soliloquy. The old man nodded. "I knew you were listening and observing wise one. I felt your presence behind me, and your power surging through my veins. Our vision was clear. Oh that my skin, wrinkled like yours, was as thick. I then could have told him the power of Saturn in Gemini. Perversity! However he calculates and plans, as he tries to protect his miserly skin, as he tries to safeguard his pompous belly, perversity will rule. Whatever he does, it will be wrong. I could not bring myself to show him that the line below the break on his palm is askew. It is not a continuation of his life line, but an indication that he will be remembered. There is nothing I could have told him which could save him. The stars have spoken. He will die as Tet is ushered in!"

Scene 5

THE ROWBOAT

2300 Hours
Tuesday, 16 January, 1968

In the ebony blackness of his bunker, Biet tossed fretfully on his metal, western style bed. The stagnant air reeked of mildew and stale urine. Fourteen more nights until Tet, he thought. Just two more weeks of sleeping in this hell-hole. I'm probably being too cautious. I could have started sleeping down here a week from now and still be safe, but it is said that one in danger cannot be too cautious, and my danger has been unquestionably revealed to me by the astrologer from Saigon.

He rolled to his side and opened his eyes to the darkness. He closed and opened them again. There was no difference. "Mother of God," he said aloud, half in wonderment at the absolute absence of light, half in supplication for his state of peril. He worked his hand under and through the surrounding mosquito net to touch his flashlight and pistol. He reassured himself that they were still beside the bed on the floor. He caressed the pistol thoughtfully. Deciding that even there it might be too far away, he pulled it through the netting and placed it under his pillow. He carefully tucked the mosquito tent back under the mattress and rolled onto his back.

Perhaps it is this mattress, he thought. A decadent western creation, comfortable to lie upon if it is not hot. But here in Vietnam it is always hot. Tomorrow I shall order a simple plank bed to be placed here in my bunker. It will be a sign to my staff that I am still Vietnamese, and it will also be more comfortable.

He sensed something moving in the blackness of the bunker!

It must be my imagination; I'm alone, he reminded himself. Another sound. A slight scratching directly above him in the timbers over the apex of the mosquito tent. Stealthily he began to reach for the flashlight, or should he get his pistol ready first? Fear paralyzed his hand. He heard it again.

It's a ghost, he thought. It is the ghost of Nguyen Van Quo! He has come to haunt me!

An eerie series of furtive sounds now echoed above him. What is it doing? Is it some kind of signal? A message? Yes! It has to be! It *is* Nguyen Van Quo! He knows of my complicity in his murder. He has returned to scratch my name from the Book of the Living. God it is so dark!

With a sudden terrifying screech, something crashed into the mosquito tent from above, ripping the ties and collapsing the gossamer web around him like an entangling trap. Something fetid and heavy plopped and writhed onto his chest. Biet screamed in terror. The ghost was alive, furry and frantic. Its long nails ripped into his neck and shoulder. The net engulfed and swallowed him. His hands tangled in the sheet and pillow. His fingers tore at the fabric. The decaying demon on his chest scratched and scrambled, but it was entangled too. Its screeches mingled with Biet's screams. The sounds thundered and echoed through the cave-like bunker. The weighted net mashed into his face, flattened his nose and filled his open mouth. His teeth caught and snagged the fibers. He felt a warm, wet stickiness on his legs. It was the ghost of Nguyen Van Quo attacking him! Slashing him! Trapping him! Killing him!

The flashlight beams of Major Hai, Colonel Tu and two frightened enlisted men stabbed into the bunker. The ugly, hairy rat, almost as large as a cat, tore itself free of the mosquito net and scurried off into the retreating shadows.

It took forever to untangle the net from the Province Chief's still flailing limbs. It took longer yet to change the sheets and clean the Dai Ta from when his bowels and bladder had failed him. But no matter how brightly they illuminated the bunker with lamplight, how many cups of coffee and Vietnamese tea were offered him, how many cigarettes he lit and snuffed immediately, nor how many soothing reassurances he received, his staff could not convince him that his attacker had only been a clumsy rodent rather than a vengeful spirit.

Jake rose early on Wednesday. His pocket sized alarm clock had sounded its feisty rattle at oh-four-thirty. He dressed without showering, donning the same fatigue trousers of the day before. An olive green tee shirt, his new Australian bush hat and his combat boots completed the task. Underwear and socks were unnecessary in Vietnam. He took the back route to province headquarters, the route the TOC crews always took despite his warnings. Shaking off the fear he, and everyone else always felt in the tropical darkness, he forced himself to think positively about the new experience which awaited him as he squinted to see the road, barely illuminated by the cat-eyes of the black out lights. Ha arrived at exactly oh-five-hundred. Colonel Tu, his counterpart, was waiting in his polished black jeep.

"You are exactly on time my friend," smiled Tu as Jake crawled into the passenger seat beside him. "You Americans are so predictable."

"What about you Troom Ta?" Jake laughed. "You were here before me. Are you trying to change the way Americans think about Vietnamese punctuality? Or is fishing the only thing that brings it out?"

"My promptness this morning was not planned for any effect but to play the good host. I knew how disappointed you would be if we started late on this, our first chance to go fishing. Besides, it was no trouble to be here at five O'clock: I have been awake since before midnight."

"What happened? Was there contact last night?"

"No!" Tu shook his head curtly as he started the jeep. He pulled into the road which led to the main highway before turning on his lights. The forcefulness with which the 'no' had been uttered made Jake realize he shouldn't press, but he was burning with curiosity. He decided to hold it in check, for a while at least. He changed the subject.

"When we made these plans, Troom Ta, you said you had only recently taken up the sport of fishing. How recent is recently?"

Tu's face, illuminated by the green dash lights, glowed with a broad smile as he stared intently ahead. "I began to fish in your country. Classmates at Leavenworth took me trout and bass fishing. I have become quite allured to the sport. When I heard you say that you also enjoy the water and, how do you say it? Wetting the line? I knew we had this in common."

Jake nodded. The jeep bounced onto MR-1 and then south through the sleeping city of Tam Ky, then left, over a groaning wooden bridge, just wide enough to pass, and sped along the sand dunes toward the sea. A shiver sliced up his spine at the thought of the two of them alone, at night, on a road that surely hadn't been swept for mines, and with the headlights on bright. If one of my men told me he was going to do this, I'd deny him permission, he thought. It's just too damn dangerous! If I had known that we would be doing this just to go fishing, I'd have found some definite reason to say no.

But the air was balmy and the polished stars overhead promised serenity and peace. The full moon had set over an hour before. The smell of saltwater and seaweed was reassuring. The war seemed far away and forgotten.

Tu parked the jeep under the rusted cannons of an old French fortress. "This old fort used to be a meeting place for the VC," Tu said off-handedly, as he and Jake grabbed their tackle and trudged to the beach. The shoreline was alive with activity. Dozens of men with flashlights and blazing torches worked and chatted in the moonless night. Their raised voices formed a raucous counterpoint to the low, slow, melody of the surf.

"This is the fishing village of Ky Phu," Tu stated. "The fishermen are beginning their day also. Our boat is here." His flashlight revealed a small, sturdy rowboat pulled well up on shore. They stacked their tackle and gear into it and pushed it toward the luminescent froth at the waterline. In the darkness, Jake could sense that other, larger boats were also putting to sea. Oil lanterns which illuminated nothing with their pale glow hung and bobbed from invisible masts. One or two gasoline engines roared into life only to mellow immediately into soft chugs. Jake heard the splashing of many feet in shallow water, and then his own boots were in the surf. He and Tu jumped into the boat and they were underway.

Behind them the sounds continued. They could hear fluttering, scraping noises as sails were raised. The steady percussion of the breaking sea pounded the beat. Musical shouts wafted from inland. Of bon voyage? Of good luck? Of warning? Jake felt as though he and Tu were somehow cheating as they set off to play while these others toiled at similar tasks for survival.

But this was authorized. King had heard Tu's invitation, and Jake's original apologetic refusal. King had ordered him to go. I still shouldn't take the day off, Jake thought. The troops only get their annual leave and one week of R&R while they're here. I'm not going to start taking advantage of my rank." But King had insisted. "Good way ta git ta know yer counterpart," he had drawled. A good point. The Vietnamese didn't get any R&R.

Sitting side by side, each with one oar, the counterparts rowed into the deeper darkness. The lights on shore dimmed and the voices faded. They were surrounded now by the sibilant ebony ocean which was restlessly alive beneath them and the obsidian sky which glittered and twinkled with jeweled eyes above them. A light breeze cooled and bathed them in the salt-fresh smell of the sea. They rowed for twenty minutes before Tu announced that they could begin.

Jake held the flashlight while Tu baited both hooks. Jake was startled to notice that the poles and tackle Tu had provided were fresh water gear. The poles were limber fiberglass, and the nylon lines were five or ten pound test at most. He wondered if this was by design, to increase the sense of sport; or for some other unfathomable reason. He decided to ask it as diplomatically as possible.

"What do you catch here?" he ventured.

"There are many fish here. There are those you call mackerel, and barracuda among others. But we are not here for food. It does not matter what we catch. We are here for recreation are we not?"

Jake decided he would wait and see what would happen, but his optimism for a fresh fish dinner dimmed. They dropped their hooks into the moving ink below them and settled into the posture of patience.

They sat bobbing slowly in the darkness.

"Last night," Tu spoke quietly, "the Province Chief was attacked by the ghost of Nguyen Van Quo, the former police chief of Ly Tin."

"What? What do you?... Are you serious?"

Tu told him the details of the incident of a few hours earlier, and Jake secretly grinned. He was grateful for the black night and the freedom to express his amusement even if it were only to himself. In the daylight, he would've had to control his facial muscles forcefully. He knew Tu was being serious. He knew he must not act superior nor ridicule the culture of his counterpart, but his astonishment forced him to ask, to make sure.

"Do you really mean he thought that rat was a ghost?" He mentally congratulated himself for asking the question in a controlled, uncritical, neutral tone.

"I can understand how you would think it to be amusing Troom Ta Jake. I also am able to see its comic nature, but you must realize its deeper significance. To the Dai Ta, it was truly an evil spirit. Not a real animal, but an evil spirit with a face and a name. Do you understand what that means?"

He could tell I was grinning, Jake thought. Can he see in the dark? The realization sobered him immediately. "No, I guess I don't Troom Ta. What does it mean?"

"Evil spirits often attack the innocent. They delight in bringing sorrow and misfortune to those who deserve it least. They hear of a beautiful child so they cause the child to fall and scar its face. They hear of a graceful dancer so they attack the dancer's legs with paralysis. That is why we Vietnamese do not openly compliment another's talents or natural blessings. We do not want an evil spirit to overhear. Evil spirits are evil, but they are almost always anonymously evil, without a face or name. Whenever they do reveal their true identities, it is invariably for the sake of vengeance. Revenge is only sweet when it falls on one who knows why and from whom it is delivered. Otherwise it is empty. You probably do not believe this. You are not Vietnamese. You could not understand."

"From my first tour, I understand a little, but does Colonel Biet believe this also? He is a catholic!"

"It does not matter if one is Catholic nor Buddhist, Protestant nor Cao Dai, Confucianist nor Hindu. If he is Vietnamese, he understands the ways of the spirits. If a spirit is recognized, it has come for vengeance. It can only be recognized by the guilty."

"What you are telling me then is that since Biet thought that this rat was the ghost of a murdered man, a former friend of his, that it means what I think it might mean?"

"It is the same as a confession to the murder!"

"Wow! That concurs with what the Hoi Chanh said. But I don't see how it can help clear Ray Gonzaga. Nothing like this would ever stand up in court."

"It might be possible to inform the Vietnamese officials who press the complaint. They would probably drop the charge of murder against the former senior advisor,." Tu said calmly. "They are Vietnamese; they would understand."

The two men sat silently in the darkness, bobbing slowly with the rolling swells. Jake could see Tu, now at the opposite end of the boat, but only as a black, almost formless, motionless silhouette against the sable sky.

"Without the moon, it is very dark at night on the sea," commented Tu. Jake wondered if Tu was reading his mind, or perhaps they had been counterparts long enough to really begin to understand the other's thoughts.

"I feel more in the dark now than ever before," smiled Jake, relishing the double meaning.

"You are referring, I suppose to the differences between Vietnamese ways and western ways."

"Well, yeah, I guess I am. There are just so many things—so different."

"American ways," Tu replied acidly, "are equally difficult to understand."

"Perhaps I can help. Which American ways are most difficult?"

"I will start with the fact that your world lies directly east from the Orient. Yet you call yourselves westerners, and 'Orient' in your language means east. Someone wants to go uptown, another wants to go downtown, and yet they both are going to the same building at the same elevation as their departure."

"Yeah. You got me Troom Ta. I guess our language can get confusing at times."

"It is not just your words; it is your belief system also. You have Catholics who believe in Christ but who are called pagan by others who also call themselves Christians. You, like Vietnam, have many religions which you call sects or denominations. But unlike Vietnam, every western sect denies the validity of all other sects. Every western Christian seems always at war with all other denominations to capture one more person into his particular set of beliefs. The beliefs of many are so similar that, while I was there, I could not for the life of me, understand where the differences lay. Yet all are intent to change someone else to switch sides and therefore be saved. The saved of one side labor mightily to save the already saved of the other side."

"All of us aren't that way," Jake said defensively.

"Many are, and they all felt compelled to save me while I was there. As a Buddhist in your country, I was often told I was lost, even though I knew exactly where I was."

Jake chuckled self consciously. "We have a saying in our country that one should never talk about religion, politics or women in polite company."

"I heard people say that while I was there, but I found that after the latest sporting event had been discussed thoroughly, men talk about little else!"

Jake laughed. "Well, we do talk about the weather. It changes over there you know. Nobody talks about it here because it's always the same. Hot!"

"I find it amusing Troom Ta Jake, that you feel heated on this cool night while we are discussing the uniqueness of your culture, especially since I am just warming up."

Jake marveled at the man's mastery of English. He knew that Tu was mostly teasing. "Sorry Troom Ta, I guess that did sound a bit defensive, I don't think I meant to be, but it came out that way. Go ahead, fire away. What else about America bothered you?"

"Are you sure you wish me to continue, my friend? I do not wish to offend."

"You are my friend also, and you are making me look at my country with new eyes. I'm a little embarrassed, that's for sure, but not offended. Go ahead. I really do want to hear your observations."

"Well, I noticed that Americans tend to believe in only one God. An unseen God who does nothing. A God who they say can perform miracles. But if a priest or follower of this God performs miracles in his name, he is branded a fake and a charlatan, because Americans do not really believe in miracles. Your God can heal the sick and raise the dead. Every western believer says this. But if he does, it is the result of trickery, or perhaps even the Devil. I do not understand how any American can believe in such a powerful God who is considered so powerless."

"Yeah, that's something some of us do know about ourselves. I heard a joke once that if someone says he talks to God, he's considered to be a good man; but if he says that God talks to him, he's considered to be crazy."

"Here in Vietnam," Tu continued flatly, "we are more practical. We know that miracles happen, and we know that man has no part in these miracles. We understand the limited nature of man. He is but a pawn to many more powerful forces; some good, some bad. We can do but what we can to survive. To, as you say, to get along."

A sudden tug at Jake's line ended the conversation. His pole bent and jerked violently in his hands. The loosened drag whizzed with a vicious zing. And then nothing. The unseen denizen of the deep was gone. There was silence.

Jake mentally cursed his lightweight fishing line. "We'll probably need a miracle to catch any fish out here," he mumbled.

"Perhaps it was an evil spirit," said Tu dryly. They both roared with laughter over the heaving black water.

They fished quietly as chromatic dawn advanced over the South China Sea. Scouting fingers of pink-tinged grey heralded the invasion by reconnoitering and interdicting the blackness, ambushing the defensive star snipers. In their wake rode cavalry legions of flame-edged scarlet and yellow, breaching the battle line and sending the forces of darkness into full scale retreat. Then came the main body, the main force, the sun itself, arriving to command the pursuit phase of the melee, exploding onto and over the horizon like a thousand tons of napalm, attacking the shadows on the sea as well as the fleeing remnants in the air.

The victory of the sun was total. Day had come again to Vietnam.

Jake marveled at nature's display. Without thinking, the lyrics of a poem learned long ago sprang to his lips:

> "O the road to Mandalay,
> Where the flyin' fishes play,
> An the dawn comes up like thunder
> Outer China 'crost the bay!"

"Kipling!" said Tu.

Jake nodded, not at all surprised by Tu's knowledge. He looked around expectantly, but no flying fish broke the smooth surface of the cobalt sea.

Tu's pole suddenly jabbed savagely toward the water which now burned with slashing silver flames. But his line also broke. He rehooked and rebaited with calm resignation.

Jake fished and mused about the Province Chief's encounter with the supernatural varmint. It surely was a confession of sorts, but can I ever prove it? Should I call General Elsin on this evidence? What would he say? Ray Gonzaga didn't kill anyone, but would the US reinstate him based upon the testimony of a ghost?

Biet is definitely the one who is into the black market. But Major Wallace only has one witness who might testify about the truck. It shouldn't be too difficult to prove the booze deals, but as of now, I don't have any hard evidence there either; and proving he's illegally selling booze by itself sure won't get Ray reinstated. So far, all I really have is the photograph. He glanced at Tu, who had donned his wrap around dark glasses and was intently gazing at the rippling circles where his line disappeared into the glistening water, now flattened as calm as a lake under the heavy sun. Tu had shown both personal integrity and courage by telling him, a foreign outsider, about the rat and Biet. Jake decided to share his news.

"I have proof, Troom Ta, that Dai Ta Biet is also the person who is guilty of taking the former PSA's code book."

"What kind of proof?"

Jake reached into his back pocket, rocking the boat slightly. He pulled out the tightly wrapped plastic bag which contained his wallet, and fumbled for the opening.

"That also amuses me about you Americans," said Tu, as Jake began to unfold the many creased bag. "Leather mildews so quickly in the tropics, yet you Americans go to any length to keep and continue using your leather wallets. Why do you not capitulate to the elements and use a plastic or fabric wallet as we do?"

Jake reached his hand into the arm deep bag and withdrew the billfold. "Good question, Troom Ta. It's just that I've had this same wallet for years. It was a gift. It would be hard to get used to another one."

Tu laughed scornfully. "I have heard many Americans scoff at Vietnamese when they tried to show us another way, your way, so of course a better way as far as you are concerned, of doing something; and when the Vietnamese gave such an answer."

Jake smiled, recognizing the truth of the barb, but he didn't respond. He handed the photograph to his counterpart.

Tu examined it closely, and he nodded. "It is not irrefutable evidence. The former senior advisor himself could have taken the picture, or he could be just outside the field of the camera."

"Is that what you believe?"

"No. You Americans guard your code books zealously. Some information within, you share with us; but much in your code books you guard from us as if we were also your enemy. Your Mr. Gonzaga would not allow the Province Chief and this enlisted man to take notes from his code book."

"That's what I thought also."

"It also proves that an American was involved in the theft."

Jake thought of Sergeant Lentz, in whose room the photos had been found. "How do you know that?"

"This photograph was developed at an American facility. The informative date on the border reveals this."

"You're right. It was Sgt. Lentz, the NCO who was killed in the last mortar attack on Camp Kronberg. That's how the pictures were discovered." He told Tu about Ba Nhur's visit.

"Pictures? More than one?"

"No. Just copies of this same picture. I've hidden the other copies."

Tu scratched the back of his neck thoughtfully. Jake could see a tiny image of himself mirrored in Tu's dark sunglasses. The direct heat was becoming intolerable. Jake was already sweating and he could see that Tu was also. The boat rocked gently. The knife edged horizon rose and fell. There was no other boat in sight.

"Who might have been the accomplice of your Sergeant Lentz?" Tu asked.

"What makes you think that Sgt. Lentz had an accomplice?"

"It is only logical. The code book was stolen. Dai Ta Biet had possession of it surely after it was stolen. That is the reason the picture was taken; that is especially the reason several copies of the photograph were made. That the Province Chief is implicated in the theft is unquestionable. Whoever took the photograph, or arranged for the photograph to be taken did so to provide himself criminal evidence against the Dai Ta. The Province Chief obviously did not pose for such a picture, nor would he grant permission for a picture to be taken. Yet it was taken. Your sergeant, a weak little man, if I remember him correctly, would not have, as you Americans so succinctly put it, the testicles to extort money or other favors from the Province Chief. Thus Sergeant Lentz must have had an accomplice. This accomplice could have been an American, although, knowing the power lust of some of my people, and the lack of any apparent motivating factor for any American, I would assume that the accomplice is Vietnamese."

Jake was stunned by the clear thinking deductions of his counterpart. Of course! He's right! Why else was the picture taken? An accomplice! But who? Who was Sergeant Lentz close to? And then he remembered. His jaw involuntarily dropped open. Colonel King had entered Sgt. Lentz's quarters during the volleyball game! Why else would King be snooping around an NCO's quarters after they were cleared? He was in the room long enough to have been looking for something. Who better to get something to hold against the PC? Who else could secure the Province Chief's cooperation in posing for the picture? Who else could command Sgt. Lentz's absolute loyalty? Who else would have such easy access to Ray Gonzaga's code book? It was King! It had to be King!

"I know who it is," he said. "It's Colonel King. That's how he got to be PSA when it's supposed to be a civilian position. He did something a couple of days ago that led me to think that he and Sgt. Lentz had something in common."

Tu sat quietly, pondering. At last he sighed and turned to Jake. "The facts fit together," he nodded without emotion. "He has the mark of Satan on his face. I was very surprised when Dai Ta Biet recommended a man with such a mark to be in such a position of closeness, of confidence."

"So now we know," Jake broke in. "The Province Chief and the senior American in the province. One is a murderer, and the other is a thief at least. What do you think we should do now?"

Tu began to reel in his line. "I think it is enough fishing for the day. I think we should do nothing more."

"But what about King? What about Biet? We can't just let them get away with it?"

Tu unhooked his bait and tossed it into the sea. "My friend, you are already closer to me than any American advisor has ever been. But you must become more like the Vietnamese, and use time to your advantage. We gain nothing by rash, unwise action. Time now works in our favor. We must wait and watch how time corrects this problem."

"Time isn't working for us," Jake sputtered. "It's working against us! Gonzaga is about to be tried for murder. Our two bosses are linked up and planning who knows what. Tet is coming fast and you know as well as I do that the time of Tet is going to be damn tough for everybody. We've got to do something, and do it quick!"

Tu shook his head. "By doing nothing, you obtained the pictures. By doing nothing, I learned of the Province Chief's guilt. These are signs that time is our benefactor. Nothing we can do will alter time. Time moves at its own pace. We must wait and allow it to work."

They began to row toward shore.

"We didn't catch any fish," Jake said spitefully, his frustration toward one subject transferring to another.

"I do not agree, Troom Ta Jake. It seems to me that we have hooked two very big fish. All that remains is for us to pull them into the boat."

"Let's hope our lines don't break this time," he said.

Act 4

Scene 1

THE PARADE FIELD

1730 Hours
Saturday, 20 January 1968

Many Americans didn't attend the event. Some, like Sergeant Mark Fellogese, couldn't because they were on duty. Others, like Major Bill Clayborne, elected to spend the evening in camp where they could watch a movie about space demons attacking earth, and then drink beer until midnight when the bar closed.

All of them had been invited, and several had chosen to come. Some because they were actually interested; others came only to break the boredom of a typical tropical evening in Vietnam.

Almost all of the citizens of Tam Ky City were here.

The Vietnamese didn't allow the Americans to sit together. With preplanned, uncharacteristic boldness, the GIs were politely but firmly separated as they arrived, and paired with their counterparts. The Vietnamese escorts who did not speak English ensured that an interpreter was nearby. This was not just a show. This was to be a demonstration of Vietnamese culture, and the Vietnamese were determined that all who saw it, savored it.

Rows of wooden bleacher seating had been erected along each side of the parade field. Ca Dor, the province capital building, dominated one end; its wide cement steps closing the horseshoe shaped stadium.

A circle of torches, on five foot bamboo poles, spaced about two feet apart, separated the crowd from the sand and sparse grass arena. Dusk still lingered in the soft azure sky, and the torches were temporarily more decorative than functional. They accented the electric feeling which hung over the crowd. It was the aura of expectation and excitement before a championship game. The atmosphere of spectacle about to happen.

Lieutenant Colonel King and Colonel Biet looked down from the portico of Ca Dor. They lounged as if on thrones, as Roman Caesars might have rested in the coliseum; as British kings of the dark ages might have sat, to be entertained by jousters, jugglers and fools. The Province Chief's wife rested with courtly maidens, on cushions, one level below.

Lieutenant Colonel Thorpe sat with his counterpart, Lieutenant Colonel Tu, one step below the Province Chief's family. Colonel Tu had thoughtfully brought a pair of comfortable straw mats, and a thermos of green tea.

In the bleachers along one side, with no Americans nearby, Co Li sat between her father and her brother Ty. Co Li and Ty spoke in hushed tones, whispered directly into the other's ear, to ensure that no one in the gathering crowd could overhear.

"The Americans know Anh Ty. I have learned that all will be working the day before Tet. They have cancelled all times of vacation and authorized absences. They know and will be prepared."

"Yes my Em, it is as we feared. The traitor Minh has informed them. I have learned that the province and district militia have also been alerted and told that they must not go to their families for the Tet celebration. It has caused much complaining. Many speak openly about their plans to desert their posts and spend the holidays traditionally despite the order, but the attack will not be the surprise we had hoped."

Li's father beckoned Ty who leaned across Co Li to listen. "I heard you mention the traitor's name. You are young; even your whispers are strident and indiscreet. This is not the place for conversation."

Ty nodded and clutched his father's arm. Placing his lips next to the elder man's ear, he whispered, "Yes, my father, but the American airplanes have been busy since Minh has spilled forth his poison against our people. The big bombs, from airplanes which are not heard, fall at least every other day now. The bombs are always very near our soldiers. They have not yet hit the main force, but there have been deaths and several wounded. The officers are worried as they must remain in the jungle. It is yet ten days before Tet."

"Today, my father," Li said, pushing her face into contact with those of her family, "I heard Dai Ta Biet request American units and government regular forces to come to Tam Ky before Tet. He sounded exceptionally concerned. We must cancel the attack. We are not strong enough to fight American infantry units."

"Hush my children. If the Americans come, we will make a concentrated but token attack. The nationwide nature of the uprising is such that we must find some suitable target in the province for the sake of credibility. We have already changed some of the planning. Our main line units will attack Hau Duc and Ly Tin within the week. We will keep attack pressure on Hau Duc until it falls. That is different enough to cast doubt on all the traitor has told them. The main attack will take place as planned and we will be victorious. We speak no more here. We must not chance being overheard."

Co Li sat back and glanced from her father to her brother. Both men were grim but relaxed. She wished she had their confidence. Somehow, since meeting Sergeant Mark, the cause, the fight for her country's freedom, the reason she existed, all had lost their former zeal. Many of the things Sergeant Mark had said confused her. He did not want to make slaves of her people. He said none of the Americans wanted to do this. She knew she shouldn't believe him, but she did. What could she do? She had no choice. She was Vietnamese; she would do her duty.

The night crept upon them. The torches seemed brighter. Shadows merged with shadows, and the faces of those nearby flickered with red from the circle of flames. A match flared in the darkness, and then another further off. Across the parade field, several pairs of spectacles, spaced among the crowd, heliographed reflected torchlight as if signaling the approach of a messenger.

A lone figure stepped into the illuminated ring. He wore knee length black trousers and a flowing green silk shirt, split at the sides like a feminine au yi. A corded rope belt held it tight at the waist; the bottom swung free at the thighs. Around his brow, he wore a multicolored scarf, knotted at the back to form a headband. It was Kor Uz Minh, the traitor, the Hoi Chanh, the patriot who had seen the light. The crowd on all three sides buzzed; the hubbub rose.

Minh held out his arm and received immediate, total silence. His voice was clear and carried easily across the sputtering line of torches. His attitude seemed submissive, perhaps even obsequious, yet the speech was delivered in a strong actor's baritone with the ring of sincerity and authority. Everyone applauded. He bowed and departed.

Tu smiled and leaned toward Jake. "He is accomplished. He says all the actors and dancers are from Quang Tin Province, but all are as good as those he worked with before in his professional troupe. He asks us to excuse the errors of a first time performance. The people like him to say this. He says the people must thank the provincial government for sponsoring the show." Tu gave the thumbs up signal in satisfaction. "And I like it that he said that!" He laughed and Jake smiled in agreement.

A group of seven in tight black trousers and short waisted yellow jackets with wide lapels bounded into the arena. While these colorful extroverts cavorted and captured most of the attention, black draped stage hands assembled musical instruments near the base of the horseshoe. The seven performers constituting the opening act, tumbled like acrobats around the circle with somersaults, back flips and cartwheels. Two rather weak spotlights tried to follow their gyrations, but there were too many quick tumblers and too few slow spotlights. The crowd roared its approval.

The group sprang to the instruments. The smallest of them, a waif of a girl, plucked a microphone from a stand, made a short introduction, and then lilted into song. Jake noticed then that the yellow jackets all had three red stripes running length ways down the left side, symbolizing the RVN flag.

Tu nudged his shoulder into Jake's. "This is one family. Father play keyboard. The mother play guitar. Two sons and two daughters play guitar also, probably other instruments as well. One girl play sinh tien; and youngest girl, she only six years old, she is one who sings."

Jake nodded. He noticed that Tu's English suffered when he tried to rush an explanation. The child musicians were like stair steps. Surely the next oldest daughter who rhythmically clapped two pieces of apparently hollow wood together was only eight, or even younger. The song was obviously modern, as the keyboard and the guitars were amplified. It was quick, lively and loud, but it was not as raucous as some stateside bands. The young entertainer's voice could clearly be heard as she belted out her song over the music. It was such a lively, happy tune.

"What's it about?" Jake semi-shouted to Tu over the din.

Tu was enjoying himself, smiling broadly. He turned without changing his expression. "It is hard to explain. It is sad song. Father run away from family to be with young girl, his mistress. Family have much hardship, much hunger, must survive without him. Very popular song. She is good singer."

"Yes she is," Jake nodded, but he wasn't smiling any longer. The paradox of tempo and crowd reception as opposed to the song's theme was a puzzle he didn't comprehend.

The music stopped to a crescendo of applause, the musical family tumbled and cart wheeled to the exit, and the instruments were cleared from the field. A blast of trumpets split the evening air. A gong clanged and resonated through the stands.

A man and a woman entered the sandy stage area. The man looked up and spoke a short speech, then squatted on his heels facing the steps of Ca Dor. The woman squatted beside him. The male actor wore a blue velvet jacket over ruby trousers; a white sash at his waist. The actress was dressed in theatrical black pajamas, made of black satin. Their headbands were brilliant gold. The crowd buzzed its approval.

Colonel Biet bent toward King. "This is Hat Bo, classical Vietnamese theatre. Some people now call it Hat Boi. It is very popular in the north and here in central Vietnam. There will be much noise and shouting. It is all very traditional. These two are man and wife. They are newly wedded. Something will happen to them I think." He was grinning happily.

King blinked his eyes in disgust. He was bored and didn't bother disguising it, but Biet seemed not to notice.

A double clash of cymbals and an ominous drum roll announced the next player: Scarlet trousers and a blazing violet jacket reflected the dancing torchlight. The face was painted deathly white with green trim. Two bamboo fangs jutted from the corners of his mouth which was adorned by a long green handlebar mustache. The elaborate black and green headdress bounced as he danced into the center of the circle directly behind the squatting couple. He made a short speech and the audience hissed and whistled.

"This is the Evil Spirit," babbled Biet gleefully. "His intent is to do harm to the newly wedded couple. But see! He has a mask. He will pretend to be the hero, the family will not know he is the evil spirit."

King noticed that the costumed player carried a red mask on a stick at his side. When the dancer whirled in a bright semi-circle around to face the pair of lovers, he held the red mask before his face. The demon shouted and roared with abandon, and these vocal bursts were accompanied by a wild clamor of gongs and drums. King lit a cigarette. He had felt obligated to attend, but he hadn't expected it to be both boring and noisy.

Another character appeared. This one's face was painted crimson with gold and black trim. A long beard hung from his chin. His costume of silver and gold blinked and twinkled in the fluttering torchlight.

His short speech of introduction was greeted by cheers and applause from the crowd.

"This is the real hero," said Biet. "The hero always has a red face. The villain in traditional drama always has a white face. But the family will be confused by the mask, they will not know who to believe."

The performance progressed with earsplitting shouts from both rival players, and a continual series of cacophonous pounding from percussion instruments. The hero and pretender fought, pushed and pulled each other around the theatrical battlefield. Whenever they were behind the couple, the evil spirit's mask was lowered, but in front of them the mask was held rigidly in place while he fought with one hand only.

The audience was rapt by the show. The watchers whistled and stomped their feet when the demon seemed to have the upper hand, and applauded and cheered uproariously when the hero seemed close to victory.

The end came suddenly, however, for in the middle of a furious flurry of noisy action, the husband and wife rose from their squatting positions, extracted rubber daggers from their clothing and simultaneously drove them into the real hero's back.

It took almost three minutes of staggering and caterwauling before the hero fell to his knees, and another minute before he died. King shook his head as if in pain. He was reminded of old fashioned stage plays where bad actors extended their death scenes in order to keep the spotlight as long as possible.

When the hero finally died to the whistles and boos of the crowd, the victorious villain did a dervish around the inside of the torch-light fence. Dramatically tossing his mask onto the fallen hero's body, he grabbed the now penitent young wife. Thrusting his long sword rather obviously between the husband's arm and body, he hoisted the wife into his arms and triumphantly danced off into the darkness while the husband staggered and died in another lingering and protracted death scene.

The audience whistled and cat-called good naturedly and then applauded the performance vigorously.

"Is it supposed to mean something?" asked King, puzzled but still not overly interested.

"It is classical Hat Bo. All Hat Bo dances portray some aspect of the history of Vietnam. This is unusual. It is the first one I've seen where the hero dies. Usually the demon dies. I do not know the historical reference for the play, but it does not matter. Hat Bo is much like your opera or ballet in that the subject of the story is not as important as the techniques which are used. The quality of the performance is what is important."

"What happens next?" King asked, failing to stifle a yawn.

"I do not know Lieutenant Colonel King. We wait to see together." Biet seemed to be enjoying King's vexation almost as much as the show.

Dusk had given way to darkness. The makeshift amphitheater was bathed in light from the flickering, smokeless torches, but the shadows among the viewers were long and deep. A few members of the audience used flashlights to help in pouring tea or to reassure themselves that the insect they felt was something other than a spider or centipede. Matches and lighters flamed. High up in the bleachers, where the torchlight could not reach, the glowing ends of cigarettes dotted the darkness with red.

The tinkle of bells and a single reverberating gong announced the next event.

"This will be Hat Cai Luong" stated Tu to Jake. "It is a more modern Vietnamese theatre style."

The play began. Black hooded stage hands assembled a bamboo and cardboard altar complete with candles and joss sticks, while a simple Vietnamese peasant family occupied the performance area. The husband and oldest son went through the motions of farming while the wife and daughter simulated cooking and washing clothes. Jake was immediately reminded of the Japanese movies he had seen while he was stationed in Okinawa as a Lieutenant. Much of the action was revealed in exaggerated facial expressions.

Kor Uz Minh, in an absurdly comic and symbolic NVA uniform with oversized red epaulets, bounced into the action. He exchanged a short, heated dialogue with the family. The wife gave the officer a bowl of rice and he departed.

"What's happening?" whispered Jake.

"The Communists ask the family to share their food with the People's Army."

"Is it a comedy?" Jake asked.

"No, not at all. The dialogue is very serious. Our new citizen of the republic, however, manages to make the Communists look comical as they act repulsive."

The officer returned. Another heated dialogue. This time with threats and a bit of shouting.

"This time they want money as well as food," Tu whispered. "They say it is duty of all families to share with People's Army and People's Government."

The money and food were provided with many exaggerated shrugs and woeful sighs.

Jake noticed that the audience listened intently to every word in total silence. No whistles, no cat-calls, no interrupting applause.

The next time the soldier came, he took away the father.

"The People's Army needs more soldiers," whispered Tu as the wife and children sobbed and wailed.

Tu didn't need to explain the next few scenes as the wife tried to manage the family farm on her own, obviously with very little success.

The buffoon-like officer once again arrived, this time to smash the family altar.

Tu was gleeful. "This is very good show. The Communists say that family's allegiance must be to the people and to government, not to the Gods and family ancestors. Do you not feel the resentment of the watchers?"

Jake did. The tension in the audience was electric. It exuded from the crowd like heat. Jake could taste it.

The distraught player wife seemed in desperation. She suddenly and unexpectedly pulled a dagger, which glinted wickedly in the torchlight, and plunged it into the comic Communist's back, to the released tension "oohs" and "aahs" of the crowd.

Jake had just begun to wonder if all Vietnamese theatre killings were accomplished with a knife of some sort, when he became aware of a commotion behind him. Madame Biet had slumped from her cushion. Her hands covered her face, muffling a scream or perhaps a moan. She struggled, but two women lifted her, half dragging, half carrying her up past her enthroned husband, back into the recesses of Ca Dor.

Those nearest in the crowd buzzed with animated half whispers while the play continued below.

"What happened?" asked Jake.

"I don't know," replied Tu, "but look at the Dai Ta."

Biet had been standing, facing the direction his wife had taken, but he now knelt before his large chair as if it were an altar. He crossed himself and began to pray.

Jake looked at the kneeling Province Chief. He felt sorry for him. The man is so reverent, he thought. It does move you to see that his first reaction to his wife's fainting spell is to fall on his knees and pray. He watched as King, took this opportunity to steal away from the makeshift theatre.

"An odd reaction to the fainting spell of a woman would you not agree my friend?" Tu murmured.

"Is that what she did? Faint?"

"Apparently, but that is odd also, is it not?"

Jake turned back to the performance just as the actress killer turned the knife on herself and died with many grimaces and emotional cries for pity. He could no longer concentrate on the drama. What was so odd about someone fainting? It could happen to anyone.

The audience loved the scene that had just ended below. They boomed their applause as both corpses came back to life and bowed to the crowd.

Tu was applauding enthusiastically beside him. "Our government theatre experiment, I think, has been successful. The dancer Minh is skilled. It was he you know who acted the demon in the hat boi. It is a good program to go to the villages. Do you not agree my friend?"

"You would know better than I," responded Jake, "but I'm still puzzled as to why Madame Biet's fainting spell struck you as being odd. She could be seriously ill. We don't really know what happened. It might even be something simple like being bitten by a mosquito. Hell, she could've fallen asleep and had a bad dream."

"The wife of the Province Chief would not sleep during Cai Luong. No Vietnamese would. We are also accustomed to mosquito bites."

"And if she's sick?"

"And if she were ill, she would have suffered quietly. She is not only the Province Chief's wife, she is a Vietnamese wife. Nothing natural would have caused her to shame her husband so. Something is amiss. Of this I am sure."

The acting troupe on the lighted field was now performing a traditional Vietnamese dance. It reminded Jake somewhat of an old fashioned western square dance as the men weaved through the line of ladies and twirled the women under their outstretched palms.

Jake, however, was still distracted. So what goes? A woman faints, and her husband starts praying in public. She's too old to be pregnant, and he's certainly not a religious zealot. Did they both see a ghost this time? Was it something about the play we were watching?

And then he knew! He remembered King's description of the fatal stab wounds suffered by the Ly Tin police chief. The actress below, unknowingly, had stabbed her antagonist in almost the same place, the same way as King had described on that first day of Jake's arrival! That had to be it.

He turned and quickly whispered his suspicions into Tu's ear.

"I think you are right," murmured Tu. "It means that Dai Ta Biet may have had an accomplice in the killing of Nguyen Van Quo. Perhaps, he himself was only the accomplice."

"That might be useful information, but it sure puts an unexpected twist on things doesn't it?"

"Unexpected; perhaps. Useful; perhaps. Interesting; surely. Now you see the wisdom of my words. Time will run its course. We must wait to see what happens next. Time is always at work. We must allow time to do its job."

Jake thought about time. Ten more days till Tet and the threatened attack. Gonzaga's trial was imminent. Was there enough time to just wait?

SCENE 2

THE TOC

2030 Hours
Monday, 22 January 1968

"Sir, Ly Tin District reports movement out in front of their wire!" Mark Fellogese didn't wait for a response. He turned back to the radio.

"Are you sure it's Ly Tin?" asked Jake. "We're not expecting anything at Ly Tin."

"It's Ly Tin all right Sir. They sound pretty edgy. They've gone to full alert. No shots yet, but one of their trip wire claymores went off."

"OK. Tell them we'll fire illumination." He turned to the other American officer in the room, the artillery advisor. "Jerry; kick out a 105 flare over Ly Tin's compound."

"Right away Sir," replied the young captain, a burly, black West Pointer from Arizona. He grabbed the direct telephone line to the artillery battery's Fire Direction Center.

Hell, I've already missed evening chow, Jake thought. I'll have to have a hamburger at the club when I do get back to camp. It had been a hell of a day. Da Nang had finally agreed to send a US battalion and maybe even a brigade to Quang Tin. But rather than send it to Tam Ky, the primary target for the enemy attack according to the hoi chanh, they were sending it to LZ Mary Ann, a bald, bomb cratered knoll about ten miles west of Hau Duc, way out in Indian Country.

Jake scratched his head. It would probably make a little sense if they were going out there today, or tomorrow even. They might catch that NVA regiment before it starts moving into government controlled land. But the US troops weren't due till this Friday, the 26th. They probably won't start the infantry sweeps until Saturday. Hell, the bad guys will be half way to Tam Ky by then.

"Illumination on the way Sir," the artillery captain shouted.

"Roger. Sergeant Fellogese! Let Ly Tin know."

"Right Sir." Fellogese quickly relayed the information.

A hush fell over the TOC as everyone waited for the response from the worried district, where American advisors and South Vietnamese militia units shared the defensive positions.

"Romeo, Romeo, this is Alpha, over." It wasn't Ly Tin. It was the other radio on the I Corps Tac Net. Da Nang was calling.

Fellogese grabbed the other mike. "Roger Alpha, this is Romeo. Over."

"Roger Romeo. Is your Three there? Over."

"Negative Alpha. But the Five is. Over."

"Roger Romeo. Switch to secure and put him on. Over."

Jake switched on the KY-109 secure voice scrambler and picked up the mike. "Alpha this is Five. Over."

"Roger Five. This is a special sit rep. The Marines at Khe Sanh on the DMZ are under heavy attack by multiple NVA divisions. G2 has received other reports of pending enemy action all up and down the country. G2 feels largest threat is at Khe Sanh, but the other reports must be considered serious. Most have been verified. The jarheads want Khe Sanh to be their show only and have refused Army reinforcements. The Third Brigade of the Fourth Infantry Division is therefore still slated for your area of operations. ETA is still 26 January. Large scale attack now under way at Kam Duc in your province. It's a Special Forces outpost near the Laos border but not under your control. Appears to be NVA battalion-size attack. The US Base at Chu Lai, also your province, also not under your control, reporting sporadic sapper probes and light mortar fire. End of message. You copy? Over."

Jake checked with Mark who had been writing furiously. Mark nodded. "Roger Alpha. This may sound like the kitten offering to help the tiger but if Chu Lai needs any help, we've got artillery in range. Be advised also that Ly Tin District, right in Chu Lai's back yard, also thinks they might have visitors tonight. Nothing tangible yet. One trip wire claymore and noise so far. Over."

"Roger Five. We'll advise Chu Lai. If they want anything, they'll come up on your tac net. Spooky will be unavailable tonight. We've sent one out to Kam Duc and the other two are now attached to the jarheads at Khe Sanh. This, of course, is Foxtrot Yankee India Oscar. Nothing further. Out."

Jake set the mike down. Too bad about Spooky. Whoever came up with the idea of mounting gatling guns in a C-47 cargo plane was a genius. It was a hell of a weapon.

"Sir, what's Foxtrot Yankee India Oscar?" asked Mark.

Jake smiled. "That's headquarters jargon. It just means for your information only. We're not expected to take any action because of what they said, and they wanted to make sure we didn't go off half cocked. One of the things you'll learn very quickly in the Army is that no matter where *you* are, the next higher headquarters never understands the situation and all the lower echelons eat stupid pills. You know how we sometimes get the feeling that we have to nursemaid the districts and spell everything out to them as if they were kids? Well Da Nang thinks the same way about us. And Saigon thinks the same thing about Da Nang. And the Pentagon probably thinks the same thing about Saigon. It's a disease that every higher headquarters catches. Anything from Ly Tin?"

"No Sir. The flare was right on target, but they didn't see anything." Mark paused, deliberating, and then blurted, "but sometimes Sir, the districts really don't understand unless we draw them a picture. I think they must pick their RTO's from the dog faces who don't need helmets."

Jake grinned. "Remind me to send you down to one of the districts for a week or two; that'll change your mind."

The field phone from Camp Kronberg grated its metallic summons. As Jake was standing right beside it, he picked up the receiver. "TOC; Colonel Thorpe."

"Sir, this is First Sergeant Prescott." The voice was breathing hard but under control. "I think we got zips probin our wire."

"Any trip flares or claymores?"

"Not yet Sir, but we got the tin cans in the concertina rattlin. We swept the area with searchlights but can't see nothun yet. The perimeter sure is jumpy though. They're sure sumpun's out there. I went out to check, and I think maybe they're right."

"Use an occasional mortar flare. Don't sweep the searchlights Top. Aim them first and then turn them on. Do you want us to do anything?"

"I guess not yet Sir, but with your permission, I'd like ta double the perimeter guard. For a while anyway."

"OK, go ahead Top. It'll at least make those who're out there now feel a little better. I want to know immediately if you spot anything real."

"Roger Sir."

Jake hung up the phone. Mark hovered at his elbow. "Sir; while you were on the phone, Hau Duc called in on the counterpart net requesting Spooky. They've got sappers probing their lines. Shots have been fired."

"Son of a Bitch!" exploded Jake. "This isn't Tet! What's going on tonight anyway? Tell your counterpart that Spooky's unavailable right now, but we'll get them something. Hey Jerry, get your eight inch guns to fire some flares over Hau Duc."

Jake walked briskly to the other end of the underground enclosure, the Vietnamese end, where Major Hai was on duty. "What's happening at Hau Duc Tieu Ta? Is it serious?"

The dapper little major nodded, but did not reply. He was bent over with his ear to a radio speaker. Jake heard the excited Vietnamese chatter coming from the radio along with the unmistakable staccato sounds of a firefight in the background. He sprang back to the American side again. "Jerry, get all your eight inchers up and ready to fire defensive support for Hau Duc! There's an actual fight going on there now!" He turned and looked at the four other Americans in the TOC, all waiting expectantly to be told what to do.

"Fellogese, you keep talking to Ly Tin. Make sure they know we're here and ready to help them. If there's a pause, inform them about Hau Duc, Chu Lai and our camp here in Tam Ky. That should keep them alert." He turned to the second. "Sergeant Smith, get on the spare radio. Switch it to the FAC freek. I want air support for Hau Duc ASAP, either night attack fighters or a gun ship/flare ship team. Tell them I don't give a purple rat's ass if the entire perimeter of Chu Lai is being penetrated. We need air support out there now! Sergeant Guererro: Call Da Nang and report what's going on. Everybody keep your logs current."

The fourth man, a tall skinny staff sergeant from Tennessee named Wilcox poised in front of him, eagerly awaiting a command. He looked like he was ready to run all the way to Camp Kronberg on foot if Jake were to give the word. Jake searched his mind for what else might need to be done. He had to say something. "Wilcox. Make some more coffee! It looks like a long night."

Wilcox bounded off.

Jake sat down, picked up the land line to the Castle and cranked the handle.

"Major Clayborne." The voice crackled over the line.

"This is Colonel Thorpe Bill. Let me speak to the PSA."

A pause. "Yeah Jake. What's cookin?" King sounded irritated.

"Hau Duc's being hit. No perimeter punctures yet. Unknown size force. That's the major thing. But Ly Tin's on full alert too. A trip wire claymore's been set off but nothing else except suspicious noises. We're giving them some artillery illumination. Camp Kronberg also thinks they've got somebody nosing around. I'm still at the TOC. Thought you should be brought up to date."

"Anythin else?" The Texas drawl now sounded bored.

"Well. The green beret outpost way out west in our AO, Kam Duc, they're under attack by an estimated battalion. Chu Lai has sappers in their wire, and, oh yeah, the marines on the DMZ are catching Hell in a big way from a multi-division NVA force."

"Who gives a fuck about the marines? Who's the TOC duty officer?"

"Captain Marcellus, the Artillery Liaison Officer."

"Sounds like he can handle it. What're you doin there?"

Jake swallowed uncomfortably. "I stayed a little late to read the Ruff Puff training reports. This all started just as I was getting ready to head back to the barn."

"OK. But it don't sound serious to me atall. Hell. Sentries on the line are always hearin stuff."

"I know, but Hau Duc is a real fight. And this along with the other activity in so many other places all at once…. It just feels like it's more than nerves. I thought you might want to come over yourself and take a look. Hear it first hand."

"Shit no. We don't have no advisors in Hau Duc. Why should I worry about that fuckin place? That's a slope show all the way. Nothin else sounds serious ta me. Probly just the wind. We got a good movie on over here. They're all waitin on me ta start it again. Gimme a call if somethin starts really happnin at our camp. Or even at Ly Tin."

"OK Dick. I'll keep you posted." He hung up wondering if the sarcasm in his thoughts had been noticeable in his voice. Except for Hau Duc, Dick was right. Nothing yet was serious. The timing could be coincidence. Hardly a night went by when some sentry somewhere didn't hear something. But Hau Duc was a real firefight. We're over here to help the Vietnamese in their war, but if no Americans are involved, he's not interested. Jake shook his head to clear away his anger.

Colonel Biet, Lieutenant Colonel Tu, and three other Vietnamese officers had entered the TOC during his talk with King. Tu had waved in greeting but both were now being briefed by Major Hai.

Jake turned to Sergeant Smith. "Have we got air support?"

"Yes Sir. A gun ship/flare ship team in the air and on the way to Hau Duc. I've got contact. Want me to tell um something Colonel?"

"No, let me talk to them. What's the call sign?"

"Brimstone One Sir. He's the flare ship and in charge of the team. We're Denmark on this net."

"Thanks…. Brimstone One this is Denmark five over."

A staccato, broken voiced gargling sound, typical of all chopper pilots' radio voices, with the thump of helicopter blades in the background, acknowledged.

"Brimstone One…. O—ver."

"Brimstone One this is Denmark Five. Be advised we're firing eight inch guns into your target area. Very high altitude trajectory. Enemy is attacking from all four directions. Our red legs will shift fire to targets only on the east side. That'll leave the other three sides for you. You should be able to fly directly over the firebase out there unless they're firing their own mortars. Just don't venture east of the base. Give me an ETA and I'll check fire their mortars. Over."

"Rog—er—Den—mark—ETA—Zero—Seven—Over."

"Roger Brimstone. I'll confirm check fire before your ETA. Out." He replaced the mike. "Sergeant Wilcox! Tell our counterparts about the helicopters; one flare ship and two gun ships. Hau Duc's got to cease fire its mortars in five minutes and I want confirmation when that happens."

"Right Sir." Wilcox bolted for the Vietnamese side.

Jake paused by Captain Marcellus who was busy on the phone to the FDC. Jake didn't disturb him. He turned instead to Mark.

"Anything new?"

"Not yet Sir. Both Ly Tin and the Camp are still hearing things. The Camp came up on our TAC net in case the land line goes down. There's a break in the fighting at Hau Duc right now, but reports are that Charlie's just restin up for another big push. Lotsa noise on every side except the one we're shellin with the eight inchers"

Jake sat down and lit a cigarette. The coffee was ready and someone brought him a cup. A lull in the action. The radios were quiet. Nothing to do now but wait. He thought of what it must be like out there on the perimeters of Hau Duc, Ly Tin and Camp Kronberg. The sentries would all be filled with terror. Straining their eyes and ears in the lurking darkness, then shielding their eyes from the blinding flares. Many will be so scared they'll forget to close one eye to save their night vision, and that'll frighten them even more. Two men to each foxhole, pushing together for mutual assurance, just touching isn't enough. Twitching and jerking at every leaf blown by the wind. Knowing that someone, somewhere out there, actually wants to kill them. They're all sweating, yet their hands, knees, feet are freezing. Their joints are aching yet numb at the same time. Every noise is amplified a thousand times. Their stomachs are churning in knots, and they feel every sensation because they think it might be the last time they do.

They'll be praying. They're out there now making promises to God they have no desires nor intentions of keeping. Asking forgiveness. Pleading to see another day. Begging God to save them. They know that here, in war, they don't have any control over their lives. Everyone wants so fervently to live, yet the soldier's job is to be ready to die.

The generals make fine speeches about living and surviving. How it's our job to live and make sure the soldier on the other side is the one to die for his country. "Make them all heros," they say. But every soldier knows from the first day of boot camp that he's training himself to die if the chips fall that way. If he's in the wrong place at the wrong time.

Even I! I stood up last week before the troops at Camp Kronberg and told them to be careful. To not take chances. I told them that none of them are expendable. Yet I sit here drinking coffee under four feet of sand bags and PSP while they're out there under a helmet and a cloud of fear. The odds are that no matter what happens tonight, I'll probably live to see the sunrise. But those guys out there don't know what their odds are. They're not sure at all. I told them they weren't expendable, but they're the ones on the line and I'm here. If they die, part of me will die with them because I'll always wonder if I made a mistake. If I could've done more. Done something better to save them. But no matter what, I'll still be breathing tomorrow. We'll get replacements, and I'll forget their names. Hell, there's nothing more expendable than a soldier. And way down deep, we all know it.

Colonel Tu eased into Jake's reverie by squatting on his heels beside him. "The Dai Ta sends his compliments and appreciation for the helicopters. The enemy is attacking again, but the mortars have ceased fire."

Jake called out to Sergeant Smith to tell the choppers about the mortars.

Still squatting, Tu lit a cigarette. "The garrison at Hau Duc is joyous at the news of the gun ships."

"Good. How's the morale of your guys at Ly Tin?"

"They are awake and alert. This is not new to them."

"No, I don't suppose it is." Jake wondered if this were a subtle jab at the American rotation system which brought new soldiers, green soldiers, every twelve months. The Vietnamese couldn't rotate out of the war zone. They stayed and fought.

On the Vietnamese side, Major Hai shouted with glee. Colonel Biet, beside him, laughed and scratched his rear end. Both were looking at the radio as if sight could help as well as hearing to understand what was happening.

"The helicopter gun ships are over Hau Duc," said Tu. He punched the air with happiness and grinned at Jake. "They are, ah, kicking the crap from them."

Jake smiled also. "Good," he said.

The Vietnamese radio crackled again. Tu interpreted. "It appears that the enemy attack has been temporarily broken off."

"Temporarily? You mean you think they'll be back tonight?"

"Yes. So does the Dai Ta. It was not just a sapper attack. It was a main force unit in strength."

"Colonel Thorpe Sir! The camp just took three RPG rockets," Fellogese shouted from the American side.

Jake grabbed the Kronberg telephone and cranked the handle. "This is Colonel Thorpe; what's happening?"

"First Sergeant Prescott Sir. We just took a few rocket rounds. Nobody hurt. Looks like we'll have ta build a new shower stall though."

"No follow up ground attack?"

"Not yet Sir. Just the rockets."

"Are you keeping the place lit up with flares?"

"Yes Sir. We got plenty of 81 illumination rounds, so we're usin um."

"OK Top. We're here if you need anything else."

"Right Sir. By the way Sir, you're not thinkin a comin back here tonight are ya? I mean, we know they're out there now."

"Well no Top, I wasn't. Too much happening. Better cancel the midnight shift change also. We'll all stick it where we are till daybreak. No need to chance a double jeep trip tonight, even through the city."

"Right Sir. I'll stay up over here too. The midnight TOC shift is on duty here now. They won't be gettin no extra sleep."

"Sir! Ly Tin is getting hit! Sappers definitely in the wire." Mark was shouting from the radio.

Jake tossed the phone aside and leaned into the radio speaker to hear. "Zulu this is Kilo. We've had several bangalores in close. RPG's and a few mortar rounds. We've got one dead sapper in our concertina. Only one friendly wounded reported so far, and he's not serious. He's still on the perimeter. No KIA's. Over." The voice was excited and frightened, but the kid was doing his job. A good report.

Jake picked up the mike. He forced himself to sound calm, confident and reassuring. "Roger Kilo. This is Zulu. Do you have any arty targets for us? Any ideas where the mortars or rockets are coming from? Over."

"Roger Zulu. Concentration three. Give us a marking round first. Over."

Jake glanced at Jerry to see if there was a need to relay the message. There wasn't. The redleg captain had heard, nodded and was sending the request to the FDC.

A pause. "On the way," he said.

"On the way," Jake repeated into the mike.

The marking round was on target, and Kilo requested fire for effect. Jake again gave the "on the way" signal and waited.

Another lull. Another empty space in time as everyone waited to react.

Jake looked at Marcellus who was poised over the artillery phones, eager, excited, but steady. "If they call for more barrages Jerry, you handle it; you're the artillery expert."

Marcellus smiled and nodded. Jake returned to Tu, still squatting as before.

"In ancient days," Tu said, "officers rode into battle with, or even in front of, their men. War was simple then. One man fought one man. Later, the long bow changed the concept of battle. The senior officers were favorite targets so they began to stay to the rear. They found that doing this, they were more effective in maneuvering their units, and their decisions could turn the tide of battle. With longer range weapons and improved communications, we no longer can sit on a hill to see the fighting. We must lock ourselves in rooms with electric machines, for that is the only way to coordinate artillery and air support, evacuate the wounded, send reinforcements if necessary, receive the latest intelligence reports, resupply, and hundreds of other activities. All without seeing or even hearing the war itself. I think it is necessary, but it is most difficult and frustrating, do you not agree my friend?"

Jake nodded silently. It was exactly what he had been thinking earlier. He lit a cigarette. He absent mindedly recalled that he had one going somewhere. He couldn't remember where he put it.

Tu continued. "Leaders used to lead by example. They wore bright clothing so all could see them. We must hide, and lead with calm voices and soft words or shouts if necessary. Some say our leadership of now is more effective. I am not sure. I would rather see and be seen."

"You're right Troom Ta. It's damn frustrating sometimes. The kids on the line would trade places with us in a minute. And most of the time, I would if I could."

"Yes, but they wouldn't believe you if you told them this."

"True, they wouldn't." He glanced back at Mark to see if anything new was happening. "Sergeant Guererro," he said. "Call the Castle. Let them know about Ly Tin and the camp's incoming. Then call Da Nang and report it."

"Yes Sir."

Tu seemed pensive, distant, preoccupied. "Something bothering you Troom Ta?" Jake asked.

"Do you know the Vietnamese customs concerning death?"

"A little, from my first tour. I remember that the dead are always buried twice."

"No, not always. Rich Vietnamese can buy their own land for a burial site and thus they have the luxury of only burying their dead once. Those of us with less money, most Vietnamese, rent a burial site until the body decays; until only bones remain. Then these are disinterred and either cremated or placed in a small compact earthenware coffin which occupies less precious earth space, allowing the first grave site to be reused."

"That seems to be very practical."

"The origin of the practicality is tradition, or superstition if you like, but we now justify the practice with practical terms."

"I'm not sure I understand."

"Our ways must seem strange. I am a Buddhist as you know. When I die, I would wish my body to be treated as in the old ways. However, I am a soldier, and therefore it surely will not be."

"What does being a soldier have to do with the way your body is treated?"

"When a Vietnamese dies, he should always die at home, surrounded by the love of his family. This will prevent his soul from wandering. Someone who dies away from home..., his soul will wander."

"Can't they bring the body back home?"

"Some do, but only a few. Usually the rich who feel that their lives are so blessed by good spirits that they can anger a few bad ones and still have good left over. Some of the more fervent Catholics also, those whose religion is strong enough to defy the old ways. For me, the old ways still have importance. My wife is very traditional, and would never allow my body to be brought home, for my soul would already be wandering."

Jake sat silently. Tu was in a gloomy mood. He seemed worried. Jake wondered if he should try to cheer him up but decided it might be taken wrong. He offered Tu a cigarette without speaking.

"After the Vietnamese dies at home," Tu continued, "there is a period of mourning while the body stays in the house. This allows the spirit to know it is wanted. To know where it belongs. Then there is the funeral and the first burial. After ten years, the bones are uncovered and carefully arranged in a small earthenware coffin, and reburied in a location dictated by the astrologers. Only in this way will the soul remain near and be able to offer its protection to the family from future evil spirits."

Jake's curiosity was boiling. He longed to ask questions, but he could tell that now was not the time. Tu was obviously not in any mood for questions. He decided reassurance was what Tu needed.

"This war will end soon Troom Ta. You and I will both die of old age surrounded by our grandchildren and great grandchildren."

"No." Tu's firm but quiet answer cut through the heavy silence inside the TOC. The 105 battery a hundred yards away boomed another barrage toward Ly Tin, emphasizing Tu's words. "I will die a soldier, away from home. I will be a wandering soul."

Jake didn't know how to respond. He took another drag from his cigarette. He heard again the agreeable sound of the artillery battery. The 8 inchers were still banging away toward Hau Duc. His plastic coffee cup was empty, but he made no move to refill it. The radio traffic in the background from both sides of the TOC was a blur of muffled, frightened, tense, determined voices. He heard the steady hum of the outside generator. The bare electric bulb over his head swarmed with buzzing insects which seemed to drown the human and machine sounds around them. He remembered the two times in the past when he had felt the grasping hand of death.

Both times I was sure I was going to die, he thought, but for some reason I didn't. Others have told me they've had the same experience at least once. Should I say this to Tu? Tu's been fighting a lot longer than I have. Surely he's felt it before. No. When the feeling's there, it's there! Nothing anyone can say will make it go away. There's nothing I can do.

"Tomorrow," said Tu. "I'm going to Hau Duc to assume command of the defenses there."

"I'll go with you," blurted Jake. "I'm your counterpart."

Tu shook his head. "The Dai Ta has ordered me to go because he is worried about Hau Duc and Dai Wi Doung's lack of experience. But he is even more worried about Tet and Tam Ky. The Hau Duc militia is doing a good job defending itself tonight. We both doubt that the VC can take over there without an attack, but it indeed will be more secure if I am there. The Province Chief has heard you work tonight, and also before at other times of tension. He feels he will need your clear head here at the time of Tet. He has ordered me to go alone."

"Don't I have anything to say about it?"

"No my friend. He will tell the senior advisor that you are not to go. Colonel King will not allow you to go against the Dai Ta's wishes."

Jake nodded. He was right. King wouldn't let him go. Not because Biet wished it, but because Hau Duc wasn't worth it. Besides that, lately for some reason, King seemed more respectful of the Province Chief. He no longer seemed to bully the Dai Ta as he did when Jake had first arrived. I wonder if the code book has anything to do with that?

"What about Biet, and what you and I know about him? What about King? We can't just let them get away with it."

"If by fate, or the mercy of the Lord Buddha, I return, we will do what we must do. If I do not return, you must do what you must do."

"God! You can say wait and see in a lot of different ways."

Tu smiled warmly. "We are friends, but we are of different cultures. We could become even stronger friends. But we would never truly understand the other."

Jake smiled. The two looked at each other intently, searching and memorizing the face that gazed back. It seemed that both were trying to absorb as much of each other as they possibly could.

Jake reached out and gently but firmly clutched Tu's arm. Tu was more than a comrade in arms. He was a friend. He was a brother. The electric realization of how close they had become flooded his chest, and a lump caught in his throat. But the sadness of Tu's premonition crushed the joy that should have been.

Tu's hands moved upward as if he were about to embrace him. They paused and hung in the air with uncertainty. Then he stood and dropped his arms. Biet was beckoning from his chair on the Vietnamese side.

Jake stood up also. They faced each other again.

"The Republic of Vietnam is worth saving my friend." Tu smiled. "It is a good cause to fight for and to die for. I will keep the gold flag with its three proud bands of red flying at Hau Duc."

"And I," said Jake. "Will make sure you get everything you ask for out there."

They smiled again.

"Sir! There's small arms fire at Ly Tin. They're under ground attack!"

"Get another gun ship/flare ship team up from Chu Lai. It's only a five minute flight from there." Sergeant Smith grabbed one mike while Jake grabbed the other to talk directly with the Ly Tin garrison.

The long night dragged on. Hours of waiting, listening, sweating. Nothing happening; no one talking. Then all Hell would pop in seconds. A flurry of commands and actions. A surge of adrenaline and excitement. The cannons outside boomed continuously. Three men reported wounded at Ly Tin. Dust offs had been quick to respond. The wounded were evacuated under fire. The attack was repulsed by 0125. One more rocket into Camp Kronberg at 0300 hours. Another probe and flurry of fire at Hau Duc at 0400.

Then nothing. Waiting. Four militiamen dead at Hau Duc. Fourteen wounded, but the Ruff Puffs had held. Two dust off helicopters had been shot down as they plucked the wounded from the firebase under constant sniper pressure. The RFPF were doing the job, and it was against an NVA main force unit. The uniforms on the enemy dead inside the wire confirmed this, but the RVN flag was still flying.

At dawn, the air in the TOC bunker was a haze of cigarette smoke which burned tired, sleepy, still nervous eyes. Jake sat in a corner resting, his back against the cool sandbags. He thought of Colonel Tu and his allegiance to his country's flag. He nodded to himself. Old Glory means as much to me. I understand.

His tired mind drifted back to Fort Bragg, where, as a Lieutenant, he had been the Officer of the Day at a flag lowering ceremony.

He and the Sergeant of the Guard; Mata, his name was Mata, saluted as Retreat sounded. The ceremonial cannon fired, and the flag detail hauled away at the lanyards. But something went wrong.

The men pulled furiously, to lower the flag by the last note of the bugle call. Jake thought it must have been a broken pulley.

But as soon as the flag was secured and their salutes terminated, Sergeant Mata made a bee line for the soldier on the other side of the pole, the one holding the guide rope.

"Soldier!" Mata shouted. "Were you holding that rope?"

The tall young recruit hung his head. "You told me to hold the guide rope Sergeant," he whined, "and I tried to, honest; but it kept burning my hands!"

Jake smiled with the memory. He had laughed out loud back then.

Dick King was standing over him.

"Did you stay here all night Jake?"

Jake got to his feet. "Yes, Dick, I did."

"I just read the log. Nothin really happened. Why'd ya stay here? Were ya afraid ta go back ta Camp Kronberg in the dark? Afraid the big bad VC were gonna getcha?"

"That might've been part of it," Jake said. He was too tired to feel angry.

"Well, that's OK then. I don't mind anyone playin it safe. Why don'tcha go home now though. Get some sleep. Come back about noon. I'll cover for ya."

"OK Dick, thanks. I think I will."

As Jake climbed the steps out into the sunlight, he heard a helicopter revving for take off from the pad. He looked up just in time to see Colonel Tu, in full battle dress, climb into the chopper. Jake waved, but Tu stared straight ahead as the bird took off. He never looked back.

Jake continued waving half heartedly until the helicopter was almost out of sight. "Good luck to you my friend," he said aloud, but there was a heaviness in his chest.

SCENE 3

OVER HAU DUC

0600 Hours
Wednesday, 24 January, 1968

"Sir, your call sign while we're up here will be Black Jerkin."

"Black Jerkin?" Jake exclaimed over the helicopter's intercom. "Wow, they're really digging deep into the dictionaries for names now aren't they?"

"Yes Sir," responded the intercom solemnly. Looking at the backs of their helmeted figures, Jake couldn't tell which man in the front was talking to him.

"Just how hairy is it supposed to get out here today Sir?" A different voice from the headphones, but he still couldn't pick the speaker. Both pilots in the cockpit stared straight ahead, their intent, sun visored faces reflecting back from the windshield like a mirror.

Jake didn't answer right away. He thought about it. It was liable to be as hairy as one of those rock and roll music festivals. "We're going to have to be on our toes," he said. "Tam Ky is still firing artillery east of the perimeter. We can fly over the base, north, west and south of it, but we've got to stay away from the east side. Those rounds will be falling almost straight down from their max ordinate. Now as for altitude, we'll have to fly high enough for me to see what's going on, and that means up where they can see us and shoot at us. It's a main force unit against us, so they have automatic weapons and rockets. Our door gunners'll have to be alert, but for God's sake, don't shoot into the compound. That's where the friendlies are." Jake checked over his shoulder to ensure that the door gunners had been listening. Both enlisted men standing behind their machine guns nodded that they understood.

Jake continued. "I need to say this too. I understand why all pilots like to buzz the tree tops. It's the safest way to fly over here, but our job is to control an air strike. We couldn't get a FAC from Da Nang, nor from Chu Lai, so that's why we're here. I've got to be high enough to see the enemy targets and direct the strike. These guys under fire out here are depending on us, especially now that the weather is OK. We couldn't get any air support yesterday because of the weather, so even if we start receiving fire, hang with it at altitude until I give the word."

"We gottcha Sir. Just don't become a sightseer and forget how our ass is hanging out when we're coasting along like a fat target drone at a thousand feet or so."

Jake thumbed the intercom button twice to signal his agreement. Seems like a good crew. Willing to get the job done. Good. He smiled in satisfaction. Funny, he thought. Here I am racing out here to get shot at and I feel good. Excited even. He analyzed his feelings of elation and exuberance. It's not just the good weather. It's because of Tu, he decided. It's not like yesterday when I sat in the TOC almost all day and couldn't do anything. I'm finally able to do something active. Something positive to help him. He sounded fine on the radio last night. Cool as a cucumber even under heavy fire. Hau Duc has been under siege for over thirty hours. He checked his watch. Thirty hours! We'll be there in about four or five minutes, just barely enough time to identify the targets before the attack aircraft get there. Only fifteen minutes to go before the zoomies are on station.

He smiled as a thought struck him. The Hoi Chanh had said that Hau Duc, along with Tien Phouc and Ly Tin would not need to be attacked. But they had probed Ly Tin without success and they had been attacking Hau Duc vainly for three days. Sure isn't what that hoi chanh told us would happen, but I still think he wasn't lying. Obviously the VC are not as strong as Minh had been told they were though. Tu was right when he scoffed at that news.

I'm beginning to understand King by now, he thought. King didn't want me to go today at first. He felt Hau Duc should mark its own position and direct the strike from the ground. Hell, that's tough to do. I know. I've done it. Someone on the perimeter usually has to get up and throw a smoke grenade right into the teeth of the enemy's main attack, or rather where they think the main attack is coming from. Then someone from the ground has to see where the smoke lands and adjust the strike from the smoke. It's scary as Hell when you're under fire. And with all the noise it's hard to make sure the jet jockeys get it right, because they sometimes don't, even when the instructions are in perfect English.

He shuddered as he remembered the near miss of a five hundred pound bomb landing just behind his position, two years before, after he had just told the pilot to hit the VC in front of him. The VC must have thought the damn bomb had actually hit us, because they jumped from cover and charged across the open field in mass so we were able to cut them down. One of the ironies of war. A dunderheaded mistake by a fly-boy that should have but didn't kill us. Instead, it turned out to be the thing that won the battle for us. If I ever meet that jerk, I still don't know whether I'll shake his hand or punch him in the schnoz.

But King doesn't know, or doesn't care how dangerous it is, and how much you need a forward air controller to direct a strike. He wasn't going to let me go until I told him I wanted to earn another medal, maybe an air medal with V device or higher, and this seemed like a good chance of getting one. He sure bought that. I knew he would. God, for a minute there, I thought he was going to go instead. Jake shook his head in wonder. I've heard of others, he thought, but he's the first one I've ever met who really would do something just so he'd get a medal.

"Arty impacting on the right Sir, I think that's Hau Duc about Two o'clock." The pilot in the right seat was pointing out the window with a green gloved hand.

"That's Hau Duc," confirmed Jake. "Let's take her up for a quick look." He noticed two quick puffs of steam-like clouds from the center of the firebase. "Son of a Bitch! They're still firing their mortars! Do a one eighty quick! I don't know which direction they're shooting." Jake's imagination visualized a friendly mortar round, intended for the VC, exploding into their chopper in mid air, sending the hulk hurtling to the earth like a wingless goose.

The big Huey lurched into a steep left bank which pressed Jake deep into the webbed seating of the open passenger compartment. He leaned into the ear of the wide eyed and open mouthed Vietnamese interpreter sitting beside him in the center of the helicopter, his radio at his feet.

"Tell Hau Duc to cease fire their mortars!"

The young man nodded. "Yes. Yes. 81 mortar. Cease fire? Cease fire?"

"Yes. Cease fire!"

The soldier bent forward and spoke rapidly into his mike. Seemingly within seconds, he looked up and smiled. "Cease fire OK. No more mortar go out."

Jake relayed this to the pilot, and the aircraft rolled heavily back toward Hau Duc.

As they circled the barren knoll, Jake could see the orange spurts of small arms fire from the perimeter. Flashes of gunfire could also be seen from the enemy, from every point of the compass. Most of these would be snipers, Jake realized. They surround the base. Makes it seem like they're everywhere, and it masks where the main force is, where the attack will come from.

At first, the small district compound looked almost the same as he had seen it only nineteen days ago. The long, low diamond shaped main bunker in the center, the mortar pits, and the circle of fortified emplacements on the perimeter. But there were differences. Several of the outer foxhole positions had been destroyed. The roofs of three storage bunkers had been caved in and scorched black by fire. Craters from incoming rounds pock marked the hill. The white flag pole had been broken in half, but the RVN flag still flew from a radio antenna on the command bunker.

Then he saw the bodies. Ten, twenty, no, more! There were at least fifty. God! Hau Duc was really putting up a good defense! This attack was serious. More yet! Maybe a hundred dead men dotted the landscape. Almost all of them wearing the khaki uniforms of the North Vietnamese Army. Many were inside the compound, even beyond the perimeter foxholes. Others were entangled in the concertina, but the majority were outside the wire. A shiver went up his spine. Gruesome, macabre, yet unreal and almost dream-like at this height. They looked like discarded plastic soldiers, the kind he used to play with as a child. Some seemed to be locked in the same strained positions as those of his former molded toys.

He blinked and looked away. Got a job to do. Which way? Where's the main attack? The main body? He searched the tree line to the west and saw only a few muzzle flashes. Snipers. Decoys. There! To the south! The blink of metal reflecting the sun. Something moved. Another movement. Got to be sure. Nothing to the east where the arty rounds were landing. Nothing to the north. "OK, I've got um!" he shouted over the intercom. "Take us down. Stay north or west of the firebase!"

He put his field glasses to his eyes to double check as the helicopter circled down and away. Another wink of sunlight south of the firebase. More movement. I've got you, you sons of bitches!

The helicopter pulled out of its dive into a screaming, terrifying, treetop level dash which the air jocks called "contour flying." Many ground grunts felt it was designed by a sadist with wings for the sole purpose of causing non flyers to lose control of all bodily functions, but despite his convulsing stomach, Jake knew it was the safest way to fly over enemy territory.

The intercom clicked. "Sir. Your covey of birds on Tac 2; call sign Viper One and Viper Two."

Jake switched his radio knob from I for intercom to the numeral two. "Viper One this is Black Jerkin, I'm your eyes for this job. Over."

"Roger Black Jerkin. You a blue suit? Over."

"Negative Viper One. Suit is green but my eyes are clear. I've got your target spotted. Can you see the friendly position yet? Over."

"Not sure Black Jerkin. We're close though. Have them pop smoke and identify. Over."

"Roger." Jake leaned again to the interpreter who had no flight helmet and thus no way of hearing Jake's conversation. "Have Hau Duc pop smoke. Pop smoke!" He wondered whether the fact that the pilots now knew he was Army instead of Air Force would make a difference in their willingness to do what he asked them to do.

The enlisted soldier beside him smiled and nodded. Popping smoke was such a common request, even Vietnamese who spoke no English at all understood it.

He soon turned again to Jake. "Green smoke Troom Ta. Green smoke."

Because of their low, tree ripping altitude and speed, Jake had lost sight of Hau Duc. He didn't even know which direction it was. He couldn't see the smoke. Had to trust what they said. "OK Viper One, Friendly unit reports green smoke on its position. I'm not in position to verify. Got it yet? Over."

A pause. Probably ten seconds no more. It seemed like ten hours. "Roger Black Jerkin. I've got green smoke on a fortified hilltop. I see it clearly. Hey, I also see a buzz saw down there. Must be you if you're in an egg beater."

"Roger Viper One. That's us. Watch our approach as I mark the target. Follow the same path. Artillery fire in area. Wait, out." He thumbed the radio quickly back to intercom. "OK, the fighters are on station and waiting for us to mark the target. Circle around to the north of Hau Duc. Fly due south right over the base and hug the turf. I'll drop a smoke grenade and then tap you on the shoulder. Don't break until I tell you to; then break right and take her up to a good spot, say due west of the base where we can watch the show."

The pilot's bright red helmet nodded and he leaned his joy stick into a right bank.

Jake switched the radio. "This is Black Jerkin again Viper One. I'm heading in for the smoke drop. What ordnance you carrying? Over."

"This is Viper One, watching your pinwheel. We've each got two 500 pounders and a nape canister. Over."

"Roger, let's spread this out as long as we can. Three runs each; napalm first, then one bomb at a time. Over."

"This is Viper One. Wilco."

Jake selected a smoke grenade from the green polyester bag at his feet. Yellow smoke. Wrong to tell them now which color I'm going to throw. Too early. The VC often had someone listening. If they knew which color, they'd have yellow smoke popped in six different places. Zoomies wouldn't know which one was mine. He waited. There's Hau Duc dead ahead. Tu, old boy, I'm right here with you like I told you. Hang in there baby. We're going to kick ass and take names.

Jake leaned his head out the open doorway to see the flight path of the helicopter. The wind tore at his face. He clutched at the smooth metal surface of the chopper's skin as if he could find a handhold. Don't think about falling out, he told himself. Think about the job. Think about Tu. Do it for Tu.

Hau Duc zipped past below; only twenty feet beneath him. He could hear the intense small arms fire clearly through his flight helmet and earphones. A splashing sound and glass breaking. Two rounds had hit the windshield high and gone out through the roof. Hope they didn't hit the rotor. They see us coming though. Here comes the tree line. Pull the pin. Get ready.

"Zing!"

A ricochet off the aircraft's skin, just a few inches from my face. Can't think about it now. Concentrate! Here's the tree line. A few more seconds. Now!

Jake leaned out the door to make sure the smoke had ignited. He watched the thin smoke stream disappear into the trees. But it was yellow. The grenade had ignited. He tapped the pilot's shoulder. "OK Viper One. This is Black Jerkin. Yellow smoke on the bad guys. Over."

"Roger Black Jerkin. Yellow smoke in sight. Also saw muzzle flashes. What were they shooting at? You? Over."

"Just small arms. We're OK. And if they couldn't hit us, they sure as Hell won't hit you. Over."

"Ho Kay. If you say so, but I always think it's unfair when the bad guys shoot back! This is Viper One heading in for first pass."

Circling west of Hau Duc at two thousand feet, Jake caught his first glimpse of the ground support fighters. A sleek, silver F-100 Saber jet roared in low over Hau Duc. A Super Saber, Jake corrected himself, and marveled at the grace and streamlined beauty of the swooping attack. The forest south of the defensive perimeter erupted in a scarlet swath of flames which merged into a single, mammoth black and red fire cloud.

"Bingo Viper One! Right on target! Well done!" he shouted happily into the lip mike.

"Roger Black Jerkin. We aim to please. Viper Two on his run now." The voice was cool, business-like and deadly.

The second Saber screamed over Hau Duc, lower, faster, looking even more vicious.

A parallel path of boiling fire butchered the verdant carpet. Black smoke billowed and tumbled into the air.

"Fantastic, Viper Two! A gorgeous hit!" bubbled Jake. The chopper pilots were laughing in the front seats, slapping each other on the knee. The door gunner behind Jake pummeled his fists into Jake's back with glee, then leaned down and screamed "Sorry Sir, guess I forgot myself for a minute."

Jake waved off his apology. What a devastating weapon! He caught his breath as the first jet banked and zoomed downward again, this time in a steep power dive. So fluid and smooth the motion; the silver wings glinting in the sunlight. It's like watching a ballet, he thrilled. Beautiful, captivating, awesome. I bet Charlie doesn't think it's so pretty.

The first 500 pound bomb shattered the tree line between Hau Duc and the still smoking scar tracks of napalm. The concussion slammed against the helicopter almost two miles away. The hot blast of wind felt fierce but invigorating on Jake's face. "Atta boy Viper One! Viper Two, put your next one to the left of the napalm trails."

"Roger."

Viper two blasted the left. Viper One ruptured the right. Then Viper Two slammed the last bomb on the far end of the twin blackened fissures in the green jungle canopy.

"Well done both of you," Jake sang. "Every pass right on target. If you need a recommendation give me a call. First class show."

"This is Viper One." The voice was emotionless, icy calm. Just another business day. "And a rebound to you Black Jerkin. You'd make a fair to middlin blue suiter if you ever get tired of the mud. By the way, Viper two reports a lot of bad guys retreating south. His last egg got um good. They're in the tall timber now so strafing runs won't be effective, but I think the pressure might be off your little people for a while anyway. We'll make a few dummy runs to urge them along. Enjoyed working with you. This is Viper One out."

Jake let out a war whoop of joy. They're running! He turned to the interpreter. "Call Hau Duc. Tell them we think the enemy is withdrawing. Ask them if the incoming fire has decreased." He could tell from the blank face that he was not understood. "Ask them if they still get shot at."

The translator nodded and chattered into his radio. "Hau Duc say no shots. No more fire from VC." He was grinning, sharing in the pride of accomplishment.

"Fantastic!" Jake picked up his own ANPRC 10 infantry radio wedged under his webbed seat, the mike on his lap. He pulled his plastic encased map from inside his fatigue jacket and pressed the push to talk button on the hand set, contacting the advisory team TOC. "This is Five. Fire Mission. 8 inch guns. Coordinates: niner four three eight; two five niner zero. Possible enemy assembly area. Fire for effect. My command. Over." They acknowledged. That should do it, he thought. If they're still going south, this barrage just might catch them. It's the spot I'd pick for an assembly area. I'll fire it right after the zoomies clear out. Elation pulled his mouth into a corner stretching grin. We did it. Hau Duc's still there and the flag's still flying. He touched the arm of the interpreter. "See if you can get Colonel Tu on your radio. I want to talk to Troom Ta Tu." Jake smiled again thinking of an appropriate wise crack to send down to his friend. I'll bet he's in a better mood now than he was the other night, he thought. I'll tell him he owes me a beer.

"Um Troom Ta." The interpreter pulled on Jake's sleeve. "Um Troom Ta. Sir. Hau Duc say Troom Ta Tu no talk. Troom Ta Tu; him die."

Nausea convulsed Jake's stomach and throat. Time stopped. The thump of rotor blades and noise of rushing wind ceased. Silence. Jake couldn't feel his hands gripping the radio, nor the sudden swelling of salty water in his eyes. The open cabin of the H-34 helicopter was out of focus. Everything diminished in size. He was a giant in a miniature doll house suspended in mid-air. The door gunners were tiny figures on a distant picture postcard. Everything moved in slow motion.

"When?" Jake asked.

"Pardon, Troom Ta? I no understand."

"When, God Damn it! When did he die?"

"Soon um Co Van. Troom Ta Tu die from last fire. Just as first airplane make fire. Him die very soon."

"Damn it! What do you mean soon? Is he dead or not? Has he already died? Or is he just expected to die soon?"

"Him die um Troom Ta. Him die dead."

Jake sunk his head in his hands. Damn language barrier! I thought for a minute there…. Jake straightened. I wonder if I could…. Tu's moody words of two nights ago cascaded into his thoughts. It's a crazy idea. It's a stupid idea, but by God I'm going to try it!

"You tell Hau Duc they're wrong! Troom Ta Tu is not dead! You hear me? You understand? He's not dead! He didn't die! Tell them to put an IV into his arm. Bandage his wounds. He's still alive!" He accompanied his words with fierce pantomime to make sure he was understood.

The interpreter stared at him in shock, not moving.

Jake grabbed the small framed man by his lapels and jerked hard. The man's eyes widened as if he thought Jake were going to throw him out of the open helicopter door. "Tell them Damn it! Tell them he's not dead! Tell them I said so! Tell them I know he's not dead! Tell them we're coming in down there to evacuate him! Do it!"

The interpreter babbled frantically into the microphone, simultaneously edging away and keeping one eye warily on Jake, obviously fearful of a more severe outbreak of caucasian madness. It evidently took a great deal of persuasion, but at last he lowered his hand set. He licked his lips nervously and reported. "Hau Duc say OK. Wounds have bandage. Needle with waterblood in arm. They say Troom Ta Tu not die yet. But maybe very soon?" His expression was hopeful.

Jake had already instructed the pilots. The chopper was on final approach to the battered Hau Duc landing pad. He smiled sardonically, and nodded. "Maybe," he said. "Tell them we have room for five or six other wounded that they can send back with us to the Tam Ky Hospital."

The helicopter landed in a swirling cyclone of dust, ammo pouches, bloody rags and mortar shell packing. Dai Wi Doung, with a bleeding bandage over one ear, ran through the dust cloud and saluted. Jake remembered that he spoke no English. He returned the salute and bowed to the District Chief. They stared at each other without speaking. Neither knew what the other was thinking, but military courtesy had been followed.

Eight severely wounded men were carried to the helipad and loaded aboard. A massive chest wound. One with both feet gone. An arm missing from the shoulder. A head wound, still bleeding, the bandage soaked with blood, dripping on the soiled uniform. The others just as bad. I said five or six, but how can I say no to any of these? They're smaller than GIs. Have to just pack them in.

Then two men brought Colonel Tu on a stretcher. Another carried the saline solution bag. Where we going to put him?, Jake thought. We're in here like sardines. There's absolutely no room. But they made room.

During the flight back, the Hau Duc veterans did not talk to each other as might have been expected after a victory. Almost all were in a morphine stupor which only partially masked the pain of embedded shrapnel, missing limbs, broken bones and abdominal wounds. They were dirty, tired, thirsty and sad, but none dared sleep. They all watched Jake as if they expected either a demonic spell or a miraculous healing. Jake held Tu's limp hand in his, patting it reassuringly. He talked to Tu in English as if he were listening and occasionally leaned his own ear near Tu's face as if a conversation were taking place. It was a charade. He knew it, and everyone on board knew it, but they didn't know why, so he played it through. If they were ever questioned, they would have to report that his actions were consistent. Once or twice he looked around as if he were looking for help. They shrank from his glance as from a cobra.

The hospital pad was the first stop where they unloaded all but Tu, Jake and the interpreter. Then they flew to the province pad where the interpreter got off and Major Hai climbed aboard. Hai knew where Tu lived. The last stop was an open field pointed out by Major Hai just a few blocks from Tu's house.

The two door gunners, under Jake's direction, carried the litter. Jake carried the saline bag in one hand and held Tu's dead hand with the other. Major Hai, confused but somewhat aware now of what was happening, ran ahead to warn Tu's wife and to prepare the house.

They were met by an open doorway and a siren-like wail from Madame Tu.

They rushed into the house, not bothering to remove their boots. In the bedroom, they set the stretcher on the floor.

"OK, thanks guys. Now get back to the chopper and take off. Tell the pilot that I said he did a damn good job." He didn't bother returning the salutes of the two door gunners, who had no idea what was going on.

He set the plastic IV bag on the bed and stepped into the large tiled main room. Madame Tu and Major Hai were in deep conversation. Madame Tu was sobbing.

"The Troom Ta says he wants a drink of water," Jake said, interrupting them. Madame Tu rushed to the outside pump and Jake returned to the bedroom. Major Hai remained where he was.

When she returned, carrying a cup of water, Major Hai followed her into the bedroom. Jake rose from his kneeling position beside Tu. "Tell her it's too late," he said. "He just died."

Madame Tu dropped the cup and fainted.

"When she comes to," Jake said, "tell her that her husband's last words were to tell his wife he would always be near to protect the family. Tell her I didn't know what he meant, and you had to explain it to me."

Hai stood in the doorway, a blank expression gave way to a fierce look of pride. He snapped to attention and saluted Jake as if on parade.

SCENE 4

THE OFFICE

1530 Hours
Wednesday, 24 January, 1968

Jake stirred as his telephone rang. It was Curly, calling from Thang Binh. "How goes it Curly?"

"Pretty good Sir. My interpreter just got back from Da Nang. I've got names, places and dates, including big Daddy himself. Do you want them over the phone or what Sir?"

"No, not over the phone. Can you get them to me tomorrow? I might be headed for Da Nang during the weekend. Colonel King told me he might send me up there for an errand or two. I'd like what you have before I go."

"Yes Sir. The District Chief and I are coming down to your location tomorrow. I'll hand carry them."

"Good. Thanks Curly, see you tomorrow."

He hung up. Biet was still pressing King to get a US battalion into or at least closer to Tam Ky before Tet. King doesn't want anybody in Da Nang upset with him, so he's sending me, hoping I'll catch any flak that flies. OK by me. It'll be my chance to call General Elsin. Haven't been able to send a message or call from here. King's so paranoid about someone going over his head, he'd flip if I did. And he's got everyone else so terrorized, someone would tell him if I tried to do it on the sly.

If Tu were alive, he'd still be telling me to wait. Telling me that time was still on our side. But Tu's dead now. My warm hearted, intelligent friend is gone. Time sure wasn't on his side. Damn I miss him. Such a terrible waste!

The heavy lump in Jake's chest ached again, as it had each time he'd relived the events of the morning.

But it's time now, Jake thought. I've waited long enough. Tu is no longer here to tell me to wait, and I need to trust my own instincts. I think I have enough on Biet's black marketeering to make a case, especially with what Curley's bringing me tomorrow, but is that enough? Tu thought that Madame Biet might've been the one who knifed Quo. Biet's surely involved, but I can't prove it….

The telephone's intrusive jangle jarred his train of thought. Race Haldane's booming voice caused Jake to hold the receiver away from his ear.

"Hey Colonel. You remember you asked me to find those two VC porters who finked on Gonzaga?"

"Yes Race, I remember."

"Well it ain't been easy but I think I found um. I figured they'd be in an RDT or PRU unit. That's where Chu Hois are usually assigned. But they weren't nowhere around up north. So I kept nosin around. Then I found um. They're in a PRU team down in Quang Nam, the province to the south a us."

"How'd they get down there?"

"Beats the shit outta me Colonel. I think somebody pulled some strings somewheres. Can you give me permission ta go down there tamorra and talk to um? I can get my own transportation."

"Hell yes Race. Do it. And let me know what you find out."

"You got it Colonel."

Jake cradled the receiver again. This might be the break we've needed, he thought. Hang on Ray, we're getting closer.

Major Hai stood in the open doorway. He saluted and bowed. Jake stood up and returned both. "Um Co Van Troom Ta Thorpe," Hai began, "I speak you please?"

"Sure, come on in Tieu Ta, but why so formal today?"

Hai entered and sat stiffly in one of the two straight back chairs in the office. Not the one beside the desk which visitors usually used, but the other one against the wall. He appeared nervous and ill at ease.

Jake walked around to the front of his desk and propped himself on the front corner nearest Hai. "I'd offer you some coffee or tea Tiu Ta, but I'm out. Would you like a cigarette?" He held out the pack.

"Thank you, no, Troom Ta."

Jake lit a cigarette and waited. Hai obviously wanted to talk, heaven only knows about what. Whatever it was though, he wouldn't come right out with it, right to the point, it wasn't the Vietnamese way.

"NVA come soon from jungle to Tam Ky. VC be very busy. Much message, much recon. For number one protection, Quang Tin must have much ambush site each night. From today to first night of Tet. Quang Tin have number one militia. Number one Ruff Puff. But maybe for now need little help. Need number one ambush against NVA. Maybe Troom Ta, America advisor help?"

"What kind of help do you need Tieu Ta?"

"Maybe one America advisor each night. Militia see, have good morale. America soldier fight with us. Militia fight better when advisor fight also."

Jake thought for a moment. Six nights. Six men. A reasonable request. We have a four man RFPF advisory unit. This is part of their job. Surely I can get two volunteers. King'll bitch about it, but what the hell, he bitches about everything. "OK Tiu Ta. I think we can help you with that. Anything else?"

"Madame Tu," Hai continued. "I tell her how you hurry to get to house before he die. She very grateful. She tell me she want you come, visit Troom Ta before bury him."

"Thank you. Tell her I will come tomorrow."

Hai looked around furtively. "No Vietnam man ever think to do what you do. I never before hear of thing like this. Yet you do. I think maybe you better Vietnam man than anybody."

"No one must ever know what I did Major Hai. You saw it, and I can't hide it from you, but you must tell no one. If you do, everything I did will be in vain. The family will feel betrayed and destroyed. It will change a good thing into a bad thing."

Hai nodded. "Do not worry Troom Ta Thorpe. I never tell. I also lie to Madame Tu. I visit hospital before I come here. I tell hurt men from Hau Duc I see Troom Ta Tu talk to you. I say him still alive when they see. Most men hurt very bad; they not remember well. I think for sure they believe I speak true."

Jake relaxed. "Good. I was worried about those guys and the word leaking out."

"Interpreter only problem. I transfer him to Pleiku today. Him already go. No problem now. I talk to Hau Duc on radio, they maybe surprised, but all believe."

"Thanks." Jake smiled, Hai had tied up all the loose ends very nicely.

"I want very much to say to all Vietnam people what you do. What good heart you have for Vietnam culture, but no can do. This make me sad, but I not worry. You have yet much time in Vietnam. Have many more chance for Vietnam people see you, know you."

"Thank you Tiu Ta." Jake was embarrassed. Hai was piling it on pretty thick. Surely neither this nor the ambush request was the reason he had come. The ambush request was routine, one he knew I'd agree to.

"I think maybe you do number one for family of Troom Ta Tu. Make feel good that spirit stay near. But I think more time. Think why you do this? Maybe you think only superstition, so OK to do. Maybe think that family who live be consider number one." Hai's eyebrows were raised. The statement had evidently been intended as a question.

A lump caught in Jake's throat. Oh God, he thought. I tried to do the right thing and now I've offended him by showing him I didn't take their spirit world seriously. How should I answer? What can I say?

Hai didn't wait for him to respond. "In helicopter to house of Tu, I see what you do. Very confused. I do what you want, not know for sure why I do. I see Madame Tu very sad Troom Ta die, but very happy him die in house. I think maybe I lie, you lie, OK little bit. But inside, not sure. What spirit of Troom Ta do for sure now? I think long time. Now have answer."

Jake took a deep breath. Here it comes, he thought. Despite his former praises, he's going to tell me how disappointed in me he really is.

Hai continued: "Troom Ta Tu die for sure in Hau Duc. But not stay Hau Duc long time. Very short time. You show love, like family in helicopter. People tell me this. Tu spirit must like this, stay close to body. Same thing as in house. Spirit must be still close when for sure in house. That make OK. That make same same Troom Ta die in house. You no believe, but do for family. But end be same. Number one. For sure, I think spirit of Troom Ta stay with family now. I come tell you no sweat. Everything number one. I know what you do for sure. I think you do number one also."

Jake swallowed. "Thanks Tiu Ta, but I do want you to know that I did it for Tu also. It's what he wanted."

Hai smiled. "I think for sure. But that only one thing. Want more to speak. OK Troom Ta?"

"Sure," gasped Jake in relief.

"You are Troom Ta America army," Hai continued. "When America fight England to get freedom for first time, many advisor from France and Germany help young America army fight."

"Yes, that's right," Jake agreed. He vaguely remembered his history lessons.

"America war for independence very much same same to our war here. Vietnam radio tell us much about this. America colony fight for freedom, for right of individual. You fight so government not come in family house anytime without papers. So government not make new taxes except by represent of people. So government not say how people must worship in one way only. Our war here for same same."

Jake nodded. There are similarities, he thought. He snuffed out his cigarette in the abalone shell ash tray on the desk. What the heck is Hai leading up to now?

"America not same same as French. French want to control country."

"Well," Jake said slowly, "many Americans back home don't understand the difference Tiu Ta. They think we're only here to control you too. Hell, some are so stupid they think we're over here fighting all the Vietnamese."

"I know. They wrong. I one time see America sergeant run two hundred meter under fire to save life of wounded Vietnam Lieutenant. Carry him back to cover. America man strong, almost get back. VC shoot him. When he fall down, he fall with care so not to hurt Vietnam man more. Very close to Army line. Many Vietnam soldier now go forward. Get sergeant and Vietnam Lieutenant. America man die. Vietnam man live."

"In my first tour here, Tiu Ta, I saw many acts of bravery by South Vietnamese soldiers. All nations have men with courage."

"Maybe so Troom Ta, but sergeant not from Vietnam. He not know name of man he save. Why he do that?"

"It was his job, at least he thought it was."

"Today, you do what you do! This your job also Troom Ta?"

Jake took a deep breath. "No. I guess it wasn't part of my job. I didn't think about it. I just did it."

"I was that Tiu Wi, Second Lieutenant. America sergeant, him save me! I never forget."

"Oh." Jake nodded, "I see." *Actually I don't see,* he thought. *I still don't get what's really bothering him.*

"Today Troom Ta, Province Chief, Dai Ta Biet, him make me Chief of Defense, Deputy to Dai Ta. I take place of Troom Ta Tu."

Jake jumped to his feet, his smile spontaneous and radiant. "Congratulations," he shouted. He shoved his hand toward the shy major.

Hai nodded and shook his hand, but continued. He wanted to finish his speech. "Before America sergeant come, I be hurt and be much, how you say, fear. I think maybe die, but he save me. Today I Tiu Ta here." He pointed to his rank insignia, an embroidered gold bar with a single silver pip above. "Dai Ta say that now I soon be Troom Ta here." His finger still pointed to the insignia. "But in here," he tapped his chest. "I still Tiu Wi, Lieutenant, with much fear. I see you today. You show me what Troom Ta is. Very strong. Very quick. Very good for people. I not ready for Troom Ta. Maybe never ready."

So that's it, thought Jake. *He lacks confidence. And because I did something instinctive that turned out right this time, he thinks he's* got to be Superman or Einstein or a combination of both to do his job. Jake thought carefully. How to bolster his ego, this man of a different culture who grew up in war. This apprehensive leader whom others must be able to trust.

Jake stepped back from the slumping, huddled major and snapped to attention. Very crisply, he saluted.

"I salute you Tiu Ta Hai. You will be the best damned Troom Ta in South Vietnam! I reacted and did something today, but so did you. I didn't tell you to call Hau Duc to confirm what we did. I didn't ask you to go to the hospital or transfer that interpreter to Pleiku. You reacted to the situation you had, and you did it all by yourself. That's what leadership is: how you react to situations. I am now your co van, your personal advisor, and I'll be at your side when you need me. But you've already proven to me that you don't need me. You can do it by yourself."

Hai stood, stunned by the salute from a superior. He returned the salute automatically and smiled broadly. "You not unhappy work with me? You not angry that new Troom Ta not come from Saigon? You think is OK we work together?"

"I am very happy about it, and proud too."

"Oh Troom Ta! I listen you always. I try hard do what must be done, as you advise me." He jumped forward and embraced Jake, then caught himself and started to withdraw, but Jake reacted and hugged him quickly. It was the Vietnamese way. Men hold hands and hug each other all the time, he thought, and I sure as hell am in Vietnam!

They separated and held each other at arm's length.

"We be good counterparts," Hai said with a broad smile.

Scene 5

---- ⊱⋆⊰ ----

THE AMBUSH SITE

1700 Hours
Friday, 26 January, 1968

"Is there more shit paper on your side Top? This roll's down to its last wipe." Mark slapped at a mosquito on his bare thigh.

"Yeah, I got some, 'n there's three more rolls in the corner here." First Sergeant Prescott had not turned his large body nor head. He had obviously checked before he sat down. Impassively, he passed a new roll to Mark.

The two men sat one hole apart on the rough cut plank, their booted feet tethered by their trousers and shorts. It was a three holer, and the abyss of the unused rumble seat yawned between them. Flies, mosquitos and a squadron of other flying insects buzzed within the shed-like structure, some of them diving into the unoccupied black hole, which, like both of the others, had been hand sawed by a sadistic wood butcher. A splinter in the gluteal region was just another of Vietnam's daily indignities. The smell, of course, was still another. The repulsive, rotten fumes of excrement and diesel fuel hung heavily within the shed. It always slugged you like a sledge hammer when you first entered, Mark thought. But by the time you dropped your drawers and settled in, you were accustomed to it.

"Big day fer you today eh?" Prescott grunted. "Gittin outta your shift by volunteerin fer an ambush patrol."

"Yeah," Mark responded nervously.

"Why'dju do it? You don't seem like the hero type."

Mark paused before replying. His first impulse was toward bravado, but he'd had other talks with this fatherly top sergeant. He could be trusted. "I'm not really sure now Top. Seemed like a good idea at the time. Finding out what war is really about. I mean, let's face it, for me so far the war has been trying to tune out static on the radio. I thought this might be a little excitement maybe. I don't know. I'll go through with it of course, because I did volunteer, but I'm sure as Hell having second thoughts now."

"Good; you are smart. I thought I pegged ju right."

Through the large crack at the bottom of the creaky wooden door, a four legged shadow appeared. One of the many camp dogs. It stopped and one of the slender shadows disappeared. The damn dog was peeing against the door! Must have a solid sense of place, Mark thought. The fourth pylon shadow reappeared and then jerked backward. Another stilt shadow jerked backward, and sand spattered against the door. The dog trotted off.

"We sure got a lotta dogs in camp," said Mark absently, trying not to think about the coming night's activities.

"Sure do," said Prescott, straining.

"Where do they all come from? I've never seen many in the ville."

"Oh, they have um there too." Prescott scratched a mosquito bite on his extended bare belly. "The thing is, a lotta the indigenous types eat dog. It's a delicacy. Kinda regional. The further north you go, the more dog's on the menu. They have a sayin. It goes: He who ain't eaten dog, ain't eaten." He chuckled. "They haveta taste good over here. Have you seen um? They're the ugliest curs on the face a the earth, all ubum. Never seen a good lookin dog over here; but they're funny bout um. A dog's a sign a' prestige. It means you got more 'n enough food ta feed yer family. So they never eat their own dogs; er at least they try not ta. Best ta catch a stray er steal a neighbor's. That's why you don't see um runnin around. They guard their pets purdy close so they don't get pinched fer a hungry neighbor's dinner."

They sat for a while in silence, staring at the unpainted boards ahead of them. Four thumb tacks still held the shredded corners of a Playboy pin up, but the picture itself was gone. GI graffiti, with its usual lack of imagination and humor, was the only interior decoration. "Vietnam, love it or leave it." "Tam Ky is the asshole of the earth, and somehow I ended up here. I guess that makes me either a queer or a piece of shit." "Yankee go home." "I would if I could." And "You're both motherfuckers, this is home!" Mark read them stoically, as he always did. I wonder if Co Li eats dog, he thought.

"Didju ever wonder why Americans over here have so many pets?" Prescott asked.

"Because we like them I guess," Mark said. "Same reason people have pets back in the world."

"Nah, it's differnt here," smiled Prescott. "Think about it. Lotsa regular pets here: dogs, cats, birds, maybe a few more types a' birds here; and even a few tanks a' tropical fish. But think a' the others. There's at least ten guys here with snakes as pets. At least three I know have pet rats. Cuppla monkeys. Probly more a' those if they were easier ta catch. Hell there's GIs in this camp with pet spiders, pet worms, and even a beetle er two."

"Yeah," Mark agreed. "I've seen them. I don't get the difference yet though."

"Well...," The huge first sergeant dreamily assumed an overweight parody of Rodin's "The Thinker" before continuing. He sighed. "It's a theory a' mine, but I think I'm right. Almost everone over here gets a pet a' some kind. Not like the states, where maybe half the people have pets. It's almost a hunnert percent over here. They're away from their families 'n loved ones, don'tchu see? They need pets."

"Need pets?" Mark stammered. Sunlight streamed through the widely spaced horizontal wall boards, blazing two bright yellow stripes across Prescott. One ran from shoulder to shoulder across the top of his balding head. The other lay in his lap, dissecting his ham-like thighs.

"Yeah, need um. Ya see, we're in a war zone. Needs a' soljers tend ta be simplified. Right down ta the basics. Air ta breathe. Food. Water 'n survival. Those are the main ones. Shelter's not! Not fer a soljer. It's a luxry. But the pets prove there's one more need. Can you guess what i'tis?"

"Well, I guess you're going to say love. That's the only thing it could be. But I don't see how a spider could give love to anyone."

"Right chu are Bucko! See, I told ju you were smart. But the need ain't ta receive love. That's where yer' wrong. The need is ta give love! That's the only way it makes sense. Think about it. Back when you were first crazy in love with someone. Didju think about the lovin she might give ya? Nah! You only thought about what chu could do fer her, right?"

He might be right, Mark thought. I do think of making Li happy. Pleasing her. Giving her things. And sex of course. I don't know whether that's getting or giving, maybe a little of both. He nodded to Prescott who was winding toilet paper around his hand.

"Yep, it all fits in," the First Sergeant said. "The human need is ta give love, and it's a basic need fer sanity as well as happiness. Almost ever philosophy talks bout it. All kindsa verses in the Bible bout it. Happiness comes from givin. You gotta give in order ta receive." He continued to wind the white paper around his hand. Around and around it went. "'N it's more blessed ta give than i'tis ta receive."

Holy cow, Mark thought. How much paper does he need? He's got a pad an inch thick front and back. Is he going to use both sides? He watched as Prescott finally tore the paper without concern, leaned forward and reached behind him. Mark's thoughts returned to the conversation.

"Then how come everyone seems to think they've got to be loved in order to be happy?" he asked, watching Prescott begin a second padded package of toilet paper, as thick as the first.

"We humans," Prescott said slowly. "Have the ability ta git everthin all screwed up. Our priorities git confused. The Bible says Seek ye first the Kingdom a' God. How many people you know actually do that? Nah! They all go after the pleasures a' the flesh. Seekin their own kingdom. Back home it's too easy ta get all tangled up wi' worldly problems that don't mean shit. We get confused. Over here though, it becomes clearer. Easier ta focus on what's important." He started his third white mitten. "That's why marriages break up. People fergit why they were happy when they concentrated on givin love and they start demandin it, er expectin it wit'out givin anythin themselves. That don't work. And even if it did, it don't make um happy. So they breakup 'n start all over again. Over here though, the guys keep their pets all through their tours. Unless someone steps on um. The only ones who don't have pets, have a thing goin with a hooch maid er another little bird somewheres, you know, onea those double breasted, split tailed, Oriental bed thrashers."

Mark smiled self consciously.

Prescott eyed him cautiously. "You got a pet Fellogese?"

"No First Sergeant, I don't."

"Thought tha' twas the case," Prescott said matter of factly. He heaved himself up to his feet, reached down, surprisingly agile for his bulk, and hoisted his shorts and trousers to his waist in one motion. "You be careful out there tonight Fellogese. Don't think about her. It'll be a distraction. You'll git lotsa chances fer love. But survival's a need too. And if you don't meet that need, you don't get no more chances fer nothin."

"OK Top, thanks." He paused as the big sergeant opened the spring loaded wooden door and sunlight flooded into the latrine. "Hey Top?"

"Yeah." Prescott stood silhouetted in the doorway.

"Do you have a pet?"

"Nah, I don't. But I don't have no piece a' tail on the side neither. I figger this camp, the men in this camp; they take up all my time. They're a big enough headache fer me."

"I thought that might be the case," said Mark.

"Break a leg out there tonight kid." The door banged shut.

Out here on the trail, Mark thought, you can see a little way at least. God it's dark! He heaved himself into several short jumps for a noise check. No sound except his boots hitting the ground. Good. The ANPRC-10 on his back was well taped; and no jangle from his pockets nor his weapon.

Eight claymore mines had been arranged to cover both directions up and down the wide trail, on either end of the linear ambush. This extended the killing zone. The twelve men had already been carefully positioned and camouflaged at a tree line along one side of the trail. Mark had selected his own position and prepared it.

Mark waited for the patrol leader, Captain Tot, to catch up. Tot was walking the trail, making a final check of the site. He was a banker during the day, a militia soldier at night. He'd already spent his tour with the ARVN, and probably would have stayed in. He was good, but he had bleeding ulcers which he couldn't cure, and field duty made them worse. The ailment had forced him to resign from regular service, but his hatred of communism caused him to be a passionate and valuable part-timer.

Tot dragged a tree branch as they walked, trashing the trail, obliterating their boot tracks. The swishing noise sounded eerie and ominous in the night stillness. Mark studied the dark tree line thirty meters to the right. Not a sign. Not a single movement. The ambush could not be seen. He glanced to his left into a wide rice paddy. Tot had chosen the site well. The rice paddy was only three inches or so below the trail, no cover for a fleeing enemy in that direction, yet a chopper could get in there to pick us out if need be.

It was so damn dark. Only a silver sickle of a moon in the sky, but once in the jungle, beyond the tree line, you couldn't even see the sky. Using filtered flashlights, Mark and Tot found their own adjacent positions in the center of the formation. Mark's was a hasty foxhole, only six inches deep, but long and narrow with two sandbags in front.

Tot's position was only five feet away, but Mark couldn't see him through the thick jungle foliage. That preparation was a waste of time, he thought, all that digging and camouflage. Hell, if I can't see him from five feet away, how's Charlie going to see us from the trail?

He had been surprised at the heavy weapons of the ambush team. All of his training had been with US units. We just use a regular rifle squad, he thought. All rifles except one machine gun and maybe two BARs. But this provisional militia unit was playing for keeps. Two M-60 machine guns, two old fashioned 30 caliber MGs, three BARs, and a grenade launcher; Captain Tot carried a 45 caliber Thompson. I've got the only rifle, except maybe for the three machine gun ammo bearers. Of course, mine is a little more than just a rifle. This new M-16 can be fired on automatic too. Five men are also carrying that new single shot rocket launcher that you throw away after you fire it. What do you call it? Oh yeah, a LAW. Hell, we could take on an army with this fire power.

He wondered what time it was. He couldn't see the numbers on his watch. Probably about twenty two hundred. We arrived just after dark and worked fast. He chuckled to himself as he recalled the

Armed Forces Radio operator's joke about time that he'd heard this afternoon before he left. "For you Army grunts out there: the time is now fourteen hundred. For you Navy swabbies: the time is now six bells. For our Air Force audience: the time is two o'clock PM. And if any Marines are listening, Mickey's short hand is on the two and his long hand is on the twelve."

Thinking of the radio, Mark remembered that he should report in. He pulled the handset from his belt. "Romeo, this is Romeo Shade. In position. Over." His voice was almost a whisper into the mike.

"Roger Romeo Shade, standing by. Out." It was Major Clayborne's voice. I wonder which NCO took my shift tonight?

He laid out his hand grenades, four of them, in a row along the right side of his shallow prone position. He then placed his hand held parachute flare tube near where his left shoulder would be when he stretched out. The five extra ammo clips for his M-16 were stacked by his left hip. He pulled out his canteen and took a long, gulping drink. Gosh, I didn't realize how thirsty I was. I'm still sweating. Hell, I'm soaked with sweat. Maybe it was the digging, he thought, or it's the damn tropics. As hot at night over here as it is in the day. He knew he was lying to himself. The jungle is cool tonight, almost chilly.

He thought about Li. Her bright smiling face, her sable hair reflecting the sunlight like polished ebony, her warm breath into his neck when she was beneath him. He remembered the Top's warning. I've got to forget about her tonight, he thought.

The string loop around his right arm jerked twice. Tot was sending the absolute silence signal. That meant it was now twenty-three-hundred. He picked up the slack and jerked his left forearm twice, feeling the tug of the taut string; sending the signal down the line.

OK, he thought, now the waiting really begins. He eased into a more comfortable sitting position, careful to make no sound. The next time the string jerked, it would mean get ready, here they come.

The trail they had chosen was one of the primary intervillage net-work trails leading into Tam Ky, four miles east. It had been a 'which shell hides the pea?' type decision. This is a main trail, but the VC would probably take a lesser trail. Thus we should ambush one of those. So many trails. The VC know we can't ambush them all, so which one would we choose? If the VC thought we'd be on one of the smaller trails, they might gamble that this main one would be unwatched, especially if they were guiding in an NVA unit. Tot had made the decision.

The NVA would be coming from the west, of course, toward Tam Ky. But we might catch a recon patrol or supply party headed west: That's why Tot had employed the linear ambush rather than an L shaped ambush. The L shape was better when you were sure which way the enemy would be coming from, but it was weak against an enemy moving the other way. The linear was versatile. Deadly either way. Tot wanted no surprises.

A distant animal roaring sound broke the jungle silence. A tiger? God, I hope he doesn't come this way. Mark was still sweating. The black and green chalk on his face felt greasy and sticky. He sud-denly realized there were no bird sounds. The jungle was almost noisy in the daytime. He had taken several short jaunts into the boondocks with civic action teams, medical aid teams and such, and the jungle was always full of bird sounds. He remembered writing about it in his journal. But now? Do the birds know we're here? Is that it? Is something else coming? Maybe the damn birds don't screech at night. Maybe it's always this quiet.

He strained his eyes at the clearing ahead, and to the trail that cut across it. He couldn't see the damn trail. Just a little patch out in front of the trees which was not quite as dark as it was in here. We need a sniper scope, he thought. But sniper scopes weren't issued to advisory teams and the militia didn't have any either. Only the US units and the ARVN.

Something crawled across his bare forearm. Shuddering inwardly, he flicked it off with his finger. What was it? A beetle? A centipede? A spider? God, the jungle's full of spiders!

His helmet seemed to weigh a ton; the straps bit into his forehead. The stiff snubbed root of a tree prodded maliciously into his buttocks. Wonder how long I've been sitting on that? Am I so scared that my ass is numb?

He slowly and stealthily shifted position away from the blunted poniard. His shirt was still soaking with sweat. Still no sounds from the jungle. God it's quiet! Like a tomb!

I wonder what time it is? How long have we been waiting? How long before dawn? God I hope no one comes!

Suddenly feeling the urge, he shifted again, this time to his knees. He fumbled with his fly and then urinated from the kneeling position, squeezing and constricting his penis to eliminate any splashing noise. The pressure caused his urine to burn uncomfortably, but at last he was finished. He rebuttoned his fly and felt a warm wetness on his leg. Hell, he hadn't finished! Who cares? His fatigues were wet from sweat anyway.

He shuddered; an almost violent convulsion, unexpected, uncontrollable. Was it the cold? Is it fear? He tried to relax. I'm a soldier damn it. God, I need a cigarette!

The cord around his right arm jerked.

God Almighty! It's going to happen! They're coming, and from the west. He jerked the cord on his left arm. It's probably a whole NVA division. He stretched out prone in his grave-like furrow, flicking the safety of his rifle to off. He groped for the flare, found it, set it down again. Checked the location of his ammo clips, still there. Checked his grenades, still there. Then he grabbed the flare tube again and waited. Sweat streamed into his eyes, burning, burning. It's so dark I can't see anyway. Should have worn a headband, I will next time. Next time? God, I've got to live through this before there'll be a next time. Damn tree root's digging into my leg now.

Fuck it. Can't move yet. Anytime now. Wait for first shot. No, it'll be a claymore. God help me! Jesus watch over me! Can't see a fucking thing. Pitch black. Was that a movement? No. Maybe it was a false alarm. God I hope so. Maybe they saw us or heard us. Maybe they're coming up behind us. God, I'm out here all alone! The fucking Ruff Puffs have all run away! I'm all by my fucking self!

The earsplitting thwack of a claymore shattered the stillness. Mark jabbed his flare tube butt into the ground. He saw that both his and Tot's flares were almost simultaneous. Twin trails of sparkle-dust arched upward through the tree line. Another claymore cracked. The machine guns on each side of him roared into action. Tracers zinged their angry red dashes outward into the clearing. Muzzle blasts lit up the tree line with blinding flashes mixed with ghostly, fleeting shadows.

Both flares ignited. Their individual pops somehow clearly audible through the thunderous din of small arms fire.

There they are! The enemy! Only a handful! Seeking cover! Throwing themselves flat! Returning fire! Black pajamas! VC, not NVA! Mark's finger jerked hard on the trigger. The rifle butt jack-hammered into his shoulder. Spent casings spewed past his cheek. One clip already expended. Change clips. Roll back into position. Fire again. Aim this time damn it; don't just shoot! Aim!

He saw a VC leap into the rice paddy and begin to run in a low crouch for the far end of the clearing. He was nimble and quick. Can just barely see him; more cover in that paddy than I thought. Mark took careful aim and squeezed off a short burst. Got him! He knew he got him. The way he fell; as if he had been a puppet and all the strings had been dropped at the same time; limp and lifeless.

A splatter of bullets zinged over Mark's head and whacked into the trees behind him. Something thumped hard into the sandbag below his chin. Only one man out there now still shooting. All the tracers converging on him. The poor bastard doesn't have a chance! There, he's stopped firing. They got him. It's over.

Mark eased his rifle from his shoulder and studied the still figures on and beside the trail. No movement. Where's the one I got? Can't see him. But we'd see him if he moves. God, I'm thirsty.

One by one, the machine guns ceased fire. Silence returned. The only sounds were of his own heavy breathing and the sputtering parachute flares hissing lower. The light dimmed. The shadows became longer. One flare went out. The other hit the ground just beyond the trail. It burned like a distant campfire for a few seconds, then darkness again. The silence was louder than ever; the blackness worse than before. I forgot to close one eye, he thought. Destroyed my night vision.

A sudden pop to his right and another trail of twinkling stars. Tot had sent up another flare. It ignited. The bodies were still there. Tot gave crisp, sharp commands in Vietnamese, and everyone began to move forward. Mark picked up his ammo and grenades, stuffing them into pockets as he walked. He checked the clip in his rifle, still half full. Another flare. Tot wanted plenty of light. Mark held his rifle at the ready. Are they really all dead? Was it really this easy? One of them might still be alive. Might throw a grenade. Might pull the pin and lay on a grenade, knowing he was dying. Then when we turn him over, the spoon will fly. No chance to get away. He'd heard of them doing that. God it was quiet. Eerie; spooky. The acrid smell of cordite and sulphur filled the air. The swinging parachute flares caused shadows to dance and play ghoulishly across the trail. The bodies appeared to be in constant motion. But they weren't.

Eight dead men were on the trail. All of them armed with AK-47's. Definitely VC. Blood saturated the area.

Tot grinned at him. "Eight VC! Ambush good!"

"Should be another over there," said Mark. He didn't really want to see the man he'd shot, but he knew he should make sure. He walked slowly into the dry paddy. The sight of the eight dead men had made him feel a bit light headed. It wasn't so bad until he saw the blood.

"Over here," he called. Tot and two others approached.

"Helicopter on way," Tot said. "Must go soon. We are in open area now. VC know for sure where we are." He caught up with Mark just as Mark reached the dead man.

"This one carry satchel with papers," chortled Tot. "Him leader!"

Mark looked at the corpse at his feet. Blood soaked the black pajamas. One foot was bare, the other wore a rubber shower slipper. I did this, he thought. I killed a man.

One of the soldiers turned it over onto its back. The dead eyes stared upward. The mouth gaped open. There was mud caked on the teeth. "I know him," said Tot. "It is Let Bal Ty. Son of rich man in Tam Ky."

"I've heard the name before," said Mark, trying to remember.

"How you know he here?" asked Tot. "You shoot him?"

"Yes, I shot him."

Tot reached for Mark and squeezed his elbow. "You do good. Him leader. Almost escape. I tell Dai Ta. Maybe you get Vietnam medal.

"Thanks," Mark grunted half heartedly. He turned his back on them and vomited into the dancing shadows.

SCENE 6

THE POLICE STATION

0900 Hours
Saturday, 27 January, 1968

Co Li folded her hands in her lap and sat stoically. Now is not the time to cry, she thought. That will come later. Yes, I will grieve for my brother later. Survival must come first! We must survive. At least until the time of Tet.

The captain of the national police sat directly across from her, toying with his mustache. His white shirt is frayed at the collar, she thought. He is stupid, and nervous too. But he doesn't have the breeding, the education, to not show it. I can see it in his eyes. He doesn't know what to do. He is evidently waiting for someone.

Slowly, forcing her features into an air of majestic calmness, she turned to glance at her father, sitting expressionless beside her. No need to worry about him. He is strong. He will not allow his grief to betray us. I am proud of him. If they only knew what he is going through. They would admire him too. My poor father. To lose his only son. And then to refuse himself the relief of grief because of being brought here for questioning. To be forced to deny his son to men he would normally spit upon. Oh, the stars are perfidious! We must have alienated a jealous evil spirit because of our health or wealth. Perhaps I caused it because I have not hidden my happiness with Sergeant Mark. But I cannot cry. I must freeze my face.

She allowed her gaze to travel to the American sitting in one corner of the room, leaning his chair against the wall in a barbaric, slouching posture.

He obviously had no parental training at all, she thought. But he isn't nervous. He wears short pants in the French manner, with long stockings and boots. But he isn't like the Frenchmen I remember. His clothing is crumpled, and he is hairy, ape-like and crude. The white beard makes him appear wise and kind, yet that childish turkey feather in his hat contradicts those qualities. His eyes are shrewd, crafty. I can almost smell him, and he would smell dangerous. He is staring at me, as if he could read my thoughts, as if he could know my secrets. Doesn't he know that it is impolite in Vietnam to stare? Of course he does. He's doing it on purpose, trying to unsettle me. Li looked away. How long must we wait?

The door opened and a short, ARVN major bustled in. The helmet under his arm bore the white QC symbol of the military police. The captain rose and bowed. The American raised a hand in a casual, sloppy greeting but did not otherwise stir from his semi-reclined position in the corner. The major sat down directly across the table from her father and pulled papers from his brief case. He arranged them in a not quite neat stack in front of him and smiled.

"Uhh, you are Let Yu Giap of Tam Ky, the owner of the Nuc Mam processing plant here and a fish products factory in Ly Tin?" he asked curtly, addressing Li's father.

"I am." Her father's voice was strong. Only she knew how much effort he was exerting to maintain his composure.

"Uhh, I am Major Phant. Chief of the Phoenix Program for Military Sector One, the Northern Sector. Are you, uhh, aware of the nature of this program?"

"I have heard of it. The fishermen are afraid of it. They say it is a government terrorist program."

Phant bristled. "It's not a terrorist organization!" he said icily. "It's an intelligence function only, designed to, uhh, identify the Viet Cong infrastructure. We seek the provisional government appointees, what is called the, uhh, shadow government. We target the, uhh, traitors among the legal citizens of South Vietnam who pretend to be loyal but work covertly for our government's destruction. We arrest the Communist sympathizers; the, uhh, spies and other subversives among the people. It is perhaps a different war than, uhh, that which is fought by the military, but it is war nonetheless. It is certainly not terrorism."

Let said nothing. Good, Li thought. My father does not deign a reply. Everyone knows of the flagrant abuses of power by members of the Phoenix mobsters. One of them need only to point a finger and say "I heard that he or she is VC," to have someone arrested. It is how many of these cockroaches settle personal, petty disputes and puff themselves into power, into believing in their own importance. But I cannot reveal my anger here.

Phant bobbed his head toward Li, but continued to address her father. "You are the father of Let Chu Li, the official secretary to the, uhh, Province Chief of Quang Tin?"

"I am."

"You are also the father of Let Bal Ty, a high ranking member of the local covert Communist cell of Quang Tin Province?"

"I am the father of Let Bal Ty. If he was Viet Cong, I did not know of it." Li breathed a small sigh of relief. It had been a trick question. A normal, automatic answer of "yes" would have confessed knowledge of Ty's Viet Cong affiliation. Her father had been alert.

"You do know, Let, that your traitorous son was shot dead last night as he tried to sneak back from a meeting with the NVA unit operating in the, uhh, western region of this province?"

"I have only been told of his death, and that the circumstances indicate he was working for the Viet Cong. I know nothing else." A lump began to form in Li's throat. She willed herself not to cry, not to think about her brother's torn body lying somewhere, unattended.

"When did you learn of his death?"

"When the police arrested me this morning."

Phant quickly turned to the captain. "Is he under arrest?"

"No, Um Tiu Ta. We have only temporarily detained them both for questioning." The captain was obviously flustered.

"So, Let, you are not under arrest,—yet!" The sarcasm and threat in the last word was unmistakable. Li noticed a small spider spinning a web in the corner of the room.

"Forgive me esteemed Tiu Ta, but as of yet, I do not think that I, nor my good friend Dai Ta Than Mak Biet, Province Chief of Quang Tin, could tell the difference." The sarcasm in Let's voice matched Phant's. Li's heart again jumped with pride at Let's response. Well done my father, she thought. You attack where they are weak and when least expected. They play cat against mouse, but you have shown them that this mouse may be big enough to eat the cat.

Phant had veiled his eyes. He shuffled studiously through the stack of papers before selecting the one already on top to read carefully. "Uhh, please inform me Um Let, how such a powerful and influential man as you, did not know that his only son was Viet Cong? Do you not see how this fact, uhh, troubles us?"

Li smiled inwardly. The stammering fool is now using the polite form, calling my father "Mister Let." We have gained ground.

"Of course," said Let, "but I did not know. I thought he was an obedient son, a trustworthy son. He has deceived me as he has deceived our country. To discover that he was Viet Cong was a great shock." He paused and lowered his gaze sadly to the floor. "Almost as great as to be told of his sudden death."

"Uhh, you realize, Um Let, that the people of Tam Ky will hear of this. They will know that your son has shamed you and dishonored his family by disobeying you. They will know that as a father, you failed to, uhh, control and guide your son."

Li cursed under her breath. *He forces my father to admit the worst thing a father could admit, and he threatens, nay he boasts, that he will advertise this lie to all in the city. My poor father. To suffer this unjust shame for the cause of the people. Oh father, what can I do to help you?*

"Yes, I know this," Let nodded.

"Is this the, uhh, story you want us to say to the people?"

"It is the truth," lied Let.

Phant jerked his head abruptly to Li. *Does he read my thoughts?* She felt the grip of fear in her chest. *Does he see my fear? Is my mask as effective as my father's?*

Sunlight streamed in from the window. Dust motes, thousands of tiny dots, swam in the illuminated beams.

"And you Co Li. Were you aware of your brother's, uhh, rebellion? Did you know of his unpatriotic activities or leftist leanings?"

"No Um Tiu Ta. He did not speak to me of such matters."

"Did he ever question you about what took place in the Province Chief's office? Was he, uhh, curious about your work? Did he ever visit you at work?"

Li tried to swallow. Her tongue stuck to the roof of her mouth. She held her back erect, her chin high. *If I show weakness now,* she thought, *I reveal my guilt. If I am suspected, my father will be drawn into the net. Vietnamese women are expected to be pretty toys for the men, without interest in politics or business. I will tell him what he wants to hear. I will be shy, while answering his questions directly. I am a woman.*

"No, Um Tiu Ta," she said in a low voice. "I was his younger sister. He only spoke to me of my safety, my conduct, and other family matters." *The office,* she thought. *He asked me if Ty had ever vis-*

ited there. He did it so often, but always at the window. Could this lackey worm know of this? Is it a trap?

Phant nodded. "Yes," he said. "I myself have two younger sisters." He turned to Let, and Li breathed again.

"The papers we found on your son's body indicate that he was very high in the local VC organization. Perhaps even the second in, uhh, seniority in the province."

"My son was ambitious and capable, but I am further shamed and dishonored by this knowledge."

Phant nodded. "His record shows that he never served in the, uhh, military service of our country. That he opposed such service is now obvious, but how, Um Let, could he have, uhh, avoided military conscription?"

Li's breath again caught in her throat. How could her father answer this without condemning himself? Ty could not have done it without his father's bribes and influence. Surely, this police capon knows this as he asks the question.

"I am to blame as well as my son for this failure," said Let without hesitation. "I manage two factories. I hoped that one day my son would assume this responsibility as my heir. I used my position, my friendship with government officials, to keep him by my side. I realize now, how selfish and foolish I was. Had he served our country under arms, he would have recognized how evil the enemy truly is."

"You say, Um Let, that you used, uhh, friendship to keep your son out of the service? How can this be?"

"Friendship, yes, mostly friendship. Many officials owed me favors. Sometimes, of course, I paid additional taxes. I can provide a written list of officials to whom I paid these additional taxes. I can give it to both you and the American advisors if you like."

A master stroke, Li exulted. He could bring down the entire provisional government for graft, and many in the ARVN and national service as well. It was a cannon shot!

"Uhh, well, uhh," stammered Phant, "we'll not worry about that list at this moment."

"I understand." Let pressed his advantage. "But I did not think at the time that I was being unpatriotic. I felt our country's industry and economy were as important to our nation's survival as the military. For, without these, what does the military protect?"

"If your son proved to be half as, uhh, patriotic as your words, Um Let, we would not be here today, and you would not be under suspicion. But such is not the case."

Li caught a whiff of the major's breath as he leaned forward. It smelled like death.

"If my son were as patriotic as I believed him to be, Um Tiu Ta, I would still have a son and my family would still have a future. I could look forward to grandchildren and great grandchildren praying for my soul to advance into heaven. But such is not the case."

"Uhh, yes, I'm truly sorry, Um Let. Allow me to express my deep sorrow. With the loss of your only son, your family indeed has no future generations."

No, Li thought, it doesn't. Only sons carry the family name. The children of daughters are considered the continuation of her husband's family. I am of the Let family only until I marry. The lackey, blood-swallowing government has killed the Let family. Oh Ty, my brother, I will miss you. I need your strength.

Phant was still questioning. "Who were your son's friends?" Again the icy fingers clutched at her. What could her father say? A father must always know who his son's friends are, and all of Ty's friends were comrades for the people's cause. Would he give someone away to save himself?

Let didn't hesitate. "Nguyen Son Sam and Nguyen Gor Gre were the two he was closest to. I know of no others. He kept mostly to himself."

Li blanched. he had given the names of two stalwart comrades. Why? Why didn't he name someone unimportant?

Phant looked at another page. "It would, uhh, appear that you speak the truth, Um Let. Both of these men were also killed last night in the same action which took your son, plus, uhh, six others."

Let nodded sadly. "Their fathers also will be shamed."

Li cheered inwardly. Oh wise my father. You remembered who went with Ty last night, and guessed they were also killed.

"Very well, Um Let, we are satisfied for now. Your name will not appear on our list of, uhh, suspects. Please forgive our initial lack of respect, but you do understand our natural, uhh, suspicions. Your family was known to be close, even for a Vietnamese family. It was our duty to investigate."

I understand and hold no ill wishes against you."

But I do, thought Li, retaining her stoic countenance. I hate you! All of you. Three days from now you will be begging my father for mercy, and I will remind him of this barbaric, insulting session. I will then turn my grief to fury and vengeance.

"Um Tiu Ta, I have a few questions of you if I might be allowed." Let had stood and now bowed politely.

"Please tell me the details of my son's death. I know only what was said before. Where was he killed? What papers was he carrying? Who killed him?"

"He was killed on the, uhh, main trail east from Ky Lam Village, just as the trail enters Tam Ky District. He was carrying a pistol of Russian manufacture. All the men with him carried Soviet AK-47 rifles. The papers were mostly in code, but one, which was not coded, identified him as the, uhh, Provisional City Chief of Tam Ky and Deputy Province Chief. The papers are being decoded now. We hope to know more soon. We may even discover the identity of your son's superior, the VC Province Chief."

Li breathed even easier now. Her father had always insisted on coded messages, while others scoffed. He always said it would take at least five days to break a code, at least enough time for escape. Her father might be identified as the senior patriot in the province when the code is broken, but there was no need to escape. Only three days until Tet. Only three days until victory.

"And who killed him?" Let was insistent.

Phant eyed him closely. "Your son was, uhh, an enemy of the South Vietnam government. He was killed in a military action. There must not be a vendetta, nor, uhh, untoward accusations."

"Who killed him?"

"Uhh, a unit of the Province regional force militia. Captain Tot was commanding. However, it séems that Captain Tot gives credit to an American advisor for shooting your son. Evidently no one else saw him. Perhaps that may make you feel better, Um Let, to know that he was not killed by a fellow countryman."

"What was the advisor's name?"

"I should not tell you Um Let, for it, uhh, worries me that you are asking, but knowing your influence, you would discover his name soon anyway so I will tell you. He is one of those with an unpronounceable American name. A sergeant. Sergeant Far-o-gaysay, or something like that."

Li stifled a scream, then choked back a moan. Tears sprang to her eyes. She pretended to cough in order to turn her face and conceal her raging emotions. Oh, break my heart! As if the pain were not enough already. My brother dead. My beloved the murderer. How can I ever again look at Sergeant Mark's handsome face without seeing the bloody ghost of my brother? How can I continue my life? She shuddered uncontrollably.

"Are you all right Co Li?" The major now stood and was leaning across the table toward her. His reeking breath engulfed her. Her father peered down at her intently, questioningly. Did he know? Could he tell? Oh spirit of my mother, spirit of my ancestors, help me to pass through this terrible period, however temporary it may be. Help me control my feelings, my tears, my anger, my grief.

"It is all right now," she gasped, the sob in her voice almost under control. "I have a chest cold, and, the thought of my brother lying dead in the jungle brought back my constriction. My stomach is also upset. I am only a woman. Please forgive my lack of control." She said it to the floor, so that the major would accept it as just a feminine reaction. However, she had certainly shamed her father by her lack of control and she might have given them both away. Survive, survive, she thought. Ahh, but is anything worth surviving for now? She wiped her eyes with a pink handkerchief which she pulled from the sleeve of her black au yi.

Let turned again to Phant. "Where is my son's body now?"

"At the, uhh, Het Roi Mortuary in Tam Ky. You may claim the body this afternoon."

"Would it be unpatriotic or disrespectful to mourn him in the traditional way and bury him in the family cemetery."

"Uhh, you have the means Um Let, to make his funeral one of the major events in the city for years. I believe I speak for the Province Chief and the government when I ask you to be, uhh, circumspect. You must not project the funeral of a hero, nor even of an honored son. However, as he was your only son, a small, unpublicized ceremony will be allowable. The Republic of South Vietnam is not without, uhh, understanding of the feelings of its people."

"Thank you Um Tiu Ta. But your warning was not necessary. My son's life was obviously tormented by the deception he lived. He has died violently, untimely, and away from home. No amount of earthly prayers nor grandeur at his funeral could set his spirit at ease. His soul will wander and cause much trouble for the living. A grand funeral would also bring unwanted publicity to the shame he has brought to our family. Do you think that I would be so foolish as to consign a large funeral?"

"Of course not. Forgive me Um Let. Uhh, I did not mean to offend."

The funeral will take place in two weeks, Li thought, while Ty lies in state at the mortuary. By that time, the people will be in control of the country. By that time we can give him a hero's funeral, the most expensive funeral ever seen in Tam Ky. I, myself, will purchase a bronze marker proclaiming him a patriot and a martyr for the people. Perhaps even a statue to his honor on the capitol grounds. Oh Sergeant Mark, how could you have done this to us. Why did it have to be you? Why did you do this to me?

"Uhh, you may go now Um Let. Again we apologize for troubling you." The major and the captain were both bowing. Li sighed with relief. She wasn't sure she could have held her poise, her grief, her anger, her frustration another second. Her emotions churned within her. She had to get outside, to breath the sea air.

"May I be permitted to ask a few questions?" It was the wooly American from the corner. She had forgotten he was there. He still hadn't moved. He spoke slowly from his half reclined posture which looked as if he were about to sleep, but his eyes were on fire. Heavy hooded eyes. Slits! Almost Asian, but savage, vicious, suspicious. The eyes of a snake about to strike. Oh not now, she thought. I can't take any more.

"Uhh, what is it Um Co Van Haldane?" asked Major Phant.

"I think you mighta forgotten something."

"What have we forgotten?"

"This chick here; she's the Dai Ta's personal secretary, right?"

"She is the, uhh, Province Chief's secretary, yes. Is this significant in some way we have overlooked?"

"As far as I'm concerned; you bet your sweet ass you did."

"Please enlighten me Mr. Haldane."

The front legs of the chair hit the floor with a sharp snap as Race leaned forward and stabbed a burly finger toward Let. "OK. You got a close family here right? I heard you say that, and he agreed, right? His son's a fuckin Commie, right? And her brother's a fuckin Commie, right? Everone in this country knows that a little sister's gotta do what her older brother tells her ta do, right?" He paused. No one said anything.

He continued. "Shit! He was a big wheel in the local VC; pulled a lotta horsepower. Had ta be pretty smart 'n cagey as a fox ta be that high, right? You mean ta tell me after all that, you believe this little bitch when she said she didn't spill her guts out about all the high brass plans she had ta hear? Bullshit! Her brother woulda hadta've been stupid to miss that gold mine right under his nose. And we've already said he wasn't stupid, right? She's lyin through her fuckin teeth!"

Li concentrated even more fiercely to maintain a composed visage. She pretended to not understand the rude, crude English the American used. Her father couldn't help her; he spoke no English. Her stomach churned. She felt a sudden, sickening sensation that she was about to lose control of her bowels. But she had to appear calm, unafraid, innocent. Oh, Sergeant Mark, why did you do this?

"And Papa Bear here," Haldane continued, "just lost his only son right? Yet he sits here as cool as a fuckin cucumber, answerin yer questions like he didn't know anyone got shot last night. Hell! Can't ya see it's all put on? I know the Vietnamese. He has ta be all broke up about loosin his boy, but he can't afford ta show it cause he might give sumpum else away."

Major Phant spoke softly, placatingly, to the bearded giant. "Before I, uhh, entered this interrogation room this morning, Co Van Haldane, I contacted Dai Ta Biet by phone for his opinion and guidance in this, uhh, matter. He assured me that he trusts his secretary implicitly. He reminded me also that if the Communists win this war, Let Yu Giap would have more to lose than any other Quang Tin citizen, after all, he is a capitalist! A Communist government would strip him of his money and his, uhh, corporate ownership. He would become merely one of the people."

"I think you all got your greedy little noses so far up this rich pinko's ass you can't see straight! I've seen you put farmers in jail with less evidence than you got on this pinko pair. I always thought that was pushin it a bit too far, but shit! You gotta at least keep this clown's name on the hot list. He already admitted he bribed his fuckin Commie bastard son's way outta the Army. Don't let his money blind you to the truth, and whatever you do, don't let this frosty assed bitch back into Ca Dor where she can really fuck things up."

"We appreciate your, uhh, advice Um Haldane. In this case, I feel you tend to exaggerate the risk because you do not yet, uhh, understand our people nor the character of this family which has been so shamed. There will be no further investigation unless new evidence appears."

Haldane sighed loudly, rose, stretched like an awakening cat, shook his head disgustedly, and strolled with obvious disgust from the room.

"Uhh, I apologize for this also Um Let. The American is always this way, he has no manners."

"What did he say?" asked Let.

"He feels we should still suspect you both of being VC. That is nothing to be, uhh, worried about. I'm sure he also suspects me and perhaps even the Dai Ta himself. I sometimes think that all Americans suspect all Vietnamese of being VC. But if we all were," he smiled, signalling an oncoming joke, "there would be no war and all the Americans would have to go home. They wouldn't have anyone left to, uhh, advise." He burst out in a loud laugh. "It almost makes it worth while for all of us to, uhh, become VC doesn't it?"

"No," the industrialist replied. "My son was a traitor."

The major sobered instantly. "I'm sorry Um Let. I meant no disrespect to your grief."

Let nodded and took Li's arm. "We will go now. If you need to speak with us again, we will be easy to locate."

Both police officers nodded and bowed.

As they left the building, Li allowed herself to tremble. Tears sprang again to her eyes and rolled down both cheeks, but she did not cry out. She would wait to wail until after she arrived inside their home. Still, one thing that was said inside bothered her. "Father, what did they mean, that you have the most to lose if the people win this struggle? They said the new government will take it from you.

Let smiled. "They said that? Well, they are correct in a way. But do not forget that I will be the government." He smiled again. "And the government will be efficient, not like those offal eating pigs in there who were blinded by their greed and fear of the power of money."

It was easier for her father, she thought. He has the cause more fervently than I. It helps to know that his son was a martyr. He also has his business which consumes him. I believe in our cause. I do. But is it worth my brother's life? Is it worth the casting away of my true love, my chance for happiness?

Her father was still muttering. "We'll send another party tonight to obtain the information Ty carried. There is no need to change plans. They won't break the code in time. We will have one day less of preparation, but that will be no problem. You will take three days away from work to grieve for your brother, and I from the factory to grieve for my son. This free time will compensate for the day lost.

The only problem is the loss of Ty. My son had several important tasks. Now he is gone. Who will accomplish his assignments?"

Li straightened. "I will replace Ty, my father. I am a woman, but I am young and strong. I will do the missions my brother would have done. It would be what Ty would have wished."

"Yes, I agree. But now we have two additional tasks."

"What are these my father?"

"I will kill Tot, the banker. I will do it personally."

"And the other?"

"You will kill that American; the murderer of your brother!"

Let watched her intently. "Do it soon!"

"I will kill him at the first opportunity," Li said. Teardrops became twin rivulets down her face, but she marched resolutely at her father's side. She must do her duty. It is what Ty would have wished.

SCENE 7

DA NANG

1200 Hours
Saturday, 27 January, 1968

Jake's ear hurt where the receiver had been pressed for so long. The phone system in Vietnam was about as up to date as the plumbing in Camp Kronberg.

The lines to Saigon were constantly busy. The local operator had actually laughed when Jake asked how long the wait would be. Most of the callers had a higher priority. He stretched in resignation and sauntered into the brightly tiled lobby of the CORDS head-quarters. He'd try again in three hours, just before his chopper left for Tam KY. Three hours to kill. Well, what the heck, he'd never been a tourist in Da Nang before.

He strolled out of the former villa onto the brick surface of a large courtyard which now served as a high fenced, VIP parking lot. The heat invaded his uniform. His legs felt heavy and dull but a persistent pain throbbed at his temples. His meeting with Lamar had been rough enough, and then the frustration of the phone system. He hadn't accomplished a damn thing yet. For the first time in his life, he felt he needed a drink, really needed one.

A stocky man in civilian clothing passed him from behind, and bustled to a waiting jeep. As the man turned to plop heavily into the driver's seat, Jake recognized him. He was a US Marine Corps gunnery sergeant with whom Jake had worked in the Pentagon six years ago. The man looked up as he was about to drive away and Jake caught his eye.

"Hello Gunny Garbino, how are you?"

The man switched off the jeep with a jerk, looked hurriedly around as if he'd been caught cheating at solitaire, and rushed over. He held out his hand warmly, but with a distinct air of furtiveness.

"Hey there Captain Thorpe. Oh! Wow! It's Colonel Thorpe now. Congratulations. You've obviously been doing well."

"Yes, good to see you too Gunny. Or should I say Top now?"

Garbino flicked his eyes back and forth like a tennis spectator before answering. "Well Sir, it's kind of yes and kind of no. What are you doing here?"

"I'm assigned to CORDS. I'm DPSA of Quang Tin Province."

Garbino sagged. "Hell Sir, I guess I'll have to tell you then; otherwise you might give it away."

"What are you talking about?"

"Lets go get a cup of coffee. There's a restaurant just down the street. It's got a view. We can talk there. I'll leave my jeep here; it's an easy walk and the lot's secure."

With curiosity broiling, Jake followed Garbino through the wrought iron courtyard gate and into the streets of the second largest city in South Vietnam. He recalled that he'd been enchanted by Da Nang two years ago on his one visit up north. The city the French had called Tourane used to attract many tourists; but it was changed now. The clean charm of back then was losing its battle against the dual pressures of overcrowding and poverty. The blight of urban deterioration added to his sense of depression.

They walked down one of the many hills of the city to a large four storied building with no sign over the door. Garbino entered first, and they trudged up the stairs to the fourth floor.

Jake was mildly shocked to find a surprisingly modern restaurant on the top floor. Two walls were decorated with lacquered abalone shell pictures and live plants. Everything else seemed to be windows. The music of Beethoven filled the room and the air was thick with the pungency of spices and smoked meat. Garbino led the way to an empty table next to a window.

Red Beach stretched out beneath them. Jake smiled as he remembered that this was where the marines had stormed ashore in an amphibious assault in sixty five, only to be met by a smiling city mayor and a group of school girls bearing gifts of flowers. It was a beautiful beach; over four miles of pink flecked white sand. Today, multicolored beach umbrellas and bright towels dotted the vista. Lawn chairs and even a few yellow cabanas sprinkled the shoreline with more color. It could be Hawaii, Jake thought. But a gigantic German hospital ship anchored in the harbor; the large bright red cross on its side jarred and marred the tranquil vacation scene below.

"They don't serve beer or alcohol here, but the coffee's great," Garbino murmured.

Jake controlled his still stabbing curiosity and continued to gaze at the view. To his right, a rugged, rocky outcropping guarded the bay. A misplaced, solitary mountain, forming a peninsula which jutted into the sea. It loomed over Da Nang City as well as the harbor; massive, menacing, and fortress-like.

"Is that the Marble Mountain that I keep hearing about on the radio, where all the relay switches are?"

"Oh no," smiled Garbino. "Marble Mountain's on the other side, further to the right. You can't see it from here. That's Monkey Mountain. Marble Mountain's just a pimple compared to Monkey Mountain. Bunch of Buddhist temples or something up on this one.

They consider it holy ground. There's VC up there too, right in our back yard so to speak. But we can't get at um because of the temples. They can use the mountain, but if we go after um we somehow desecrate their holy ground. If it was up to me, I'd blast the Hell outta them with air strikes and naval gunfire, but Saigon's afraid of the Buddhists. They might start burnin themselves up again and topple the government like they did before. So we just try to keep them bottled up."

Jake continued to gaze out the window at the peaceful, idyllic sights below him. The sunlight blinked warmly off the sapphire blue bay. He looked at the bathers on the beach. Almost all were GIs. What a wonderful day. Even his headache seemed a bit better.

The coffee arrived, European style, thick, dark and bitter with a cream pitcher beside each demitasse cup. Nothing like this in Quang Tin, thought Jake.

"Look, Colonel, you recognized me and I gave it away, so I gotta tell you. I shoulda just said I got outta the Corps. You wouldn'a known any better; but I spoke before I thought, so you'll just hav'ta keep my secret."

"Your secret?" Jake had to refocus on Garbino's face after the blinding sunshine of the window.

"Yeah, you see, I'm still in the Corps, kinda. I'm officially a master sergeant, but I'm not on duty as a Marine over here. Haven't been for over three years, almost four. I'm on loan to the State Department."

"On loan?" Jake realized he sounded like a parrot.

"Yeah, I'm a civilian DPSA, same job you got, only up in Quang Tri Province. My boss is an Army colonel. But I've got a lieutenant colonel, Army type, and several majors report'n to me. They have to call me Sir. It just wouldn't do for um to find out their boss is a Marine master sergeant would it? Hell, the PSA don't even know, and sometimes he and I get into disagreements ya know. And, well, it'd really piss him off if he found out. So you gotta promise me not to say anything to anybody OK? I wouldn't be able to do my job at all."

Jake smiled, thinking of the black emblems on his own shoulders which represented silver leaves, and were also, at least temporarily, misrepresenting who he really was. Everybody's fooling everybody, he thought. What kind of war is this anyway?

"You can trust me Gunny, er, I guess... Hell, what do I call you now, Mister Garbino? Or have you changed your name too?"

Garbino grinned. "No. It's Mister Garbino. I've been that for so long I'm getting used to it." He paused and smoothed out one bushy eyebrow. "And thanks Colonel, I really appreciate it. It's not easy you know, to pretend you're something you're not. Sometimes I feel like a spy or something."

Jake was still smiling. "I guess if we're going to make this charade believable, you'd better call me Jake. What's your first name?" Jake was tempted to share his own secret, but he couldn't; he was under orders not to.

"Thanks Sir, er... Jake," Garbino grinned. But you don't want to know. I go by a nickname. Diji. I've been called Diji all my life. It's my initials, see, D-G; and since I've got an unpronounceable first name, everybody's always taken the easy way out. Hell, my first name is a twelve letter Bohunk or German name." He grinned again.

"How'd it happen?" asked Jake, "this loan business."

"Well, it's a long story. I know someone. They were short handed. He asked me to help out. He filled out a request to Eighth and I, the Corps Headquarters. It got approved and I came over. Then I got a promotion on the civilian job, and then another one. Like I said, they were short handed. Then I got this job. I've been here a year and a half, almost halfway through my tour.

"Well, I won't tell anyone, but every time we meet, you've got to buy the coffee."

"Agreed," smiled Garbino. "Was that you ahead of me in Lamar's office today, getting your butt chewed out?"

"Yes, I was trying to get an American unit in close to Tam Ky City for the Tet holidays."

"Ill be damned. That's the main reason I'm here too. We're expectin all hell to break loose the night Tet turns. We got an NVA regiment for Christ's sake, sittin on our door step.

"Join the crowd. We have the same thing."

"Shit! No wonder Lamar ain't receptive. Everyone's askin for the same thing. I just spoke to someone in G2 up here from Saigon. Evidently, they're expectin the sierra to fly all up and down the country that same night."

"How can that be? How can Charlie mount an offensive of that scale? I thought we had them on the run."

"I got no idea. All I know is they got the horsepower to do it in Quang Tri."

Jake nodded. "In Quang Tin also."

Who's the PSA in your province? Is it Mr. Heath?"

"No, we don't have a top level civilian. We used to, Ray Gonzaga. He, ahh, he got into a little trouble." Jake decided he shouldn't go into details.

"Gonzaga? Hell I remember now! He's a great guy. He's more than a prince, he's a friend a mine. Hell of a shame what's happnin to him. I heard all about it. Haven't they straightened all that shit out yet? What a frame up. Somebody had it in for him."

Jake felt a surge of relief. "No. They haven't straightened it out yet, but I think they will. He's a friend of mine too. I've known him since college. He was one of my professors." Jake felt relieved telling someone. He knew he could trust this burly fraud.

Garbino chatted on. "Gonzaga's, well, kinda like a big brother to me. We went through the MATA course together. He could tell I was having trouble with all the homework and stuff. Really took me under his wing and helped me get through. Our names both start with G, and you know the old government way of doin everything alphabetically, so we always ended up in the same classes and shit. We really became close."

"Yes, Ray's like that." He really is, thought Jake. Always taking in strays. Always the teacher. Always the father figure.

The conversation continued through the strong, rich coffee, the classical music, the clatter of china and crystal, and the bright play-land scenery below. They spoke of Pentagon friends and former experiences, the tumultuous confusion of high level headquarters, and the danger facing both provinces on the eve of the lunar new year. And they spoke of Ray Gonzaga and the unfairness of life.

At 1430 they walked back to CORDS, and Garbino plopped into his jeep. With a warm feeling of renewed friendship, Jake watched him wave and drive off.

Hustling into the headquarters, Jake had an awakening sensation as if he were just arriving back to duty from leave, or a weekend pass. Wow, he thought, that little break really did me some good. Just time enough to make that phone call. Thinking of Garbino as he began dialing, he remembered what he had said to Sergeant Fellogese just a few weeks ago. Nothing in Vietnam is as it seems.

"Da Nang CORDS Operator," a feminine Oriental voice said.

"I'm calling Saigon for General Elsin, priority two."

"I'll connect you Sir."

A pause. He glanced around the room. The walls were totally bare except for the ever present pictures of General Westmoreland and President Thieu, hanging side by side at one end of the room. I wonder if they're counterparts, Jake thought. Or would it be Thieu and the Ambassador? But it was Westmorland's picture on every wall, usually along side Thieu's.

"MR-1 Regional Switchboard." This time it was a masculine voice. A southerner, from Georgia or Alabama, Jake guessed.

"I want to speak to General Elsin in Saigon."

"I'll put ya raat through, Suh."

Another pause. Damn; that meeting with Lamar today was absolute disaster. Lamar! He's a sharp cookie all right. Made me feel like a ten year old getting his ass chewed out by the principal for skipping school.

"MR-3 Regional Switchboard." A north easterner, Jake thought. Either Vermont or New Hampshire. "I'm trying to get through to General Elsin in CORDS Headquarters, Saigon."

"I'm a' connectinya right now Sir."

Again silence from the phone. Damn that Lamar. He's tough. He probably knew that Garbino would be asking for support for Quang Tri, and I can see why he couldn't send reinforcements to everybody, but Hell, he's already sending troops to Quang Tin; just to the wrong part. But he still turned me down flat on getting the Army to send that battalion into Tam Ky City rather than out in the boonies. Made me feel like a whining child just for asking. It must be some kind of political problem that's out of his control.

He also knew King had sent me to be his messenger. Actually chewed me out for doing King's dirty work for him. Hell, he's a civilian, but he must know that I didn't have any choice. Sure didn't act like it though, acted like asking for protection was some kind of sin. Hell, he missed the whole point. The U.S. should change their plans. They're going to waste their time on LZ Mary Ann.

And he wouldn't listen to any complaints about Biet either. Said it would have to come through channels, from me, to King, to Lamar; the chain of command. He could tell I didn't want to do that. He didn't know why, and he didn't ask. Good thing I guess, because I couldn't have told him. Would've made me look like a bigger fool yet.

"Saigon CORDS Operator," another Vietnamese female.

"General Elsin please, Colonel Thorpe calling from Da Nang."

"One moment please."

I was tempted to tell Lamar what I suspect about King though. He gave me a chance when he ripped me a new one because of my Aussie bush hat. Really blew his stack when he heard the whole team was wearing them. "Is this one of King's stupid ideas?" he'd asked. I told him King had approved it, which was obvious if we all wear them. It's the least damaging answer I could have given. There's bad blood between King and Lamar. I could tell by the way he flamed. He'd really have been pissed if he knew that it was not only King's idea, but also a profit making venture. Curly had one of his team check the price in Sydney. Probably should have let the profit matter kind of accidently slip. That would be one way to get King relieved from command. But I need to talk to General Elsin first. If what I think happened really happened, I'm going to get King up front with formal UCMJ charges of something a lot more serious than profiteering.

I guess the bush hat is history though. Lamar said he's sending a message today to Tam Ky and will follow it up with a letter. I hope King gets the message early so he has a chance to cool off before I get back.

"General Elsin's office, Captain Bernardo Sir."

"Captain Bernardo? This is Colonel Thorpe, I met you on New Year's Day, right after I came in country. Is the General in?"

"Yes Sir, I remember. You, er, got promoted. Yes Sir, the General's in, I'll tell him you're on the line."

"Thank you. By the way, weren't you a lieutenant when I met you?"

"Yes Sir, I was. Shiny new railroad tracks as of last week. Had the wetting down party last night."

"Congratulations. Sorry I missed it."

"I'll get the General for you Sir."

Another pause. More waiting. Getting the secret promotion, the way I did saved me money, he thought. I couldn't throw the traditional party to "wet down" the new rank insignias. I wonder if Bernardo got his promotion early the same way I did. As General Elsin's aide, he probably did.

"Hello Jake, Elsin here. What news do you have?"

"Well, sir; I've got a skull I'd like to talk about."

"Forget about the cloak and dagger shit Jake, something just happened today. I'll tell you later. But I'm busy. For what you're going to say, I don't give a fuck who's listening. I don't have time to play guessing games by talking in circles. I want it straight out. No code. No ambiguities."

Jake told him. He told him of the truck; the black market booze which had been confirmed by Curley; the knife wound; the ghost rat; the report of Minh, the Hoi Chanh; the pictures of Biet with the code book; King's entry into Sergeant Lentz's room; Madame Biet's actions at the play; and Tu's suspicions. He also told him of his failure to get Lamar's ear in regard to Biet. "I didn't tell him what I suspect about King Sir. Thought I should tell you first."

"Anything else?" asked Elsin

"Perhaps Sir. Our police Advisor, Race Haldane, discovered that the two VC porters who reported the code book in enemy hands had been sent to another province. He went down there to question them about their statements. We think someone paid them to tell that story of the captured code book. I understand Race got back to Tam Ky first thing this morning, but he had an important interrogation of suspects that he felt he should sit in on and I had to catch a helicopter to come up here, so I haven't heard yet what he's found out."

"Well, I hear you, but it's not going to be as simple as you'd like it to be Jake. Than Mak Biet's not the only Province Chief who deals in the black market, and he's certainly not the only one who lines his pockets with graft. Mr. Lamar probably should have explained it to you. There's really not much we can do. Unless we can pin the murder on him, it's going to be up to the Vietnamese government. Hell, they might even let him get away with murder; and I know they won't relieve him just because his wife might've committed murder.

"But surely it's enough to clear Ray Gonzaga isn't it? Enough to get him his job back."

A silence from the other end of the wire. "I'm sorry to be the one to tell you this Jake. Ray Gonzaga died about two hours ago. Heart attack. The doctor's already confirmed it was natural causes."

Jake couldn't breathe. God, oh God! First Tu and now Ray. But this was the worst. He felt that someone had just delivered a blow to his solar plexus. Two hours ago? Jesus, I was drinking coffee! Tears streamed down his face.

"Jake? Jake? You all right? Jake? You still there?"

"Yes General, I'm still here." His voice was hoarse. It wasn't his voice. It was scratchy and broken, but he didn't feel like trying to control it. Christ, everybody's dying!

"You all right Jake?"

"Yes General, I'm OK."

"OK. Real sorry about this Jake. Maybe next month you can come down here. I'll take you to dinner. I especially want to hear more about King. I don't think that picture and your sighting of him going into a room is nearly enough evidence to get him charged, much less relieved. Keep snooping around a bit. Do your job, and don't be disloyal or anything. What you said really bothers me though. We don't want officers who have no honor. Keep your eyes peeled."

"I'll try General."

"OK Jake. And keep your powder dry. Look's like the shit's going to hit the proverbial you know what in a coupla days."

"Jesus General, you know about that?"

"You're probably referring to your local situation, but no, I've not yet heard of the specifics in your province. I was talking about spraying shit over the whole God Damned country. But I'm not surprised at all that Tam Ky is also sitting in front of that damned fan."

"Oh, I get it. Well good luck General."

"You too! Hang in there Jake. See you soon."

Jake hung up. His neck and shoulders were stiff, as if he'd been on the phone for hours. His headache was returning with titanic vengeance. His mouth was dry. Ray! God Damn it Ray! I'm so sorry. You didn't die of a heart attack, you died of a broken heart, a broken spirit. And I could've helped, if only I'd been faster. I didn't even get to see you. Didn't get to say goodbye. Oh Damn it Ray, why couldn't you have waited?

Act 5

SCENE 1

THE CONFERENCE ROOM

1400 Hours
Sunday, 28 January, 1968

"Dung Noi!" Major Hai's high pitched shout screeched through the room. Even the Americans who didn't understand the words halted their conversations in mid sentence and stared at him. A few papers rustled. The monotonous droning of several large flies was suddenly audible as the ebony insects dived and zig-zagged through the thick layers of cigarette smoke. All eyes looked toward the head of the conference table where Jake and Hai sat.

"This is meeting for plan," Hai announced in English, his voice calm now and tuned to normal volume. "No need for all to talk with big noise please. We work today with cool heart, make better plan. Need plan good today, win victory tomorrow. Please to continue, but quiet! Cool heart! Please to remember."

The pre-occupied officers immediately hunched again into their several groups over their maps, charts, and written plans. The hum of the now lowered voices of busy men totally drowned the insect noises, but Jake couldn't help but notice the similarity of the sound, the sameness of tone. It was the buzz of mortal beings striving for survival.

"What does dung noi mean?" he asked, as Hai sat down again beside him.

"It mean be quiet," smiled Hai. "I could not hear your words although your face was near to my ear."

"Good job," Jake responded with an encouraging smile. "I especially liked that bit about the cool heart. You're right too. It's a good way to put it. Nice choice of words."

"Not my words," grinned Hai. "Words of Buddha. Buddha say men must always take middle path. Must avoid show any strong emotion such as angry, hate, fear, jealous, too strong grief, or even, how you say, big joy? Start with x letter."

"Excitement? Ecstasy? Exuberance?" Jake proposed.

"Yes. Ecstasy word I mean. Maybe all three. Buddha say all strong emotion lead to craving which is root of all sorrow and suffering in world. Extreme emotion disrupt social harmony. He say man who show emotion have hot heart. Hot heart not virtue. Cool heart is virtue. That is what gentle smile on all Buddha statue mean."

Jake grinned, hoping his smile was not a parody of the statues he'd seen, but unable to resist the irony of the instant. "Yes, I see, but was Buddha ever expecting a full scale attack by an NVA regiment within thirty six hours?"

"Not sure," beamed Hai. "But you make joke at this time. Show you have cool heart. Is very good."

Jake grinned again and shrugged off the compliment as the engineer advisor and two Vietnamese officers approached with a stack of papers.

Jake and Hai had poured over the plans by themselves yesterday until the wee hours. This morning they had assembled the entire staff and their counterpart advisors and redistributed the various plan sections for last minute changes and final detailed coordination. There had been few flaws detected, but many omissions of details, and many points of confusion. It was a Vietnamese plan, but Jake had privately instructed the advisors to make sure there were no mistakes, even if they had to take over the decision making themselves. He had done this without asking King. This wasn't a matter of following orders or not following orders, he had decided, this was survival time.

Jake and Hai had situated themselves centrally to act as final decision makers, arbiters of disputes, and problem solvers.

"If we blow up these bridges Sir, the NVA can't get across the river," said the young engineer advisor, a first lieutenant.

"Yes, but neither could the farmers. The VC blew those same bridges two years ago to disrupt trade. We can't do the VC's work for them. The bridges stay!"

A Vietnamese officer asked, "Troom Ta? My counterpart want me to put land mine in field here and here to protect my position. OK to do?"

"Those are cultivated rice fields. We can't keep people out of their own rice fields. Tell him good idea, but no dice. That's going a bit too far."

Hai nodded his approval.

Another question: "Sir. How about retractable barbed wire gates on these trails? They can be closed after dark."

"Good thinking. Place them in series. Several in a row with different locking devices. Hang tin cans on them with rocks inside so we can hear if they're moved or cut."

"Sir. The hospital's not mentioned in the plan. Who's going to guard it?" This question was from Major Buckingham, the S2 advisor. A West Pointer whose astuteness and clear thinking Jake had noticed before. A good question. Jake made a mental note to remember his sharpness at rating time.

"Major Hai and I discussed that. We don't see that as a target. There'll be the normal guard of five QC policemen. We're gambling that there's no need to reinforce it."

A Vietnamese officer approached. "Troom Ta, are we to receive no American support at all?"

"There's a Navy destroyer off the coast. We might be able to get some naval gunfire support. Depending on what happens elsewhere, we might be able to get Spooky and helicopter gunships."

"But no American soldiers Troom Ta?"

"No. The militia will have to protect the city."

Hai leaned forward. "Excuse me Troom Ta, I just learn that we get one regiment of ARVN. It is on trucks now from Quang Nam. It maybe arrive midnight tonight."

"Hey that's good. Where you planning to put them?"

"South of capital as we discussed, between Province Headquarters and city of Tam Ky. One battalion will be reserve. This allow us to concentrate our militia forces in other areas more critical."

"Excellent. Good news."

There was a pause in the incessant questions. Jake glanced at Hai. He looked tired. "Did you sleep at all last night Tieu Ta?"

"Little bit." Hai answered sheepishly, yawning as he remembered. He snapped his mouth shut with determination. "But I sleep enough Troom Ta; enough."

"We'd both better get a good night's sleep tonight. It's liable to be our last chance for a while."

"Yes, I agree Troom Ta Jake."

Jake smiled at Hai's use of his first name. He and his new counterpart had grown closer during this period of enforced togetherness. "What do you think Tiu Ta? Is there any chance the NVA will hit us tonight instead of tomorrow night?"

"I no believe so Troom Ta. All ARVN and militia units still one hundred percent strength. Even units which no listen to our warnings and plan to give leaves of absence no do until after daylight tomorrow. Maybe NVA not attack tomorrow also. You know already they say temporary cease fire from twenty four hundred last night through February three of your calendar. They do this every year, and they never before break this Tet truce."

"Yeah, but they have broken other cease fire agreements."

"Many times. But never at Tet."

"Well, the whole US intelligence network thinks they'll attack tomorrow as planned."

"Yes, our intelligence people also, but I pray they not attack. It mean very bad year if such violence happen on first day of new year."

"You're not Catholic, are you Tiu Ta?"

"No, I am Buddhist."

"I thought so. I think you're the first Buddhist officer I've met over here. Are there that many Catholics in South Vietnam?"

"Yes. I think maybe ten percent of South Vietnam is now Catholic but over forty percent be Buddhist."

"Then why do I meet so many more Catholic officers in the Army than Buddhist? Is it just coincidence?"

"No Troom Ta, you see true. Especially officer. There be more Catholic than Buddhist. There be several reason. First, true Buddhist, not like me. I believe, but no be, how you say, devout? True Buddhist never kill. He no kill animal for food. Not even insect who bite him. We believe in many lives, you say, I think, reincarnation. Every live thing have soul. If I be bad in this life, I be pig or dog in next. If I be bad dog and not do what dog should do, I be mosquito in next life. You can see, true Buddhist be no good in military where we think death of other people each day for job. Catholic no have trouble with think this. Can kill people, still be Catholic.

Also, when Ho Chi Minh fight against French, maybe half his soldier be Catholic, who get much war experience. Almost all Catholic run from Communism in 1954 to south. These now be most of senior officer for South Vietnam military. Almost all general be Catholic. This good, as they very qualified. But bad too because there be much talk of Catholic help each other."

"You mean discrimination?"

"Yes, I before think much thought of discrimination when I not get assignment or promotion as I think should happen. But now I get promotion. Now I think maybe discrimination be more just talk than for sure."

"Aren't the VC and NVA mostly Buddhist?"

"Yes."

"How do they get around their beliefs about killing?"

"They do as I do. During this life, I must give loyalty and duty to country. Country need me to fight. It what I should do. My duty. Therefore correct for me to do. I am not priest. I am not devout. So maybe is more easy for me than to choose gentle way of Buddha. But both ways be correct. So I choose. If it be my karma to be born pig in next life because I do my duty in this life, then it my karma. I will have many life to correct this mistake. I think people from north same. Maybe little different. Communist want people to worship government. Very close to natural way of Vietnam people to think. Communist leaders say all Vietnam people one family. Government be head of family. That why people in north believe they be right. They think they fight for family as same same fight for country. It close to way I feel, but different. After war, they find out difference. Communism hurt family, hurt country. But then too late."

"For what it's worth, I sure do agree with you."

"Thank you Troom Ta, but easy for you to feel this way. You not Vietnamese and not believe in karma. You know many Catholic here still believe in karma?"

"Yes, I did know that."

"Vietnam people be Vietnam people first. What religion we be, be second. To be Vietnam people almost same as religion."

"I'm beginning to understand this. Is it true for those who are Protestant as well as Catholic?"

"Yes, but only few Protestant. Vietnam people difficult to become Protestant, but easy to become Catholic."

Jake glanced around. The murmuring clumps of planners remained busy. Neither he nor Hai were needed as yet. "Really? Why is that Tiu Ta?"

"Both offer strong attraction to any Vietnam person. They say everyone must repent and confess. All bad deed done in past be forgiven by God. This allow everyone to go to heaven after death. All Vietnam people believe there should be consequence for every act. Must suffer consequence of every bad act. If one be Christian, either Catholic or Protestant, is maybe OK. Just confess and God forget. Very strong argument. But Protestant priest call himself Pastor. It mean leader of sheep. No Vietnam people want to be sheep in this life while they be yet human. Catholic priest call himself father. Family very important to Vietnam people. Catholic say God is father in heaven. Also pray to Mother Mary. If Catholic, one belong to big family of God. Make Vietnam people feel good."

"I see the appeal."

"I think much about this. I think Buddha correct. Man must suffer consequence of action. If all action good, man can become Buddha in this life. But if do one bad thing, must have consequence of bad thing. I believe this more like true. Man always cause bad thing that happen to him.

Jake nodded absently. There we really part company, he thought. Ray didn't deserve what happened to him in his last few months. His actions should surely have made him a Buddha if that way were true. And my actions? I wonder if I should suffer any other consequences more than the guilt I feel for letting Ray down. I wish I knew for sure if I did let him down or not. Hai was still talking. The eternal chatter box! Now he's saying something about rocks and trees having souls too, only different. What's the difference? I missed it. I'll have to ask him.

The telephone jangled. He could just hear the muffled caller over the hubbub of the planners.

"Race Haldane Colonel."

"Yes Race, what did you find out?"

"Those Commie monkeys were paid off all right. The porters, you know? They admitted it, but they don't know who it was what paid um. Some Goddamned fat gook in civilian clothes is all they know. Paid um half before, and half after their interrogation. Told um exactly what ta say. Just between you and me, I think it was the Dai Ta himself, but can't be sure. After this damn Tet scare is over and done with, I'll run over there again with some photographs. See if they can recognize someone. I'll make sure and take a picture of the Province Chief as well as somma the other chubby ones around here."

"Sounds good Race. What about the NPFF? Are your white shirts all set for tomorrow?"

"Yeah, think so. I managed to requisition a cuppla machine guns and hand grenades on the sly. Don't ask where I got um. We'll give um back after tomorrow, maybe. By the way, in case you're won-derin, we just got another rat faced Chu Hoi in today. He's main line VC from the 123rd Battalion, but a real pansy. Wants to see his mama. He came over because she lives here in Tam Ky and he says there will be an attack tomorrow! He wants her ta get outta town before the attack. Ain't that sweeta him? It should erase all fuckin doubts if you had any. If he's a Commie plant, he's the best I ever saw. All he talks about is his mama. Looks like the shit's gonna fly for sure."

"Thanks Race." Jake hung up. And no American unit to help us, he thought. He gritted his teeth in determination.

Suddenly, King stormed into the conference room. "Have ya-all seen this?" he shouted. He waved a paper. His eyes bulged. His jaw jutted with pugnacious fury. "Do ya know who the fuck wrote this?" He threw the page into Jake's lap. "They're all over the place. On every fuckin bulletin board. I'll court marital the Son of a Bitch myself, so help me Christ!"

Jake picked up the paper. It appeared to be a poem run off on a purple inked mimeograph. He read it:

"The Ballad of the Bush Hat"

"There are stories galore about the war in far off Vietnam.
Stories of gore, and l'amour, extolled and told adnauseum.
But the saddest of all, of all tales tall, that I heard anyone spin,
I read on the wall of a shit-house stall while I was flogging my skin.
I read The Ballad of the Hat, there while I sat, of the men of Team Number Two.
Twas called a bush hat. Nothing bush league about that, claimed the scrawl in the wall residue;
Worn by men who were free, with high esprit, in the Province of Quang Tin.
And there was glee in old Tam Ky, but that was way back then.
Now as I had my fun and got my gun (without getting any on me),
I bemoaned the fate of those men in 68, on the coast of the South China Sea.
Soldiers of pride, and men who tried, wearing their jaunty chapeau,
And I almost cried as my dick I dried (more wild oats that I wouldn't sow."

"See whad I mean? See whad I mean?" shouted King.

Jake glanced up, vanely suppressing his grin, but King wasn't looking. He glared at the assembled officers in the room. They stared back, not knowing what was happening.

King jerked back to Jake. "Read it! Read the whole Goddamned fuckin thing. Then you'll see whad I mean."

Relieved that King hadn't totally disrupted the planning session by his yelling, Jake quickly read the remaining stanzas. His smile hidden by his lowered head:

> "For this gallant crew, with courage true blue, in their dashing and debonair bonnet,
> Admiring glances did draw, filling others with awe, for it had the RVN rank symbol on it.
> And they all wore a smile, for the hat had a style that just had something about it.
> It was versatile not juvenile, and it might have been legal, but I doubt it.
> But Team Number Two had to pass in revue between the proverbial rock and hard place.
> Colonel King said "DaNang didn't give a hang" whether they wore helmets or lace,
> But someone told Lamar, of course from afar (he never came close to Quang Tin).
> He was shining his pate as he baldly did state: "Don't ever wear it again!"
> So King and his troop got the 'get with it' poop, and it was useless to parlezvous.
> They got the shaft, up the aperture abaft, and to their Aussie hats they bid adieu.
> Their jungle hats they doffed, a few team members coughed,
> Taps were played so charmy-
> The music was soft, bitter beers were quaffed, for Team Two had to rejoin the Army!

Now my face I hide. A little of me just died, as I read that tale of woe.
I'm still bleary eyed from that day I cried about the victory of the status quo.
I was still in a trance as I zipped up my pants and stepped away from the vat.
I took a belt of likker and gave a silly snicker, as I vowed never to forget

'The Ballad of the Hat.'"

The poem was signed "Robert Serviceman, Team Two."

Jake had finished reading, but continued to stare at the page in order to mask and control the smile which involuntarily surged to his face. King was so angry he could spit. Not only had his icon been disallowed, someone had now stepped on it. I wonder who the poet is? I wonder if he knew how much it would goad King? Probably. That might be why he didn't sign his real name, although the allusion to Robert Service was clever enough to have been motive in itself.

King interrupted his thoughts. "Haven't ya-all finished that shit yet? Whadda you tryin ta do? Memorize it? They're all over the fuckin place. On every bulletin board. And desks and other walls. It's a Goddamned waste a taxpayer money, and I'll court martial the bastard for it. Do you know who the fuck is responsible? Do you?"

Jake looked up to meet King's fierce gaze directly. "Sorry Dick, but I sure don't." I honestly wish I did, he thought. I'd like to compliment him on his style. He had resolved not to grin, but his resolve failed him.

"You do know!" screamed King, seeing the smile. "Who is the ass hole? Is it you?"

"No Dick, it wasn't me, and I don't know who it was. But it's funny. It's not that big of a deal is it?"

"Not that big a deal? Jesus Christ! Not that big a deal? We've lost our team emblem. The thing that set us apart!" His eye patch birthmark had turned bright crimson. His mouth twisted with fury. Specks of saliva bubbled at the corners of his lips. "Holy fuckin shit! How can ya take it so calmly? That fuckin Lamar castrated us! And he did it on purpose! And we gotta fuckin asshole traitor on our team who agrees with him! And you don't think it's a big deal? Jesus Fuckin Christ!"

"It's just somebody making a joke Dick. What else is there to do about the hats? It's a lost cause. Besides, he really never said anything bad about the hats if you really read the poem."

"It's not a jokin issue Goddamn it! I want ever fuckin copy taken down and burned. You hear me? Burned! And I'm gonna go over to the Castle now and write a proper goodbye to our team symbol. I'll make it a Goddamned epitaph. A eulogy. So everone'll see how noble it was, and how much a loss it was, and how much it hurt us ta lose it. We'll post my version all around, 'n I'll send a copy to Lamar by God and let'im know how much he's fucked up our morale! And you! You find out who wrote this fuckin thing! I want his ass! An I don' wanna hear any more backtalk!"

King wheeled about and stomped out of the conference room.

"What happen?" asked Hai. "You be in trouble?"

"No, I don't think so Tiu Ta. Colonel King is just upset that we can no longer wear those soft bush hats."

"That bring such anger? Why he not concentrate on danger of tomorrow? For sure, problem of what hat to wear not so important as enemy threat, no?"

"Of course it isn't Tiu Ta. Don't worry. We'll all be ready." Jake's glance took in the Conference room, again all business.

Mollified, Hai settled back to answer another staff question.

God, Jake thought. King really doesn't realize the difference in priorities! Or at least he hasn't yet. How can such arrogant stupidity go unnoticed by his superiors? He's a five percenter by God! Got promoted to LC ahead of his contemporaries. How can I work for such a self centered, two faced Janus, even if he didn't sabotage Ray as I think he did? Oh well, maybe when General Elsin reads the report I wrote for him, something might happen. Jake reached out to accept the list of figures placed in front of him. "Yes," he said. "Issue every advisor a double basic load of ammo for tomorrow.

SCENE 2

THE BUNKER

1900 Hours
Sunday, 28 January, 1968

Co Li trudged determinedly forward toward the low square mound of sandbags which marked the opening to the TOC. In the darkness, silhouetted by the distant headlights of a jeep, the mound resembled an empty raised dais or a stage between performances. With each step, she could feel the hardness of the thin dagger in its sheath, sewn into the inside of the front panel of her flowing au yi. It thumped against her thigh, a goading, irritating, constant reminder of what she was about to do.

It does not have to be tonight, she thought. I could probably do it tomorrow morning in his room. But they might not let me into the American camp tomorrow, and the closer to Tet, the more they all will be on guard. It must be tonight.

How will I do it? Should I allow him to kiss me in the darkness and stab him in the heart as we are close? Should I wait until his back is turned? Yes, it would be best if he turns his back. Even in the darkness, I do not want to chance seeing his face as he realizes I have killed him.

"Halt!" The militia sentry's voice pierced the stillness of the evening.

"It is I, Co Let Chu Li, Secretary of the Province Chief of Quang Tin. I want to speak with the American, Sergeant Mark Fellogese."

"Wait here please."

The faceless shadow that was the sentry blended into the deeper shadows of the TOC wall. Another sentry, she knew, was posted at the other end of the wall. But even now, so early after twilight, he was indistinguishable from the merged shades of the moonless night. After I kill him, she thought, I will say that one of the guards did it.

A foot scraped gravel in front of her, and someone cleared his throat. "Sergeant Mark? Is it you Sergeant Mark?"

"Yes Co Li, where are you?"

"Here." She held out her hands, her heart racing in spite of her wishes. She felt the glow of joy swell in her chest, to her neck and to her face. She was smiling. Don't smile, she commanded herself, but she couldn't help but disobey. His hands found hers and he pulled her to him.

Resist, she told herself, and this time her body obeyed. She stiffened. He felt her resistance and immediately stopped pulling, but he held her hands in his.

"Co Li," Mark said, his voice choked with sadness. "I'm sorry about your brother. I heard after. I didn't know at the time. Christ I'm sorry. What can I say? What can I do?"

Li said nothing. Why am I not crying? she thought. I'm here to kill the man I love, my only love. He reminds me that he has killed my dear brother who is yet awaiting his funeral, yet my eyes are dry. The dagger lay heavy against her thigh, waiting.

"Co Li, please believe me, I couldn't help it. It's this damned war. I was just at the wrong place at the wrong time. I had to shoot. I'm a soldier for Christ's sake. What else could I do?"

"They say you are hero," she said, knowing that her pointed words were cutting him, preparing the way for her dagger.

He released her hands. She could feel his nervousness; hear his shuffling feet.

"God, I'm not a hero Co Li. I just went where I was supposed to go. I did what I was supposed to do."

"They say you did not have to go. They say you ask to go."

"Oh God! Yes I did. I went because I wanted to, because I wanted to be more of a soldier. If I had even the slightest thought that my going would affect us, would cause me to lose you, I'd never have gone. But I did go, and I did my job. I'm sorry for your grief Co Li, and I'm sorry I caused it. But I can't be sorry for doing my job."

Now!, she thought. Now, while he is only a voice in the shadows. Better to remember after, that I thrust out at a voice, an unseen enemy. His voice is strong yet tender. He makes me remember other nights. Nights I will always remember. But no. Better to not remember him as when his weight was upon me, or how his face smiled when he touched my breast. Her hand closed tightly around the knife handle. So dark. He cannot see me, but I cannot see him either.

"Co Li please understand. I was just doing what I had to do. I was just doing my duty."

Duty? Yes, he's right. It was his duty. As Anh Ty was doing his duty. As I must do my duty. But he's right. It wasn't malice. It was duty. He should not be punished for doing his duty should he? What is my duty now? I must tell him that I understand. Because of our love, I owe him that much. Besides, I still don't know exactly where he is.

"I understand duty Sergeant Mark. Everyone must do his duty."

"You do? God. I hope you really do. I need that."

She felt his relief in the air about her. It was tangeble, alive.

"Co Li?" His voice was tentative. "I feel so close to you, most of the time, yet—sometimes—I feel like I don't really know you at all. But—I have to ask—I know it's difficult now—right after it's happened, but, do you think you could forgive...? Do you think we could ever be—lovers again? Or at least friends again?"

Her fingers tightened once more around the handle. Never, she thought. No matter what happens. We could never be lovers again. But he started to ask if I can forgive him. Can I? Should I? "Yes, maybe forgive," she said. "It is difficult now. Tomorrow difficult. Next day difficult. Maybe next year difficult. Yet all this is now, as you speak it. Now is not good word. Mean nothing. You speak now word now, but before I hear it, that now gone. Gone forever. When I hear word, is at different now than now of before. Now I cannot forgive you. But now I can. And now I do. I forgive you Sergeant Mark. Must forgive. You only do your duty."

"Thank you Co Li," Mark said solemnly. "I know how hard it must be for you. I know how you must feel. Your brother was so close...."

"You know how I feel Sergeant Mark?" she interrupted. Again deliberately wounding him with words, reminding herself of her own duty.

"No, I'm sorry. I didn't mean that I guess. I just meant I know you're grieving and I'm sorry. I feel sorry for you. It's all I can think about. How it was me who caused it. I didn't mean to, but it happened. I can't undo it. God I wish I could. You say you forgive me, but I can't forgive myself for hurting you. I wish your brother had killed me instead of the other way round. But what can I do now?"

Li was stunned. It could have been so! Ty could have killed Sergeant Mark instead! It might have been, and then I would have been forced to see my hated brother every day, knowing that he had killed my only love. Such unending torture that would have been.

What? What am I thinking? Hating my dead brother for something he did not do? Oh! There is a capricious spirit controlling my thoughts, finding new ways of torturing me. My love is still alive yes, standing somewhere in front of me. Somewhere near. But it is my duty to kill him. She shuddered. Away spirit, away. I must do my duty with a clear head.

"Co Li, I love you. I love you with all my heart. I'll make it up to you somehow. I don't know how, but I will."

"I have already forgive you. It was duty," she said coldly, still grasping the knife. Forgive is only a word, she thought. Love is only a word.

"Yes. Yes, it was my duty, but there were so many elements of chance involved. I volunteered for one night. It was that night. Of the three ambush patrols that night, I was in that particular one. We chose that specific trail. He chose the same trail. God, so many points of pure chance."

"We say that karma. You say fate. It no could be not happen." But I brought it about, she thought. It was my happiness. I allowed my love to make me happy and an evil spirit became jealous. It's more my fault than it is his. Her grip softened and relaxed. The blade hung loose in the au yi. Later, I'll do it later, she thought.

"I'm glad you understand," he murmured. "I'm still not sure I do."

"You kill enemy in war," she said, confused by her jumbled thoughts and emotions.

His hand touched her arm, gently. "Yeah, I killed an enemy. A VC. I didn't even think about the possibility that it might be your brother. He had a gun." His voice mumbled in front of her. His hand now tight around her elbow.

"Did you know?" he asked. "Did you know your brother was a VC?"

She paused. The sudden question surprised her and blasted through her confusion. Should she admit it? Would that resolve anything? No. She could never trust an American with that secret, not even her beloved.

"You did know didn't you?" She had waited too long to respond. He knew her too well. It doesn't matter now if he knows. After all, she was here to kill him.

"Yes, I know. I know all VC in Tam Ky."

"God, it must be tough on you. To have a member of your own family on the side of the enemy. And knowing other friends who are also enemies. Jesus, you must live in misery, like on the edge of a sword. It's a hell of a war for you. I'm sorry."

"Yes," she said, realizing he would not understand what she was about to say. "There is one special friend. Man who was very dear to me. Yet he is enemy. He always be enemy. It is very hard time to live." She felt a tear on her cheek. Her hand sadly but resolutely regripped the hilt of the dagger. When he draws near again, she thought. And he will.

"When my tour is over here," he continued. "Only eleven more months. I'll take you back with me. You'll be my wife. We'll make our new lives together in America, away from war, away from all this sadness."

"You want to marry with me?" The knife felt heavy, overfilling her hand.

"I sure do! We'll get married here before we leave. As soon as possible. It'll be easier that way."

"You marry me after you kill my brother?" Li's head was spinning. Voices echoed in her ear. He loves me. Do your duty! He wants to marry me. Obey your father! He wants to take me to America. Avenge your brother.

"Li. My little Em. You say you have forgiven me, and maybe you have. Maybe you can. I don't know. I just know it's a terrible war. I know you loved your brother. You told me you did, and how he watched over you. At any other time, in any other place, I would have loved your brother too. But it can't happen now, and we might never be able to pick up the pieces, but I want to try. God help me, I love you. I can't stop loving you."

He was closer now. Standing very near. She could feel his breath on her upturned face. He was so tall, so strong. He took her other arm and pulled her to him again. Now! She felt tears streaming down her face.

Resist. Resist, she told herself. But she went willingly into the warmth of his embrace. I could do it now, so easy, she thought. But I couldn't do it now. He is so trusting, so kind, so loving. He wants to marry with me! He squeezed her to him, gently crushing her small frame against his. Duty! she reminded herself. Now! she decided. It must be now. I cannot miss. Now!

But that now passed. And then another, and the blade remained sheathed. In Co Li's inner war, duty, in the end, was conquered by love.

SCENE 3

―――――――― ✦ ――――――――

THE ORPHANAGE

0930 Hours
Monday, 29 January, 1968

"OK," Jake said. "According to their original plan, one company is supposed to come through here. One platoon will split off to hit the radio station, and the other two will attack the main Regional Force compound over there." Jake pointed across the short open field to the militia compound.

"Yes," Major Hai nodded. "We before add the more barbed wire. Three lines."

Jake studied the short forty yards of rough, open terrain between the jungle edge and the outskirts of the city. It was one of four places where the jungle grew close in, making it an obvious avenue of approach by the enemy. Two new rows of triple strand concertina had been strung behind the original, leaving about ten yards between each. Three razor sharp fences to keep the wolves out. "Have we placed any trip flares?" he asked.

"Yes Troom Ta. Some at edge of jungle in trees. Some in open in front of barbed wire."

"What kind of fire power do we have covering this approach?"

Hai told him. Artillery and mortars. Too far removed for small arms protection. It was the best they could do.

Jake asked several more questions. Detailed questions about deadly force, the same type of questions he'd asked at the other sites this morning. The planning time had passed. Now the line had to be walked. Everything had to be inspected.

There hadn't been enough time for planning, there never was. Now, there's not enough time to check everything. But we've got to check, Jake thought. We have to make time. Otherwise we die.

Jake looked around at the shacks and houses nearby. Most of them bare hovels, only just habitable. "What about the civilians who live in this area?"

"We already move them," Hai responded. "All building here now empty. We give many tent; set up new village on east side of highway. All civilian, they stay tonight. Come back tomorrow if no attack. We tell them can stay longer if want. Some people, they like tent house better."

"Good, you've done well, Tiu Ta." Yes, Jake thought, Hai and the other Vietnamese had indeed done well. This was the seventh defensive sector he'd inspected this morning. It was a good defense here, as it was at the others. The enemy would have to attack across open terrain, lit up by trip flares, through a mortar barrage. They would have to cut their way through the first barbed wire barrier while mortar shells were falling.

Once past this wire, they would bunch up to cut the knife edged wire strands of the second obstacle; and while doing this, they would be doused with five blasts of flaming, thickened gasoline from fougasse canisters. As they penetrated that second barbed wire fence silhouetted by the flames behind them, they would be blasted by command detonated claymore mines.

Then they had to cut their way through the third barbed wire fence before launching their attack against the main defenses of the militia compound where more wire, larger fougasse canisters, more claymores, and aimed small arms fire awaited them.

No one should live through all that, Jake thought, but they always do. Somehow the enemy gets through everything we throw at them. Their ranks are thinned, but that's the best we can hope for.

"You have more suggestion Troom Ta?" Hai's attitude was that of a teenager showing off his prize winning science project to his high school teacher. Cocky, proud, eager for praise.

"No, Tiu Ta, I don't. I wish we had more troops to actually defend this approach. But without them, I think you've done as well as it could be done."

"We could do more better Troom Ta. But you tell me no use land mine or booby trap. We could have many punji stake pit in open area, and even between wire, but you no like."

"No, I don't Tiu Ta. Those things can't just be aimed at the NVA. They could catch our own people, either before, or perhaps even long after the attack is over. I especially think it's a bad idea to place punji pits this close in to the city."

"Maybe so Troom Ta. I no put here because you say so, but punji pit good against VC in night attack."

Jake nodded silently and gritted his teeth. His jaw tightened. This was an aspect of the Vietnamese mentality he remembered from his first tour. They never seemed to consider the aftermath of battle. If the fight begins tonight, it might be over by morning; or it might go on for three days or even a week. But sooner or later, it would be over. The soldiers on both sides would regroup, and the civilians would come back to their homes.

A single punji pit with dung dipped bamboo spears or nails in the bottom could injure ten attacking men in one night, but the next day it would still be armed; as dangerous as ever. Waiting for a young mother picking herbs. Waiting for a small child to come exploring through the dusty battle ground. Waiting to send the sharpened spikes ripping through tiny bare feet.

He saw it happen early in his first tour. He never let it happen again, but they always wanted to. Anything to hurt the enemy and make him bleed. Anything to protect themselves just a little bit better, regardless of the cost to others. And civilian casualties were not something to worry about.

I recognize the anomaly, he thought. Hai and I are both soldiers. It's our duty, our job, to plan and carry out the mass slaughter of other human beings who oppose us. It requires a deliberate mental perversion. What other profession thinks only of better ways to kill other people. What other profession thinks such bloody thoughts as it's better to maim or cripple an opponent than it is to kill him because if you cripple him, it takes someone else, at least one, maybe more, out of the battle to carry or drag him away. Or thinks of cannon shells called "bee hive" which send thousands of needle shaped fleshettes in a five hundred yard death spray. Or canister bombs which drop thousands of grenade-like explosives in a pattern that would cut the grass on ten football fields. Thoughts of napalm, and five hundred pound bombs. Of machine guns and bayonets, and if a machine gun can't kill fast enough, use a six-barreled gattling gun. Every conceivable way of mayhem has been created and used. Yet even these are not enough for the modern soldier. We still make other weapons by hand in the field. Like the fougasse. An explosion detonated, one shot flame thrower which spews syrup-like thickened fuel in a flaming cascade that adheres to skin and clothing like glue. Burning glue.

God! Why am I a soldier? And even worse, why am I good at it?

"This is last position, Troom Ta." Hai interrupted his thoughts.

"Are you sure all the civilians from threatened areas have been evacuated Tiu Ta?"

"We cannot evacuate all of city Troom Ta. We not know all area maybe in danger. We evacuate all civilian from near targets in NVA plan. Most civilian." He shrugged as if in apology. "Except one place. Refugee Reception Center. We move many, but many come every day. Many now come from Hau Duc. No can move everybody same time. Many refugee still there. Also Catholic orphanage. It be same compound as Refugee Reception Center. It be very near Province Headquarters. People still there. Catholic mother who be chief of Sisters there, she say they no go."

"Why not?" asked Jake.

"Who know why not? She not say. She not go. She not listen."

"Let's go talk to her again."

Hai rolled his eyes upward in pained resignation and crawled into his black jeep. He started it and shifted into reverse as Jake hopped into the passenger seat. Jake glanced at the green leather seats. Tu's former jeep, he thought. He remembered other rides to other places in this jeep. Silent rides. Tu had never been as verbose as Hai, but especially while driving. Riding with Tu had always been a time for thinking. Hai hardly ever kept quiet. He was talking now. What did he say? Something about a gunfight in downtown Tam Ky?

"Whoa, I missed part of that Tiu Ta. Who was it that was fighting?"

"The National Police Field Force, you call them NPFF. They fight with QC, ARVN military police."

"And it happened last night in Tam Ky?"

"Yes, no one die, but two QC and one NPFF policeman have wound.

The jeep bounced around a corner into another dirt back street. A large pig and two geese scurried out of the jeep's path. The air was shattered with squeals and angry barnyard honking. Hai, concentrating on the conversation, acted as if he did not see the fluttering wings and scrambling hooves. Jake gripped the dashboard handle and swallowed hard.

"How did it start?" he asked.

"QC and NPFF both try to set up roadblock at same street corner. QC there first. NPFF go one block away, set up roadblock in front of QC roadblock. QC send to ARVN for reinforcements. ARVN send QC armored car. This crash through NPFF roadblock."

"Jesus! How did they get it resolved?"

Hai shrugged. "Report say they shoot maybe twenty, thirty minutes. Many bullet holes in Tam Ky buildings. Police not good shooter. QC number ten also. Maybe pretty lucky eh?" He jerked the wheel to avoid a platoon of Tam Ky militia assembled in the street for an equipment inspection.

"Damn lucky," agreed Jake. "Who got them to stop shooting?"

"Nobody stop. NPFF run out of ammunition. They get in jeeps and drive away."

"Is anything being done now to smooth it over? There's got to be cooperation by tonight or we're really in trouble. That QC platoon and the NPFF make up almost twenty percent of our total fighting force."

"Yes Troom Ta. Big co van with beard, police advisor, he talk this morning with QC platoon commander and NPFF commander. He make both men go in one room. He go in also. Stay there. No let them come out to eat. No let them go out for nothing. He say must work together or starve together."

Jake smiled. That would be a typical Race Haldane tactic. Good! If anyone could pound cooperation into somebody's head by tonight, it would be Race. God what a stupid thing to happen now. Just when we need everyone's full support.

He had made one more try last night to get Americans in close to the city. He had flown to LZ Mary Ann to talk to the Regimental Commander there. King had given the OK. No one had visited the Americans yet, since they had come into the Province last Friday.

He had asked for a company or even just a platoon. But they had turned him down. They were beating the bush in the jungle looking for Charlie. They wouldn't accept the fact that Charlie was no longer in the boonies. Only US intelligence sources were to be trusted, as far as they were concerned, and US G2 reports didn't specifically say that Tam Ky was going to be attacked. So they were going to continue searches in the jungle.

By now, the VC are just outside Tam Ky! He bit his lower lip as the jeep pulled to a stop in the circular driveway of a three storied, almond colored brick building. It looked more like a fortress than an orphanage, with barred windows and a massive stone staircase leading up to a heavy wooden door. A large black cross hung over the arched doorway.

Jake recoiled at the sight of a statue beside the stairway. It had, evidently, once been a statue of a cowled monk leading a small child by the hand, away from the building. The unpainted dull grey granite statue had, however, been severely defaced, and, Jake realized ruefully, defaced was the correct word.

The nose and lower portion of the Monk's face had been chipped off rather recently, leaving only the blind eyes and ashen grey forehead. Where the face was fractured, the granite was bright and sparkling, making the wound even more obvious and gruesome; making the statue a hideous, hooded monster.

Additionally, Jake realized, the arm of the Monk had been severed quite cleanly, so that now, rather than pulling the child, with its lusterless grey innocent face, the hewn rock youth followed willingly, proffering the useless limb to its former owner, the monster who never looked back.

As Hai stepped out of the jeep, he grinned at the statue. "This be souvenir of last time NVA attack Tam Ky, only four month ago. We have ARVN division in Tam Ky then. ARVN fight very well. NVA come in, but ARVN drive them back out in same day." He paused and glanced again at the statue. "This bad statue. Many Buddhist say it show Catholic steal children. Some other people say it prove Catholic not be trusted, because statue be man priest who take child away. Do in secret, because only sister work here in orphanage. Most Buddhist happy when statue break with bullets in fighting."

"Do you think Catholics steal children?" Jake asked.

"No. Before maybe not so sure. But I go inside to talk with Reverend Mother. See all other sister. See children. All good thing. Catholic do good here at orphanage."

"I'm proud of you Tiu Ta." Jake reached out to touch Hai's elbow. "It would have been easy to be prejudiced, and see evil things because you expected to see evil things. You have an open mind. I'm proud to be your friend."

Hai beamed with the compliment. As they started the long climb up the steps, he slipped his arm around Jake's waist. Jake smiled tolerantly. He reminded himself that the gesture was merely one of overt friendship, common in Vietnam, yet his western background didn't allow him to feel comfortable. He started to push away, but resisted the urge, forcing himself to walk placidly up the steps. Taking a deep lungfull of resolve, he put his arm around Hai's shoulders. He felt silly, out of place, embarrassed, but he was in Vietnam, and such things are done in Vietnam with friends.

Hai's natural acceptance of Jake's embrace melted away the uneasiness Jake felt. They grinned at each other, and clamored up the stairs laughing. They arrived at the door still locked like Siamese twins. Jake waited for Hai to knock, as it was a Vietnamese institution, and Hai was Vietnamese. But Hai didn't knock. It took a moment for Jake to realize that Hai was waiting for him to knock, probably because he was the senior officer.

They looked at each other expectantly, still waiting, still locked side by side in each other's arms. They laughed again and then both knocked simultaneously. This coincidence sent them both into convulsions of renewed laughter. Neither man noticed that the door had opened until she spoke.

"Et alohrs Messieurs?" Her voice was cool and calm, but rang with authority. The surprise of hearing that voice and seeing her appear so suddenly before them, caused them both to react with juvenile guilt. Jake felt himself blushing. Without thinking, he automatically snapped to attention, and he realized that Hai had done the same thing. He was still grinning. He couldn't stop. Wow. What must she be thinking? Grown men, soldiers, officers, acting like small children.

Hai stammered something in Vietnamese, while Jake studied the regal looking nun who stood before them. She was dressed in a bright white habit which glinted brilliantly in the direct sunlight. A wooden cross hung between her breasts, and a cord of woven twine circled her waist. She wore a high peaked headdress with a flowing train which formed a kind of half cape around her shoulders.

She was Vietnamese, Jake saw, but taller than most. Almost as tall as he was. Her face was remarkable, the color of fine parchment, but smooth and free from both worry and guilt. The thick eyeglasses she wore magnified her black eyes into deep liquid pools, but there was no hardness, no bitterness. These are soft eyes, Jake thought. Kind, gentle eyes.

"Yes, of course we can talk," she said to Hai, "but let us speak in English, as I suspect your—playmate does not speak our native tongue." The corners of her mouth twitched upward, but it was those gentle eyes which gave away her amusement. She has a sense of humor too, thought Jake. He realized he was still grinning. She must think I'm a Cheshire cat, he thought.

She led the way into the building to a small sitting room.

"I'm Mother Angela," she began, as they all sat down. "I have met Major Hai before,..." She let her voice trail off expectantly.

"I'm Lieutenant Colonel Jake Thorpe, Major Hai's advisor."

"He my counterpart Reverend Mother," Hai interjected.

"Your counterpart? An interesting word. Perhaps it helps to explain the childish behavior I witnessed at the entrance."

"I apologize for the horseplay Reverend Mother," Jake said, "but we are here to persuade you to evacuate this building. There will be trouble tonight. Your orphanage is in danger."

"I have been informed of this possibility. We will not evacuate!"

"But why Reverend Mother?"

"There are two reasons. The first is that I have prayed to Saint Nicholas, the Patron Saint for Children. From him I have received guidance, and this guidance was to keep the children here in the home. I will not go against his guidance."

"We could move you with force Reverend Mother," Hai said, tentatively. Jake could tell that the Reverend Mother saw through the empty threat.

"You must do what your duty says you must do; as must I," she said, matter of factly. There was no note of triumph at all. She did not regard this as a test of wills. She was looking at the floor.

"What is the second reason?" asked Jake.

She looked up to meet his gaze and smiled. "This is the eve of Tet. New Year's Eve, as you call it. Tet is the most important holiday in Vietnam, as I'm sure you've heard. The superstitions of Vietnam hold that anyone who is away from their home at the turn of the year is doomed to have an unhappy year. I am a Catholic and reject this superstition. But many of the children here, perhaps all who are old enough to know, still cling to this belief. This orphanage is their home. For many, it is the only home they have ever known. It would cause extreme unhappiness to send them away from here this night."

"But Reverend Mother, we're talking about war! Bombs and real bullets. We're talking about the possibility of children being killed. Are you willing to risk their lives just so they might not be unhappy for a while?" Jake was aghast.

"The reality of war has been with these children all of their lives. It has been with me all of my life. War holds no special terror for any of us. Not being in their home at Tet does! Life and death for me and for these children is in God's hands, not mine. In this case, however, their happiness or unhappiness is my responsibility."

Jake and Hai exchanged helpless glances. Hai shrugged. "Cannot move nuns and children with bayonet," he said. "Nobody understand. Everyone think wrong. Everyone mad with us."

Jake nodded. "OK," he said. "Let's walk around and see if there's some way we can make it as safe as possible for them."

The two men walked outside to look at the windows and walls. The stately, white robed nun followed discreetly behind. "I maybe bring one platoon of militia, from reserve. Put some men on roof. Some in windows. Some outside," Hai exclaimed with enthusiasm. "Give good protection."

"Sure it would Tiu Ta, but that would really cut our reserve strength wouldn't it?"

"Still have two platoon. One north of city. One west or south of city."

"Which direction would you leave without a reserve Tiu Ta? West? Or south?"

"Not sure Troom Ta. Which you say?"

"Neither. We're facing an NVA regiment Tiu Ta! If a battalion or even a company breaks through, a one platoon counter-attack will probably be ineffective, but it's sure better than nothing."

"ARVN have two company in reserve Troom Ta!"

"Sure Tiu Ta, but they've got a different mission. They've got the responsibility for the entire built up area of the city in case of a break through. We've got all the known targets and all the militia compounds. The police are the usual security for the Refugee Center, which includes the orphanage. We'll have to let them handle it."

"I no agree Troom Ta. These be children."

"Well the ultimate decision is yours Tiu Ta, but it seems to me the Reverend Mother knows the risk she's taking. I sure wouldn't short my reserve strength for this. It's like the hospital. We have to take some risks ourselves. We just don't have enough troops."

"Barbed wire then?" asked Hai

"No, that wouldn't stop bullets. The odds are they won't attack this building. It's not located in a good place to be an observation post, and it certainly has no military function. What I think we must protect against is stray gunfire and accidental destruction. Why don't we get some sandbags and stack them up around the bottom floor. It will look the same as several banks and other civilian buildings, so it won't stand out as a target, but it will give better protection. I'll ask the Reverend Mother to keep the kids on the ground floor during the attack.

"Can do Troom Ta. We have many extra sandbags."

"Well Reverend Mother," Jake said turning to Mother Angela. "Can you keep the children on the ground floor?"

"Yes Colonel, that can be arranged. And, for what it's worth, I agree with your decision. I would not want my stubbornness to reduce the effectiveness of your defense. Besides, as you said, the orphanage has no military significance. The VC have no reason to attack children."

"Don't be so sure about that Reverend Mother." Jake was remembering brutal, savage scenes from his previous tour.

"You not know VC!" interjected Hai. "You woman of peace and love, Reverend Mother. You not understand VC and NVA. NVA especially bad. I see before many times. They make many children, women, old people die on purpose. NVA very bad."

"Nonsense!" scoffed Mother Angela. "This war is about the land and the right to govern the people. Neither side would deliberately make war on children."

Jake and Hai glanced at each other with sadness.

Mother Angela continued. "Everyone knows this building is an orphanage. Tonight I will turn on all the lights. The children will like it, and it will advertise to all sides that we are here. In this way, we will be safer. There will be no mistakes."

Hai rolled his eyes upward. "You still think we should no send platoon?" he said to Jake.

Jake shook his head with frustration and sadness. "As much as her naivete makes me want to protect her for her own good, Tiu Ta, I still don't think we should reduce our reaction force. I'll call Co Van Haldane and have him double the police guard out here."

Hai was still shaking his head.

"Would you like to see the children Colonel? There is an American Sergeant inside now playing with some of them. He has been coming almost every day for a week now. The children have come to look forward to his visits."

"An American Sergeant?"

"Yes. His name is Sergeant Fellogese."

"Fellogese? He's here? Why has he been coming here?"

Mother Angela smiled knowingly and led Jake in by his arm. Hai remained at the jeep, using the radio to call for sand bags and a work detail.

"This is the playroom for some of the smaller children," Mother Angela said, as she opened a door. Jake was surprised at the noise. It had been so quiet in the hallway. Sergeant Fellogese was on his back in the center of the floor. At least ten toddlers swarmed over and around him like bees on a honeycomb. Whoops of joy and squeals of delight pealed through the room. The children rocked on their unsteady legs and dropped onto his face and stomach. Three of them crawled across his chest. Others clung to his arms and legs, another was pulling his hair. Mark was grinning and giggling, enjoying the fracas as much as the children. Two nuns stood against the far wall, smiling and nodding with approval.

"Sergeant Fellogese," Mother Angela said, softly. "We have a visitor."

"Don't get up Sergeant. Go ahead. Don't let me spoil your fun."

Fellogese had started to scramble to his feet, but smiled and relaxed. "Hi ya Colonel. These little tykes just can't get enough of this. They really like beating up on me."

"So I see. Looks like you enjoy a bit of masochism yourself."

"Well Sir," he winced as an elbow jabbed near his eye, "I can't think of anything to do that they'd like better. What time is it Sir?"

Jake looked at his watch. "Eleven ten."

"Thanks Sir, I gotta get going pretty soon. My shift starts at noon."

"Take your sleeping bag with you. The roads will be closed tonight. You'll have to sleep at the TOC if you sleep at all," said Jake as he tickled a youngster.

"It's already there Sir. Took it yesterday."

Jake smiled. He nodded to Mother Angela who was beaming as she watched Mark. "He is so good with the children," she said.

They turned and walked down the corridor to another doorway. "The older children are upstairs," she whispered, with a forefinger to her lips. "This is the infants' room. They will all be sleeping."

She opened the door to a crescendo of bleating and bawling from tiny babies. Jake's ears ached with the noise. A very young girl in a grey and white nun's habit sat in the corner rocking two infants. One was sound asleep, the other was red faced and screaming. The girl is probably a novice, Jake thought, so dedicated and peaceful at her task. Another nun, in a solid grey habit, was changing the linen in a crib.

"These are our newest charges," said Mother Angela nodding and smiling toward the row of cribs. She was now almost shouting to be heard. Four of them came to us just a few days ago from Hau Duc, when their parents were killed in the fighting."

A lump caught in Jake's throat. He remembered the children he'd seen when he first visited the westernmost district. He didn't recognize any of these as the same, but realized he hadn't really focused on the faces. They might be the same, but it didn't matter. This damned war, he thought. Nobody thinks of this. He looked down on one waif in a crib. He was asleep and covered with a mound of dirty oily rags. Why do I think it's a boy? he wondered. "What's wrong with this child?" he asked.

"That is a burned child," answered Mother Angela. "We have put salve on the burns. The bandages are loose but necessary to keep away the flies and mosquitos."

Jake was shocked. This isn't the way to treat burns. It used to be, he remembered, but not anymore. "Who is your doctor?" he asked.

"One of the doctors from the Province Hospital comes to visit once a week. He is very old, but a good doctor."

"Would you like to have another one visit you from time to time?" he asked.

"That would be nice, yes," she said.

He made a mental note to try to get an American doctor from China Beach or Chu Lai out here, at least on an occasional basis. He looked at his watch. "Reverend Mother, I'm happy that I came here. I'm glad that I met you, but I have to leave now as there is much to do."

She nodded understandingly. Looking at her serene face, Jake felt a warm glow inside his chest. This is what Christianity really means, he thought. In spite of the raucous noise around him, he thrilled at the atmosphere, the feel of the orphanage. This place, this woman. This is true goodness. This is peace. This is what peace is all about. "I'll see you again Reverend Mother. And that's a promise," he said.

"Thank you Colonel. You have a gentle soul, but it is troubled. It is not often I see a gentle soul in the body of a soldier. You are the type to offer your life for the lives of others. You probably think this is a noble and soldierly attitude; but it is rare. I see it as a Christ-like trait. I will pray today to Saint Sebastian, the Patron Saint of soldiers, for your safety."

Jake nodded, a bit disconcerted. He was not accustomed to have anyone praying for him. He had certainly never thought of himself as Christ-like. He didn't know how to respond. "Thank you," he said, "and tell the Saint thank you also."

Mother Angela laughed. "Saint Sabastian will be pleased with your thanks," she said, her magnified eyes twinkling. "And you are welcome at any time." She gazed at him directly, seriously now; unwaveringly. "You are very different for a westerner. Obviously you are not Catholic, but your heart is good. I think I shall also pray to Saint Joan of Arc for you. She was a soldier also you know. She has always been one of my favorite saints."

Jake swallowed and felt himself blushing. "Thank you again Reverend Mother."

She accompanied him to the steps leading down to the jeep, where they were joined by Mark. "Any possibility of a lift Sir? Over to the TOC?"

"Sure Sergeant, hop in."

They trotted down the steps to meet Hai, but at the sight of Hai's face, they both stopped cold. "What's the matter?" Jake asked.

"They be shooting in town. On radio now. Sniper with rifle shoot from window. Kill regional force captain; Him my captain. Him banker, work in bank in daytime. Good officer. Him long time friend. Captain Tot him name."

"Captain Tot?" blurted Mark. "I knew him. He was on my patrol."

"Yes, same Captain Tot," said Hai grimly.

"Has there been any other shooting?" asked Jake. "Any way to tell if it's started already?"

"National police there now. They say no attack. Just one shot."

"Jesus Sir, what a shame! He really was a good man." Mark's eyes were moist. "I was only with him that one time, but Hell, Sir. He's gone now. I really liked him. I never even told him what a good job he did on the ambush. I always meant to." He wiped his eyes. "Jesus, I'm crying. I guess I'm kind of stupid or weak or something."

Jake put his hand on Mark's shoulder. "No son, you're none of those. You fought with him. You make friends quickly in wartime. It's OK to cry; you've lost a friend."

"God Sir, what a waste." Mark put his hands on the hood of the jeep and hung his head. Hai reached and placed his hand on one of Mark's. "He was my friend also. I know for long time. I sad for him also." Hai and Jake exchanged glances and nodded. Mark was young, the glances said. His first loss of a friend in war.

Hai gripped Mark's hand harder. "Many people think soldier not cry," he said. "Not true. All soldier cry every time. Never get used to death of friend." His own eyes were wet, verifying his words.

Jake reached out and caught Hai's other hand. The three stood for a moment in silence, locked in bereavement, and locking in their own friendship.

Mark finally raised his head. "I've got to get to work," he said.

"Let's go," Jake said softly. They climbed into the jeep. All of them seemed to have heavy, cumbersome legs which made getting in awkward and clumsy. Jake glanced up at the top step. Mother Angela still stood there, serenely, sadly. Could she hear us? Did she know what happened? He waived at her and watched as she made the sign of the cross, blessing them.

The jeep coughed into life and jolted noisily down the street. Hai, for once, was silent as he drove.

It was a short drive, only six or seven hundred meters. They pulled up to the TOC and Mark jumped out. "Thanks Sir," he said. His voice was now clear and steady. "Thanks to both of you." He turned and ducked inside the bunker.

Hai then drove Jake to Camp Kronberg. Jake wanted to check the US defenses there one more time in detail. "I'll meet you at the TOC at sixteen hundred hours," he said to Hai as they parted.

"Yes Troom Ta. Midnight come very soon tonight."

"Right, and we've got much to do before then," Jake said as Hai started the jeep and rolled away. Much to do and miles to go. Miles to go before I sleep, Jake thought. But no time to rest for me today and surely no sleep tonight. Old Robert Frost wasn't fighting a war when he wrote those lines. The woods here are just as deep and dark, but they sure aren't lovely tonight. Twelve hours to go before all hell breaks loose, and those twelve hours will pass so quickly it'll probably seem like only an hour or so. For some reason, a line of Christopher Marlow's "Dr. Faustus" jumped to his memory:

"Now hast thou but one bare hour to live,
And then thou must be damned perpetually:
Stand still you ever moving spheres of heaven,
That time may cease, and midnight never come."

He shuddered. Why did I remember that line? It was in the one play I acted in back in school. The line wasn't even one of mine. I played a prince. Gruesome thought to think of now. Is the Devil out there waiting for me? Waiting to take me at midnight? Probably a whole bunch of devils, and they're all wearing NVA pith helmets.

It took him four and a half hours to check everything at Camp Kronberg, but he was satisfied. They were as ready as possible. Despite his tardy arrival back at the TOC, Major Hai still hadn't arrived. Only about an hour till sunset, he thought. Where is he? The damned Vietnamese sense of time, he remembered. But surely today he'd remember. Should I go looking for him? Or should I wait here? Jake sat in his jeep drumming his fingers on the steering wheel. Men scurried in all directions. Everyone was armed and anxious. Dust and tension hung in the still hot air.

Major Buckingham's face appeared in the TOC doorway. He squared his shoulders resolutely and walked to Jake's jeep. Buckingham nervously stopped beside Jake and saluted.

"Colonel Thorpe Sir: may I talk to you Sir?"

"Sure Buck, go ahead," Jake said returning the salute.

"Sir. It's bad news. I'm sorry."

"Spill it Buck. What is it?"

"Sir. We just got a message from Da Nang Red Cross."

"Yes?"

"It's your wife Sir." Buckingham deliberately looked away, avoiding eye to eye contact.

"Come on Buck; what is it?"

"Sir, maybe you'd like to come in outta the sun and sit down first."

"OK, OK," Jake said, half amused by Buck's hesitancy and half irritated by it. "You've convinced me. It's really bad news. Now tell me what it is."

"Sir. Your wife. She committed suicide Sir. She's dead. God I'm sorry I had to be the one to tell you Sir. Anything I can do?"

Jake sat frozen to the jeep. He couldn't move. Delores dead? Suicide? "How did she do it?" he asked stiffly.

"The telegram says she jumped off a bridge and drowned Sir. They have recovered the body."

"Did she leave a note?"

"The message didn't say Sir. Just what I told you. Anything you want me to do?"

"No, just give me a few minutes here, I'll be in in a minute."

"Yes Sir, I will. I've already informed Colonel King Sir. He says to convey his sympathy. Says you can go back on emergency leave on the first bird outta here tomorrow."

"OK. Thanks Buck. I'll have to go back. We were separated you know, but I'll have to go back. I'll leave tomorrow." What am I jabbering about? he thought. I'm not making sense. She's dead. At peace at last. Poor tortured woman. I can't even cry, but I feel it in my chest. Hard to breathe. Hard to swallow. Mouth's dry. Need a drink of water. Why'd she do it? Damn her! Why'd she do it now? God, I knew she was mixed up. She threatened to do it so often, but I didn't expect her to ever really go through with it. She always said she wanted to, but I never thought she would.

"Colonel Thorpe Sir?"

Jake looked up to see Buckingham still standing there. Major Hai was now standing beside him. "Yes Buck?"

"Sir, you've been sitting here over half an hour now. Don't you think you should come on in? I can't leave you here Sir. It'll be dark soon, and it's Tet. There'll be an attack tonight."

Jake climbed out of the jeep woodenly. "Sorry Buck, I guess I lost track of the time." He nodded at Hai, who hovered nearby looking concerned and worried. "I'm OK Tiu Ta. I'll get it together before the fight starts. I need a drink of water."

Hai nodded, but didn't look convinced.

Jake looked up at the blue sky, already taking on a slightly darker hue. The sky to the east was covered with crimson colored clouds reflecting the sun. Red sky at night; a sailor's delight, he thought. But there's no sailors in Tam Ky!

SCENE 4

CA DOR

2330 Hours
Monday, 29 January, 1968

Co Li clutched her purse tightly to her breasts with both arms. It was heavy. Only two grenades, she thought, almost as small as duck eggs, but so heavy in my purse. Two little eggs to be hatched, she smiled wryly, one to give birth to the new year and one to the new era of independence.

Despite her anxiety, she forced herself to walk unhurriedly across the smooth surface of the parade field toward Ca Dor. The soft breeze smelled like rain. It pressed the front panel of the au yi against her legs. She felt the firmness of the hidden dagger. It reminded her of the last time she carried it. Had it only been yesterday? I must not fail tonight, she thought. It will not be the same as before. I have no feelings for these pigs, for any of them. They are enemies of my country. They are my enemies! She hugged her purse tighter. Ty would not fail. He would not be feeling fear now as I am, but I will do my duty and do what he had planned to do himself. Ty's spirit is with me. My father depends upon us both.

There is no moon tonight. It is the death night of the twelfth month. The period of the new moon. She looked up and smiled, feeling the mist-like spray of light rain. The dark clouds cover the sky like winter blankets. Not a single star in sight. Even the heavens, she thought, are allied with our cause tonight.

The dark shadow-shape of Ca Dor loomed ahead. Sentries would be posted as always, she knew, and tonight they would have been specially chosen for their alertness. "I approach," she called out confidently before they challenged her. "I am the Dai Ta's personal secretary. He has summoned me."

"Advance Co Let Chu Li," a voice announced from the deeper shadows beside the stairway, "You may enter."

Li did not break stride as she purposefully marched up the stairs. She never saw the sentries, but she felt their wary eyes boring into her. She could hear one of them breathing. Would they call the Dai Ta to check on her story? Would they believe that she left her family on this eve of Tet to come to work? She shuddered as the suserrations of the wind whispered behind her.

Inside the front entrance, she drew a quick breath. She was surprised though, at the heat. It dawned on her that it had been refreshing and almost cool outside. Inside the capital building, however, the stone walls still held the afternoon heat. She glanced into her office. The windows had been closed and shuttered. Another reason for the heat and the heaviness of the air, she realized. She blinked in the bright lights of the corridor and noticed two Americans walking toward her. It was Troom Ta King, the mismarked devil, and his deputy.

Their presence did not worry her. She knew they would suspect nothing. They would never realize that she was out of place here on this holiday night. Americans never notice anything strange or out of place. Unconsciously, however, she clutched her purse tighter. The two long noses were talking to each other intently, seriously. She looked at the floor. She could not chance seeing the evil eye look at her tonight. She hoped he had not driven Ty's spirit away from her.

They walked past without pausing and exited the building. She breathed again.

Up the stairs. Slowly, slowly. Don't draw attention. Which room would he be in? The bedroom? The sitting room? I must be sure. Two weeks ago he announced that he would spend every night in his bunker. That would have made it more difficult. But it had been that one night only. Something must have happened. He has never gone into his bunker since then. He would be somewhere on this floor. Somewhere in his living quarters.

On the next tread of the stairs, her eyes came level with the landing on the second floor. She paused. A very young Vietnamese sentry in polished boots and a white leather belt relaxed halfway down the hall, in front of the sitting room door. He was leaning casually against the door frame, lost in his own thoughts. He had not heard her.

Li froze. A sentry? Up here? There had never been a sentry on the second floor. She forced herself to be calm. Think! Think! A new plan must be formed. We never considered that they would increase the number of interior guards, and place them in new positions. Think! Her eyes were even with the soldier's boots. She noted his neatly tied white laces. The walls also seemed exceptionally white. She sniffed the odor of fresh paint. All of her senses seemed to be in needle sharp focus. She saw that the hardwood floor had been recently waxed and polished. A mosquito hummed past her ear. The long hallway runner had been carefully vacuumed, but the lackey soldiers who had cleaned Ca Dor for Tet had left several wrinkles which marred the evenness of the carpet's surface. A radio somewhere below played holiday music for Tet.

Squaring her shoulders resolutely, she continued up the stairs. The young guard glanced in her direction and immediately straightened to a military posture. Their eyes met.

Li smiled. Remain calm, she reminded herself. She recognized him as one of the guards usually assigned outside the building. He's unaccustomed to being inside, she thought. He's probably nervous. I must show confidence.

The guard smiled back and nodded his head in a token bow of greeting. As she reached the top of the stairs, she nodded in return, slightly deeper than his had been. A mistake, she thought. They had exchanged bows before, and Li's position, so close to the Dai Ta, had allowed her to bow less obsequiously. She was the Dai Ta's secretary. A person of importance. If he is truly alert, she thought, he will notice the change. He will know that I am lacking confidence here tonight. He will know there is something different about my presence. Should I speak to him? What should I say?

She walked toward him. A quick plan only half formed in her mind. She looked at the floor demurely, as a proper Vietnamese woman should do; but out of the corner of her eye, she saw him appraising her.

All of the guards are chosen for their sense of duty, she remembered. They must never abandon their posts. She thought of walking seductively, but quickly dismissed the thought. Whatever I do, she realized, must be natural for me to do. I must play the part of myself.

She walked past him feeling his eyes burning into her. Her own eyes searching the corridor ahead. Where? Where should I make it happen? There! she thought. At the intersection of the two hallways. It's far enough away to muffle the sound, yet close enough to make him feel that he might still be on his post, still on guard. A sudden fear clutched at her throat. Could there be another sentry in the other hallway? That would change everything. I must look down the other passage before I go into my act. She swallowed. Her mouth was dry. Her tongue seemed to cling to her teeth.

She reached the corner. Her eyes hurriedly swept the connecting corridor. Clear. No guards. She swallowed again and took a deep breath. She glanced boldly back at the sentry. He was still watching her. Good! Now I must be the actress. She smiled again, still looking at the young soldier. As she stepped toward the entrance of the second passage, she deliberately toed down her foot so that the rubber thong caught on the loose carpet runner. She dropped her purse and sprawled awkwardly to her knees. She glanced again at the young militiaman.

He was poised to come to her aid, but he hadn't yet moved from his post by the sitting room door. She could read the indecision on his face. Yes, she thought, he wants to come. He wants to play the protective male. Just a bit more coaxing. Just a few more rice grains to attract the hungry rodent toward the trap.

She started to get to her feet but winced obviously as she put weight on her foot. She slumped to a sitting position and began to rub her ankle.

He still hadn't moved. The unfeeling insect! Doesn't he see that I am in pain? She grimaced for his benefit as she massaged her leg. He took a step toward her but hesitated. Through lowered lashes she could see his anxiety. He wouldn't call out to her, she knew, for fear of disturbing the Dai Ta on the eve of Tet. He was torn between his duty as a soldier and his desire to be of help. But his duty is winning, she realized. He's not going to come.

One more ploy, she thought. If it fails, I will have to abandon this plan and do something else, more desperate, with greater risk. She rose again to her feet, winced again, sat down again, and dropped her head as if she were crying. Most men cannot resist a weeping woman, she thought. She sniffed loudly in the quiet hallway.

It worked. The guard approached. "Are you injured Co Li?" he asked gently.

Li wiped her eyes and face as if to dry them. "It is my ankle." she said. "I feel it must be badly sprained." She was not surprised that he knew her name. All the guards knew who she was. She did not know his name.

"Would you like me to call someone. Should I get you a ride to the hospital?"

"No, not now," she said quickly, startled that he might shout for assistance despite the Dai Ta. "No, it is almost Tet. I cannot allow my misfortune to take someone else away from their family. Perhaps if I lean on your shoulders, only to that door there." She pointed down the connecting corridor. "That will be all I need for now."

"Yes, certainly," he smiled proudly. "I can carry you if you would like."

"No. I will be satisfied to lean on you and remove the weight from my ankle. Help me to my feet please." She held her hands up to him.

He pulled her up easily and she leaned against him, pretending shyness but remembering to act as if she were in severe pain.

"Your purse remains on the floor," he said. "Should I carry it for you?"

"No, later please. Help me to my door first. You may bring my purse to me after that." She smiled up at him. I can't allow him to pick up my purse, she thought. The weight might cause suspicion. Yet I also cannot pick it up, for I must have both hands free.

He put his arm around her waist and lifted, helping to carry her as she limped past the intersection and down the other hall. He is strong, she thought, and polite. Such a pity that he has been misled to work against his own people.

They reached the door. Now, she thought. It must be now while he is so close. One hand groped for the dagger and found it. I must not look at his face. The sight of his young face might dissuade me.

"Here we are," he said. "Is the door locked? Do you have the key?"

"Freedom from imperialism is the key," she replied, and slashed the knife upward, viciously, into his abdomen. She heard his surprised, pain filled grunt and felt him buckle as he continued to try to support her weight. She lifted her arm from his shoulder and stepped back. The blade slipped out of him easily. A man's belly is like a bag of wet rice, she thought; and then she looked at his face.

His startled eyes stared at her, uncomprehending, questioning. Li fought against the automatic gag reflex. His eyes began to glaze. "I did you—no harm," he stammered. "Why...?" His mouth jerked open as if to scream.

Li froze. He mustn't shout. I should stick it into him again, but his eyes are so accusing. Her stomach still churned. Don't shout. Don't shout. Please don't shout, she thought.

But the guard only grunted again and gasped for air. He crumpled at her feet, gurgling and moaning softly. I have killed a man, she thought. A countryman. I wish I could have offered him the opportunity to join our cause. He surely would have joined. But there was no time. He was my enemy and thus my act was not murder. But he was so young. It is probable that he had never yet fought against our people. His only crime was that he was chosen to be here tonight. If another had been chosen, this one would still be alive. Life was unfair to him. Death was unfair to him. Why is my stomach so upset? I think I'm going to be sick! She looked down at him. May his restless spirit treat me with mercy. She shuddered as she felt his spirit standing beside her, accusing her.

Li looked at the knife in her hand. Blood covered the blade and saturated the handle. Her hand and wrist were bloody. The arm of her blue au yi was soaked and stained almost to the elbow.

I must wash it off before Tet, she thought. The new year must not come while I have blood on my skin. She shuddered again. No time to waste. Our people have waited long enough. Tonight we taste of victory; and my duty is not yet completed.

Li wiped the dagger on the uniform of the soldier and re-sheathed it. Picking up her purse, she squared her shoulders and marched resolutely around the corner and down the quiet hallway to the sitting room door. She knocked softly.

"Who is it?" A female voice. Madame Biet was with him. Of course! I should have expected it. It is Tet, when families are together. I must determine where they both are in the room before I throw the grenade. "Co Let Chu Li," she responded. "Your husband's secretary. I have been working late and am going home now. I thought to wish you and the Dai Ta my best wishes just before Tet."

"Come in my child." It was the Dai Ta.

She turned the knob and opened the door. Colonel Biet sat against the wall in an easy chair. He was wearing a silk brocade smoking jacket with velvet collar. His wife stood like a bejeweled queen beside him. A bottle of scotch whiskey sat on the coffee table in front of them. Each of them held a glass.

"Forgive me for interrupting the harmony of your home Dai Ta. I only want to wish you happiness and peace in the new year." She bowed in the doorway.

Biet smiled and inclined his head without rising. "Thank you Co Li, and may the year of the monkey be happy for you also."

Li withdrew and closed the door, but not all the way. Quickly, she pulled the grenade from her purse and tucked the purse under her arm. She pulled the pin and the spoon twanged away onto the carpet. "One, two, three," she counted to herself as she pushed the door open again. Stooping, she rolled the grenade toward the startled couple, then stood and reclosed the door. She had not looked at their faces. She heard muffled shouts from the room as she began running toward the stairway. She held her breath. I do my duty, she reminded herself, for the people of Vietnam.

But an evil spirit bunched another wrinkle in the carpet runner and her rubber thong again snagged. This time she was not acting as she tripped and sprawled heavily to the floor.

The explosion ripped the door from its hinges and thundered through Ca Dor.

Fear clutched her heart and throat as men began running up the stairs toward her.

Ty where are you? she thought with panic. I should have been half way down the stairs by the time the guards reached me. They would have run right past me. But now they will see me near the door.

The men bolted into view. Four of them. The captain of the guard at their head.

Li sat up and pointed at the door. "An explosion," she stammered. "It must have been a mortar or a rocket from outside. See to the Dai Ta! See if he is hurt!"

The captain hesitated, his men bunching up behind him. "Where is the sentry?" he asked curtly.

"The sentry?" Li responded, pretending surprise. "I saw no sentry. There was no sentry here when I arrived."

The captain swore, then he and two men rushed past her to the sitting room. The fourth man stopped to help her. "Are you all right Co Li?" he asked.

"Yes, I think so. Please see to the Dai Ta." Fear and guilt combined forces to claw at her nerves. She could not look directly at him. He really was concerned.

"Are you sure you are well?"

"Yes, yes. Please look to the others. I think the Dai Ta may be injured."

He gazed into her face kindly, worriedly. She recognized him then. It was Sergeant Lam, a merchant from Tam Ky, and one of the oldest soldiers in the province militia. He was a long time guard at Ca Dor; a friend who often brought her flowers.

"What are you doing here in the capital at this time of night, on the eve of Tet?" he asked. The gentleness of his voice indicating no suspicion, only curiosity and concern.

"The Dai Ta called me here to do a bit of work." She had answered automatically but realized it was the best answer. If she had said she had been working late, he might have known she was lying. He often looked in on her office.

Lam nodded. "Strange," he said. "He told me he was not going to work tonight."

Li shrugged. "He sent for me. I had just arrived when the explosion happened."

He helped her to her feet. A twinge of pain stabbed from her ankle. It is the spirit of the young soldier, she thought, already seeking revenge. She hid her bloody arm behind her. Lam must not see that, she warned herself.

He was nodding again, but Li imagined that she saw a faint glimmer of suspicion in the friendly eyes. "You had best go home now to be with your family at Tet," he said. "Can you walk?"

"Yes," she said, but she paused as he moved away from her toward the sitting room. She felt compelled to watch him. Did he see the blood on my au yi? On my hand? She could hear the soldiers in the sitting room shouting and talking excitedly. When Lam was only a few feet away, she saw him stop and look at something on the carpet. What could it be? Her eyes swept over the floor, now littered with bits of plaster and wall fragments. Then she saw it too. The grenade spoon!

Li wheeled about to face away from Sergeant Lam. She did not want him to see the guilt that would be on her face.

"Co Li!" Lam commanded, gruffly. "Please halt where you are. Do not move. I must ask you more questions!"

Calmly, stoically, Li reached into her purse for the final grenade. This second little egg was intended for the message center, she thought. But now it must hatch prematurely. Clutching the spoon so that it would not fly, she pulled the pin and turned.

He had drawn his pistol, but when he saw the grenade in her hand, his eyes widened with surprise.

"Drop that!—No! Don't drop it! he stammered. "Don't do anything or I'll shoot!"

She held up the pin for him to see, and tossed it over her shoulder. "If you shoot me, I must drop the grenade," she said with thick sarcasm. She took a limping step toward him, threateningly. "If you try to run away, I will throw it at you. Tell me, lackey of the long noses, how do you feel knowing you are about to die?"

He took a step backward, still aiming his pistol at her. "Stop!" he commanded lamely. "You can't do this. You also will die."

The captain and both guards came running out of the room. They stood together, stunned by what they had blundered into.

"I am told it takes seven seconds to explode from the time the spoon flies," Li said as if in a trance. "Seven is a lucky number. Does anyone feel lucky on this eve of Tet?"

She looked at their eyes. No one felt lucky.

"Tonight the people of Vietnam arise to throw off the yoke of colonialism. Tonight The Peoples' Army will defeat the lackey forces. Join us. Swear your allegiance to a united Vietnam, and you will all be spared. You can share in the victory."

Li watched their eyes. Their eyes had hardened! They were all unwilling to switch sides. Didn't they understand? She was confused. She had always known, for a fact, that every Vietnamese at least secretly supported her cause. Was this fact wrong? Could her father be wrong? She made the offer again, making sure they knew it was in earnest.

The three men stood silently, watching her. They appeared more resolute now. More steadfast. Less fearful.

She held up her chin. "Then so be it," she said. "When we are born again, you will all be cattle."

The ping of the grenade spoon resonated loudly along the narrow hallway as she dropped the grenade onto the carpet at her feet.

The men crashed and jostled each other frantically as they bolted away toward the opposite end of the corridor. They run like chickens before the hawk, she thought.

"Long live the Peoples' Republic of Vietnam," she announced proudly. Then she thought of Mark. "Forgive me Sergeant Mark," she murmured quietly. "I love you as the clouds love the wind. But it was not to be."

The thunderclap of the blast shook the walls of Ca Dor.

SCENE 5

THE BATTLEGROUND

0200 Hours
Wednesday, 31 January, 1968

"You no sleep Troom Ta? Need sleep! You no sleep for long time." Major Hai's voice was worried, concerned.

"I'm not sleepy Tiu Ta." Jake answered.

The two men sat in the darkness on wooden ammo boxes and leaned back against the sandbagged outer wall of the TOC. The heavy clouds still hung ominously over them, blanketing the moonless sky, but the rain had finally stopped. The night air smelled brisk and clean. In the distance, a nighthawk's plaintive cry wailed lonely and lost.

The dull red glow of the two men's cigarettes were the only breaks in the total blackness before them.

"You no sleep last night; you no sleep all day today," Hai continued. "Maybe I get blanket, you sleep here near TOC. I wake you anything happen."

"No thanks, Tiu Ta. I'm really not sleepy; but what about you? You haven't slept in two nights either."

"You need sleep Troom Ta," said Hai, ignoring Jake's question. "I fear for you. You have grief inside from death of wife, yet you not go home today like you should. I know you inside, Troom Ta. You no go home because you think attack come. You very like Vietnam man. Think of duty number one. But grief sit on head. I see behind eyes. Better you sleep for short time Troom Ta. You must go home tomorrow."

Jake dragged on his cigarette. Major Hai was only half right, he thought. He felt no grief, at least no grief that he was aware of; but he had refused to leave on the helicopter which was sent for him. The attack was indeed pending. He had been awake now for forty four hours. "I won't sleep Tiu Ta. You sleep. Don't stay awake just because I do."

"I no sleep even if lay down Troom Ta. Too much happen. NVA no attack last night like should. We know NVA very near. Hoi Chanh say they attack. Many VC show self, do sabotage. We kill many; capture many. They very surprise NVA no attack. They think last night be attack also, but NVA no come. I think why not? I think many maybe. Maybe they know we ready. Maybe they celebrate first day of New Year before attack on second day. Maybe they think more big surprise if wait one day more. Maybe they have radio no work, no get word from Hanoi to attack. Maybe they hit by many arclight bomb, all die. I think too many maybe."

Jake smiled in the darkness. "Well, if you have to worry Tiu Ta, it's better to worry about why they didn't attack, than why they did."

"But I think that too Troom Ta. Why VC attack last night? If we not know before, these tell us something big in plans. Today first day of Tet. All VC of last night give up one year bad luck by do act of violence on first day. Why they do? Even they think NVA come same day, today be wrong day for Veitnam people. Why they do?

"Well, both of the Hoi Chanhs we captured said they thought all the South Vietnamese, even the ARVN and militia would give up and join the Communists if there was an all out Tet offensive. Obviously that's what they were told, and evidently most of them believed it."

"Aaah!" Hai's disgusted grunt split the silent night air. "How they believe that Troom Ta? We fight many years already. We not slave to America. You here to advise me. You no tell me must do, have to do. We fight NVA and VC for South Vietnam. Americans help us. I always think maybe they say this colonial war just for propaganda. I never think they believe what they say."

Hai's cigarette made a glowing red arc in the blackness as he raised it to his lips. Jake watched the glow brighten as Hai drew on it. It retraced the arc, descending to lap level as Hai exhaled in a long rushing whisper. "I think VC crazy," he blurted.

"Maybe all they wanted was a little publicity here and in the few other provinces they hit last night." Jake said, his voice calm. He watched a star appear from behind a moving black cloud only to disappear again behind another. "If so, they've already got that here when they killed the Province Chief last night."

"That maybe make sense for other province Troom Ta, but not for here. That show how crazy VC be. Dai Ta Biet not good Province Chief. I can say now him dead. He steal from Quang Tin people. Steal from militia. Steal from everybody. Everybody know. Him very bad man, and wife very bad woman. Many people join VC to fight against Dai Ta Biet. VC do South Vietnam big favor when kill Dai Ta Biet."

Jake was stunned. He had known of course, from his own sources of intelligence, but he had no idea the Vietnamese themselves felt this way. Whenever the subject of government graft had come up, the Vietnamese had always seemed to shrug their shoulders, as if it didn't matter. "Hell Tiu Ta, why didn't you report him?"

"You not understand Troom Ta. Hard to explain because Americans not understand Vietnam way. Dai Ta Biet steal for sure, but is OK for Province Chief to steal. All Province Chief steal little bit. No can run province with money from Saigon government. Saigon expect Province Chief to steal what need to run province. If little bit money find Province Chief pocket, that OK too. Everybody know. You understand Troom Ta?"

"Well, it confirms my suspicions Tiu Ta. I guess I didn't really know that the Saigon central government approved of graft. Why don't they just insist on honesty and then refund what is necessary to run the provincial government?"

"Not know Troom Ta. But is this way all districts, all province, all region governments. Probably true in Saigon also."

No wonder, Jake thought, that they didn't listen to me in Da Nang. Biet was doing what they all were doing. "So why was Biet so bad then?" he asked.

"Biet go too far. Dai Ta take too much. Him take money for weapons, put in pocket, no buy weapons. Him take supply from Saigon and sell, not give to people like should. Him steal from Americans and sell. Much black market. Some steal OK. Him and wife steal too much. Sometime take land from farmer, sell land, keep money. Farmer become VC. Biet very bad Province Chief."

Jake didn't respond. Hai was right, he didn't understand. An entire government system designed to operate on graft. It reminded him of the Latin American concept of the "mordida." Same idea. Systemitized corruption. Resented by everyone, but accepted by everyone. That's why it will never change.

They sat in silence surrounded by the darkness. Jake was suddenly aware of a slight rustling noise off to his left, and realized that someone else was sitting there, listening, about ten feet away. It wasn't a sentry. There was no sentry post on this side. It was probably someone from the TOC. Someone off shift. The TOC had been double shifted since noon the previous day.

"We arrest um Giap last night. Him try blow up bridge on highway. Father of Co Li. We search house, find many document. Him VC Province Chief of Quang Tin." Hai was speaking quietly, thoughtfully. "Document say many more name of legal VC in Quang Tin. Document say NVA and VC plan attack Tam Ky last night. That maybe not true because not happen, but other document maybe number one. First day of new year already very bad for VC in this province."

Jake shook his head. "I'm still flabbergasted that the Province Chief's personal secretary was a VC. How could that have happened Tiu Ta? How could she have slipped past all the security checks?"

"So sorry Troom Ta. What mean fabbergas?"

Jake laughed. "It means surprised Tiu Ta. If I'm flabbergasted, I'm very surprised."

Hai laughed also. "I am fabbergassed Troom Ta, to hear such a word."

"Flabber; flabbergasted Tiu Ta."

"Yes, just so. I am flabbergassed," laughed Hai.

At that moment, the poncho curtain of the TOC doorway rustled. A shaft of light from the TOC stabbed out onto the open ground and then snuffed out. A man with a small flashlight climbed the steps and approached. "Tiu Ta? he asked.

Hai grunted his presence, and the two chattered earnestly and rapidly in Veitnamese.

"Troom Ta," Hai turned to Jake, outposts report movement. I go check. I call you if anything happen. Maybe you sleep for short time, OK?"

"I'll be OK Tiu Ta. I'll be right here if you need me."

Hai shuffled away with the man carrying the flashlight. All was silence and darkness again.

Jake lit another cigarette. He was suddenly conscious of fatigue dragging at his body. The muscles in his shoulders ached, and his legs felt leaden and awkward. But sleep would be impossible. He was not ready to rest. I know they're still going to attack, he thought. But then he was assailed by doubts. Do I think they're going to attack, or do I want them to attack? Am I being stubborn?

Or is it that I just want to be right in predicting the attack? They should have attacked last night as their plans indicated, but they didn't. Why didn't I just go home today to the funeral like I should've? Hell, if they didn't attack last night, they won't attack now. They know we're ready for them now. They'd be stupid to attack tonight. But they will, he thought. I know they will.

"Colonel Thorpe Sir?" The voice came from his left. The person he'd sensed was there a few moments ago. It sounded like Sergeant Fellogese.

"That you Fellogese?"

"Yes Sir. I can't sleep either."

Jake remembered the rumors that linked the young sergeant to Co Li, and immediately realized why Fellogese could not sleep. "How you holding up Sergeant? You OK?"

"I'm OK Sir. I guess everybody knows don't they?"

"Hard to keep that kind of rumor secret. Especially after what happened last night. They giving you a bad time?"

"Oh no Sir. No one's said a word. Not yet anyway. But I can tell by their eyes. Been a lot of whispering that's stopped suddenly as I walked by today. I hear Colonel King's going to give me the third degree about what I might have told her."

"Not much I can do to help you there Sergeant."

"I know Sir. But that's no problem really. I never really knew anything that might have helped them. The problem is with me Sir. I still can't believe it. I can't believe that she really did it. Are they really sure it was her Sir?"

"From what I hear, they are. Four guards just barely got away from the grenade she dropped. One guard was killed by a knife, and she had a knife on her. They said she deliberately killed herself."

"How do they know the guards are telling the truth Sir? They could be VC. They could've killed the PC and her both."

"You probably heard Major Hai telling me that her father was VC. So was her brother. You know that. I'm afraid, son, that she was VC." Jake wondered why he had used the word "son". Somehow, he was feeling paternalistic because of the Sergeant's grief. He probably shouldn't, he thought; after all, Fellogese had disobeyed official orders when he had become involved with an "indiginous female personnel." He smiled to himself at the officious military terminology, and then sobered as he realized how stupid and inept such regulations were. No military force or government could order someone not to fall in love, and soldiers away from home in a combat situation are especially vulnerable because they live with fear for their lives on a daily basis. It was an order that couldn't be enforced and thus enforcement was hardly ever attempted.

Mark spoke again. "She wasn't VC when she was with me Sir. I know! She loved me. I know she did; and, God help me, I loved her too. I wanted to marry her!"

Jake detected the checked emotion behind the words. Mark had been crying here in the darkness. He was just barely controlling his sobs now, as he talked.

"It's OK son," Jake said. "You knew her. I didn't. None of us did. None of us know why she did it. Maybe her father made her do it." And maybe she was just a good actress and a dedicated enemy, he thought. He wondered if she had been able to get information from this youthful sergeant without being obvious enough to arouse suspicion. He wondered if they would attack tonight using that information.

"God Sir, I hate this fucking war!"

Jake didn't answer. There was nothing he could say. But he had been reached. Gone were the thoughts of the sergeant's possible foolishness. Gone were any military considerations of a man betrayed by an enemy spy. There was only young Mark Fellogese, one of his men, hurting inside, needing succor. He stood up to walk closer to Mark.

"I'll never forget her Sir." Mark said, his voice still catching in his throat. "She was the best thing that ever happened to me."

Jake nodded. He realized Fellogese couldn't see him nodding, but he was unable to think of anything to say that could help. He was unable to ease the pain of grief; unable to offer words of advice that would be accepted. He felt helpless.

Fellogese sniffed. "God I'm sorry Sir. Here I am blubbering about Co Li, and I just realized you just lost you wife too. You must feel even worse that I do. God I'm sorry Sir."

Jake was surprised. He wasn't in grief at all, but it would certainly not be appropriate to explain why to Fellogese just now. Jake was not in the mood for long explanations and niether was Fellogese. It would be best to let him continue to believe that we are both suffering, Jake thought. He'll accept being comforted by someone he thinks is going through the same feelings of loss.

"That's OK Fellogese, thanks. You know you said you'd never forget her? That's good, because you won't. Just concentrate on the small things. Remember what her eyes looked like when she laughed. Remember how she moved her hands or walked toward you. Remember the details. As long as you remember the small things, she'll be alive and with you. It'll make it easier."

"Thanks Sir, I'll try."

Jake didn't know if it would really help or not, but inside, he somehow, now felt better. He felt that he had done what a good officer, a good leader must do. He hoped it would help.

The poncho curtain moved again, and Hai's voice carried into the darkness. "Troom Ta. Maybe you better come. I thank maybe NVA attack tonight."

After the briefing, King yawned, stretched and stood up from the green metal chair in front of the sit-map. "Well," he drawled. "They ain't attackin us yet. Jake, let's you and me go outside for some fresh air b'fore they do." He turned and walked out of the TOC. Jake followed.

Outside, the darkness of the night swallowed them. Jake blinked his eyes at the blackness, trying to force his pupils to expand and adjust. King's voice called to him. "Over here Jake."

Here it comes, thought Jake, as he groped toward the exaggerated drawl. The glow of King's cigarette told him where the PSA stood waiting.

"OK," King began, "why'd ya wake me up? Had ta be more 'n what I heard in that fuckin briefin. All they mentioned was a bunch a fuckin noises heard by shit-scared Gook sentries who think God Damn lonesome ghosts are wailin all around tonight cause it's fuckin Tet."

Jake sighed softly. "No Dick. There isn't anything else. Just all those outposts hearing movement. But considering all the evidence, the enemy plans, the attacks last night, I felt it was serious. I think we're going to get hit sometime between now and dawn."

"Shit! You thought we were gonna get hit last night too! I stayed up till two inna fuckin mornin just cause a' your fuckin feelins, 'n nuthin happened. I told ya then we wouldn't get hit, and we didn't. What makes tonight so fuckin differnt?"

"Two things Dick. One: They may not have hit us here, but you heard the briefing; even Da Nang is now warning of a country-wide offensive tonight. Just like Minh, the Hoi Chanh, said there would be. Second, of course, is all this movement that's going on. Somebody is prowling around out there in a lot of places, and that to me is a strong indication of a pending attack."

"Well fuck! The only reason I got up was cause a' all the shit that happened yesterday. If they hadn't hit with those fuckin gorilla attacks here 'n at all those other places last night, I'da hung up the fuckin phone and gone back ta sleep. Now that I've been briefed on all your fuckin indications of a pendin attack, I'm pissed off at myself for gettin up. It's nothun!"

"I thought it was best to wake you Dick. You'd've been even more pissed off if we heard these noises but didn't call you until they were in the wire."

King didn't respond. Jake watched his superior's cigarette glow brighten as he sucked smoke into his lungs. Jake glanced at his new Army issue watch, on the thick leather band which protected it from the electricity in his body. In the darkness the luminescent dial was so brilliant that it took a few seconds to focus his eyes. The hands of the dial almost formed a horizontal line as they stretched and pulled away from each other. Three-forty-five. Two hours to go before the sun comes up.

"Well Jake, I just dono what I'm a gonna do about you. I knew from the git go there wouldn't be no major fuckin attack here. My experience tole me there wouldn't. Last night, when all the little shit started, 'n then later when that commie bitch blasted Biet all ta hell, I started thinkin that maybe I might'a been wrong. Maybe they might attack after all, but they didn't, so I was right. Sure, I was surprised when they hit all those puny piss-ass places. I was even surprised when they hit Khe Sanh. But I wasn't at Khe Sanh! If I hadda been, I wouldn'a been surprised. I'd'a smelled the fuckin attack before it came. I always do. I got good fuckin instincts bout that kinda shit. And the NVA didn't hit us here did they? So I was fuckin right waddn't I? Well, I'm still right. And they won't hit us tonight neither!"

"Tonight's not over yet," said Jake lamely.

"Shit! I dono if you're just stubborn or if ya just can't unnerstand these fuckin Gooks. Gooks are Gooks no matter which fuckin side they're on. This is their fuckin Tet period. They wait all year for this week a partyun. Those fuckin slopeheads out there gainst us mighta thought once or twice bout hittin us, but that fuckin poster we sent out sayin we knew bout it sure as all hell killed that idea." He stopped short. "Hey that reminds me. I still see that God-damned hat poem stuck up all round here. I thought I tole ya ta get rid a all of um."

"Yes, you did Dick," Jake said dispiritedly. "But I've been so busy with the defense preparations, I haven't had time yet."

"Have ya found out who wrote the fuckin thing?"

"Not yet. Haven't even tried yet."

"God Damn it! I knew it. Your fuckin judgement is all fucked up Jake. You hear some fuckin Gook turncoat talk bout an attack and ya panic. You go off all half cocked and forget your priorities. I'm your fuckin CO God Damn it! What I say should mean somethun, even if we are the same rank. No wonder everbody round here's been laughin atcha behind your back. The way you been hoppin around preparin defenses. They all know there's not gonna be no fuckin attack."

Jake remained silent. He seethed inside. This stupid, pompous ass! This imbecile! This egotistical paranoid is indeed my CO, and there's not a damn thing I can do about it. God! Maybe we're not so different from the Vietnamese after all. We allow guys like King to come into power and stay there even though they abuse the power and are exactly the wrong type of man to have the job.

"You're really pissed off at me aren'tcha?"

"Sure I am Dick. I'm not the only one who thought there was going to be an attack. Biet thought it too. That's why he shut himself into Ca Dor for two weeks. Tu thought there would be an attack. Hai still thinks one is coming tonight. But even if I were the only one, I'd have done exactly as I did. Because if an attack were to come, we had to be ready for it. The consequences of not being ready if the rumor were true far outweighed the embarrassment of being unnecessarily ready if the attack didn't come. It had to have a higher priority than catching some jokester poet."

"No."

"No? No? You mean you really think chasing this poet is more important than defending ourselves?"

"No. I mean that's not it. That's not the real reason yer so pissed at me."

Jake stopped and swallowed. He was always shocked at King's eerie ability to read other people's thoughts.

"Somethun to do about Ray Gonzaga iddn' it?" King continued.

Jake stared hard at the dark, still indistinguishable, shape in front of him. He couldn't see King's face. In his mind, Jake imagined he could see King's eyes, cat's eyes, glowing in the dark. "Yes it is," he said. "How did you know?"

"Just a fuckin guess. Whatchur bitch?"

"Gonzaga's dead. Did you know that?" Jake asked, his voice low and choked with emotion.

"Yeah, I heard. So what?"

"The way I figure it, you killed him," Jake hissed.

"What the fuck ya talkin bout? Gonzaga died of a heart attack in Da Nang."

"That's right. A heart attack caused by being lied about, wrongly accused of murder, black marketing and aiding the enemy. Gonzaga was a good man, a proud man. Being accused like that broke his heart, and I'm talking literally as well as figuratively"

"And you think I had somethun ta do with that? Fuck! I remember tellin ya I thought he was innocent a' mosta that shit. What the fuck makes you think I had anythin ta do with it? King's voice was calm, innocent.

I could almost believe him, Jake thought. "I saw you in Camp Kronberg," he said. "After Sergeant Lentz got it. I saw you go into his room."

"So what?"

"So you didn't find the pictures you were looking for did you?"

A pause. I have just given King a dose of his own medicine, he thought.

"Whadda you know bout any fuckin pitchers?"

"I've got them!" Jake could sense King's tenseness.

"So what if ya do? I'm not in those fuckin pitchers. What does any a this have ta do with me?"

"You were looking for them. That means you know what they were. That connects you. That makes you an accomplice."

"Bullshit! That duddn't prove a fuckin thing. Sure I was lookin for um. Sergeant Lentz took the shot and showed it to me. So I knew. Hell, he showed it to me after Gonzaga had been relieved. It sure don't prove I had anythun ta do with the code book, but it does prove that that fat turd Biet did! That's why I wanted the pitchers. Ta prove Biet was a thief and that he framed Gonzaga." The voice was still calm, but there was a detectable new edge to it.

"You're lying Dick. If you knew, it was your duty to confiscate the picture when you saw it and stand up for Ray. But you didn't. You never reported it. You wanted everyone to blame Ray."

Another pause. "Ok," King said. "So I saw a chance ta become the PSA. What's that ta you? Gonzaga was a weakling. A piss-poor excuse for a PSA. He let the fuckin Gooks get away with everthing they wanted. He didn't have the balls for this job. When I saw the pitcher, I knew all I had ta do was keep my mouth shut and the fuckin Army'd have a good PSA for once. And I've proven that. I've straightened this fuckin province out since I took over."

Jake didn't answer. he stepped forward toward the shadow which had been drawling its self praise and aimed a short, wicked right fist at the source of the voice. He felt the satisfying, bone jarring crunch as his fist smashed into King's face. The blow slammed the shadow backward into a prattfall on the sand. King jumped to his feet and Jake could see him crouched in a boxer's stance. The two began circling each other in the darkness. My night vision's adjusting just in time, Jake realized.

"So it was Gonzaga!" King muttered. "What was he, your daddy or somethun?"

"You might say that. He wasn't really, but he might as well have been. We had that kind of relationship."

"Well tough shit, you stupid asshole! You've assaulted a superior officer now, and I'll have your fuckin ass up for a general court martial. You'll leave Quang Tin the same way that fuckin Gonzaga did, behind bars. Now I don't have nuthun ta fear from ya. You're as good as fuckin gone, so I might as well rub it in a bit. I took the fuckin code book myself, and gave it ta Biet! How does that make ya feel? You can yell bout it all ya want, cause ya can't prove it. Just reportin it'll make ya sound crazy and stupid."

Fury filled Jake's soul. He stopped circling. He straightened and drew his pistol. King kept in his crouch, obviously unaware in the dark of what Jake had done. Jake drew back the slide and released it, chambering a round and cocking the hammer. The unmistakable metallic sound was shockingly loud in the still blackness. King froze.

"What the fuck ya doin?" he asked.

"We're all alone here Dick. We can just barely see each other. No one else can see us. You're just as stupid as you think I am if you think you could prove that I assaulted you. It's my word against your's and you'd need more than that to get me on assault. But as you said, I can't prove you're guilty either, even though you've confessed to me that you're a thief and a liar. But after you explained how nobody can prove anything that might have happened out here, I realized that I can do something about you after all. I'll just shoot you myself and do the Army a favor. I'll get away with it of course, because who would even begin to suspect me?"

"Hey Jake, wait a fuckin minute!" King's voice wasn't calm at all now. It was an octave higher than normal and tinged with fear.

"You wouldn't shoot me, I'm American. I'm a fellow fuckin officer Goddamnit!"

Jake smiled. The rush of total power surged through his veins. This was true revenge. He no longer had to kow-tow to this strutting idiot. He felt elated, exhalted, thrilled. He still had anger, but never before had he felt so supreme, so in control of the moment. He saw the dark blur in front of him move slightly and he knew that King was reaching for his own pistol. "Don't do it Dick! You'll be dead before it's halfway out of the holster." The shadow froze.

"You're just upset Jake. It's cause a' your wife's suicide. You wouldn't be doin this otherwise."

"My wife's death has nothing to do with this. Nothing to do with you. All that means is that if, for some reason, I do get caught, I'll have a reason to plead temporary insanity; and I'll go free. You might as well face it Dick, your last horse just ran away. You might as well bend over and kiss your butt goodbye." Jake's finger tightened on the trigger. His mind was crystal clear. Every sense was alive and alert. He relished this moment and wanted to savor it. He wanted it to last forever.

"Whadda ya want me ta do?" The dark voice pleaded. "You want me to confess? Fuck; I'll give ya a written confession. You want me to resign my commission? I'll resign tomorrow."

"No. Tomorrow you'll be in control again," Jake said flatly. It's got to happen tonight. It's got to end now. You saw your chance with Ray and you took it. Tonight is my chance."

"For Christ's sake Jake! Please! Ya can't do this!"

"Oh yes I can," Jake said, and his finger tightened on the trigger. Jake's voice was a deadly purr. "It's like killing a rattlesnake," he said. I can too, he thought. I can do it. Just a tiny bit more of a squeeze on this trigger. It'll all be over. I will have avenged Ray. Quang Tin and South Vietnam will be better off. The Army will be purged of an internal cancer. Jake realized he was grinning. The skin at his fingertips tingled; alive, exquisitely alive. Every breath increased his power and strength. He knew he was calm, icily under control. His mind exuberantly on fire and aware of every sensation: the cool damp and the soft whispering of the misty rain which had just started again; the bold distinction of dark shadow-devil against the black back-curtain of night; the salty smell of the South China Sea; the weight of the pistol in his hand; the solid heft of total, absolute power. I won't feel this way after I kill him, Jake thought. I'll feel guilt, but it'll be worth it.

King cleared his throat. "Jake, please, I..." he stopped suddenly. "Wait. Listen!"

Jake listened. Nothing but the rain. "You can't bullshit me now Dick. It's too late."

"No listen!" King pleaded. "It's about ta happen. Here it comes. You'll hear it too."

Three hollow pops, like champaign corks across a room, sounded in the distance. It was the unmistakable distinctive pop of incoming mortars.

Jake looked at his watch. Oh-four-hundred. It's beginning, he thought, marveling again at King's psychic ability.

Three more pops, then a fourth and fifth. Simultaneously, a trip flare blossomed its tangerine fire near the northern perimeter, followed by wild screams and a burst of machine gun fire. A fougasse exploded off to the left.

Instinctively, both men sprawled to the damp earth. The first three mortar rounds screeched their arrival and exploded near the Castle, approximately one hundred meters away.

"Ground assault at the northern perimeter," yelled King. "I'll get over there and control that situation. You get ta the TOC and take command there!"

Jake reached over and grabbed King's shirt. He pushed the 45 barrel into one nostril of King's nose. "Now tell me who's judgement was poor, Shithead!"

King's response was calm and even. "Go ahead. Shoot. No question but you'd get away with it now. But I'm the best man in a firefight you ever saw. I can help save everone's ass tonight and ya know it. Shootin me might make ya feel better, but it might lose us this fuckin province!"

Jake swallowed hard. He's right. We need every man. "You are a lucky son of a bitch," he said. "We'll have to take this up later."

"Later!" King roared with laughter. "Fuck! You just rolled snake eyes. It's my roll now. My dice and my table."

He bolted to his feet but immediately sprawled again as the second wave of mortar shells screamed and crashed around them. "Karumph, karumph." They both hugged the ground. "Karumph." More pops in the distance. "Kablam." Another fougasse burst in flaming scarlet against the blackness of the night. "Pukka. Pukka. Pukka. Pukka." Several machine guns were now dueling.

As if on cue, both men were up and running in different directions. Jake heard King's laughter, wild, crazy laughter, fade away to the north. I've lost him, he thought. He knows he's won.

He threw himself flat again as another volly of mortar rounds whistled through the dark clouds above him. The ground rocked and heaved under him as they exploded. "Karumph, karumph, karumph."

Then up and running again. Didn't realize the TOC was so far away. "Kapow." Another fougasse. They're in the wire. A claymore mine ripped its deep throated roar into the percussion crescendo, and then another claymore. They're already beyond the second wire! Too fast! Too fast! We're not even slowing them up. He threw himself into another headfirst dive as more mortar rounds screamed and blasted around him. These were closer. They cracked in a single shock wave. Mud from one or more blasts rained down upon him. He glanced up to get his bearings. There's the TOC! Only five or six meters away. Several parachute flares now illuminated the battleground. He glanced over his shoulder and saw King clearly. King was almost to the northern perimeter. Mortar rounds fell around the PSA and a stream of tracers raced past his ear, but King kept running. That lucky bastard, Jake thought. He should be dead at least twice already tonight.

Jake leaped and ran the short distance to the TOC. He glanced around one more time before entering. Explosions and small arms fire seemed all around him. Suddenly, however, the earth buckled as a titanic blast ruptured the air. It was like an earthquake. Jake jerked his head to the east. A great ball of fire mushroomed skyward a thousand yards away. By the glow of the many flares, he could see the giant pillar of smoke bellow upward following the flames. What the hell? Was it an ammo dump? We don't have an ammo dump over there, he thought. That's over near the refugee camp. Then the truth struck him. It was the orphanage! Several timed satchel charges would create such a blast. He was dumbstruck. Those filthy, dirty sons of bitches! They destroyed it on purpose. Hai had been right, we should have protected it. And I was wrong. Dead wrong! He gritted his teeth in fury and frustration. He bolted down the steps and into the TOC. Don't think of the children, he thought. Don't think of Mother Angela. Think of them later, there's a job to do now!

The bunker was a flurry of activity. Three times the normal staff were shuffling against one another. Every radio had two or three men leaning over it. Everyone had a clipboard and a lighted cigarette.

Jake headed for the four radios on the American side. Major Clayborne was on the mike of the first one. "Roger Uniform. This is Bravo Three. Understand two kilos. How many whiskeys? Over." He looked up at Jake as if Jake had been standing there for hours. "Thang Binh is getting hit too Sir. Two US types are already KIA. Don't know who. I'm getting the WIAs now."

Jake nodded.

Beside Clayborne, Captain Marcellus was coordinating an artillery fire mission. "Keep at least one tube angled high Goddamn it!" he shouted into the mike. "We need continious illumination, at least one flare burning at all times. Roger that! Level the others and load with beehive. Let's show the blue legs what the arty can do in a pinch."

Captain Hastings was on the net to higher. "Tango this is Echo. Affirmative. Affirmative. We have ground attack at three locations. This headquarters, ARVN compound directly south, and Thang Binh District compound. Penetration at this location. I say again perimeter has been breached at this location. Suspected penetration also at Thang Binh. Reserve has not been committed either location. No other contact. Over."

The fourth radio operator was vainly trying to obtain some type of air support from Chu Lai.

A Vietnamese messenger rushed from the other side of the TOC and handed a message to Jake. Jake read it and passed it to Hastings. "Better tell Da Nang this too," he said flatly.

Hastings nodded. "Tango this is Echo. Railroad Bridge Number Six south of city is now under attack. Estimate one company sized element. Perimeter holding so far, over."

Jake lit a cigarette. The smoke haze inside was so thick the Vietnamese side was almost obliterated.

A mortar round exploded near the TOC starting a cascade of sand falling like tiny multiple waterfalls from between the sandbags. Dust mixed with the smoke in the cloudy room.

Major Hai appeared at Jake's elbow. "All military compound in city under attack now," he said quietly.

Jake wheeled to face him. "All compounds? What about Camp Kronberg?"

Hai bowed apologetically. "Ah, not know. So sorry Troom Ta. All Vietnam military compound under attack."

Jake nodded. "Ground attack?" he asked.

Hai shrugged. "Not know yet Troom Ta. Everybody on radio. Everybody shout. Everybody excite much. Cannot tell which is big attack, or which is only diversion."

Another explosion just outside. The walls again rained sand; the work inside didn't pause. No one even flinched.

Hai leaned toward the Veitnamese side, listening to the radio. He straightened and looked up at Jake. "Reserve platoon on north perimeter, attack. We no give word. Other co van, Troom Ta King, him get reserve platoon, lead counterattack. They fight now. VC still inside perimeter. Platoon leader, him report just now, say Troom Ta King fight good. Very brave man."

Jake nodded. It figures, he thought. He must think he leads a charmed life. Hell, maybe he does. Damn him though! He shouldn't be out there on the perimeter. That's not his job. He's the commander, and he should be here in the command center, not out there playing cowboy. He should be here! Gotta give him credit though, he's a hellova soldier. "Tell Da Nang we just committed the reserve here," he shouted to Hastings.

Jake looked around at the bustle of intense activity on both sides. Here, he thought, where there is nothing to do but wait and pray. No plans to make; too late for plans now. No air support to coordinate. No artillery to adjust because they're right on top of us. One of the reserve units already committed, so only two small ones remain to deploy or command. Sit on your hands. Just wait and keep Da Nang informed. Damn King! He should be here where he belongs, and I should be out there where I could do something.

"Jesus!" Hastings shouted. "Da Nang reports the whole country's getting hit! Da Nang's being attacked, Hue, Quang Tri, Quang Ngai, Quang Nam, Nha Trang, Pleiku, everywhere! Even Saigon! Just like they've been saying."

Everyone paused to listen, then shrugged and went back to work. No time to think what it might mean. Their fight was here and now.

"Sir! The zips are in the perimeter of Kronberg."

"Which direction did they come in?"

"West side Sir. The fence is blown. They're pouring through.

"OK, commit the Kronberg reserve unit. Tell them to kick um outta there."

"Roger Sir."

Hastings waved to signal that he'd heard and was passing it on to Higher.

"Sir! The deputy police advisor's on the land line. He says the NPFF compound is being hit!" The voice was strident.

"How's his police force doing? Are they holding?"

"He says they are so far Sir, but he says all hell's a poppin.'"

"OK, tell him to keep us informed. Jake thought of Race. Sure must be different from being a police captain in Minnesota, he thought. He's never really been trained for this, but I can't think of a better man for the job.

"Sir! First Sergeant Prescott says it's hand to hand in Camp Kronberg. He's asking for reinforcements."

"Tell him we don't have any. Everybody's engaged. No! Wait! Don't tell him that! Tell him to do the best he can. We're working on it and we'll send somebody as soon as we can." Gotta keep his spirits up, he thought. Worst thing I could do would be to let him think we don't care. Make him lose hope.

Hai lit a cigarette and offered another to Jake. Jake started to refuse it, knowing he had one lit somewhere, but accepted it anyway. Who knows where it is now, he thought. He lit it and inhaled deeply. He noticed Sergeant Fellogese standing by the door of the TOC. His twitching jaw signalling his nervousness.

"No can do nothing," Hai said helplessly. "Want to do some thing, but nothing can do."

"I know," Jake said. "How's everyone doing at your end?" He motioned toward the Vietnamese side of the TOC.

"Much fighting. Little more sabotage in city, but ARVN drive armed VC away from city already. Everyone hold ground. Nobody run. Everybody call for American help."

"What are you telling them?"

"I tell them Americans come soon."

"But they're not! We can't get anybody to respond. Your guys have got to hold all by themselves."

"Yes. I know this. But they not know."

"What are you going to tell them when they find out you've lied to them?"

Hai grinned. "If they alive tomorrow, I say sorry. But they not angry tomorrow, because still alive. If not alive, trick no work anyway."

Jake grinned. "You're a hell of a soldier Hai, I just did the same thing."

Hai reached up and touched Jake's arm. "You good soldier too Troom Ta. Many American no think VC attack tonight. Many Vietnam people also. You think so. You make me believe. Turn out true. Who know what happen maybe soon, but if you no think so, we not be ready. Everybody die for sure. I think you number one."

Jake smiled. He started to tell Hai about the orphanage, and how he should have listened to him. That would have made me an even better soldier, he thought, but now is not the time.

Another mortar blast filled the room with dust. The bare electric bulb swung and danced at the end of its tether.

Jake was suddenly aware of a hush gradually capturing the bunker. The radio speakers continued to blare, Vietnamese on one side, English on the other. But one by one, the men inside ceased their own conversations and lifted their heads to listen. Jake forced himself to listen. What was it?

Outside, the generator hummed. The cannons roared. Mortar rounds exploded. Machine guns chattered. Rifles barked. Then he heard it. It was not loud at all, but it was different, unique. It was so distinctive, he wondered why he hadn't noticed it earlier. It sounded a little like raindrops. Heavy raindrops. Irregular spaced thuds, only just audible, outside on the sand-bags.

They all knew what it was. Incoming small arms fire! Bullets! Bullets, slamming into the sandbags! The enemy was close. Well inside the perimeter! Perhaps just outside the bunker! They were in danger of being overrun! Any moment a grenade could bounce into the TOC, and concussion alone could kill everyone in such a tightly enclosed space!

Now at last, there was something to do. Something that had to be done. "Keep working everyone. I'll check it out," he said. He picked up a rifle and ducked past Sergeant Fellogese, through the blackout curtain.

He was surprised at the light. At least ten parachute flares filled the air at different heights. Rain still fell. The odor of cordite choked him. An acrid, burning smell, seering his nostrils and throat, stinging his eyes. Muzzle flashes everywhere he looked. A white phosphorous grenade boomed and added a lingering lacy, fleecy-white fan with sparkling tips to the spectrum of orange, peach, and pumpkin colored flashes. A stream of angry red tracers from an old water cooled heavy machine gun flashed across the parade ground. The friendly Vietnamese militia units were definitely fighting hard. He could hear the impact of the small arms rounds clearer, louder now that he was outside. He looked at the sandbags. There! Along the west wall. Ripped to shreds. Puffs of dry sand popping out onto the wet green canvas.

He crouched. Probably a machine gun. He scanned the dark backdrop to the west. There it is! The multiflashes of an AK-47 on full automatic. He leveled his M-16 and squeezed off two short bursts. The flashes stopped. The thudding stopped. He stood up to survey the battlefield. Shell craters dotted the parade ground, pock marking the land like a giant face ravished in the past by uncontrollable acne. They're using impact fuses, he thought. Delay fuses. They know we're not out in the open.

Sergeant Fellogese appeared at his side, crouching, ready for combat.

"Sir! Stay down! Stay down Sir!"

Good advice, he thought. No need to take any more risks than I have to. He crouched to one knee and glanced to the north where King had disappeared. Frenzied muzzle flashes tore the shadows like several strings of firecrackers. "He's still at it," he said, "That asshole King is still alive. It's still in doubt over there."

"Sir! Watch out! B-40! B-40!" Mark's voice shrieked beside him. Fellogese was crawling forward, trying to throw himself in front like a shield.

Jake jerked his eyes to the left to see a man in black pajamas crouching on one knee about two hundred meters away. The cannon-like bore of a B-40 rocket launcher aimed his way. Jake swung up his rifle, but too late. The swishing flame of the rocket ripped straight at him. He flung himself prone just as the earth split and shattered around him.

His ears rang. He shook his head to clear the fog and numbness. Suddenly, he noticed that the firing had stopped. It was quiet. So totally quiet. Too quiet! He looked up from the wet sand. Mark Fellogese lay crumpled beside him.

Jake's ears still rang, but he could hear. He wasn't deaf. He knew he wasn't deaf, but there were no sounds of fighting. No explosions. No incoming. No outgoing.

Something moved out there on the parade field. People! Several people moving this way, but they are walking so slowly. Proudly, determinedly. What in Heaven's name is going on? Who is it for Christ's sake?

They drew nearer. A figure in white was leading, stepping out confidently. Jesus! It's Mother Angela!

Mother Angela was smiling. Her magnificent, magnified eyes twinkled as they reflected the glow from the last parachute flare. Someone beside her. Who is that beside her? It's Curly! Curly Danby! What's he doing here in Tam Ky for Christ's sake?

Several others. They were closer now. He began to recognize a few more faces. They were all smiling.

Another man in a South Vietnamese officer's uniform stepped out beside Mother Angela. His olive green fatigues were neatly starched and pressed. His boots brightly polished.

It was Lieutenant Colonel Tu! "Oh my God, Troom Ta, what's happening?"

Tu beckoned for him to follow.

Scene 6

CURTAIN CALL

<u>Major Jacob Thorpe</u>'s funeral took place on the same day as that of his wife Dolores. At the request of family members, the two services were held in the same church, but separated by two hours. Jake was buried in Tahoma National Cemetary, near Auburn Washington, and Dolores was buried in a large cemetery in Tacoma. Major Thorpe was posthumously awarded the Bronze Star for Gallantry; his name can be found on the second granite slab from the left on the Vietnam War Memorial, in Washington, D.C.

<u>Sergeant Mark Amory Fellogese</u> survived his wounds of the Tet offensive. He was treated extensively at Letterman General Hospital near San Francisco and did not return to Vietnam during his Army tour of duty. After his discharge, he again attended Rutgers University, this time under the GI Bill and eventually received a PhD in Literature specializing in Shakespeare. He is currently teaching classes on this subject at the University of Georgetown. He has been offered the English Department Dean's chair three times and has refused all three opportunities. He lives alone and has never married. He does not even date.

<u>Lieutenant Colonel Richard C. King</u> was awarded the Silver Star for Gallantry for his actions in the battle for Quang Tin during Tet of 68.

He completed a lustrous military career by being promoted and promoted again, and then again. He retired in 1989 with the rank of Lieutenant General (2 stars). During the Desert Storm war, General King became somewhat famous as a media advisor, appearing on several network television talk shows. His easy mannerisms and descriptive southern eloquence earned him high praise from media critics and the general public, primarily as he was perceived to be so unpretentious and self-effacing. He lives quietly now on his 22 acre ranch in Texas and occasionally appears as a paid speaker on the subject of international relations.

Major Bill Clayborne also survived his Vietnam tour. However, he was passed over for promotion to LTC, and resigned his commission after twelve years of service. He was hired by the US Postal Service in 1972 and served well and honorably as a postman in Atlanta Georgia until 1983 when he died of lung cancer. He left his wife, three grown children and two grandchildren.

Major Roger (Buck) Buckingham survived the Tet battle, but stepped on a Viet Cong land mine three months later. He lived in pain for five weeks and died in the military hospital in Honolulu. He left a loving wife and four year old daughter.

First Lieutenant Clarence George resigned from the Army shortly after returning from Vietnam. He was accepted at the University of California (Berkley) and almost immediately became active in the anti-Vietnam demonstrations there. Because of his status as a Vietnam veteran, his eyewitness (but self-created) testimonies of US Army war crimes were credible and he became a significant spokesman for the SDS radicals on the campus. He was arrested four times for vandalism, and twice for assault on police officers, but ultimately graduated with an advanced degree in economics. He is now a successful CPA in San Diego; a Rotary Club, Republican Party and VFW member and very respected in his community. His veteran's classification allows him access to the local VA hospital which is a considerable monetary benefit.

<u>Captain John Hastings</u>, although slightly wounded during the Tet Offensive, completed his tour and returned to the United States. He was passed over for promotion to Major and resigned from the Army. He had difficulties adjusting to civilian life and found it difficult to hold a steady job. Four years later, he was diagnosed with severe Post Traumatic Stress Syndrome. He is now a permanent residential patient at the VA hospital in Chicago.

<u>Brigadier General Eugene P. Elsin</u> was re-assigned to the Pentagon after his Vietnam tour. In 1972, after an office Christmas party, several of the women officers filed sex discrimination and sexual abuse charges against five senior male officers (Major and above). Although General Elsin did not attend the party, he was considered responsible because he was in charge of that office. He was summarily asked to retire immediately without honors. He died of prostate cancer two years later.

<u>First Sergeant Lawrence Prescott</u> retired from the Army in 1970 and after attending seminary on the GI bill, was ordained as an Episcopal Minister. He is now the Senior Pastor of St. Mary's Episcopal Church in Sandusky Ohio. His son, Dan, (First Lieutenant Daniel Prescott) was killed in action during Desert Storm. His daughter-in-Law, shortly thereafter, was killed in an automobile accident. Pastor Prescott and his wife Susan have adopted their two grandsons and are raising them in Sandusky.

<u>Ba Mai</u> (The house servant at The Castle) was captured by the Viet Cong during the Tet attack. She was raped, tortured and murdered.

Major Benh Lah Hai was promoted to Lt. Colonel and continued serving as the Deputy Province Chief of Quang Tin until the fall of South Vietnam in 1972. He spent five years in a concentration camp of the type the new government of Vietnam called "Re-Education Camps." His wife was sent to a similar but separate camp for the same period of time. Shortly after being released, the couple escaped Vietnam in a small, ill equipped boat to Australia, and then on to the USA. The exodus was filled with such danger, hardships and misery that the writer of this novel is considering another book about that real life adventure. Hai, who now calls himself Hi, works as a fishing boat skipper along the east coast of Texas. His oldest son is serving a four year sentence in prison for a drug offence.

Captain Doung (of Hau Duc) not only survived Tet, but was promoted to major for his actions on that night. The Hau Duc militia completely crushed the local VC uprisings. Doung, however, was killed three years later when Quang Tin fell to the Communists.

Major Cecil Doyle (Senior advisor for the District of Tien Phouc) earned a bronze star for heroism during the Tet action. He and his advisors fought alongside the district militia and completely routed the local VC uprising. He returned home after his Vietnam tour to find that his wife had run off with another man. Major Doyle began drinking excessively and was thrown out of the Army. At age 37, while driving under the influence of alcohol, he hit and killed a small child. He has been in and out of jail ever since.

Major Ken Wallace (Senior Advisor for the District of Ly Tin) survived the Tet uprising in his district as there also the militia fought well and won the day. He rotated to the US at the end of his tour. He remained in the Army as a career officer and retired in 1979 as a Lt. Colonel. He found it difficult, however, to adjust to civilian life and found it difficult to remain employed. He divorced, re-married, divorced again and re-married again. He and his third wife are now separated while he is employed part time as a cashier in a grocery store.

Major Dang (District Chief of the District of Thang Binh) was promoted to Lieutenant Colonel immediately after the Tet offensive. He was advanced to the position of Province Chief of Quang Tin province, replacing the deceased Col. Biet. Lt. Col Dang was as effective as a province chief as he had been as a district chief. The province became a model of efficiency and graft free government. When the country fell to the North Vietnamese in 1973, the province chief was listed as MIA. He was never seen again.

<u>Major Conrad (Curly) Danby</u> (Senior Advisor for the District of Thang Bien), was killed in action during the battle of Tet in 1968. He was posthumously recommended to receive two major awards for courage during this action: The pentagon downgraded the first submission from a Congressional Medal of Honor to a Silver Star. Major Dang (above paragraph) submitted Danby for the RVN Cross of Gallantry with gold star (Highest bravery award of RVN), which Danby's widow proudly received. Major Danby's name appears low on the farthest right slab of black marble on the Washington DC memorial.

Race Haldane (the National Police Advisor) lost a hand and both legs from wounds suffered during the Tet offensive in Quang Tin. After extensive surgeries and recuperation in the states, he retired completely in his small house on a lake in Minnesota. He occasionally fishes from his wheelchair and watches television. For the most part, however, he lives in the past with his memories.

Sergeant Kor Uz Minh (the Hoi Chanh dancer) was prepared for the Tet attacks. Because of the lack of reinforcements to the province, he had again become certain that the attacks would succeed. His troupe had just completed a show that day in Thang Binh. Dressed in black pajamas like the attackers, Minh joined the VC cadre battalion as it swept into the village. He was killed by a South Vietnamese militia marksman. This saved him from shame and torture, however, for the VC knew of his duplicity.

Mister "Diji" Garbino (the US Marine sergeant temporarily assigned to the State Department) survived the Tet attacks in his province and remained at his duty station until late 1971 when he was forced to evacuate under State Department orders. Upon arriving in the US, Garbino was given a choice whether to re-join the Marine Corps at his former rank or become a permanent employee of the State Department. He chose the latter and has been assigned to staff positions in Laos, Cambodia and Thailand. He has recently retired with the pay grade equivalent to a brigadier general.

Let Yu Giap of Tam Ky (Co Li's father) was captured during the first phase of the Tet conflict. After the battle, he was tried, convicted and sentenced to death for treason, but because of a strong and meticulous legal defense which with his wealth he could afford, he had not yet been executed when the Communists overran the Province in 1972. He immediately became the Revolutionary Province Chief with all benefits. Although now an old man, he retains this position of power and influence and rules with vicious and unchallenged brutality.

The defense of Quang Tin Provence, Tam Ky City, and Thang Bien City during the battle of the 1968 Tet holiday cease fire period was an unequivocal success. After-action reports show 3 Americans KIA, and 13 WIA. There were 4 ARVN KIA's and 12 WIA, and the combined province, district and other level South Vietnamese militia suffered 23 KIA and 51 WIA. During the clean up, they counted over 250 NVA and VC bodies left behind. The effectiveness of both attacking units was eliminated for over a year. The fact that the legal cadre VC (such as Co Li's father) exposed themselves and were mostly killed or captured one full day before the military attack decimated the covert VC effort for the remainder of the war. Even more important, when the populace of the provence (and the country) did not rise up and join the Communists as truly expected, the leadership at all levels lost face and surely would have capitulated had not the news media and general population of the United States reacted to the battle with sensationalism and renewed determination to end the conflict as quickly as possible, thus causing the beginning of the American retreat.

ABOUT THE AUTHOR

With an MA in Literature from the University of Oregon, Jim McDaniel is a former College Instructor, Newspaper Columnist, Army officer and Corporate Sales Manager. He has written two non-fiction books and several magazine articles in addition to this novel. He is now a full time professional writer. As an Army Lieutenant Colonel, he completed two combat tours in Vietnam including one as the Deputy Senior Advisor of Quang Tin Province (same job as the protagonist in this story). Jim lives near Tacoma Washington with his wife, Jan, and their grandson, Christopher. Christopher is also their adopted son and is in the 6th grade.

0-595-25405-5